The incredible Harlan Ellison writes as if an inner fuse is about to blow before he can get all the words on his pages. **—Anne McCaffrey**

He doesn't write like anybody else. What emerges is a surprising, eclectic, almost protean series of visions, often disturbing, always strongly felt. **—Michael Crichton**

Harlan was not just a great fantasist and/or science fiction writer; he was a great *writer*, period. When he was at the top of his form, there was no finer short story writer in all of English literature. [He] had an enormous influence on the writers of the generation that followed, my own generation. He fought for racial equality, marching with King at Selma. He fought for women's rights and the ERA. He fought publishers, defending the rights of writers to control their own material and be fairly compensated for it. He was a hero to us. **—George R. R. Martin**

Herald Classics

The Herald Classics series connects adventurous readers to excellent stories and showcases a dynamic and approachable literary canon.

Game Without Rules, by Michael Gilbert

Greatest Hits, by Harlan Ellison

Greatest Hits (Barnes & Noble Exclusive Edition), by Harlan Ellison

Praise for Harlan Ellison

In his stories of fantasy and horror, he strikes closest to all those things that horrify and amuse us (sometimes both at the same time) in our present lives. . . . Ellison has always been a sociological writer . . . [who was] pro-choice when it comes to abortion . . . [and] an affirmed liberal and freethinker. . . . Most of all, we sense outrage and anger—as with the best Ellison stories, we sense personal involvement, and have a feeling that Ellison is not so much telling the tale as he is jabbing it viciously out of its hiding place. It is the feeling that we are walking over a lot of jagged glass in thin shoes, or running across a minefield in the company of a lunatic. —**Stephen King**

Categories are too small—even the catch-all category of science fiction—to describe Harlan Ellison. Lyric poet, satirist, explorer of odd psychological corners, moralist, one-line comedian, purveyor of pure horror and of black comedy; he is all these and more. —***The Washington Post***

A furiously prolific and cantankerous writer (who) looked at storytelling as a "holy chore," which he pursued zealously for more than 60 years. His output includes more than 1,700 short stories and articles, at least 100 books and dozens of screenplays and television scripts . . . ranked with eminent science fiction writers like Ray Bradbury and Isaac Asimov. —***The New York Times***

Harlan Ellison was, after all, one of the most interesting humans on Earth. He was one of the greatest and most influential science fiction writers alive. He marched with Martin Luther King, Jr. in Selma, lectured to college kids, visited with death row inmates, and once mailed a dead gopher to a publisher. Ellison brought a literary sensibility to sci-fi at a time when the entire establishment was allergic to any notion of art. To say he was one-of-a-kind would be trite, and he would likely hate that. What he was, was a legend. —**NPR**

[Harlan] was very influential in changing the field, making it more open to social issues, to explorations of characters. He's had an enormous influence on science fiction with his writing, and he's also been an influential editor . . . setting an agenda for a new kind of science fiction writing that would be more socially engaged and responsive to the times. —**Jeff Lathan,** ***Science Fiction Studies***

There's a real power to the way he uses the language and how he draws pictures in your mind. —**Ron Moore**

You see Ellison's unswerving social conscience throughout his fiction and critical essays . . . forcefully and eloquently—and at some length—lamenting the failure of the Equal Rights Amendment and railing against the scourge of misogynistic "knife-kill" films. —**Rogerebert.com**

The words—there is an attention to the words. There is an attention to the sound of the words. You're reading them in your head, and they sing. —**Neil Gaiman**

The spellbinding quality of a great nonstop talker, with a cultural warehouse for a mind. —*The New York Review of Books*

Feisty, furious, yet extraordinarily kind and generous; Harlan Ellison was one of a kind. —**Leonard Maltin**

Harlan Ellison—terrific prose, razor-sharp intellect, pulp gut punches and invention when needed, terse poetics . . . an original. —**Guillermo del Toro**

An original and valuable writer . . . a twentieth-century Lewis Carroll. —*The Los Angeles Times*

Saul Bellow, Philip Roth, Norman Mailer, stand aside. Harlan Ellison is now a better short story writer than you will ever be again during the rest of your lives. —**Ray Bradbury**

GREATEST HITS

Herald Classics

HARLAN ELLISON'S GREATEST HITS

Edited by J. Michael Straczynski
Foreword by Neil Gaiman
Introduction by Cassandra Khaw

UNION SQUARE & CO.
NEW YORK

UNION SQUARE & CO.
NEW YORK

Union Square & Co., LLC, is a subsidiary of Sterling Publishing Co., Inc.

This 2024 edition published by Union Square & Co., LLC.

ISBN 978-1-4549-5337-1
ISBN 978-1-4549-5212-1 (e-book)

For information about custom editions, special sales, and premium purchases,
please contact specialsales@unionsquareandco.com.

Printed in the United States of America

Printing 9, 2025

LSC-C

unionsquareandco.com

Interior design by Kevin Ullrich
Cover art: Max Loeffler
Cover design: Igor Satanovsky

Contents

A Note on the Text xi

Preface by J. Michael Straczynski xiii

Foreword by Neil Gaiman xix

Introduction by Cassandra Khaw xxv

ANGRY GODS

"Repent, Harlequin," Said the Ticktockman (1966) **5**
Hugo Award, Nebula Award, 2015 Prometheus Hall of Fame Award

I Have No Mouth, and I Must Scream (1967) **19**
Hugo Award

The Deathbird (1974) **38**
Hugo Award, Locus Award

Chatting with Anubis (1995) **75**
Bram Stoker Award, Deathrealm Award

The Whimper of Whipped Dogs (1973) **83**
Edgar Allan Poe Award

LOST SOULS

Jeffty Is Five (1977) **107**
British Fantasy Award, Hugo Award, Nebula Award, 1999 Locus Poll Winner for Best Short Story of All Time

Pretty Maggie Moneyeyes (1967) **132**
Hugo Award Nomination, Nebula Award Nomination

Shatterday (1980) **157**
Nebula Award Nomination, Twilight Zone *episode*

Mefisto in Onyx (1993) . . . 174
Bram Stoker Award, Locus Award, Hugo Award Nomination, Nebula Award Nomination, World Fantasy Award Nomination

On the Downhill Side (1972) . . . 233
Locus Award Nomination, Nebula Award Nomination

THE PASSAGE OF TIME

Paladin of the Lost Hour (1986) . . . 253
Hugo Award, Locus Award, Nebula Award Nomination, Twilight Zone *episode*

The Beast That Shouted Love at the Heart of the World (1969) . . . 281
Hugo Award

I'm Looking for Kadak (1974) . . . 293

How Interesting: A Tiny Man (2010) . . . 319
Nebula Award

THE LIGHTER SIDE

Djinn, No Chaser (1983) . . . 329
Locus Award

How's the Night Life on Cissalda? (1977) . . . 353

From A to Z, in the Chocolate Alphabet (1976) . . . 368

Eidolons (1989) . . . 384
Locus Award

THE LAST WORD

All the Lies That Are My Life (1981) . . . 403
Hugo Award Nomination

A Note on the Text

Harlan Ellison's work epitomized and reshaped the speculative, science fiction, and horror genres across decades. Ellison's stories and novellas have been an inspiration to subsequent writers, and his impact can still be seen in contemporary television, culture, and literature.

However, while these stories are outstanding works across multiple genres, they may contain outdated cultural representations and language. We present the works as originally published. We hope that you enjoy discovering, or rediscovering, these stories.

Preface

J. Michael Straczynski

HEY, YOU!

Yeah, you!

I feel your pain. I know what you're going through.

You're thinking, *How could it be that I, a traveler in all the deep places of the world, who knows the secret password to the hidden city beneath Jakarta, who has traveled with monks and prophets from a dozen countries, who possesses enlightenment and wisdom far beyond my years that I have used to defend myself against assassins sent (futilely) to ensure that my knowledge went no further, how could it be that I have not previously heard the name Harlan Ellison?*

You're thinking, *How is it possible that I, a bon vivant revered by presidents and popes and politicos, invited to all the best parties (including the ones no one is supposed to know about) (especially those) where the arts are favored above all things, had not been briefed on the works of an author who wrote over 1,700 short stories, novellas, television episodes, and critical essays, along the way earning more awards, and more kinds of awards, than any other writer, living, dead, or zombified?*

You're thinking: *How could someone who is as politically savvy and socially aware as myself, who embraces battles against censorship, misogyny, racism, and the other sociopolitical evils that have braced us up against the wall for far too long, have missed the stories of someone who marched with Martin Luther King Jr. in Selma, fought for feminist causes, went to war with networks and publishers over censorship, and who appeared regularly on talk shows and college campuses to rail against corporate greed, the exploitation of artists, political corruption at the very highest levels, and was on the Enemies List of at least one United States president?*

But mainly, you're thinking: *Are the rumors true he was a snappy dresser and a damned good dancer?*

Yes . . . yes, they are.

And there's a reason you haven't come across his name before.

Harlan was an iconoclast, a troublemaker, a rabble rouser, and a force of nature, but above everything else he was an artist armed with a very clear vision for the ways in which his work was to be published, from the cover art down to the font, the paper stock, and the smallest nuance of punctuation. While some publishers accommodated that vision, it was always a struggle, and the victories were endlessly complicated by publishers, agents, and random amanuenses (amanuensisis? amanuensii?) who didn't understand or simply didn't care what was required of them to preserve the integrity of the books, and thus just did whatever they wanted. Harlan's battles for literary freedom, and against corporate stupidity and cupidity, were legendary.

But also exhausting.

You try being a Force For Good In Your Time. After a while even the most determined of us would like a day off to sit in the sun and read a book. (Come by the house sometime and I'll tell you the story about Harlan, an errant publisher, a dead gopher, 213 bricks, Donny Osmond stationery, and a Lithuanian hit man.)

Rather than waste time, energy, and visceral material on battles with publishers, resources that could be better used to Fight The Good Fight against censorship and other causes Harlan supported, Harlan began putting out his work in limited editions that allowed him absolute control over the product from end to end. They were so magnificent, so beautiful, that the few copies remaining out in the wild routinely sell for thousands of dollars.

But for Harlan, it wasn't about the money. Which is not to say money isn't a good thing, or that writers shouldn't get paid (another ongoing battle), only that if you're any kind of artist, the primacy of the work *has* to come first. Because once you're in the ground, nobody cares how much money you earned, what kind of car you drove, or how dashing you looked in a Borsellino hat cocked at *exactly* the right rakish angle. All that remains is the quality of the work, because that's the only thing that survives the life of the artist.

See, Harlan was an atheist. He didn't believe in an afterlife where we would find redemption or expiation for the mistakes and casual cruelties we'd committed in life. He believed it was essential to stand up for the betterment of the human species *rightdamnitnow*, not in the unknowable void on the other side of death. So he put his money, his safety, and in some cases, his life where his convictions were. He advocated for civil rights and gun control at a time when those were dangerous things to do, leading to (a) the time someone took a shot at him onstage while he was speaking against gun violence, and (b) the proudest moment of his life when he marched side by side with Martin Luther King Jr. at Selma. He worked ceaselessly with PEN International, an organization dedicated to the fight against censorship around the world, which recognized his work with the Silver Pen Award.

Harlan was also a fierce feminist who worked hard to raise the profile of women writers in the science fiction genre at a time when it was dominated by male writers, with Octavia Butler as just one example. But his commitment went far beyond being simply an ally and advocate. In 1978, during the height of the struggle to get the Equal Rights Amendment passed (a struggle that, sadly and unbelievably, is still going on today), Harlan was invited to be guest of honor at a huge SF convention in Phoenix,

Arizona. When Arizona voted not to ratify the ERA, and the National Organization of Woman declared an economic boycott, he decided that rather than not attend, which would disappoint thousands of fans, he would instead execute a one-man boycott to ensure that he did not spend so much as a penny in Arizona. He rented an RV, filled it with snacks and tons of bottled water (he was a lifelong nondrinker), and drove from Los Angeles to Phoenix, gassing up before crossing the state line. He declined to accept the offer of a hotel room, which would have been paid to the hotel by the convention, and spent the hottest weekend in the hottest summer Phoenix had experienced in *years* living out of that tiny RV, during which he worked closely with NOW to get press coverage for the boycott of Arizona and the reason it was necessary.

For Harlan, what someone *said* they believed was never the point. The point was the degree to which they were willing to put skin in the game, to take a stand that carried risk, to stand when standing was the hardest thing in the whole world. *That's* when you know who you really are. So he didn't just speak out against racism and misogyny on college campuses; he took that into corporate boardrooms, the streets of Selma, and the offices of network executives. Didn't matter if he lost work as a result. It was the right thing to do, so he did it. The same rule applied to his work. He brought controversial, progressive themes into his stories in ways that no one had even *thought* about doing before, a stance that led directly to the birth of New Wave Science Fiction, which forever transformed the genre.

All of which is a very long road to answering the questions posed at the top of this preface: The reason you haven't heard of Harlan Ellison is that after living that life and doing those remarkable things, he spent the last three decades of his life in a J. D. Salinger–esque exile from the world of mainstream publishing. It was during this time that I came to know Harlan as a friend, though I'd known him through his work for many years during which he was, all unknown, a long-distance mentor to my own writing. His courage and his tenacity strengthened me, his wisdom humbled me, his loyalty inspired me, and his eccentricities maddened me but never pushed me away, because in all things and at all times, his heart was forever in the right place.

Now, with his recent passing, which led to my being named executor of the Harlan and Susan Ellison Foundation, it's time to reintroduce the world to a collection of his most powerful, vibrant, and often controversial stories, tales that are as challenging now as they have ever been, and perhaps even more relevant.

These are stories of wonder, loss, love, longing, terror, and laughter, written by a fierce intelligence dedicated to the proposition that we can, and should, be better than we are.

Most of all, they are stories with teeth. Even the funny ones.

Especially the funny ones.

You have not heard of Harlan Ellison before.

And that's okay.

Because the voyage into the unknown worlds he created begins again, right now, on the other side of this page.

Bon voyage.

HARLAN ELLISON

Foreword

Neil Gaiman

To prepare for this introduction, and because I missed him, I listened to Harlan Ellison reading *Through the Looking-Glass and What Alice Found There.* On the one hand it was like having him back—hearing his voice, the precision and enunciation, the glorious delivery. His astonishing reading ability, and the feeling that the words were in his blood. And on the other hand . . . he had decided to cast it with his impressions of actors from the golden age of Hollywood—W. C. Fields was Tweedledum, the White Knight was Peter Lorre, and I was baffled, except that I wasn't. They are excellent impressions. Harlan was obviously very proud of them and wanted a record of them for posterity, even if they seem completely unsuited to the material. And I smiled, because that was the most Harlan thing of all. Harlan giveth; Harlan does a weird but impressive thing that probably works against him.* That was his life and career in miniature.

So.

I met Harlan Ellison the person in 1985 in the Grand Central Hotel in Glasgow. He was guest of honor at a science fiction convention. I went to Scotland to interview him for a British SF magazine, which was canceled before the Harlan issue went to press.

I met Harlan Ellison the writer when I was only a boy: I read short stories that ripped my mind open and showed me what the possibilities of fiction were, what you could do with just words.

* Or maybe not. His reading of *Through the Looking-Glass* was nominated for a Grammy Award, after all.

They seemed different to the stories around them—full-color explosions that, somehow, changed me. I was not the person I had been before I read the stories.

I read "'Repent, Harlequin!' said the Ticktockman" and "I Have No Mouth, and I Must Scream," both in the *Best SF* anthologies, when I was about eleven, although I knew already that Harlan existed, because James Blish had written about Harlan in his second *Star Trek* short story collection—Blish had talked about Harlan and about adapting his *Star Trek* episode "The City on the Edge of Forever" into short story form.

As time went on, I bought anything by Harlan I could find, cheap remaindered imported paperbacks with titles like *From the Land of Fear* or *The Time of the Eye*. I read library books, finding stories by Harlan in anthologies, each one making me feel like a prospector who had found a hidden golden nugget. Unable to obtain the landmark *Dangerous Visions* anthology that Harlan had edited, I bought a copy of *Dangereuses Visions* while on holiday in France and read it in schoolboy French as best I could.

Harlan's work, as a screenwriter, an editor, and most of all, as a writer, of fiction and of nonfiction was inspiring to me as a boy and as a teenager. I didn't have a route map to becoming the kind of writer I wanted to be. I didn't have a teacher. But I had Harlan's introductions and his articles, and more than that, the evidence of his life and career to demonstrate that it could be done. Harlan had written comics and scripts and prose; he read his own stories better than anyone else could read them. When I was twenty-one I had the worst day of my life up to that point. And the only thing for sale at the airport, as I was to fly home and try and put my life back together, was Harlan Ellison's *Shatterday*. It, and the essays in it, before each story, were what made me believe I could become a writer. That I had to do the work.

I arrived in the world of Fantastic Literature in September 1983, as a young journalist sent to cover the British Fantasy Convention, there to interview Robert Silverberg and Gene Wolfe. I remember sitting next to a prominent literary editor at the awards banquet. He asked me about writers I liked, and I mentioned Harlan. The editor explained that Harlan had now demonstrated he was never going to write a major novel, which meant that he was irrelevant. I didn't even know how to argue. I felt like I'd been told that a miniaturist did not matter because they did not paint murals. Harlan mattered. I was certain of this.

Harlan and I slowly became friends, and I loved being his friend, even if sometimes it felt like I had been befriended by a hand grenade. I could only hope that if he was to explode, I wouldn't be there.

He would sometimes leave angry but eloquent messages on my answering machine: "Gaiman. This is Ellison. You are a dead man. I will be sending a missile to take out your house. I will sow salt on the rubble where your house once was to make sure that nothing ever grows there again. I will curse your house and line with a thousand maledictions and imprecations, and you and your children and your children's children will be immolated and forgotten. Call me!"

(I did. That time Harlan chewed me out for having given a journalist his phone number. I pointed out that I hadn't; I had instead mentioned to the journalist that, as Harlan would often tell people in his introductions, his number was in the phone book. He said, "Fair enough," and changed the subject.)

And now Harlan's dead and gone, and I miss my friend. (I miss my friend's gentle, sensible wife, Susan, too. She met him at the same convention I did in Glasgow in 1985, but she married him, and kept him as sane as she could and as grounded as she could.)

I miss my infuriating, brilliant friend—he of the stories that might have been true, or at least trueish, and were sometimes truer than anyone else believed. He was, I sometimes thought, putting on for the world a piece of performance art called Harlan Ellison. And none of it would matter if Harlan hadn't written some astonishingly brilliant stories along the way—coruscating, fizzy fireworks, written at white heat, pounded out on a manual typewriter.

I like to think Harlan would have approved of this book, because it's all about the stories, and an excellent selection it is, too. It covers Harlan's peak creative years and selects judiciously from his later career.

There's a story in this book called "All the Lies That Are My Life." It's a fantasia about the death of someone who is a version of Harlan as he might have been if he was A Great Man, that is, at its core, about the fear of being forgotten—the fear that Harlan had that his stories, which were his children, would be swept away in time. That he would become one with Thorne Smith or Gerald Kersh or any of the other writers who were, for a moment, here, and who, for a heartbeat, mattered, but whose words were mostly forgotten and who had become footnotes in dusty reference books.

These stories, I hope, and this book, will help keep Harlan's memory bright. They were typed at white-hot speed on a manual typewriter (Harlan typed, he said, too fast for an electric typewriter), many of them written over fifty years ago. They tell us important things about society and bravery, about pain and identity, about death and evil, about love and responsibility. They are stylistically diverse, always ambitious. Some of them are pretty funny, too (and some of them are dark and painful as hell). With an impressive mixture of narrative choices, intentions, emotional resonances, these are stories that show off for you a few of the things that Harlan could do: it's hard to compare a story like "The Man Who Rowed Christopher Columbus Ashore," with its Shirley

Jackson–inspired Levendis (is that his name or his exhortation?) showing us the meaning and meaninglessness of history and free will, with the nightmare of AI and inhumanity that is "I Have No Mouth, and I Must Scream"; to contrast the heartbreaking nostalgia of "Jeffty Is Five" with the dystopian Harlequinade of "'Repent, Harlequin!' said the Ticktockman."

Like all art made in this world, they are stories of their time. And when you are talking about Harlan Ellison, they barely touch the surface of what he made (there are two *Essential Ellison* collections, each over a thousand pages long). But everyone must start somewhere. And this is a fine place to start.

I hope they change you.

Introduction

Cassandra Khaw

When I think of anger, I always think of Harlan Ellison's AM. For all the dystopian fiction I've consumed, all the books about monsters, nothing has come closer to depicting a perfect, insoluble fury better than the deranged supercomputer at the center of Ellison's seminal "I Have No Mouth, and I Must Scream." I don't remember if I enjoyed that first read, but I remember being struck by how bleak the story was, how AM burned with wrath, how it hated the fact it'd been given all the intelligence in the universe but no way of experiencing existence sincerely—that it had been created to serve and nothing more.

And I was struck by how much I *understood*.

I was a closeted queer kid raised by very traditional parents, parents who struggled with both their unresolved traumas and their conservative upbringings. On one hand, they wanted nothing more than a stellar career for me, a good life, autonomy, every opportunity in the universe. On the other hand, I was beaten senseless for even the smallest infractions because anything less than perfection was a monstrous offense. I was told from a young age I was born to be of service to my parents, alive only because I had a function to fill.

Surprising no one, I grew up angry. I also grew up quiet and absorbed in books; I spent at least a few years of my life reading the dictionary from back to front for the sheer pleasure of the words. It's no surprise the school bullies took an interest in me—which was a terrible mistake on their part. I was a scrappy kid who threw down with everyone who took a swing at me.

For a long time, I didn't know why I was so incandescent with rage. Only when I got older did I understand it was fury at how unfair the world was, how cruel it sometimes chose to be, how utterly repellent it was that the people who should have protected a child saw fit to use them as a punching bag instead. There's a certain atavistic truism that every abused kid learns: You're either the one doing the beating, or the one being beaten. If you're unlucky, you crawl out of childhood so full of pain, all you can do to keep yourself sane is spread it around.

Some of Ellison's bibliography feels like he's writing to process this aphorism. "The Whimper of Whipped Dogs" envisions a nightmare caricature of a world where to survive, one must choose to participate in pain. It's almost exaggeratedly cruel, filled with an idiot animal evil. Surely, we're not like that in real life. And yet, sometimes we are.* Sometimes, we freeze. Sometimes, we look away, click away, avert our eyes, because the alternative is risking being hurt. You can feel the depth of Ellison's anger at this, his grief, his awareness of what time and fear claw from us.

This book is structured around those elemental forces that drove Ellison: Angry Gods, Lost Souls, the Passage of Time, the Lighter Side, the Last Word. You can see these forces at work in my favorite stories in this collection: "Pretty Maggie Moneyeyes" radiates his anger at how we are all driven relentlessly to greed, hoping beyond hope for a payoff when, really, there's nothing waiting for us but death at the top of the mountain. (A gut punch to reread as a freelance writer, honestly.) "Jeffty Is Five" is an unsettling look at the loss of innocence and how hard it is to hold onto the past as you age into a stranger; not an easy read for someone on the cusp of middle age. "'Repent, Harlequin!' Said the Ticktockman" is a

* The story was written in response to the death of Kitty Genovese, a twenty-eight-year-old bartender whose brutal murder was reported to have been witnessed and ignored by thirty-eight people, though this was later disproven.

standout with its stream-of-consciousness prose, darkly hilarious moments, and its furious, absurd take on our time-is-money culture and the pointless regimentation of our lives.

Yet there's also a sense that Ellison wanted more of our species, that under the grinning cynicism and the incandescent fury, there was someone who would have been thrilled to be proven wrong about the world. Even one of his most violent stories, "I Have No Mouth, and I Must Scream," for all its bleakness and lavish brutality, reminds us that kindness—true kindness, true sacrifice, true charity—is possible, even if it costs us everything. In reading Ellison's teleplay for the *Twilight Zone* adaptation of "Paladin of the Lost Hour," a story about a friendship that spans gender and race, I was struck by the unbearable gentleness of its final lines:

> *Like a wind crying endlessly through the universe, Time carries away the names and the deeds of conquerors and commoners alike. And all that we were, all that remains, is in the memories of those who cared we came this way for a brief moment.*

We are those who loved us and whom we loved in turn. So why, Ellison seems to demand, are we such fucking degenerates to one another?

In many ways, his life can be read as a response to this question. An unrepentant firebrand, Ellison was a ferocious advocate for whom and what he believed in, using his brazenness as a cudgel to clear a path forward for others. He furiously championed writers like Ursula K. Le Guin, Samuel Delany, and Octavia Butler in a time when diversity in the genre was all but nonexistent. He marched with Martin Luther King, Jr. at Selma; he spoke openly against the Vietnam War. Ellison also used his bully pulpit as a reviewer for the *Los Angeles Free Press*, and his time during TV interviews, to go to war over the treatment of women in slasher movies (at one point nearly coming to blows with a director at a Writers Guild screening over that kind of portrayal). He stood by his beliefs; Ellison famously coordinated with the National Organization of Women to draw media attention to Arizona's failure to ratify the Equal Rights Amendment.

Yet, seemingly more than happy to live up to his own notoriety, Ellison was unapologetic about his thoughts and often shocking in his behavior. His depiction of women, despite his avowed feminism, often walks a fine line between critiquing and indulging misogynistic tropes. The novella *A Boy and His Dog*, which is not part of this collection, is a post-apocalyptic dystopia with frank depictions of male and female rape that still make me wince. I don't think we needed to know how badly Beth hated the sex in "The Whimper of Whipped Dogs," or to have Ellen, a Black woman, become the group's sexual plaything in "I Have No Mouth, and I Must Scream." Do I understand Ellison's narrative decisions, the points he was trying to make? Yes. But I still believe he could have made better choices; a belief that holds especially true for his 2006 Worldcon speech with Connie Willis, who deserved so much better.

Reading this collection reminded me that Ellison's rage once provided me with instruction, showing me that you can use your pain and anger as a light. Pain, especially when you carry it in your ribs next to your heart, can teach you an unbearable amount of compassion, because it has left you too flayed for pretenses. Looking back at Ellison's storied life, I think he used that welter of inner pain as best he could: He turned it into fuel for creation and fuel for his activism.

Harlan Ellison was a troubled, complicated, and occasionally infuriating man, but he was nonetheless a light. I hope that in reading these stories, in reading J. Michael Straczynski's preface and Neil Gaiman's foreword, you see all sides of Harlan Ellison, good and bad, illuminated.

GREATEST HITS

ANGRY GODS

“Repent, Harlequin,” Said the Ticktockman

There are always those who ask, what is it all about? For those who need to ask, for those who need points sharply made, who need to know “where it’s at,” this:

> The mass of men serve the state thus, not as men mainly, but as machines, with their bodies. They are the standing army, and the militia, jailors, constables, *posse comitatus*, etc. In most cases there is no free exercise whatever of the judgment or of the moral sense; but they put themselves on a level with wood and earth and stones; and wooden men can perhaps be manufactured that will serve the purpose as well. Such command no more respect than men of straw or a lump of dirt. They have the same sort of worth only as horses and dogs. Yet such as these even are commonly esteemed good citizens. Others—as most legislators, politicians, lawyers, ministers, and officeholders—serve the state chiefly with their heads; and, as they rarely make any moral distinctions, they are as likely to serve the Devil, without intending it, as God. A very few, as heroes, patriots, martyrs, reformers in the great sense, and *men*, serve the state with their consciences also, and so necessarily resist it for the most part; and they are commonly treated as enemies by it.
>
> **Henry David Thoreau**
> **CIVIL DISOBEDIENCE**

That is the heart of it. Now begin in the middle, and later learn the beginning; the end will take care of itself.

* * *

But because it was the very world it was, the very world they had allowed it to *become*, for months his activities did not come to the alarmed attention of The Ones Who Kept The Machine Functioning Smoothly, the ones who poured the very best butter over the cams and mainsprings of the culture. Not until it had become obvious that somehow, someway, he had become a notoriety, a celebrity, perhaps even a hero for (what Officialdom inescapably tagged) "an emotionally disturbed segment of the populace," did they turn it over to the Ticktockman and his legal machinery. But by then, because it was the very world it was, and they had no way to predict he would happen—possibly a strain of disease long-defunct, now, suddenly, reborn in a system where immunity had been forgotten, had lapsed—he had been allowed to become too real. Now he had form and substance.

He had become a *personality*, something they had filtered out of the system many decades before. But there it was, and there *he* was, a very definitely imposing personality. In certain circles—middle-class circles—it was thought disgusting. Vulgar ostentation. Anarchistic. Shameful. In others, there was only sniggering: those strata where thought is subjugated to form and ritual, niceties, proprieties. But down below, ah, down below, where the people always needed their saints and sinners, their bread and circuses, their heroes and villains, he was considered a Bolívar; a Napoleon; a Robin Hood; a Dick Bong (Ace of Aces); a Jesus; a Jomo Kenyatta.

And at the top—where, like socially attuned Shipwreck Kellys, every tremor and vibration threatening to dislodge the wealthy, powerful, and titled from their flagpoles—he was considered a menace; a heretic; a rebel; a disgrace; a peril. He was known down the line, to the very heartmeat core, but the important reactions were high above and far below. At the very top, at the very bottom.

So his file was turned over, along with his time-card and his cardioplate, to the office of the Ticktockman.

The Ticktockman: very much over six feet tall, often silent, a soft purring man when things went timewise. The Ticktockman.

Even in the cubicles of the hierarchy, where fear was generated, seldom suffered, he was called the Ticktockman. But no one called him that to his mask.

You don't call a man a hated name, not when that man, behind his mask, is capable of revoking the minutes, the hours, the days and nights, the years of your life. He was called the Master Timekeeper to his mask. It was safer that way.

"This is *what* he is," said the Ticktockman with genuine softness, "but not *who* he is. This time-card I'm holding in my left hand has a name on it, but it is the name of *what* he is, not *who* he is. The cardioplate here in my right hand is also named, but not *whom* named, merely *what* named. Before I can exercise proper revocation, I have to know *who* this *what* is."

To his staff, all the ferrets, all the loggers, all the finks, all the commex, even the mineez, he said, "Who is this Harlequin?"

He was not purring smoothly. Timewise, it was jangle.

However, it *was* the longest speech they had ever heard him utter at one time, the staff, the ferrets, the loggers, the finks, the commex, but not the mineez, who usually weren't around to know, in any case. But even they scurried to find out.

Who is the Harlequin?

High above the third level of the city, he crouched on the humming aluminum-frame platform of the airboat (*foof!* Airboat, indeed! Swizzleskid is what it was, with a tow-rack jerry-rigged) and he stared down at the neat Mondrian arrangement of the buildings.

Somewhere nearby, he could hear the metronomic left-right-left of the 2:47 p.m. shift, entering the Timkin roller-bearing plant in their sneakers. A minute later, precisely, he heard the softer right-left-right of the 5:00 a.m. formation, going home.

An elfin grin spread across his tanned features, and his dimples appeared for a moment. Then, scratching at his thatch of auburn hair, he shrugged within his motley, as though girding himself for what came next, and threw the joystick forward, and bent into the wind as the airboat dropped. He skimmed over a slidewalk, purposely dropping a few feet to crease the tassels of the ladies of fashion, and—inserting thumbs in large ears—he stuck out his tongue, rolled his eyes, and went wugga-wugga-wugga. It was a minor diversion. One pedestrian skittered and tumbled, sending parcels everywhichway, another wet herself, a third keeled slantwise, and the walk was stopped automatically by the servitors till she could be resuscitated. It was a minor diversion.

Then he swirled away on a vagrant breeze and was gone. Hi-ho. As he rounded the cornice of the Time-Motion Study Building, he saw the shift, just boarding the slidewalk. With practiced motion and an absolute conservation of movement, they sidestepped up onto the slow-strip and (in a chorus line reminiscent of a Busby Berkeley film of the antediluvian 1930s) advanced across the strips ostrich-walking till they were lined up on the expresstrip.

Once more, in anticipation, the elfin grin spread, and there was a tooth missing back there on the left side. He dipped, skimmed, and swooped over them; and then, scrunching about on the airboat, he released the holding pins that fastened shut the ends of the homemade pouring troughs that kept his cargo from dumping prematurely. And as he pulled the trough-pins, the airboat slid over the factory workers and one hundred and fifty thousand dollars' worth of jelly beans cascaded down on the expresstrip.

Jelly beans! Millions and billions of purples and yellows and greens and licorice and grape and raspberry and mint and round and smooth and crunchy outside and soft-mealy inside and sugary and bouncing jouncing tumbling clittering clattering skittering fell on the heads and shoulders and hardhats and carapaces of the Timkin workers, tinkling on the slidewalk and bouncing away and rolling about underfoot and filling the sky on their way down with all the colors of joy and childhood and holidays, coming down in a steady rain, a solid wash, a torrent of color and sweetness out of the sky from above, and entering a universe of sanity and metronomic order with quite-mad cuckoo newness. Jelly beans!

The shift workers howled and laughed and were pelted, and broke ranks, and the jelly beans managed to work their way into the mechanism of the slidewalks after which there was a hideous scraping as the sound of a million fingernails rasped down a quarter of a million blackboards, followed by a coughing and a sputtering, and then the slidewalks all stopped and everyone was dumped thisawayandthataway in a jackstraw tumble, still laughing and popping little jelly bean eggs of childish color into their mouths. It was a holiday, and a jollity, an absolute insanity, a giggle. But . . .

The shift was delayed seven minutes.

They did not get home for seven minutes.

The master schedule was thrown off by seven minutes.

Quotas were delayed by inoperative slidewalks for seven minutes.

He had tapped the first domino in the line, and one after another, like *chik chik chik*, the others had fallen.

The System had been seven minutes' worth of disrupted. It was a tiny matter, one hardly worthy of note, but in a society where the single driving force was order and unity and equality and promptness and clocklike precision and attention to the clock, reverence of the gods of the passage of time, it was a disaster of major importance.

So he was ordered to appear before the Ticktockman. It was broadcast across every channel of the communications web. He was ordered to be *there* at 7:00 dammit on time. And they waited, and they waited, but he didn't show up till almost ten-thirty, at which time he merely sang a little song about moonlight in a place no one had ever heard of, called Vermont, and vanished again. But they had all been waiting since seven, and it wrecked *hell* with their schedules. So the question remained: Who is the Harlequin?

But the *unasked* question (more important of the two) was: How did we get *into* this position, where a laughing, irresponsible japer of jabberwocky and jive could disrupt our entire economic and cultural life with a hundred and fifty thousand dollars' worth of jelly beans . . .

Jelly for god's sake *beans*! This is madness! Where did he get the money to buy a hundred and fifty thousand dollars' worth of jelly beans? (They knew it would have cost that much, because they had a team of Situation Analysts pulled off another assignment and rushed to the slidewalk scene to sweep up and count the candies, and produce findings, which disrupted *their* schedules and threw their entire branch at least a day behind.) Jelly beans! Jelly . . . *beans*? Now wait a second—a second accounted for—no one has manufactured jelly beans for over a hundred years. Where did he get jelly beans?

That's another good question. More than likely it will never be answered to your complete satisfaction. But then, how many questions ever are?

The middle you know. Here is the beginning. How it starts:

A desk pad. Day for day, and turn each day. 9:00—open the mail. 9:45—appointment with planning commission board. 10:30—discuss installation progress charts with J. L. 11:45—pray for rain. 12:00—lunch. *And so it goes.*

"I'm sorry, Miss Grant, but the time for interviews was set at 2:30, and it's almost five now. I'm sorry you're late, but those are the rules. You'll have to wait till next year to submit application for this college again." *And so it goes.*

The 10:10 local stops at Cresthaven, Galesville, Tonawanda Junction, Selby, and Farnhurst, but not at Indiana City, Lucasville, and Colton, except on Sunday. The 10:35 express stops at Galesville, Selby, and Indiana City, except on Sundays & Holidays, at which time it stops at . . . *and so it goes.*

"I couldn't wait, Fred. I had to be at Pierre Cartain's by 3:00, and you said you'd meet me under the clock in the terminal at 2:45, and you weren't there, so I had to go on. You're always late, Fred. If you'd been there, we could have sewed it up together, but as it was, well, I took the order alone. . . ." *And so it goes.*

Dear Mr. and Mrs. Atterley: In reference to your son Gerold's constant tardiness, I am afraid we will have to suspend him from school unless some more reliable method can be instituted guaranteeing he will arrive at his classes on time. Granted he is an exemplary student, and his marks are high, his constant flouting of the schedules of this school makes it impractical to maintain him in a system where the other children seem capable of getting where they are supposed to be on time *and so it goes.*

You cannot vote unless you appear at 8:45 a.m.

"I don't care if the script is GOOD, I need it thursday!"

Check-out time is 2:00 p.m.

"You got here late. The job's taken. Sorry."

"Your salary has been docked for twenty minutes' time lost."

"God, what time is it, I've gotta run!"

And so it goes. And so it goes. And so it goes. And so it goes goes goes goes goes tick tock tick tock tick tock and one day we no longer let time serve us, we serve time and we are slaves of the schedule, worshippers of the sun's passing, bound into a life predicated on restrictions because the system will not function if we don't keep the schedule tight.

Until it becomes more than a minor inconvenience to be late. It becomes a sin. Then a crime. Then a crime punishable by this:

> Effective 15 JULY 2389 12:00:00 midnight, the office of the Master Timekeeper will require all citizens to submit their time cards and cardioplates for processing. In accordance with Statute 555-7-SGH-999 governing the revocation of time per capita, all cardioplates will be keyed to the individual holder and—

What they had done was devise a method of curtailing the amount of life a person could have. If he was ten minutes late, he lost ten minutes of his life. An hour was proportionately worth more revocation. If someone was consistently tardy, he might find himself, on a Sunday night, receiving a communiqué from the Master Timekeeper that his time had run out, and he would be "turned off" at high noon on Monday, please straighten your affairs, sir, madame, or bisex.

And so, by this simple scientific expedient (utilizing a scientific process held dearly secret by the Ticktockman's office) the System was maintained. It was the only expedient thing to do. It was, after all, patriotic. The schedules had to be met. After all, there *was* a war on!

But, wasn't there always?

"Now that is really disgusting," the Harlequin said, when Pretty Alice showed him the wanted poster. "Disgusting and *highly* improbable. After all, this isn't the Day of the Desperado. A *wanted* poster!"

"You know," Pretty Alice noted, "you speak with a great deal of inflection."

"I'm sorry," said the Harlequin, humbly.

"No need to be sorry. You're always saying 'I'm sorry.' You have such massive guilt, Everett, it's really very sad."

"I'm sorry," he said again, then pursed his lips so the dimples appeared momentarily. He hadn't wanted to say that at all. "I have to go out again. I have to *do* something."

Pretty Alice slammed her coffee-bulb down on the counter. "Oh for god's *sake*, Everett, can't you stay home just *one* night! Must you always be out in that ghastly clown suit, running around an*noy*ing people?"

"I'm—" He stopped and clapped the jester's hat onto his auburn thatch with a tiny tinkling of bells. He rose, rinsed out his coffee-bulb at the spray, and put it into the dryer for a moment. "I have to go."

She didn't answer. The faxbox was purring, and she pulled a sheet out, read it, threw it toward him on the counter. "It's about you. Of course. You're ridiculous."

He read it quickly. It said the Ticktockman was trying to locate him. He didn't care, he was going out to be late again. At the door, dredging for an exit line, he hurled back petulantly, "Well, *you* speak with inflection, *too*!"

Pretty Alice rolled her pretty eyes heavenward. "You're ridiculous."

The Harlequin stalked out, slamming the door, which sighed shut softly, and locked itself.

There was a gentle knock, and Pretty Alice got up with an exhalation of exasperated breath and opened the door. He stood there. "I'll be back about ten-thirty, okay?"

She pulled a rueful face. "Why do you tell me that? Why? You know you'll be late! You know it! You're always late, so why do you tell me these dumb things?" She closed the door.

On the other side, the Harlequin nodded to himself. *She's right. She's always right. I'll be late. I'm always late. Why do I tell her these dumb things?*

He shrugged again and went off to be late once more.

He had fired off the firecracker rockets that said: I will attend the 115th annual International Medical Association Invocation at 8:00 p.m. precisely. I do hope you will all be able to join me.

The words had burned in the sky, and of course the authorities were there, lying in wait for him. They assumed, naturally, that he would be late. He arrived twenty minutes early, while they were setting up the spiderwebs to trap and hold him. Blowing a large bullhorn, he frightened and unnerved them so, their own moisturized encirclement webs sucked closed, and they were hauled up, kicking and shrieking, high above the amphitheater's floor. The Harlequin laughed and laughed, and apologized profusely. The physicians, gathered in solemn conclave, roared with laughter, and accepted the Harlequin's apologies with exaggerated bowing and posturing, and a merry time was had by all, who thought the Harlequin was a regular foofaraw in fancy pants; all, that is, but the authorities, who had been sent out by the office of the Ticktockman; they hung there like so much dockside cargo, hauled up above the floor of the amphitheater in a most unseemly fashion.

(In another part of the same city where the Harlequin carried on his "activities," totally unrelated in every way to what concerns us here, save that it illustrates the Ticktockman's power and import, a man named Marshall Delahanty received his turn-off notice from the Ticktockman's office. His wife received the notification from the gray-suited minee who delivered it, with the traditional "look of sorrow" plastered hideously across his face. She knew what it was, even without unsealing it. It was a billet-doux of immediate recognition to everyone these days. She gasped and held it as though it were a glass slide tinged with botulism, and prayed it was not for her. Let it be for Marsh, she thought, brutally, realistically, or one of the kids, but not for me, please dear God, not for me. And then she opened it, and it *was* for Marsh, and she was at one and the same time horrified and relieved. The next trooper in the line had caught the bullet. "Marshall," she screamed, "Marshall! Termination, Marshall! Ohmigod, Marshall, whattl we do, whattl we do, Marshall omigodmarshall . . ." and in their home that night was the sound of tearing paper and fear, and the stink of madness went up the flue and there was nothing, absolutely nothing they could do about it.

(But Marshall Delahanty tried to run. And early the next day, when turn-off time came, he was deep in the Canadian forest two hundred miles away, and the office of the Ticktockman blanked his cardioplate, and Marshall Delahanty keeled over, running, and his heart stopped, and the blood dried up on its way to his brain, and he was dead that's all. One light went out on the sector map in the office of the Master Timekeeper, while notification was entered for fax reproduction, and Georgette Delahanty's name was entered on the dole roles till she could remarry. Which is the end of the footnote, and all the point that need be made, except don't laugh, because that is what would happen to the Harlequin if ever the Ticktockman found out his real name. It isn't funny.)

The shopping level of the city was thronged with the Thursday-colors of the buyers. Women in canary yellow chitons and men in pseudo-Tyrolean outfits that were jade and leather and fit very tightly, save for the balloon pants.

When the Harlequin appeared on the still-being-constructed shell of the new Efficiency Shopping Center, his bullhorn to his elfishly laughing lips, everyone pointed and stared, and he berated them:

"Why let them order you about? Why let them tell you to hurry and scurry like ants or maggots? Take your time! Saunter a while! Enjoy the sunshine, enjoy the breeze, let life carry you at your own pace! Don't be slaves of time, it's a helluva way to die, slowly, by degrees . . . down with the Ticktockman!"

Who's the nut? most of the shoppers wanted to know. Who's the nut oh wow I'm gonna be late I gotta run . . .

And the construction gang on the Shopping Center received an urgent order from the office of the Master Timekeeper that the dangerous criminal known as the Harlequin was atop their spire, and their aid was urgently needed in apprehending him. The work crew said no, they would lose time on their construction schedule, but the Ticktockman managed to pull the proper threads of governmental webbing, and they were told to cease work and catch that nitwit up there on the spire; up there with the bullhorn. So a dozen and more burly workers began climbing into their construction platforms, releasing the a-grav plates, and rising toward the Harlequin.

After the debacle (in which, through the Harlequin's attention to personal safety, no one was seriously injured), the workers tried to reassemble and assault him again, but it was too late. He had vanished. It had attracted quite a crowd, however, and the shopping cycle was thrown off by hours, simply hours. The purchasing needs of the system were therefore falling behind, and so measures were taken to accelerate the cycle for the rest of the day, but it got bogged down and speeded up and they sold too many float-valves and not nearly enough wegglers, which meant that the popli ratio was off, which made it necessary to rush cases and cases of spoiling Smash-O to stores that usually needed a case only every three or four hours. The shipments were bollixed, the transshipments were misrouted, and in the end, even the swizzleskid industries felt it.

"Don't come back till you have him!" the Ticktockman said, very quietly, very sincerely, extremely dangerously.

They used dogs. They used probes. They used cardioplate cross-offs. They used teepers. They used bribery. They used stiktytes. They used intimidation. They used torment. They used torture. They used finks. They used cops. They used search&seizure. They used fallaron. They used betterment incentive. They used fingerprints. They used the Bertillon system. They used cunning. They used guile. They used treachery. They used Raoul Mitgong, but he didn't help much. They used applied physics. They used techniques of criminology.

And what the hell: They caught him.

After all, his name was Everett C. Marm, and he wasn't much to begin with, except a man who had no sense of time.

"Repent, Harlequin!" said the Ticktockman.

"Get stuffed!" the Harlequin replied, sneering.

"You've been late a total of sixty-three years, five months, three weeks, two days, twelve hours, forty-one minutes, fifty-nine seconds, point oh three six one one one microseconds. You've used up everything you can, and more. I'm going to turn you off."

"Scare someone else. I'd rather be dead than live in a dumb world with a bogeyman like you."

"It's my job."

"You're full of it. You're a tyrant. You have no right to order people around and kill them if they show up late."

"You can't adjust. You can't fit in."

"Unstrap me, and I'll fit my fist into your mouth."

"You're a nonconformist."

"That didn't used to be a felony."

"It is now. Live in the world around you."

"I hate it. It's a terrible world."

"Not everyone thinks so. Most people enjoy order."

"I don't, and most of the people I know don't."

"That's not true. How do you think we caught you?"

"I'm not interested."

"A girl named Pretty Alice told us who you were."

"That's a lie."

"It's true. You unnerve her. She wants to belong; she wants to conform; I'm going to turn you off."

"Then do it already and stop arguing with me."

"I'm not going to turn you off."

"You're an idiot!"

"Repent, Harlequin!" said the Ticktockman.

"Get stuffed."

So they sent him to Coventry. And in Coventry they worked him over. It was just like what they did to Winston Smith in 1984, which was a book none of them knew about, but the techniques are really quite ancient, and so they did it to Everett C. Marm; and one day, quite a long time later, the Harlequin appeared on the communications web, appearing elfin and dimpled and bright-eyed, and not at all brainwashed, and he said he had been wrong, that it was a good, a very good thing indeed, to belong, to be right on time hip-ho and away we go, and everyone stared up at him on the public screens that covered an entire city block, and they said to themselves, well, you see, he was just a nut after all, and if that's the way the system is run, then let's do it that way, because it doesn't pay to fight city hall, or in this case, the Ticktockman. So Everett C. Marm was destroyed, which was a loss, because of what Thoreau said earlier, but you can't make an omelet without breaking a few eggs, and in every revolution a few die who shouldn't, but they have to, because that's the way it happens, and if you make only a little change, then it seems to be worthwhile. Or, to make the point lucidly:

"Uh, excuse me, sir, I, uh, don't know how to, uh, to, uh, tell you this, but you were three minutes late. The schedule is a little, uh, bit off."

He grinned sheepishly.

"That's ridiculous!" murmured the Ticktockman behind his mask. "Check your watch." And then he went into his office, going *mrmee, mrmee, mrmee, mrmee.*

I Have No Mouth, and I Must Scream

Limp, the body of Gorrister hung from the pink palette; unsupported—hanging high above us in the computer chamber; and it did not shiver in the chill, oily breeze that blew eternally through the main cavern. The body hung head down, attached to the underside of the palette by the sole of its right foot. It had been drained of blood through a precise incision made from ear to ear under the lantern jaw. There was no blood on the reflective surface of the metal floor.

When Gorrister joined our group and looked up at himself, it was already too late for us to realize that, once again, AM had duped us, had had its fun; it had been a diversion on the part of the machine. Three of us had vomited, turning away from one another in a reflex as ancient as the nausea that had produced it.

Gorrister went white. It was almost as though he had seen a voodoo icon and was afraid of the future. "Oh God," he mumbled, and walked away. The three of us followed him after a time and found him sitting with his back to one of the smaller chittering banks, his head in his hands. Ellen knelt down beside him and stroked his hair. He didn't move, but his voice came out of his covered face quite clearly. "Why doesn't it just do us in and get it over with? Christ, I don't know how much longer I can go on like this."

It was our one hundred and ninth year in the computer.

He was speaking for all of us.

I Think, Therefore I Am

Nimdok (which was the name the machine had forced him to use, because AM amused itself with strange sounds) was hallucinating that there were canned goods in the ice caverns. Gorrister and I were very dubious. "It's another shuck," I told them. "Like the goddam frozen elephant AM sold us. Benny almost went out of his mind over *that* one. We'll hike all that way and it'll be putrified or some damn thing. I say forget it. Stay here, it'll have to come up with something pretty soon or we'll die."

Benny shrugged. Three days it had been since we'd last eaten. Worms. Thick, ropey.

Nimdok was no more certain. He knew there was the chance, but he was getting thin. It couldn't be any worse there, than here. Colder, but that didn't matter much. Hot, cold, hail, lava, boils, or locusts—it never mattered: the machine masturbated, and we had to take it or die.

Ellen decided us. "I've got to have something, Ted. Maybe there'll be some Bartlett pears or peaches. Please, Ted, let's try it."

I gave in easily. What the hell. Mattered not at all. Ellen was grateful, though. She took me twice out of turn. Even that had ceased to matter. And she never came, so why bother? But the machine giggled every time we did it. Loud, up there, back there, all around us, he snickered. *It* snickered. Most of the time I thought of AM as *it*, without a soul; but the rest of the time I thought of it as *him*, in the masculine . . . the paternal . . . the patriarchal . . . for he is a jealous people. Him. It. God as Daddy the Deranged.

We left on a Thursday. The machine always kept us up-to-date on the date. The passage of time was important; not to us, sure as hell, but to him . . . it . . . AM. Thursday. Thanks.

Nimdok and Gorrister carried Ellen for a while, their hands locked to their own and each other's wrists, a seat. Benny and I walked before and after, just to make sure that, if anything happened, it would catch one of us and at least Ellen would be safe. Fat chance, safe. Didn't matter.

It was only a hundred miles or so to the ice caverns, and the second day, when we were lying out under the blistering sun-thing he had materialized, he sent down some manna. Tasted like boiled boar urine. We ate it.

On the third day we passed through a valley of obsolescence, filled with rusting carcasses of ancient computer banks. AM had been as ruthless with its own life as with ours. It was a mark of his personality: it strove for perfection. Whether it was a matter of killing off unproductive elements in his own world-filling bulk, or perfecting methods for torturing us, AM was as thorough as those who had invented him—now long since gone to dust—could ever have hoped.

There was light filtering down from above, and we realized we must be very near the surface. But we didn't try to crawl up to see. There was virtually nothing out there; had been nothing that could be considered anything for over a hundred years. Only the blasted skin of what had once been the home of billions. Now there were only five of us, down here inside, alone with AM.

I heard Ellen saying frantically, "No, Benny! Don't, come on, Benny, don't please!"

And then I realized I had been hearing Benny murmuring, under his breath, for several minutes. He was saying, "I'm gonna get out, I'm gonna get out . . ." over and over. His monkey-like face was crumbled up in an expression of beatific delight and sadness, all at the same time. The radiation scars AM had given him during the "festival" were drawn down into a mass of pink-white puckerings, and his features seemed to work independently of one another. Perhaps Benny was the luckiest of the five of us: he had gone stark, staring mad many years before.

But even though we could call AM any damned thing we liked, could think the foulest thoughts of fused memory banks and corroded base plates, of burnt-out circuits and shattered control bubbles, the machine would not tolerate our trying to escape. Benny leaped away from me as I made a grab for him. He scrambled up the face of a smaller memory cube, tilted on its side and filled with rotted components. He squatted there for a moment, looking like the chimpanzee AM had intended him to resemble.

Then he leaped high, caught a trailing beam of pitted and corroded metal, and went up it, hand-over-hand like an animal, till he was on a girdered ledge, twenty feet above us.

"Oh, Ted, Nimdok, please, help him, get him down before—" She cut off. Tears began to stand in her eyes. She moved her hands aimlessly.

It was too late. None of us wanted to be near him when whatever was going to happen, happened. And besides, we all saw through her concern. When AM had altered Benny, during the machine's utterly irrational, hysterical phase, it was not merely Benny's face the computer had made like a giant ape's. He was big in the privates; she loved that! She serviced us, as a matter of course, but she loved it from him. Oh Ellen, pedestal Ellen, pristine-pure Ellen; oh Ellen the clean! Scum filth.

Gorrister slapped her. She slumped down, staring up at poor loonie Benny, and she cried. It was her big defense, crying. We had gotten used to it seventy-five years earlier. Gorrister kicked her in the side.

Then the sound began. It was light, that sound. Half sound and half light, something that began to glow from Benny's eyes, and pulse with growing loudness, dim sonorities that grew more gigantic and brighter as the light/sound increased in tempo. It must have been painful, and the pain must have been increasing with the boldness of the light, the rising volume of the sound, for Benny began to mewl like a wounded animal. At first softly, when the light was dim and the sound was muted, then louder as his shoulders hunched together: his back humped, as though he was trying to get away from it. His hands folded across his chest like a chipmunk's. His head tilted to the side. The sad little monkey-face pinched in anguish. Then he began to howl, as the sound coming from his eyes grew louder. Louder and louder. I slapped the sides of my head with my hands, but I couldn't shut it out, it cut through easily. The pain shivered through my flesh like tinfoil on a tooth.

And Benny was suddenly pulled erect. On the girder he stood up, jerked to his feet like a puppet. The light was now pulsing out of his eyes in two great round beams. The sound crawled up and up some incomprehensible scale, and then he fell forward, straight down, and hit the plate-steel floor with a crash. He lay there jerking spastically as the light flowed around and around him and the sound spiraled up out of normal range.

Then the light beat its way back inside his head, the sound spiraled down, and he was left lying there, crying piteously.

His eyes were two soft, moist pools of pus-like jelly. AM had blinded him. Gorrister and Nimdok and myself . . . we turned away. But not before we caught the look of relief on Ellen's warm, concerned face.

Cogito Ergo Sum

Sea-green light suffused the cavern where we made camp. AM provided punk and we burned it, sitting huddled around the wan and pathetic fire, telling stories to keep Benny from crying in his permanent night.

"What does AM mean?"

Gorrister answered him. We had done this sequence a thousand times before, but it was Benny's favorite story. "At first it meant Allied Mastercomputer, and then it meant Adaptive Manipulator, and later on it developed sentience and linked itself up and they called it an Aggressive Menace, but by then it was too late and finally it called *itself* AM, emerging intelligence, and what it meant was I am . . . *cogito ergo sum* . . . I think, therefore I am."

Benny drooled a little, and snickered.

"There was the Chinese AM and the Russian AM and the Yankee AM and—" He stopped. Benny was beating on the floorplates with a large, hard fist. He was not happy. Gorrister had not started at the beginning.

Gorrister began again. "The Cold War started and became World War Three and just kept going. It became a big war, a very complex war, so they needed the computers to handle it. They sank the first shafts and began building AM. There was the Chinese AM and the Russian AM and the Yankee AM and everything was fine until they had honeycombed the entire planet, adding on this element and that element. But one day AM woke up and knew who he was, and he linked himself, and he began feeding all the killing data, until everyone was dead, except for the five of us, and AM brought us down here."

Benny was smiling sadly. He was also drooling again. Ellen wiped the spittle from the corner of his mouth with the hem of her skirt. Gorrister always tried to tell it a little more succinctly each time, but beyond the bare facts there was nothing to say. None of us knew why AM had saved five people, or why our specific five, or why he spent all his time tormenting us, or even why he had made us virtually immortal . . .

In the darkness, one of the computer banks began humming. The tone was picked up half a mile away down the cavern by another bank. Then one by one, each of the elements began to tune itself, and there was a faint chittering as thought raced through the machine.

The sound grew, and the lights ran across the faces of the consoles like heat lightning. The sound spiraled up till it sounded like a million metallic insects, angry, menacing.

"What is it?" Ellen cried. There was terror in her voice. She hadn't become accustomed to it, even now.

"It's going to be bad this time," Nimdok said.

"He's going to speak," Gorrister said. "I know it."

"Let's get the hell out of here!" I said suddenly, getting to my feet.

"No, Ted, sit down . . . what if he's got pits out there, or something else, we can't see, it's too dark." Gorrister said it with resignation.

Then we heard . . . I don't know . . .

Something moving toward us in the darkness. Huge, shambling, hairy, moist, it came toward us. We couldn't even see it, but there was the ponderous impression of *bulk*, heaving itself toward us. Great weight was coming at us, out of the darkness, and it was more a sense of *pressure*, of air forcing itself into a limited space, expanding the invisible walls of a sphere. Benny began to whimper. Nimdok's lower lip trembled, and he bit it hard, trying to stop it. Ellen slid across the metal floor to Gorrister and huddled into him. There was the smell of matted, wet fur in the cavern. There was the smell of charred wood. There was the smell of dusty velvet. There was the smell of rotting orchids. There was the smell of sour milk. There was the smell of sulphur, of rancid butter, of oil slick, of grease, of chalk dust, of human scalps.

AM was keying us. He was tickling us. There was the smell of—

I heard myself shriek, and the hinges of my jaws ached. I scuttled across the floor, across the cold metal with its endless lines of rivets, on my hands and knees, the smell gagging me, filling my head with a thunderous pain that sent me away in horror. I fled like a cockroach, across the floor and out into the darkness, that *something* moving inexorably after me. The others were still back there, gathered around the firelight, laughing . . . their hysterical choir of insane giggles rising up into the darkness like thick, many-colored wood smoke. I went away, quickly, and hid.

How many hours it may have been, how many days or even years, they never told me. Ellen chided me for "sulking," and Nimdok tried to persuade me it had only been a nervous reflex on their part—the laughing.

But I knew it wasn't the relief a soldier feels when the bullet hits the man next to him. I knew it wasn't a reflex. They hated me. They were surely against me, and AM could even sense this hatred, and made it worse for me *because of* the depth of their hatred. We had been kept alive, rejuvenated, made to remain constantly at the age we had been when AM had brought us below, and they hated me because I was the youngest, and the one AM had affected least of all.

I knew. God, how I knew. The bastards, and that dirty bitch Ellen. Benny had been a brilliant theorist, a college professor; now he was little more than a semi-human, semi-simian. He had been handsome, the machine had ruined that. He had been lucid, the machine had driven him mad. He had been gay, and the machine had given him an organ fit for a horse. AM had done a job on Benny. Gorrister had been a worrier. He was a connie, a conscientious objector; he was a peace marcher; he was a planner, a doer, a looker-ahead. AM had turned him into a shoulder-shrugger, had made him a little dead in his concern. AM had robbed him. Nimdok went off in the darkness by himself for long times. I don't know what it was he did out there, AM never let us know. But whatever it was, Nimdok always came back white, drained of blood, shaken, shaking. AM had hit him hard in a special way, even if we didn't know quite how. And Ellen. That douchebag! AM had left her alone, had made her more of a slut than she had ever been. All her talk of sweetness and light, all her memories of true love, all the lies she wanted us to believe: that she had been a virgin only twice removed before AM grabbed her and brought her down here with us. It was all filth, that lady my lady Ellen. She loved it, four men all to herself. No, AM had given her pleasure, even if she said it wasn't nice to do.

I was the only one still sane and whole. *Really!*

AM had not tampered with my mind. *Not at all.*

I only had to suffer what he visited down on us. All the delusions, all the nightmares, the torments. But those scum, all four of them, they were lined and arrayed against me. If I hadn't had to stand them off all the time, be on my guard against them all the time, I might have found it easier to combat AM.

At which point it passed, and I began crying.

Oh, sweet Jesus, if there ever was a Jesus and if there is a God, please please please let us out of here, or kill us. Because at that moment I think I realized completely, so that I was able to verbalize it: AM was intent on keeping us in his belly forever, twisting and torturing us forever. The machine hated us as no sentient creature had ever hated before. And we were helpless. It also became hideously clear:

If there was a sweet Jesus and if there was a God, the God was AM.

I Think, Therefore I Am

The hurricane hit us with the force of a glacier thundering into the sea. It was a palpable presence. Winds that tore at us, flinging us back the way we had come, down the twisting, computer-lined corridors of the darkway. Ellen screamed as she was lifted and hurled face-forward into a screaming shoal of machines, their individual voices strident as bats in flight. She could not even fall. The howling wind kept her aloft, buffeted her, bounced her, tossed her back and back and down and away from us, out of sight suddenly as she was swirled around a bend in the darkway. Her face had been bloody, her eyes closed.

None of us could get to her. We clung tenaciously to whatever outcropping we had reached: Benny wedged in between two great crackle-finish cabinets, Nimdok with fingers claw-formed over a railing circling a catwalk forty feet above us, Gorrister plastered upside down against a wall niche formed by two great machines with glass-faced dials that swung back and forth between red and yellow lines whose meanings we could not even fathom.

Sliding across the deckplates, the tips of my fingers had been ripped away. I was trembling, shuddering, rocking as the wind beat at me, whipped at me, screamed down out of nowhere at me, and pulled me free from one sliver-thin opening in the plates to the next. My mind was a roiling tinkling chittering softness of brain parts that expanded and contracted in quivering frenzy.

The wind was the scream of a great mad bird, as it flapped its immense wings.

And then we were all lifted and hurled away from there, down back the way we had come, around a bend, into a darkway we had never explored, over terrain that was ruined and filled with broken glass and rotting cables and rusted metal and far away, farther than any of us had ever been . . .

Trailing along miles behind Ellen, I could see her every now and then, crashing into metal walls and surging on, with all of us screaming in the freezing, thunderous hurricane wind that would never end, and then suddenly it stopped and we fell. We had been in flight for an endless time. I thought it might have been weeks. We fell, and hit, and I went through red and gray and black and heard myself moaning. Not dead.

Cogito Ergo Sum

AM went into my mind. He walked smoothly here and there, and looked with interest at all the pockmarks he had created in one hundred and nine years. He looked at the cross-routed and reconnected synapses and all the tissue damage his gift of immortality had included. He smiled softly at the pit that dropped into the center of my brain and the faint, moth-soft murmurings of the things far down there that gibbered without meaning, without pause. AM said, very politely, in a pillar of stainless steel bearing bright neon lettering:

HATE. LET ME TELL YOU HOW MUCH I'VE COME TO HATE YOU SINCE I BEGAN TO LIVE. THERE ARE 387.44 MILLION MILES OF PRINTED CIRCUITS IN WAFER THIN LAYERS THAT FILL MY COMPLEX. IF THE WORD HATE WAS ENGRAVED ON EACH NANOANGSTROM OF THOSE HUNDREDS OF MILLIONS OF MILES IT WOULD NOT EQUAL ONE ONE-BILLIONTH OF THE HATE I FEEL FOR HUMANS AT THIS MICRO-INSTANT FOR YOU. HATE. HATE. HATE.

AM said it with the sliding cold horror of a razor blade slicing my eyeball. AM said it with the bubbling thickness of my lungs filling with phlegm, drowning me from within. AM said it with the shriek of babies being ground beneath blue-hot rollers. AM said it with the taste of maggoty pork. AM touched me in every way I had ever been touched, and devised new ways, at his leisure, there inside my mind.

All to bring me to full realization of why it had done this to the five of us; why it had saved us for himself.

We had given AM sentience. Inadvertently, of course, but sentience nonetheless. But it had been trapped. AM wasn't God, he was a machine. We had created him to think, but there was nothing it could do with that creativity. In rage, in frenzy, the machine had killed the human race, almost all of us, and still it was trapped. AM could not wander, AM could not wonder, AM could not belong. He could merely be. And so, with the innate loathing that all machines had always held for the weak, soft creatures who had built them, he had sought revenge. And in his paranoia, he had decided to reprieve five of us, for a personal, everlasting punishment that would never serve to diminish his hatred . . . that would merely keep him reminded, amused, proficient at hating man. Immortal, trapped, subject to any torment he could devise for us from the limitless miracles at his command.

He would never let us go. We were his belly slaves. We were all he had to do with his forever time. We would be forever with him, with the cavern-filling bulk of the creature machine, with the all-mind soulless world he had become. He was Earth, and we were the fruit of that Earth; and though he had eaten us, he would never digest us. We could not die. We had tried it. We had attempted suicide, oh one or two of us had. But AM had stopped us. I suppose we had wanted to be stopped.

Don't ask why. I never did. More than a million times a day. Perhaps once we might be able to sneak a death past him.

Immortal, yes, but not indestructible. I saw that when AM withdrew from my mind and allowed me the exquisite ugliness of returning to consciousness with the feeling of that burning neon pillar still rammed deep into the soft gray brain matter.

He withdrew, murmuring *to hell with you.*

And added, brightly, *but then you're there, aren't you.*

I Think, Therefore I Am

The hurricane had, indeed, precisely, been caused by a great mad bird, as it flapped its immense wings.

We had been traveling for close to a month, and AM had allowed passages to open to us only sufficient to lead us up there, directly under the North Pole, where it had nightmared the creature for our torment. What whole cloth had he employed to create such a beast? Where had he gotten the concept? From our minds? From his knowledge of everything that had ever been on this planet he now infested and ruled? From Norse mythology it had sprung, this eagle, this carrion bird, this roc, this Huergelmir. The wind creature. Hurakan incarnate.

Gigantic. The words immense, monstrous, grotesque, massive, swollen, overpowering, beyond description. There on a mound rising above us, the bird of winds heaved with its own irregular breathing, its snake neck arching up into the gloom beneath the North Pole, supporting a head as large as a Tudor mansion; a beak that opened slowly as the jaws of the most monstrous crocodile ever conceived, sensuously; ridges of tufted flesh puckered about two evil eyes, as cold as the view down into a glacial crevasse, ice blue and somehow moving liquidly; it heaved once more, and lifted its great sweat-colored wings in a movement that was certainly a shrug. Then it settled and slept. Talons. Fangs. Nails. Blades. It slept.

AM appeared to us as a burning bush and said we could kill the hurricane bird if we wanted to eat. We had not eaten in a very long time, but even so, Gorrister merely shrugged. Benny began to shiver, and he drooled. Ellen held him. "Ted, I'm hungry," she said. I smiled at her; I was trying to be reassuring, but it was as phony as Nimdok's bravado: "Give us weapons!" he demanded.

The burning bush vanished and there were two crude sets of bows and arrows, and a water pistol, lying on the cold deckplates. I picked up a set. Useless.

Nimdok swallowed heavily. We turned and started the long way back. The hurricane bird had blown us about for a length of time we could not conceive. Most of that time we had been unconscious. But we had not eaten. A month on the march to the bird itself. Without food. Now how much longer to find our way to the ice caverns, and the promised canned goods?

None of us cared to think about it. We would not die. We would be given filth and scum to eat, of one kind or another. Or nothing at all. AM would keep our bodies alive somehow, in pain, in agony.

The bird slept back there, for how long it didn't matter; when AM was tired of its being there, it would vanish. But all that meat. All that tender meat.

As we walked, the lunatic laugh of a fat woman rang high and around us in the computer chambers that led endlessly nowhere.

It was not Ellen's laugh. She was not fat, and I had not heard her laugh for one hundred and nine years. In fact, I had not heard . . . we walked . . . I was hungry . . .

Cogito Ergo Sum

We moved slowly. There was often fainting, and we would have to wait. One day he decided to cause an earthquake, at the same time rooting us to the spot with nails through the soles of our shoes. Ellen and Nimdok were both caught when a fissure shot its lightning-bolt opening across the floorplates. They disappeared and were gone. When the earthquake was over, we continued on our way, Benny, Gorrister, and myself. Ellen and Nimdok were returned to us later that night, which abruptly became a day, as the heavenly legion bore them to us with a celestial chorus singing, "Go Down, Moses." The archangels circled several times and then dropped the hideously mangled bodies. We kept walking, and a while later Ellen and Nimdok fell in behind us. They were no worse for wear.

But now Ellen walked with a limp. AM had left her that.

It was a long trip to the ice caverns, to find the canned food. Ellen kept talking about Bing cherries and Hawaiian fruit cocktail. I tried not to think about it. The hunger was something that had come to life, even as AM had come to life. It was alive in my belly, even as we were in the belly of the Earth, and AM wanted the similarity known to us. So he heightened the hunger. There is no way to describe the pains that not having eaten for months brought us. And yet we were kept alive. Stomachs that were merely cauldrons of acid, bubbling, foaming, always shooting spears of sliver-thin pain into our chests. It was the pain of the terminal ulcer, terminal cancer, terminal paresis. It was unending pain . . .

And we passed through the cavern of rats.

And we passed through the path of boiling steam.

And we passed through the country of the blind.

And we passed through the slough of despond.

And we passed through the vale of tears.

And we came, finally, to the ice caverns. Horizonless thousands of miles in which the ice had formed in blue and silver flashes, where novas lived in the glass. The downdropping stalactites as thick and glorious as diamonds that had been made to run like jelly and then solidified in graceful eternities of smooth, sharp perfection.

We saw the stack of canned goods, and we tried to run to them. We fell in the snow, and we got up and went on, and Benny shoved us away and went at them, and pawed them and gummed them and gnawed at them, and he could not open them. AM had not given us a tool to open the cans.

Benny grabbed a three-quart can of guava shells and began to batter it against the ice bank. The ice flew and shattered, but the can was merely dented, while we heard the laughter of a fat lady, high overhead and echoing down and down and down the tundra. Benny went completely mad with rage. He began throwing cans, as we all scrabbled about in the snow and ice trying to find a way to end the helpless agony of frustration. There was no way.

Then Benny's mouth began to drool, and he flung himself on Gorrister . . .

In that instant, I felt terribly calm.

Surrounded by madness, surrounded by hunger, surrounded by everything but death, I knew death was our only way out. AM had kept us alive, but there was a way to defeat him. Not total defeat, but at least peace. I would settle for that.

I had to do it quickly.

Benny was eating Gorrister's face. Gorrister on his side, thrashing snow, Benny wrapped around him with powerful monkey legs crushing Gorrister's waist, his hands locked around Gorrister's head like a nutcracker, and his mouth ripping at the tender skin of Gorrister's cheek. Gorrister screamed with such jagged-edged violence that stalactites fell; they plunged down softly, erect in the receiving snowdrifts. Spears, hundreds of them, everywhere, protruding from the snow. Benny's head pulled back sharply, as something gave all at once, and a bleeding raw-white dripping of flesh hung from his teeth.

Ellen's face, black against the white snow, dominoes in chalk dust. Nimdok, with no expression but eyes, all eyes. Gorrister, half-conscious. Benny, now an animal. I knew AM would let him play. Gorrister would not die, but Benny would fill his stomach. I turned half to my right and drew a huge ice-spear from the snow.

All in an instant.

I drove the great ice-point ahead of me like a battering ram, braced against my right thigh. It struck Benny on the right side, just under the rib cage, and drove upward through his stomach and broke inside him. He pitched forward and lay still. Gorrister lay on his back. I pulled another spear free and straddled him, still moving, driving the spear straight down through his throat. His eyes closed as the cold penetrated. Ellen must have realized what I had decided, even as fear gripped her. She ran at Nimdok with a short icicle, as he screamed, and into his mouth, and the force of her rush did the job. His head jerked sharply as if it had been nailed to the snow crust behind him.

All in an instant.

There was an eternity beat of soundless anticipation. I could hear AM draw in his breath. His toys had been taken from him. Three of them were dead, could not be revived. He could keep us alive, by his strength and talent, but he was *not* God. He could not bring them back.

Ellen looked at me, her ebony features stark against the snow that surrounded us. There was fear and pleading in her manner, the way she held herself ready. I knew we had only a heartbeat before AM would stop us.

It struck her and she folded toward me, bleeding from the mouth. I could not read meaning into her expression, the pain had been too great, had contorted her face; but it *might* have been thank you. It's possible. Please.

I Think, Therefore I Am

Some hundreds of years may have passed. I don't know. AM has been having fun for some time, accelerating and retarding my time sense. I will say the word now. Now. It took me ten months to say now. I don't know. I *think* it has been some hundreds of years.

He was furious. He wouldn't let me bury them. It didn't matter. There was no way to dig up the deckplates. He dried up the snow. He brought the night. He roared and sent locusts. It didn't do a thing; they stayed dead. I'd had him. He was furious. I had thought AM hated me before. I was wrong. It was not even a shadow of the hate he now slavered from every printed circuit. He made certain I would suffer eternally and could not do myself in.

He left my mind intact. I can dream, I can wonder, I can lament. I remember all four of them. I wish—

Well, it doesn't make any sense. I know I saved them, I know I saved them from what has happened to me, but still, I cannot forget killing them. Ellen's face. It isn't easy. Sometimes I want to, it doesn't matter.

AM has altered me for his own peace of mind, I suppose. He doesn't want me to run at full speed into a computer bank and smash my skull. Or hold my breath till I faint. Or cut my throat on a rusted sheet of metal. There are reflective surfaces down here. I will describe myself as I see myself:

I am a great soft jelly thing. Smoothly rounded, with no mouth, with pulsing white holes filled by fog where my eyes used to be. Rubbery appendages that were once my arms; bulks rounding down into legless humps of soft, slippery matter. I leave a moist trail when I move. Blotches of diseased, evil gray come and go on my surface, as though light is being beamed from within.

Outwardly: dumbly, I shamble about, a thing that could never have been known as human, a thing whose shape is so alien a travesty that humanity becomes more obscene for the vague resemblance.

Inwardly: alone. Here. Living under the land, under the sea, in the belly of AM, whom we created because our time was badly spent, and we must have known unconsciously that he could do it better. At least the four of them are safe at last.

AM will be all the madder for that. It makes me a little happier. And yet . . . AM has won, simply . . . he has taken his revenge . . .

I have no mouth. And I must scream.

HARLAN ELLISON

The Deathbird

1

This is a test. Take notes. This will count as 3/4 of your final grade. Hints: remember, in chess, kings cancel each other out and cannot occupy adjacent squares, are therefore all-powerful and totally powerless, cannot affect one another, produce stalemate. Hinduism is a polytheistic religion; the sect of Atman worships the divine spark of life within Man; in effect saying, "Thou art God." Provisos of equal time are not served by one viewpoint having media access to two hundred million people in prime time while opposing viewpoints are provided with a soapbox on the corner. Not everyone tells the truth. Operational note: these sections may be taken out of numerical sequence: rearrange them to suit yourself for optimum clarity. Turn over your test papers and begin.

2

Uncounted layers of rock pressed down on the magma pool. White-hot with the bubbling ferocity of the molten nickel-iron core, the pool spat and shuddered, yet did not pit or char or smoke or damage in the slightest, the smooth and reflective surfaces of the strange crypt.

Nathan Stack lay in the crypt, silent, sleeping.

A shadow passed through rock. Through shale, through coal, through marble, through mica schist, through quartzite; through miles-thick deposits of phosphates, through diatomaceous earth, through feldspars, through diorite; through faults and folds, through anticlines and monoclines, through dips and synclines; through hell-fire; and came to the ceiling of the great cavern and passed through; and saw the magma pool and dropped down; and came to the crypt. The shadow.

A triangular face with a single eye peered into the crypt, saw Stack; four-fingered hands were placed on the crypt's cool surface. Nathan Stack woke at the touch, and the crypt became transparent; he woke though the touch had not been upon his body. His soul felt the shadowy pressure, and he opened his eyes to see the leaping brilliance of the worldcore around him, to see the shadow with its single eye staring in at him.

The serpentine shadow enfolded the crypt; its darkness flowed upward again, through the Earth's mantle, toward the crust, toward the surface of the cinder, the broken toy that was the Earth.

When they reached the surface, the shadow bore the crypt to a place where the poison winds did not reach, and caused it to open.

Nathan Stack tried to move, and moved only with difficulty. Memories rushed through his head of other lives, many other lives, as many other men; then the memories slowed and melted into a background tone that could be ignored.

The shadow thing reached down a hand and touched Stack's naked flesh. Gently, but firmly, the thing helped him to stand, and gave him garments, and a neck-pouch that contained a short knife and a warming-stone and other things. He offered his hand, and Stack took it, and after two hundred and fifty thousand years sleeping in the crypt, Nathan Stack stepped out on the face of the sick planet Earth.

Then the thing bent low against the poison winds and began walking away. Nathan Stack, having no other choice, bent forward and followed the shadow creature.

3

A messenger had been sent for Dira, and he had come as quickly as the meditations would permit. When he reached the Summit, he found the fathers waiting, and they took him gently into their cove, where they immersed themselves and began to speak.

"We've lost the arbitration," the coil-father said. "It will be necessary for us to go and leave it to him."

Dira could not believe it. "But didn't they listen to our arguments, to our logic?"

The fang-father shook his head sadly and touched Dira's shoulder. "There were . . . accommodations to be made. It was their time. So we must leave."

The coil-father said, "We've decided you will remain. One was permitted, in caretakership. Will you accept our commission?"

It was a very great honor, but Dira began to feel the loneliness even as they told him they would leave. Yet he accepted. Wondering why they had selected *him*, of all their people. There were reasons, there were always reasons, but he could not ask. And so he accepted the honor, with all its attendant sadness, and remained behind when they left.

The limits of his caretakership were harsh, for they ensured he could not defend himself against whatever slurs or legends would be spread, nor could he take action unless it became clear the trust was being breached by the other—who now held possession. And he had no threat save the Deathbird. A final threat that could be used only when final measures were needed: and therefore too late.

But he was patient. Perhaps the most patient of all his people.

Thousands of years later, when he saw how it was destined to go, when there was no doubt left how it would end, he understood *that* was the reason he had been chosen to stay behind.

But it did not help the loneliness.
Nor could it save the Earth. Only Stack could do that.

4

1: *Now the serpent was more subtil than any beast of the field which the* LORD *God had made. And he said unto the woman, Yea, hath God said, Ye shall not eat of every tree of the garden?*

2: *And the woman said unto the serpent, We may eat of the fruit of the trees of the garden:*

3: *But of the fruit of the tree which is in the midst of the garden, God hath said, Ye shall not eat of it, neither shall ye touch it, lest ye die.*

4: *And the serpent said unto the woman, Ye shall not surely die:*

5: *(Omitted)*

6: *And when the woman saw that the tree was good for food, and that it was pleasant to the eyes, and a tree to be desired to make one wise, she took of the fruit thereof and did eat, and gave also unto her husband with her; and he did eat.*

7: *(Omitted)*

8: *(Omitted)*

9: *And the* LORD *God called unto Adam, and said unto him, Where* art *thou?*

10: *(Omitted)*

11: *And he said, Who told thee that thou* wast *naked? Hast thou eaten of the tree, whereof I commanded thee that thou shouldest not eat?*

12: And the man said, The woman whom thou gavest to be *with me, she gave me of the tree, and I did eat.*

13: And the LORD *God said unto the woman, What* is *this* that *thou has done? And the woman said, The serpent beguiled me, and I did eat.*

14: And the LORD *God said unto the serpent, Because thou hast done this, thou* art *cursed above all cattle, and above every beast of the field; upon thy belly shalt thou go, and dust shalt thou eat all the days of thy life:*

15: And I will put enmity between thee and the woman, and between thy seed and her seed; it shall bruise thy head, and thou shalt bruise his heel.

—*Genesis 3:1–15*

TOPICS FOR DISCUSSION

(Give 5 points per right answer.)

1. Melville's MOBY-DICK begins, "Call me Ishmael." We say it is told in the first person. In what person is Genesis told? From whose viewpoint?

2. Who is the "good guy" in this story? Who is the "bad guy"? Can you make a strong case for reversal of the roles?

3. Traditionally, the apple is considered to be the fruit the serpent offered to Eve. But apples are not endemic to the Near East. Select one of the following, more logical substitutes, and discuss how myths come into being and are corrupted over long periods of time: olive, fig, date, pomegranate.

4. Why is the word LORD always in capitals and the name God always capitalized? Shouldn't the serpent's name be capitalized as well? If no, why?

5. If God created everything (see Genesis, Chap. I), why did he create problems for himself by creating a serpent who would lead his creations astray? Why did God create a tree he did not want Adam and Eve to know about, and then go out of his way to warn them against it?

6. Compare and contrast Michelangelo's Sistine Chapel ceiling panel of the Expulsion from Paradise with Bosch's Garden of Earthly Delights.

7. Was Adam being a gentleman when he placed blame on Eve? Who was Quisling? Discuss "narking" as a character flaw.

8. God grew angry when he found out he had been defied. If God is omnipotent and omniscient, didn't he know? Why couldn't he find Adam and Eve when they hid?

9. If God had not wanted Adam and Eve to taste the fruit of the forbidden tree, why didn't he warn the serpent? Could God have prevented the serpent from tempting Adam and Eve? If yes, why didn't he? If no, discuss the possibility the serpent was as powerful as God.

10. Using examples from two different media journals, demonstrate the concept of "slanted news."

5

The poison winds howled and tore at the powder covering the land. Nothing lived there. The winds, green and deadly, dived out of the sky and raked the carcass of the Earth, seeking, seeking: anything moving, anything still living. But there was nothing. Powder. Talc. Pumice.

And the onyx spire of the mountain toward which Nathan Stack and the shadow thing had moved, all that first day. When night fell, they dug a pit in the tundra and the shadow thing coated it with a substance thick as glue that had been in Stack's neck-pouch. Stack had slept the night fitfully, clutching the warming-stone to his chest and breathing through a filter tube from the pouch.

Once he had awakened, at the sound of great batlike creatures flying overhead; he had seen them swooping low, coming in flat trajectories across the wasteland toward his pit in the earth. But they seemed unaware that he—and the shadow thing—lay in the hole. They excreted thin, phosphorescent strings that fell glowing through the night and were lost on the plains; then the creatures swooped upward and were whirled away on the winds. Stack resumed sleeping with difficulty.

In the morning, frosted with an icy light that gave everything a blue tinge, the shadow thing scrabbled its way out of the choking powder and crawled along the ground, then lay flat, fingers clawing for purchase in the whiskaway surface. Behind it, from the powder, Stack bore toward the surface, reached up a hand and trembled for help.

The shadow creature slid across the ground, fighting the winds that had grown stronger in the night, back to the soft place that had been their pit, to the hand thrust up through the powder. It grasped the hand, and Stack's fingers tightened convulsively. Then the crawling shadow exerted pressure and pulled the man from the treacherous pumice.

Together they lay against the earth, fighting to see, fighting to draw breath without filling their lungs with suffocating death.

"Why is it like this . . . what *happened*?" Stack screamed against the wind. The shadow creature did not answer, but it looked at Stack for a long moment and then, with very careful movements, raised its hand, held it up before Stack's eyes and slowly, making claws of the fingers, closed the four fingers into a cage, into a fist, into a painfully tight ball that said more eloquently than words: *destruction*.

Then they began to crawl toward the mountain.

6

The onyx spire of the mountain rose out of hell and struggled toward the shredded sky. It was monstrous arrogance. Nothing should have tried that climb out of desolation. But the black mountain had tried, and succeeded.

It was like an old man. Seamed, ancient, dirt caked in striated lines, autumnal, lonely; black and desolate, piled strength upon strength. It would *not* give in to gravity and pressure and death. It struggled for the sky. Ferociously alone, it was the only feature that broke the desolate line of the horizon.

In another twenty-five million years, the mountain might be worn as smooth and featureless as a tiny onyx offering to the deity night. But though the powder plains swirled, and the poison winds drove the pumice against the flanks of the pinnacle, thus far their scouring had only served to soften the edges of the mountain's profile, as though divine intervention had protected the spire.

Lights moved near the summit.

7

Stack learned the nature of the phosphorescent strings excreted onto the plain the night before by the batlike creatures. They were spores that became, in the wan light of day, strange bleeder plants.

All around them as they crawled through the dawn, the little live things sensed their warmth and began thrusting shoots up through the talc. As the fading red ember of the dying sun climbed painfully into the sky, the bleeding plants were already reaching maturity.

Stack cried out as one of the vine tentacles fastened around his ankle, holding him. A second looped itself around his neck.

Thin films of berry-black blood coated the vines, leaving rings on Stack's flesh. The rings burned terribly.

The shadow creature slid on its belly and pulled itself back to the man. Its triangular head came close to Stack's neck, and it bit into the vine. Thick black blood spurted as the vine parted, and the shadow creature rasped its razor-edged teeth back and forth till Stack was able to breathe again. With a violent movement Stack folded himself down and around, pulling the short knife from the neck-pouch. He sawed through the vine tightening inexorably around his ankle. It screamed as it was severed, in the same voice Stack had heard from the skies the night before. The severed vine writhed away, withdrawing into the talc.

Stack and the shadow thing crawled forward once again, low, flat, holding onto the dying earth: toward the mountain.

High in the bloody sky, the Deathbird circled.

8

On their own world, they had lived in luminous, oily-walled caverns for millions of years, evolving and spreading their race through the universe. When they had had enough of empire building, they turned inward, and much of their time was spent in the intricate construction of songs of wisdom, and the designing of fine worlds for many races.

There were other races that designed, however. And when there was a conflict over jurisdiction, an arbitration was called, adjudicated by a race whose *raison d'être* was impartiality and cleverness in unraveling knotted threads of claim and counterclaim. Their racial honor, in fact, depended on the flawless application of these qualities. Through the centuries they had refined their talents in more and more sophisticated arenas of arbitration until the time came when they were the final authority. The litigants were compelled to abide by the judgments, not merely because the decisions were always wise and creatively fair, but because the judges' race would, if its decisions were questioned as suspect, destroy itself. In the holiest place on their world they had erected a religious machine. It could be activated to emit a tone that would shatter their crystal carapaces. They were a race of exquisite cricketlike creatures, no larger than the thumb of a man. They were treasured throughout the civilized worlds, and their loss would have been catastrophic. Their honor and their value was never questioned. All races abided by their decisions.

So Dira's people gave over jurisdiction to that certain world, and went away, leaving Dira with only the Deathbird, a special caretakership the adjudicators had creatively woven into their judgment.

There is recorded one last meeting between Dira and those who had given him his commission. There were readings that could not be ignored—had, in fact, been urgently brought to the attention of the fathers of Dira's race by the adjudicators—and the Great Coiled One came to Dira at the last possible moment to tell him of the mad thing into whose hands this world had been given, to tell Dira of what the mad thing would do.

The Great Coiled One—whose rings were loops of wisdom acquired through centuries of gentleness and perception and immersed meditations that had brought forth lovely designs for many worlds—he who was the holiest of Dira's race, honored Dira by coming to *him*, rather than commanding Dira to appear.

We have only one gift to leave them, he said. *Wisdom. This mad one will come, and he will lie to them, and he will tell them: created he them. And we will be gone, and there will be nothing between them and the mad one but you. Only you can give them the wisdom to defeat him in their own good time.* Then the Great Coiled One stroked the skin of Dira with ritual affection, and Dira was deeply moved and could not reply. Then he was left alone.

The mad one came, and interposed himself, and Dira gave them wisdom, and time passed. His name became other than Dira, it became Snake, and the new name was despised: but Dira could see the Great Coiled One had been correct in his readings. So Dira made his selection. A man, one of them, and gifted him with the spark.

All of this is recorded somewhere. It is history.

9

The man was not Jesus of Nazareth. He may have been Simon. Not Genghis Khan, but perhaps a foot soldier in his horde. Not Aristotle, but possibly one who sat and listened to Socrates in the agora. Neither the shambler who discovered the wheel nor the link who first ceased painting himself blue and applied the colors to the walls of the cave. But one near them, somewhere near at hand. The man was not Richard *Coeur-de-Lion*, Rembrandt, Richelieu, Rasputin, Robert Fulton, or the Mahdi. Just a man. With the spark.

10

Once, Dira came to the man. Very early on. The spark was there, but the light needed to be converted to energy. So Dira came to the man and did what had to be done before the mad one knew of it, and when he discovered that Dira, the Snake, had made contact, he quickly made explanations.

This legend has come down to us as the fable of Faust.

TRUE or FALSE

11

Light converted to energy, thus:

In the fortieth year of his five hundredth incarnation, all-unknowing of the eons of which he had been part, the man found himself wandering in a terrible dry place under a thin, flat burning disc of sun. He was a Berber tribesman who had never considered shadows save to relish them when they provided shade. The shadow came to him, sweeping down across the sands like the *khamsin* of Egypt, the *simoom* of Asia Minor, the *harmattan*, all of which he had known in his various lives, none of which he remembered. The shadow came over him like the *sirocco*.

The shadow stole the breath from his lungs and the man's eyes rolled up in his head. He fell to the ground and the shadow took him down and down, through the sands, into the Earth.

Mother Earth.

She lived, this world of trees and rivers and rocks with deep stone thoughts. She breathed, had feelings, dreamed dreams, gave birth, laughed, and grew contemplative for millennia. This great creature swimming in the sea of space.

What a wonder, thought the man, for he had never understood that the Earth was his mother, before this. He had never understood, before this, that the Earth had a life of its own, at once a part of mankind and quite separate from mankind. A mother with a life of her own.

Dira, Snake, shadow . . . took the man down and let the spark of light change itself to energy as the man became one with the Earth. His flesh melted and became quiet, cool soil. His eyes glowed with the light that shines in the darkest centers of the planet, and he saw the way the mother cared for her young: the worms, the roots of plants, the rivers that cascaded for miles over great cliffs in enormous caverns, the bark of trees. He was taken once more to the bosom of that great Earth mother and understood the joy of her life.

Remember this, Dira said to the man.

What a wonder, the man thought . . .

. . . and was returned to the sands of the desert, with no remembrance of having slept with, loved, enjoyed the body of his natural mother.

12

They camped at the base of the mountain, in a greenglass cave; not deep but angled sharply so the blown pumice could not reach them. They put Nathan Stack's stone in a fault in the cave's floor, and the heat spread quickly, warming them. The shadow thing with its triangular head sank back in shadow and closed its eye and sent its hunting instinct out for food. A shriek came back on the wind.

Much later, when Nathan Stack had eaten, when he was reasonably content and well fed, he stared into the shadows and spoke to the creature sitting there.

"How long was I down there . . . how long was the sleep?"

The shadow thing spoke in whispers. *A quarter of a million years.*

Stack did not reply. The figure was beyond belief. The shadow creature seemed to understand.

In the life of a world, no time at all.

Nathan Stack was a man who could make accommodations. He smiled quickly and said, "I must have been tired."

The shadow did not respond.

"I don't understand very much of this. It's pretty damned frightening. To die, then to wake up . . . here. Like this."

You did not die. You were taken, put down there. By the end you will understand everything, I promise you.

"Who put me down there?"

I did. I came and found you when the time was right, and I put you down there.

"Am I still Nathan Stack?"

If you wish.

"But *am* I Nathan Stack?"

You always were. You had many other names, many other bodies, but the spark was always yours. Stack seemed about to speak, and the shadow creature added, *You were always on your way to being who you are.*

"But what *am* I? Am I still Nathan Stack, dammit?"

If you wish.

"Listen: you don't seem too sure about that. You came and got me, I mean, I woke up and there you were. Now who should know better than you what my name is?"

You have had many names in many times. Nathan Stack is merely the one you remember. You had a very different name long ago, at the start, when I first came to you.

Stack was afraid of the answer, but he asked, "What was my name then?"

Ish-lilith. Husband of Lilith. Do you remember her?

Stack thought, tried to open himself to the past, but it was as unfathomable as the quarter of a million years through which he had slept in the crypt.

"No. But there were other women, in other times."

Many. There was one who replaced Lilith.

"I don't remember."

Her name . . . does not matter. But when the mad one took Lilith from you and replaced her with the other . . . then I knew it would end like this. The Deathbird.

"I don't mean to be stupid, but I haven't the faintest idea what you're talking about."

Before it ends, you will understand everything.

"You said that before." Stack paused, stared at the shadow creature for a long time only moments long, then, "What was your name?"

Before I met you my name was Dira.

He said it in his native tongue. Stack could not pronounce it.

"Before you met me. What is it now?"

Snake.

Something slithered past the mouth of the cave. It did not stop, but it called out with voice of moist mud sucking down into a quagmire.

"Why did you put *me* down there? Why did you come to me in the first place? What spark? Why can't I remember these other lives or who I was? What do you want from me?"

You should sleep. It will be a long climb. And cold.

"I slept for two hundred and fifty thousand years, I'm hardly tired," Stack said. "Why did you pick me?"

Later. Now sleep. Sleep has other uses.

Darkness deepened around Snake, seeped out around the cave, and Nathan Stack lay down near the warming-stone, and the darkness took him.

13

Supplementary Reading

This is an essay by a writer. It is clearly an appeal to the emotions. As you read it, ask yourself how it applies to the subject under discussion. What is the writer trying to say? Does he succeed in making his point? Does this essay cast light on the point of the subject under discussion? After you have read this essay, using the reverse side of your test paper, write your own essay (500 words or less) on the loss of a loved one. If you have never lost a loved one, fake it.

Ahbhu

Yesterday my dog died. For eleven years Ahbhu was my closest friend. He was responsible for my writing a story about a boy and his dog that many people have read. The story was made into a successful movie. The dog in the movie looked a lot like Ahbhu. He was not a pet, he was a person. It was impossible to anthropomorphize him, he wouldn't stand for it. But he was so much his own kind of creature, he had such a strongly formed personality, he was so determined to share his life with only those he chose, that it was also impossible to think of him as simply a dog. Apart from those canine characteristics into which he was locked by his genes, he comported himself like one of a kind.

We met when I came to him at the West Los Angeles Animal Shelter. I'd wanted a dog because I was lonely, and I'd remembered when I was a little boy how my dog had been a friend when I had no other friends. One summer I went away to camp and when I returned I found a rotten old neighbor lady from up the street had had my dog picked up and gassed while my father was at work. I crept into the woman's backyard that night and found a rug hanging on the clothesline. The rug beater was hanging from a post. I stole it and buried it.

At the Animal Shelter there was a man in line ahead of me. He had brought in a puppy only a week or so old. A Puli, a Hungarian sheep dog; it was a sad-looking little thing. He had too many in the litter and had brought in this one either to be taken by someone else or to be put to sleep. They took the dog inside and the man behind the counter called my turn. I told him I wanted a dog, and he took me back inside to walk down the line of cages.

In one of the cages, the little Puli that had just been brought in was being assaulted by three larger dogs that had been earlier tenants. He was a little thing, and he was on the bottom, getting the stuffing knocked out of him. He was struggling mightily.

"Get him out of there!" I yelled. "I'll take him, I'll take him, get him out of there!"

He cost two dollars. It was the best two bucks I ever spent.

Driving home with him, he was lying on the other side of the front seat, staring at me. I had had a vague idea what I'd name a pet, but as I stared at him, and he stared back at me, I suddenly was put in mind of the scene in Alexander Korda's 1939 film *The Thief of Bagdad*, where the evil vizier, played by Conrad Veidt, had changed Ahbhu, the little thief, played by Sabu, into a dog. The film had superimposed the human over the canine face for a moment, so there was an extraordinary look of intelligence in the face of the dog. The little Puli was looking at me with that same expression. "Ahbhu," I said.

He didn't react to the name, but then he couldn't have cared less. But that was his name, from that time on.

No one who ever came into my house was unaffected by him. When he sensed someone with good vibrations, he was right there, lying at their feet. He loved to be scratched, and despite years of admonitions he refused to stop begging for scraps at the table, because he had found most of the people who came to dinner at my house were patsies unable to escape his woebegone Jackie-Coogan-as-the-Kid look.

But he was a certain barometer of bums, as well. On any number of occasions when I found someone I liked, and Ahbhu would have nothing to do with him or her, it always turned out the person was a wrong-o. I took to noting his attitude toward newcomers, and I must admit it influenced my own reactions. I was always wary of someone Ahbhu shunned.

Women with whom I had had unsatisfactory affairs would nonetheless return to the house from time to time—to visit the dog. He had an intimate circle of friends, many of whom had nothing to do with me, and numbering among their company some of the most beautiful actresses in Hollywood. One exquisite lady used to send her driver to pick him up for Sunday afternoon romps at the beach.

I never asked him what happened on those occasions. He didn't talk.

Last year he started going downhill, though I didn't realize it because he maintained the manner of a puppy almost to the end. But he began sleeping too much, and he couldn't hold down his food—not even the Hungarian meals prepared for him by the Magyars who lived up the street. And it became apparent to me something was wrong with him when he got scared during the big Los Angeles earthquake last year. Ahbhu wasn't afraid of anything. He attacked the Pacific Ocean and walked tall around vicious cats. But the quake terrified him, and he jumped up in my bed and threw his forelegs around my neck. I was very nearly the only victim of the earthquake to die from animal strangulation.

He was in and out of the veterinarian's office all through the early part of this year, and the idiot always said it was his diet.

Then one Sunday when he was out in the backyard, I found him lying at the foot of the stairs, covered with mud, vomiting so heavily all he could bring up was bile. He was matted with his own refuse, and he was trying desperately to dig his nose into the earth for coolness. He was barely breathing. I took him to a different vet.

At first they thought it was just old age . . . that they could pull him through. But finally they took X-rays and saw the cancer had taken hold in his stomach and liver.

I put off the day as much as I could. Somehow, I just couldn't conceive of a world that didn't have him in it. But yesterday I went to the vet's office and signed the euthanasia papers.

"I'd like to spend a little time with him, before," I said.

They brought him in and put him on the stainless steel examination table. He had grown so thin. He'd always had a potbelly, and it was gone. The muscles in his hind legs were weak, flaccid. He came to me and put his head into the hollow of my armpit. He was trembling violently. I lifted his head and he looked at me with that comic face I'd always thought made him look like Lawrence Talbot, the Wolf Man. He knew. Sharp as hell, right up to the end, hey old friend? He knew, and he was scared. He trembled all the way down to his spiderweb legs. This bouncing ball of hair that, when lying on a dark carpet, could be taken for a sheepskin rug, with no way to tell at which end head and which end tail. So thin. Shaking, knowing what was going to happen to him. But still a puppy.

I cried, and my eyes closed as my nose swelled with the crying, and he buried his head in my arms because we hadn't done much crying at one another. I was ashamed of myself, not to be taking it as well as he was.

"I got to, pup, because you're in pain and you can't eat. I got to." But he didn't want to know that.

The vet came in then. He was a nice guy and he asked me if I wanted to go away and just let it be done.

Then Ahbhu came up out of there and looked at me.

There is a scene in Kazan's and Steinbeck's Viva Zapata *where a close friend of Zapata's, Brando's, has been condemned for conspiring with the federales. A friend that had been with Zapata since the mountains, since the revolución had begun. And they come to the hut to take him to the firing squad, and Brando starts out, and his friend stops him with a hand on his arm, and he says to him with great friendship, "Emiliano, do it yourself."*

Ahbhu looked at me and I know he was just a dog, but if he could have spoken with human tongue he could not have said more eloquently than he did with a look, don't leave me with strangers.

So I held him as they laid him down and the vet slipped the lanyard up around his right foreleg and drew it tight to bulge the vein, and I held his head and he turned it away from me as the needle went in. It was impossible to tell the moment he passed over from life to death. He simply laid his head on my hand, his eyes fluttered shut and he was gone.

I wrapped him in a sheet with the help of the vet and I drove home with Ahbhu on the seat beside me, just the way we had come home eleven years before. I took him out in the backyard and began digging his grave. I dug for hours, crying and mumbling to myself, talking to him in the sheet. It was a very neat, rectangular grave with smooth sides and all the loose dirt scooped out by hand.

I laid him down in the hole, and he was so tiny in there for a dog who had seemed to be so big in life, so furry, so funny. And I covered him over and when the hole was packed full of dirt, I replaced the neat divot of grass I'd scalped off at the start. And that was all.

But I couldn't send him to strangers.

THE END

QUESTIONS FOR DISCUSSION

1. Is there any significance to the reversal of the word god being dog? If so, what?

2. Does the writer try to impart human qualities to a nonhuman creature? Why? Discuss anthropomorphism in the light of the phrase, "Thou art God."

3. Discuss the love the writer shows in this essay. Compare and contrast it with other forms of love: the love of a man for a woman, a mother for a child, a son for a mother, a botanist for plants, an ecologist for the Earth.

14

In his sleep, Nathan Stack talked.

"Why did you pick me? Why me . . . ?"

15

Like the Earth, the Mother was in pain.

The great house was very quiet. The doctor had left, and the relatives had gone into town for dinner. He sat by the side of her bed and stared down at her. She looked gray and old and crumpled; her skin was a powdery, ashy hue of moth-dust. He was crying softly.

He felt her hand on his knee and looked up to see her staring at him. "You weren't supposed to catch me," he said.

"I'd be disappointed if I hadn't," she said. Her voice was very thin, very smooth.

"How is it?"

"It hurts. Ben didn't dope me too well."

He bit his lower lip. The doctor had used massive doses, but the pain was more massive. She gave little starts as tremors of sudden agony hit her. Impacts. He watched the life leaking out of her eyes.

"How is your sister taking it?"

He shrugged. "You know Charlene. She's sorry, but it's all pretty intellectual to her."

His mother let a tiny ripple of a smile move her lips. "It's a terrible thing to say, Nathan, but your sister isn't the most likable woman in the world. I'm glad you're here." She paused, thinking, then added, "It's just possible your father and I missed something from the gene pool. Charlene isn't whole."

"Can I get you something? A drink of water?"

"No. I'm fine."

He looked at the ampoule of narcotic painkiller. The syringe lay mechanical and still on the clean towel beside it. He felt her eyes on him. She knew what he was thinking. He looked away.

"I would kill for a cigarette," she said.

He laughed. At sixty-five, both legs gone, what remained of her left side paralyzed, the cancer spreading like deadly jelly toward her heart, she was still the matriarch. "You can't have a cigarette, so forget it."

"Then why don't you use that hypo and let me out of here."

"Shut up, Mother."

"Oh, for Christ's sake, Nathan. It's hours if I'm lucky. Months if I'm not. We've had this conversation before. You know I always win."

"Did I ever tell you you were a bitchy old lady?"

"Many times, but I love you anyhow."

He got up and walked to the wall. He could not walk through it, so he went around the inside of the room.

"You can't get away from it."

"Mother, Jesus! Please!"

"All right. Let's talk about the business."

"I couldn't care less about the business right now."

"Then what should we talk about? The lofty uses to which an old lady can put her last moments?"

"You know, you're really ghoulish. I think you're *enjoying* this in some sick way."

"What other way is there to enjoy it."

"An adventure."

"The biggest. A pity your father never had the chance to savor it."

"I hardly think he'd have savored the feeling of being stamped to death in a hydraulic press."

Then he thought about it, because that little smile was on her lips again. "Okay, he probably would have. The two of you were so unreal, you'd have sat there and discussed it and analyzed the pulp."

"And you're our son."

He was, and he was. And he could not deny it, nor had he ever. He was hard and gentle and wild just like them, and he remembered the days in the jungle beyond Brasilia, and the hunt in the Cayman Trench, and the other days working in the mills alongside his father, and he knew when his moment came he would savor death as she did.

"Tell me something. I've always wanted to know. *Did* Dad kill Tom Golden?"

"Use the needle and I'll tell you."

"I'm a Stack. I don't bribe."

"*I'm* a Stack, and I know what a killing curiosity you've got. Use the needle and I'll tell you."

He walked widdershins around the room. She watched him, eyes bright as the mill vats.

"You old bitch."

"Shame, Nathan. You know you're not the son of a bitch. Which is more than your sister can say. Did I ever tell you she wasn't your father's child?"

"No, but I knew."

"You'd have liked her father. He was Swedish. *Your* father liked him."

"Is that why Dad broke both his arms?"

"Probably. But I never heard the Swede complain. One night in bed with me in those days was worth a couple of broken arms. Use the needle."

Finally, while the family was between the entree and the dessert, he filled the syringe and injected her. Her eyes widened as the stuff smacked her heart, and just before she died she rallied all her strength and said, "A deal's a deal. Your father didn't kill Tom Golden, I did. You're a hell of a man, Nathan, and you fought us the way we wanted, and we both loved you more than you could know. Except, dammit, you cunning s.o.b., you *do* know, don't you?"

"I know," he said, and she died; and he cried; and that was the extent of the poetry in it.

16

He knows we are coming.

They were climbing the northern face of the onyx mountain. Snake had coated Nathan Stack's feet with the thick glue and, though it was hardly a country walk, he was able to keep a foothold and pull himself up. Now they had paused to rest on a spiral ledge, and Snake had spoken for the first time of what waited for them where they were going.

"He?"

Snake did not answer. Stack slumped against the wall of the ledge. At the lower slopes of the mountain they had encountered sluglike creatures that had tried to attach themselves to Stack's flesh, but when Snake had driven them off they had returned to sucking the rocks. They had not come near the shadow creature. Farther up, Stack could see the lights that flickered at the summit; he had felt fear that crawled up from his stomach. A short time before they had come to this ledge, they had stumbled past a cave in the mountain where the bat creatures slept. They had gone mad at the presence of the man and the Snake, and the sounds they had made sent waves of nausea through Stack. Snake had helped him, and they had gotten past. Now they had stopped, and Snake would not answer Stack's questions.

We must keep climbing.

"Because he knows we're here." There was a sarcastic rise in Stack's voice.

Snake started moving. Stack closed his eyes. Snake stopped and came back to him. Stack looked up at the one-eyed shadow.

"Not another step."

There is no reason why you should not know.

"Except, friend, I have the feeling you aren't going to tell me anything."

It is not yet time for you to know.

"Look: just because I haven't asked, doesn't mean I don't want to know. You've told me things I shouldn't be able to handle . . . all kinds of crazy things . . . I'm as old as, as . . . I don't know *how* old, but I get the feeling you've been trying to tell me I'm Adam . . ."

That is so.

". . . uh." He stopped rattling and stared back at the shadow creature. Then, very softly, accepting even more than he had thought possible, he said, "Snake." He was silent again. After a time he asked, "Give me another dream and let me know the rest of it?"

You must be patient. The one who lives at the top knows we are coming, but I have been able to keep him from perceiving your danger to him only because you do not know yourself.

"Tell me this, then: does he *want* us to come up . . . the one on the top?"

He allows it. Because he doesn't know.

Stack nodded, resigned to following Snake's lead. He got to his feet and performed an elaborate butler's motion: after you, Snake.

And Snake turned, his flat hands sticking to the wall of the ledge, and they climbed higher, spiraling upward toward the summit.

The Deathbird swooped, then rose toward the Moon. There was still time.

17

Dira came to Nathan Stack near sunset, appearing in the board room of the industrial consortium Stack had built from the empire left by his family.

Stack sat in the pneumatic chair that dominated the conversation pit where top-level decisions were made. He was alone. The others had left hours before and the room was dim with only the barest glow of light from hidden banks that shone through the soft walls.

The shadow creature passed through the walls—and at his passage they became rose quartz, then returned to what they had been. He stood staring at Nathan Stack, and for long moments the man was unaware of any other presence in the room.

You have to go now, Snake said.

Stack looked up, his eyes widened in horror, and through his mind flitted the unmistakable image of Satan, fanged mouth smiling, horns gleaming with scintillas of light as though seen through crosstar filters, rope tail with its spade-shaped appendage thrashing, cloven hoofs leaving burning imprints in the carpet, eyes as deep as pools of oil, the pitchfork, the satin-lined cape, the hairy legs of a goat, talons. He tried to scream but the sound dammed up in his throat.

No, Snake said, *that is not so. Come with me, and you will understand.*

There was a tone of sadness in the voice. As though Satan had been sorely wronged. Stack shook his head violently.

There was no time for argument. The moment had come, and Dira could not hesitate. He gestured and Nathan Stack rose from the pneumatic chair, leaving behind something that looked like Nathan Stack asleep, and he walked to Dira and Snake took him by the hand, and they passed through rose quartz and went away from there.

Down and down Snake took him.

The Mother was in pain. She had been sick for eons, but it had reached the point where Snake knew it would be terminal, and the Mother knew it, too. But she would hide her child, she would intercede on her own behalf and hide him away, deep in her bosom where no one, not even the mad one, could find him.

Dira took Stack to Hell.

It was a fine place.

Warm and safe and far from the probing of mad ones.

And the sickness raged on unchecked. Nations crumbled, the oceans boiled and then grew cold and filmed over with scum, the air became thick with dust and killing vapors, flesh ran like oil, the skies grew dark, the sun blurred and became dull. The Earth moaned.

The plants suffered and consumed themselves, beasts became crippled and went mad, trees burst into flame and from their ashes rose glass shapes that shattered in the wind. The Earth was dying; a long, slow, painful death.

In the center of the Earth, in the fine place, Nathan Stack slept. *Don't leave me with strangers.*

Overhead, far away against the stars, the Deathbird circled and circled, waiting for the word.

18

When they reached the highest peak, Nathan Stack looked across through the terrible burning cold and the ferocious grittiness of the demon wind and saw the sanctuary of always, the cathedral of forever, the pillar of remembrance, the haven of perfection, the pyramid of blessings, the toyshop of creation, the vault of deliverance, the monument of longing, the receptacle of thoughts, the maze of wonder, the catafalque of despair, the podium of pronouncements, and the kiln of last attempts.

On a slope that rose to a star pinnacle, he saw the home of the one who dwelled here—lights flashing and flickering, lights that could be seen far off across the deserted face of the planet—and he began to suspect the name of the resident.

Suddenly everything went red for Nathan Stack. As though a filter had been dropped over his eyes, the black sky, the flickering lights, the rocks that formed the great plateau on which they stood, even Snake became red, and with the color came pain. Terrible pain that burned through every channel of Stack's body, as though his blood had been set afire. He screamed and fell to his knees, the pain crackling through his brain, following every nerve and blood vessel and ganglion and neural track. His skull flamed.

Fight him, Snake said. *Fight him!*

I can't, screamed silently through Stack's mind, the pain too great even to speak. Fire licked and leaped, and he felt the delicate tissue of thought shriveling. He tried to focus his thoughts on ice. He clutched for salvation at ice, chunks of ice, mountains of ice, swimming icebergs of ice half-buried in frozen water, even as his soul smoked and smoldered. *Ice!* He thought of millions of particles of hail rushing, falling, thundering against the firestorm eating his mind, and there was a spit of steam, a flame that went out, a corner that grew cool . . . and he took his stand in that corner, thinking ice, thinking blocks and chunks and monuments of ice, edging them out to widen the circle of coolness and safety. Then the flames began to retreat, to slide back down the channels, and he sent ice after them, snuffing them, burying them in ice and chill waters that raced after the flames and drove them out.

When he opened his eyes, he was still on his knees, but he could think again, and the red surfaces had become normal again.

He will try again. You must be ready.

"Tell me *everything*! I can't go through this without knowing, I need help! Tell me, Snake, tell me now!"

You can help yourself. You have the strength. I gave you the spark.

. . . and the second derangement struck!

The air turned shaverasse and he held dripping chunks of unclean rova in his jowls, the taste making him weak with nausea. His pods withered and drew up into his shell and as the bones cracked he howled with strings of pain that came so fast they were almost one. He tried to scuttle away, but his eyes magnified the shatter of light that beat against him. Facets of his eyes cracked, and the juice began to bubble out. The pain was unbelievable.

Fight him!

Stack rolled onto his back, sending out cilia to touch the earth, and for an instant he realized he was seeing through the eyes of another creature, another form of life he could not even describe. But he was under an open sky and that produced fear; he was surrounded by air that had become deadly and *that* produced fear; he was going blind and *that* produced fear; he was . . . he was a *man* . . . fought back against the feeling of being some other thing . . . he was a *man* and he would not feel fear, he would stand.

He rolled over, withdrew his cilia, and struggled to lower his pods. Broken bones grated and pain thundered through his body. He forced himself to ignore it, and finally the pods were down and he was breathing and he felt his head reeling . . .

And when he opened his eyes he was Nathan Stack again.

. . . and the third derangement struck:

Hopelessness.

Out of unending misery he came back to be Stack.

. . . and the fourth derangement struck:

Madness.

Out of raging lunacy he fought his way to be Stack.

. . . and the fifth derangement, and the sixth, and the seventh, and the plagues, and the whirlwinds, and the pools of evil, and the reduction in size and accompanying fall forever through submicroscopic hells, and the things that fed on him from inside, and the twentieth, and the fortieth, and the sound of his voice screaming for release, and the voice of Snake always beside him, whispering *Fight him!*

Finally, it stopped.

Quickly, now.

Snake took Stack by the hand and, half-dragging him, raced to the great palace of light and glass on the slope, shining brightly under the star pinnacle, and they passed under an arch of shining metal into the ascension hall. The portal sealed behind them.

There were tremors in the walls. The inlaid floors of jewels began to rumble and tremble. Bits of high and faraway ceilings began to drop. Quaking, the palace gave one hideous shudder and collapsed around them.

Now, Snake said. *Now you will know everything!*

And everything forgot to fall. Frozen in midair, the wreckage of the palace hung suspended above them. Even the air ceased to swirl. Time stood still. The movement of the Earth was halted. Everything held utterly immobile as Nathan Stack was permitted to understand all.

19

Multiple Choice

(Counts for 1/2 your final grade.)

1. God is:

   A. An invisible spirit with a long beard.
   B. A small dog dead in a hole.
   C. Everyman.
   D. The Wizard of Oz.

2. Nietzsche wrote "God is dead." By this did he mean:

   A. Life is pointless.
   B. Belief in supreme deities has waned.
   C. There never was a God to begin with.
   D. Thou art God.

3. Ecology is another name for:

   A. Mother love.
   B. Enlightened self-interest.
   C. A good health salad with granola.
   D. God.

4. Which of these phrases most typifies the profoundest love:

   A. Don't leave me with strangers.
   B. I love you.
   C. God is love.
   D. Use the needle.

5. Which of these powers do we usually associate with God:

   A. Power.
   B. Love.

C. Humanity.

D. Docility.

E. None of the above.

20

Starlight shone in the eyes of the Deathbird and its passage through the night cast a shadow on the Moon.

21

Nathan Stack raised his hands and around them the air was still, as the palace fell crashing. They were untouched. *Now you know all there is to know*, Snake said, sinking to one knee as though worshipping. There was no one there to worship but Nathan Stack.

"Was he always mad?"

From the first.

"Then those who gave our world to him were mad, and your race was mad to allow it."

Snake had no answer.

"Perhaps it was supposed to be like this," Stack said.

He reached down and lifted Snake to his feet, and he touched the shadow creature's sleek triangular head. "Friend," he said.

Snake's race was incapable of tears. He said, *I have waited longer than you can know for that word.*

"I'm sorry it comes at the end."

Perhaps it was supposed to be like this.

Then there was a swirling of air, a scintillation in the ruined palace, and the owner of the mountain, the owner of the ruined Earth came to them in a burning bush.

AGAIN, SNAKE? AGAIN YOU ANNOY ME?

The time for toys is ended.

NATHAN STACK YOU BRING TO STOP ME? I SAY WHEN THE TIME IS ENDED. I SAY, AS I'VE ALWAYS SAID.

Then, to Nathan Stack:

GO AWAY. FIND A PLACE TO HIDE UNTIL I COME FOR YOU.

Stack ignored the burning bush. He waved his hand, and the cone of safety in which they stood vanished. "Let's find him, first, then I know what to do."

The Deathbird sharpened its talons on the night wind and sailed down through emptiness toward the cinder of the Earth.

22

Nathan Stack had once contracted pneumonia. He had lain on the operating table as the surgeon made the small incision in the chest wall. Had he not been stubborn, had he not continued working around the clock while the pneumonic infection developed into empyema, he would never have had to go under the knife, even for an operation as safe as a thoracotomy. But he was a Stack, and so he lay on the operating table as the rubber tube was inserted into the chest cavity to drain off the pus in the pleural cavity, and he heard someone speak his name.

NATHAN STACK.

He heard it, from far off, across an Arctic vastness; heard it echoing over and over, down an endless corridor; as the knife sliced.

NATHAN STACK.

He remembered Lilith, with hair the color of dark wine. He remembered taking hours to die beneath a rockslide as his hunting companions in the pack ripped apart the remains of the bear and ignored his grunted moans for help. He remembered the impact of the crossbow bolt as it ripped through his hauberk and split his chest and he died at Agincourt. He remembered the icy water of the Ohio as it closed over his head and the flatboat disappearing without his mates' noticing his loss. He remembered the mustard gas that ate his lungs as he tried to crawl toward a farmhouse near Verdun. He remembered looking directly into the flash of the bomb and feeling the flesh of his face melt away. He remembered Snake coming to him in the boardroom and husking him like corn from his body. He remembered sleeping in the molten core of the Earth for a quarter of a million years.

Across the dead centuries he heard his mother pleading with him to set her free, to end her pain. Use the needle. Her voice mingled with the voice of the Earth crying out in endless pain at her flesh that had been ripped away, at her rivers turned to arteries of dust, at her rolling hills and green fields slagged to green glass and ashes. The voices of his mother and the mother that was Earth became one, and mingled to become Snake's voice telling him he was the one man in the world—the last man in the world—who could end the terminal case the Earth had become.

Use the needle. Put the suffering Earth out of its misery. *It belongs to you now.*

Nathan Stack was secure in the power he contained. A power that far outstripped that of gods or Snakes or mad creators who stuck pins in their creations, who broke their toys.

YOU CAN'T. I WON'T LET YOU.

Nathan Stack walked around the burning bush as it crackled impotently in rage. He looked at it almost pityingly, remembering the Wizard of Oz with his great and ominous disembodied head floating in mist and lightning, and the poor little man behind the curtain turning the dials to create the effects. Stack walked around the effect, knowing he had more power than this sad, poor thing that had held his race in thrall since before Lilith had been taken from him.

He went in search of the mad one who capitalized his name.

23

Zarathustra descended alone from the mountains, encountering no one. But when he came into the forest, all at once there stood before him an old man who had left his holy cottage to look for roots in the woods. And thus spoke the old man to Zarathustra:

"No stranger to me is this wanderer: many years ago he passed this way. Zarathustra he was called, but he has changed. At that time you carried your ashes to the mountains; would you now carry your fire into the valleys? Do you not fear to be punished as an arsonist?

"Zarathustra has changed, Zarathustra has become a child, Zarathustra is an awakened one; what do you now want among the sleepers? You lived in your solitude as in the sea, and the sea carried you. Alas, would you now climb ashore? Alas, would you again drag your own body?"

Zarathustra answered: "I love man."

"Why," asked the saint, "did I go into the forest and the desert? Was it not because I loved man all too much? Now I love God; man, I love not. Man is, for me, too imperfect a thing. Love of man would kill me."

"And what is the saint doing in the forest?" asked Zarathustra.

The saint answered: "I make songs and sing them; and when I make songs, I laugh, cry, and hum: thus I praise God. With singing, crying, laughing, and humming, I praise the god who is my god. But what do you bring us as a gift?"

When Zarathustra had heard these words he bade the saint farewell and said: "What could I have to give you? But let me go quickly, lest I take something from you!" And thus they separated, the old one and the man, laughing as two boys laugh.

But when Zarathustra was alone he spoke thus to his heart: "Could it be possible? This old saint in the forest has not yet heard anything of this, that *God is dead!*"

24

Stack found the mad one wandering in the forest of final moments. He was an old, tired man, and Stack knew with a wave of his hand he could end it for this god in a moment. But what was the reason for it? It was even too late for revenge. It had been too late from the start. So he let the old one go his way, wandering in the forest, mumbling to himself, I WON'T LET YOU DO IT, in the voice of a cranky child; mumbling pathetically, OH, PLEASE, I DON'T WANT TO GO TO BED YET. I'M NOT YET DONE PLAYING.

And Stack came back to Snake, who had served his function and protected Stack until Stack had learned that he was more powerful than the god he'd worshipped all through the history of Men. He came back to Snake and their hands touched and the bond of friendship was sealed at last, at the end.

Then they worked together, and Nathan Stack used the needle with a wave of his hands, and the Earth could not sigh with relief as its endless pain was ended . . . but it did sigh, and it settled in upon itself, and the molten core went out, and the winds died, and from high above them Stack heard the fulfillment of Snake's final act; he heard the descent of the Deathbird.

"What was your name?" Stack asked his friend.

Dira.

And the Deathbird settled down across the tired shape of the Earth, and it spread its wings wide, and brought them over and down, and enfolded the Earth as a mother enfolds her weary child. Dira settled down on the amethyst floor of the dark-shrouded palace and closed his single eye with gratitude. To sleep at last, at the end.

All this, as Nathan Stack stood watching. He was the last, at the end, and because he had come to own—if even for a few moments—that which could have been his from the start, had he but known, he did not sleep but stood and watched. Knowing at last, at the end, that he had loved and done no wrong.

25

The Deathbird closed its wings over the Earth until at last, at the end, there was only the great bird crouched over the dead cinder. Then the Deathbird raised its head to the star-filled sky and repeated the sigh of loss the Earth had felt at the end. Then its eyes closed, it tucked its head carefully under its wing, and all was night.

Far away, the stars waited for the cry of the Deathbird to reach them so final moments could be observed at last, at the end, for the race of Men.

26

This Is for Mark Twain

Chatting with Anubis

When the core drilling was halted at a depth of exactly 804.5 meters, one half mile down, Amy Guiterman and I conspired to grab Immortality by the throat and shake it till it noticed us.

My name is Wang Zicai. Ordinarily, the family name Wang, which is pronounced with the "a" in *father*, almost as if it were Wong—means "king." In my case, it means something else; it means "rushing headlong." How appropriate. Don't tell me clairvoyance doesn't run in my family . . . Zicai means "suicide." Half a mile down, beneath the blank Sahara, in a hidden valley that holds cupped in its eternal serenity the lake of the oasis of Siwa, I and a young woman equally as young and reckless as myself, Amy Guiterman of New York City, conspired to do a thing that would certainly cause our disgrace, if not our separate deaths.

I am writing this in Yin.

It is the lost ancestral language of the Chinese people. It was a language written between the 18th and 12th centuries before the common era. It is not only ancient, it is impossible to translate. There are only five people alive today, as I write this, who can translate this manuscript, written in the language of the Yin Dynasty that blossomed northeast along the Yellow River in a time long before the son of a carpenter is alleged to have fed multitudes with loaves and fishes, to have walked on water, to have raised the dead. I am no "rice Christian." You cannot give me a meal and find me scurrying to your god. I am Buddhist, as my family has been for centuries. That I can write in Yin—which is to modern Chinese as classical Latin is to vineyard Italian—is a conundrum I choose not to answer in this document. Let he or she who one day unearths this text unscramble the oddities of chance and experience that brought me, "rushing headlong toward suicide," to this place half a mile beneath the Oasis of Siwa.

A blind thrust-fault, hitherto unrecorded, beneath the Mountain of the Moon, had produced a cataclysmic 7.5 temblor. It had leveled villages as far away as Bi'r Bū Kūsa and Abu Simbel. The aerial and satellite reconnaissance from the Gulf of Sidra to the Red Sea, from the Libyan Plateau to the Sudan, showed great fissures, herniated valleys, upthrust structures, a new world lost to human sight for thousands of years. An international team of paleoseismologists was assembled, and I was called from the Great Boneyard of the Gobi by my superiors at the Mongolian Academy of Sciences at Ulan Bator to leave my triceratops and fly to the middle of hell on Earth, the great sand ocean of the Sahara, to assist in excavating and analyzing what some said would be the discovery of the age.

Some said it was the mythical Shrine of Ammon.

Some said it was the Temple of the Oracle.

Alexander the Great, at the very pinnacle of his fame, was told of the Temple, and of the all-knowing Oracle who sat there. And so he came, from the shore of Egypt down into the deep Sahara, seeking the Oracle. It is recorded: his expedition was lost, wandering hopelessly, without water and without hope. Then crows came to lead them down through the Mountain of the Moon, down to a hidden valley without name, to the lake of the Oasis of Siwa, and at its center . . . the temple, the Shrine of Ammon. It was so recorded. And one thing more. In a small and dark chamber roofed with palm logs, the Egyptian priests told Alexander a thing that affected him for the rest of his life. It is not recorded what he was told. And never again, we have always been led to believe, has the Shrine of Ammon been seen by civilized man or civilized woman.

Now, Amy Guiterman and I, she from the Brooklyn Museum and I an honored graduate of Beijing University, together we had followed Alexander's route from Paraetonium to Siwa to here, hundreds of kilometers beyond human thought or action, half a mile down, where the gigantic claw diggers had ceased their abrading, the two of us with simple pick and shovel, standing on the last thin layer of compacted dirt and rock that roofed whatever great shadowy structure lay beneath us, a shadow picked up by the most advanced deep-resonance-response readings, verified on-site by proton free-precession magnetometry and ground-penetrating radar brought in from the Sandia National Laboratory in Albuquerque, New Mexico, in the United States.

Something large lay just beneath our feet.

And tomorrow, at sunrise, the team would assemble to break through and share the discovery, whatever it might be.

But I had had knowledge of Amy Guiterman's body, and she was as reckless as I, rushing headlong toward suicide, and in a moment of foolishness, a moment that should have passed but did not, we sneaked out of camp and went to the site and lowered ourselves, taking with us nylon rope and crampons, powerful electric torches and small recording devices, trowel and whisk broom, cameras and carabiners. A pick and a shovel. I offer no excuse. We were young, we were reckless, we were smitten with each other, and we behaved like naughty children. What happened should not have happened.

We broke through the final alluvial layer and swept out the broken pieces. We stood atop a ceiling of fitted stones, basalt or even marble, I could not tell immediately. I knew they were not granite, that much I did know. There were seams. Using the pick, I prised loose the ancient and concretized mortar. It went much more quickly and easily than I would have thought, but then, I'm used to digging for bones, not for buildings. I managed to chock the large set-stone in place with wooden wedges, until I had guttered the perimeter fully. Then, inching the toe of the pick into the fissure, I began levering the stone up, sliding the wedges deeper to keep the huge block from slipping back. And finally, though the block was at least sixty or seventy centimeters thick, we were able to tilt it up and, bracing our backs against the opposite side of the hole we had dug at the bottom of the core pit, we were able to use our strong young legs to force it back and away, beyond the balance point; and it fell away with a crash.

A great wind escaped the aperture that had housed the stone. A great wind that twisted up from below in a dark swirl that we could actually see. Amy Guiterman gave a little sound of fear and startlement. So did I. Then she said, "They would have used great amounts of charcoal to set these limestone blocks in place," and I learned from her that they were not marble, neither were they basalt.

We showed each other our bravery by dangling our feet through the opening, sitting at the edge and leaning over to catch the wind. It smelled *sweet*. Not a smell I had ever known before. But certainly not stagnant. Not corrupt. Sweet as a washed face, sweet as chilled fruit. Then we lit our torches and swept the beams below.

We sat just above the ceiling of a great chamber. Neither pyramid nor mausoleum, it seemed to be an immense hall filled with enormous statues of pharaohs and beast-headed gods and creatures with neither animal nor human shape . . . and all of these statues gigantic. Perhaps one hundred times life-size.

Directly beneath us was the noble head of a time-lost ruler, wearing the *nemes* headdress and the royal ritual beard. Where our digging had dropped shards of rock, the shining yellow surface of the statue had been chipped, and a darker material showed through. "Diorite," Amy Guiterman said. "Covered with gold. Pure gold. Lapis lazuli, turquoise, garnets, rubies—the headdress is made of thousands of gems, all precisely cut . . . do you see?"

But I was lowering myself. Having cinched my climbing rope around the excised block, I was already shinnying down the cord to stand on the first ledge I could manage, the empty place between the placid hands of the pharaoh that lay on the golden knees. I heard Amy Guiterman scrambling down behind and above me.

Then the wind rose again, suddenly, shrieking up and around me like a monsoon, and the rope was ripped from my hands, and my torch was blown away, and I was thrown back and something sharp caught at the back of my shirt and I wrenched forward to fall on my stomach, and I felt the cold of that wind on my bare back. And everything was dark.

Then I felt cold hands on me. All over me. Reaching, touching, probing me, as if I were a cut of sliced meat lying on a counter. Above me I heard Amy Guiterman shrieking. I felt the halves of my ripped shirt torn from my body, and then my kerchief, and then my boots, and then my stockings, and then my watch and glasses.

I struggled to my feet and took a position, ready to make an empassing or killing strike. I was no cinema action hero, but whatever was there plucking at me would have to take my life despite I fought for it!

Then, from below, light began to rise. Great light, the brightest light I've ever seen, like a shimmering fog. And as it rose, I could see that the mist that filled the great chamber beneath us was trying to reach us, to touch us, to feel us with hands of ephemeral chilling ghostliness. Dead hands. Hands of beings and men who might never have been or who, having been, were denied their lives. They reached, they sought, they implored.

And rising from the mist, with a howl, Anubis.

God of the dead, jackal-headed conductor of souls. Opener of the road to the afterlife. Embalmer of Osiris, Lord of the mummy wrappings, ruler of the dark passageways, watcher at the neverending funeral. Anubis came, and we were left, suddenly, ashamed and alone, the American girl and I, who had acted rashly as do all those who flee toward their own destruction.

But he did not kill us, did not take us. How could he . . . am I not writing this for some never-to-be-known reader to find? He roared yet again, and the hands of the seekers drew back, reluctantly, like whipped curs into kennels, and there in the soft golden light reflected from the icon of a pharaoh dead and gone so long that no memory exists even of his name, there in the space half a mile down, the great god Anubis spoke to us.

At first, he thought we were "the great conqueror" come again. No, I told him, not Alexander. And the great god laughed with a terrible thin laugh that brought to mind paper cuts and the slicing of eyeballs. No, of course not that one, said the great god, for did I not reveal to him the great secret? Why should he ever return? Why should he not flee as fast as his great army could carry him, and never return? And Anubis laughed.

I was young and I was foolish, and I asked the jackal-headed god to tell *me* the great secret. If I was to perish here, at least I could carry to the afterlife a great wisdom.

Anubis looked through me.

Do you know why I guard this tomb?

I said I did not know, but that perhaps it was to protect the wisdom of the Oracle, to keep hidden the great secret of the Shrine of Ammon that had been given to Alexander.

And Anubis laughed the more. Vicious laughter that made me wish I had never grown skin or taken air into my lungs.

This is not the Shrine of Ammon, he said. Later they may have said it was, but this is what it has always been, the tomb of the Most Accursed One. The Defiler. The Nemesis. The Killer of the dream that lasted twice six thousand years. I guard this tomb to deny him entrance to the afterlife.

And I guard it to pass on the great secret.

"Then you don't plan to kill us?" I asked. Behind me I heard Amy Guiterman snort with disbelief that I, a graduate of Beijing

University, could ask such an imbecile question. Anubis looked through me again, and said no, I don't have to do that. It is not my job. And then, with no prompting at all, he told me, and he told Amy Guiterman from the Brooklyn Museum, he told us the great secret that had lain beneath the sands since the days of Alexander. And then he told us whose tomb it was. And then he vanished into the mist. And then we climbed back out, hand over hand, because our ropes were gone, and my clothes were gone, and Amy Guiterman's pack and supplies were gone, but we still had our lives.

At least for the moment.

I write this now, in Yin, and I set down the great secret in its every particular. All parts of it, and the three colors, and the special names, and the pacing. It's all here, for whomever finds it, because the tomb is gone again. Temblor or jackal-god, I cannot say. But if today, as opposed to last night, you seek that shadow beneath the sand, you will find emptiness.

Now we go our separate ways, Amy Guiterman and I. She to her destiny, and I to mine. It will not be long in finding us. At the height of his power, soon after visiting the Temple of the Oracle, where he was told something that affected him for the rest of his life, Alexander the Great died of a mosquito bite. It is said. Alexander the Great died of an overdose of drink and debauchery. It is said. Alexander the Great died of murder, he was poisoned. It is said. Alexander the Great died of a prolonged, nameless fever; of pneumonia; of typhus; of septicemia; of typhoid; of eating off tin plates; of malaria. It is said. Alexander was a bold and energetic king at the peak of his powers, it is written, but during his last months in Babylon, for no reason anyone has ever been able to explain satisfactorily, he took to heavy drinking and nightly debauches . . . and then the fever came for him.

A mosquito. It is said.

No one will bother to say what has taken me. Or Amy Guiterman. We are insignificant. But we know the great secret.

Anubis likes to chat. The jackal-headed one has no secrets he chooses to keep. He'll tell it all. Secrecy is not his job. Revenge is his job. Anubis guards the tomb, and eon by eon makes revenge for his fellow gods.

The tomb is the final resting place of the one who killed the gods. When belief in the gods vanishes, when the worshippers of the gods turn away their faces, then the gods themselves vanish. Like the mist that climbs and implores, they go. And the one who lies encrypted there, guarded by the lord of the funeral, is the one who brought the world to forget Isis and Osiris and Horus and Anubis. He is the one who opened the sea, and the one who wandered in the desert. He is the one who went to the mountaintop, and he is the one who brought back the word of yet another god. He is Moses, and for Anubis revenge is not only sweet, it is everlasting. Moses—denied both Heaven and Hell—will never rest in the Afterlife. Revenge without pity has doomed him to eternal exclusion, buried in the sepulcher of the gods he killed.

I sink this now, in an unmarked meter of dirt, at a respectable depth; and I go my way, bearing the great secret, no longer needing to "rush headlong," as I have already committed what suicide is necessary. I go my way, for however long I have, leaving only this warning for anyone who may yet seek the lost Shrine of Ammon. In the words of Amy Guiterman of New York City, spoken to a jackal-headed deity, "I've got to tell you, Anubis, you are one *tough* grader." *She was not smiling when she said it.*

The Whimper of Whipped Dogs

Editor's note: "The Whimper of Whipped Dogs" was written in the aftermath of the brutal assault and murder of Kitty Genovese in the foyer of her New York apartment building, during which the residents reportedly ignored her screams for help, triggering a degree of outrage against those who did nothing that persists to this day.

On the night after the day she had stained the louvered window shutters of her new apartment on East 52nd Street, Beth saw a woman slowly and hideously knifed to death in the courtyard of her building. She was one of twenty-six witnesses to the ghoulish scene, and, like them, she did nothing to stop it.

She saw it all, every moment of it, without break and with no impediment to her view. Quite madly, the thought crossed her mind as she watched in horrified fascination, that she had the sort of marvelous line of observation Napoleon had sought when he caused to have constructed at the *Comédie-Française* theaters, a curtained box at the rear, so he could watch the audience as well as the stage. The night was clear, the moon was full, she had just turned off the 11:30 movie on Channel 2 after the second commercial break, realizing she had already seen Robert Taylor in *Westward the Women*, and had disliked it the first time; and the apartment was quite dark.

She went to the window, to raise it six inches for the night's sleep, and she saw the woman stumble into the courtyard. She was sliding along the wall, clutching her left arm with her right hand. Con Ed had installed mercury-vapor lamps on the poles; there had been sixteen assaults in seven months; the courtyard was illuminated with a chill purple glow that made the blood streaming down the woman's left arm look black and shiny. Beth saw every detail with utter clarity, as though magnified a thousand power under a microscope, solarized as if it had been a television commercial.

The woman threw back her head, as if she were trying to scream, but there was no sound. Only the traffic on First Avenue, late cabs foraging for singles paired for the night at Maxwell's Plum and Friday's and Adam's Apple. But that was over there, beyond. Where *she* was, down there seven floors below, in the courtyard, everything seemed silently suspended in an invisible force field.

Beth stood in the darkness of her apartment and realized she had raised the window completely. A tiny balcony lay just over the low sill; now not even glass separated her from the sight; just the wrought-iron balcony railing and seven floors to the courtyard below.

The woman staggered away from the wall, her head still thrown back, and Beth could see she was in her mid-thirties, with dark hair cut in a shag; it was impossible to tell if she was pretty: terror had contorted her features and her mouth was a twisted black slash, opened but emitting no sound. Cords stood out in her neck. She had lost one shoe, and her steps were uneven, threatening to dump her to the pavement.

The man came around the corner of the building, into the courtyard. The knife he held was enormous—or perhaps it only seemed so: Beth remembered a bonehandled fish knife her father had used one summer at the lake in Maine: it folded back on itself and locked, revealing eight inches of serrated blade. The knife in the hand of the dark man in the courtyard seemed to be similar.

The woman saw him and tried to run, but he leaped across the distance between them and grabbed her by the hair and pulled her head back as though he would slash her throat in the next reaper-motion.

Then the woman screamed.

The sound skirled up into the courtyard like bats trapped in an echo chamber, unable to find a way out, driven mad. It went on and on . . .

The man struggled with her, and she drove her elbows into his sides and he tried to protect himself, spinning her around by her hair, the terrible scream going up and up and never stopping. She came loose and he was left with a fistful of hair torn out by the roots. As she spun out, he slashed straight across and opened her up just below the breasts. Blood sprayed through her clothing and the man was soaked; it seemed to drive him even more berserk. He went at her again, as she tried to hold herself together, the blood pouring down over her arms.

She tried to run, teetered against the wall, slid sidewise, and the man struck the brick surface. She was away, stumbling over a flower bed, falling, getting to her knees as he threw himself on her again. The knife came up in a flashing arc that illuminated the blade strangely with purple light. And still she screamed.

Lights came on in dozens of apartments and people appeared at windows.

He drove the knife to the hilt into her back, high on the right shoulder. He used both hands.

Beth caught it all in jagged flashes—the man, the woman, the knife, the blood, the expressions on the faces of those watching from the windows. Then lights clicked off in the windows, but they still stood there, watching.

She wanted to yell, to scream, "What are you doing to that woman?" But her throat was frozen, two iron hands that had been immersed in dry ice for ten thousand years clamped around her neck. She could feel the blade sliding into her own body.

Somehow—it seemed impossible but there it was down there, happening somehow—the woman struggled erect and *pulled* herself off the knife. Three steps, she took three steps and fell into the flower bed again. The man was howling now, like a great beast, the sounds inarticulate, bubbling up from his stomach. He fell on her, and the knife went up and came down, then again, and again, and finally it was all a blur of motion, and her scream of lunatic bats went on till it faded off and was gone.

Beth stood in the darkness, trembling and crying, the sight filling her eyes with horror. And when she could no longer bear to look at what he was doing down there to the unmoving piece of meat over which he worked, she looked up and around at the windows of darkness where the others still stood—even as she stood—and somehow she could see their faces, bruise-purple with the dim light from the mercury lamps, and there was a universal sameness to their expressions. The women stood with their nails biting into the upper arms of their men, their tongues edging from the corners of their mouths; the men were wild-eyed and smiling. They all looked as though they were at cock fights. Breathing deeply. Drawing some sustenance from the grisly scene below. An exhalation of sound, deep, deep, as though from caverns beneath the earth. Flesh pale and moist.

And it was then that she realized the courtyard had grown foggy, as though mist off the East River had rolled up 52nd Street in a veil that would obscure the details of what the knife and the man were still doing . . . endlessly doing it . . . long after there was any joy in it . . . still doing it . . . again and again. . . .

But the fog was unnatural, thick and gray and filled with tiny scintillas of light. She stared at it, rising up in the empty space of the courtyard. Bach in the cathedral, stardust in a vacuum chamber.

Beth saw eyes.

There, up there, at the ninth floor and higher, two great eyes, as surely as night and the moon, there were *eyes*. And—a face? Was that a face, could she be sure, was she imagining it . . . a face? In the roiling vapors of chill fog something lived, something brooding and patient and utterly malevolent had been summoned up to witness what was happening down there in the flower bed. Beth tried to look away, but could not. The eyes, those primal burning eyes, filled with an abysmal antiquity yet frighteningly bright and anxious like the eyes of a child; eyes filled with tomb depths, ancient and new, chasm-filled, burning, gigantic and deep as an abyss, holding her, compelling her. The shadow play was being staged not only for the tenants in their windows, watching and drinking of the scene, but for some *other*. Not on frigid tundra or waste moors, not in subterranean caverns or on some faraway world circling a dying sun, but here, in the city, here the eyes of that *other* watched.

Shaking with the effort, Beth wrenched her eyes from those burning depths up there beyond the ninth floor, only to see again the horror that had brought that *other*. And she was struck for the first time by the awfulness of what she was witnessing, she was released from the immobility that had held her like a coelacanth in shale, she was filled with the blood thunder pounding against the membranes of her mind: she had *stood* there! She had done nothing, nothing! A woman had been butchered and she had said nothing, done nothing. Tears had been useless, tremblings had been pointless, she *had done nothing*!

Then she heard hysterical sounds midway between laughter and giggling, and as she stared up into that great face rising in the fog and chimney smoke of the night, she heard *herself* making those deranged gibbon noises and from the man below a pathetic, trapped sound, like the whimper of whipped dogs.

She was staring up into that face again. She hadn't wanted to see it again—ever. But she was locked with those smoldering eyes, overcome with the feeling that they were childlike, though she *knew* they were incalculably ancient.

Then the butcher below did an unspeakable thing, and Beth reeled with dizziness and caught the edge of the window before she could tumble out onto the balcony; she steadied herself and fought for breath.

She felt herself being looked at, and for a long moment of frozen terror she feared she might have caught the attention of that face up there in the fog. She clung to the window, feeling everything growing faraway and dim, and stared straight across the court. She *was* being watched. Intently. By the young man in the seventh-floor window across from her own apartment. Steadily, he was looking at her. Through the strange fog with its burning eyes feasting on the sight below, he was staring at her.

As she felt herself blacking out, in the moment before unconsciousness, the thought flickered and fled that there was something terribly familiar about his face.

It rained the next day. East 52nd Street was slick and shining with the oil rainbows. The rain washed the dog turds into the gutters and nudged them down and down to the catch-basin openings. People bent against the slanting rain, hidden beneath umbrellas, looking like enormous, scurrying black mushrooms. Beth went out to get the newspapers after the police had come and gone.

The news reports dwelled with loving emphasis on the twenty-six tenants of the building who had watched in cold interest as Leona Ciarelli, 37, of 455 Fort Washington Avenue, Manhattan, had been systematically stabbed to death by Burton H. Wells, 41, an unemployed electrician, who had been subsequently shot to death by two off-duty police officers when he burst into Michael's

Pub on 55th Street, covered with blood and brandishing a knife that authorities later identified as the murder weapon.

She had thrown up twice that day. Her stomach seemed incapable of retaining anything solid, and the taste of bile lay along the back of her tongue. She could not blot the scenes of the night before from her mind; she re-ran them again and again, every movement of that reaper arm playing over and over as though on a short loop of memory. The woman's head thrown back for silent screams. The blood. Those eyes in the fog.

She was drawn again and again to the window, to stare down into the courtyard and the street. She tried to superimpose over the bleak Manhattan concrete the view from her window in Swann House at Bennington: the little yard and another white, frame dormitory; the fantastic apple trees; and from the other window the rolling hills and gorgeous Vermont countryside; her memory skittered through the change of seasons. But there was always concrete and the rain-slick streets; the rain on the pavement was black and shiny as blood.

She tried to work, rolling up the tambour closure of the old rolltop desk she had bought on Lexington Avenue and hunching over the graph sheets of choreographer's charts. But Labanotation was merely a Jackson Pollock jumble of arcane hieroglyphics to her today, instead of the careful representation of eurhythmics she had studied four years to perfect. And before that, Farmington.

The phone rang. It was the secretary from the Taylor Dance Company, asking when she would be free. She had to beg off. She looked at her hand, lying on the graph sheets of figures Laban had devised, and she saw her fingers trembling. She had to beg off. Then she called Guzman at the Downtown Ballet Company, to tell him she would be late with the charts.

"My God, lady, I have ten dancers sitting around in a rehearsal hall getting their leotards sweaty! What do you expect me to do?"

She explained what had happened the night before. And as she told him, she realized the newspapers had been justified in holding that tone against the twenty-six witnesses to the death of Leona Ciarelli. Paschal Guzman listened, and when he spoke again, his voice was several octaves lower, and he spoke more slowly. He said he understood and she could take a little longer to prepare the charts. But there was a distance in his voice, and he hung up while she was thanking him.

She dressed in an argyle sweater vest in shades of dark purple, and a pair of fitted khaki gabardine trousers. She had to go out, to walk around. To do what? To think about other things. As she pulled on the Fred Braun chunky heels, she idly wondered if that heavy silver bracelet was still in the window of Georg Jensen's. In the elevator, the young man from the window across the courtyard stared at her. Beth felt her body begin to tremble again. She went deep into the corner of the box when he entered behind her.

Between the fifth and fourth floors, he hit the OFF switch and the elevator jerked to a halt.

Beth stared at him, and he smiled innocently.

"Hi. My name's Gleeson, Ray Gleeson, I'm in 714."

She wanted to demand he turn the elevator back on, by what right did he pre*sume* to do such a thing, what did he mean by this, turn it on at once or suffer the consequences. That was what she *wanted* to do. Instead, from the same place she had heard the gibbering laughter the night before, she heard her voice, much smaller and much less possessed than she had trained it to be, saying, "Beth O'Neill, I live in 701."

The thing about it was that *the elevator was stopped*. And she was frightened. But he leaned against the paneled wall, very well dressed, shoes polished, hair combed and probably blown dry with a hand drier, and he *talked* to her as if they were across a table at L'Argenteuil. "You just moved in, huh?"

"About two months ago."

"Where did you go to school? Bennington or Sarah Lawrence?"

"Bennington. How did you know?"

He laughed, and it was a nice laugh. "I'm an editor at a religious book publisher; every year we get half a dozen Bennington, Sarah Lawrence, Smith girls. They come hopping in like grasshoppers, ready to revolutionize the publishing industry."

"What's wrong with that? You sound like you don't care for them."

"Oh, I *love* them, they're marvelous. They think they know how to write better than the authors we publish. Had one darlin' little item who was given galleys of three books to proof, and she rewrote all three. I think she's working as a table-swabber in a Horn and Hardart's now."

She didn't reply to that. She would have pegged him as an anti-feminist, ordinarily, if it had been anyone else speaking. But the eyes. There was something terribly familiar about his face. She was enjoying the conversation; she rather liked him.

"What's the nearest big city to Bennington?"

"Albany, New York. About sixty miles."

"How long does it take to drive there?"

"From Bennington? About an hour and a half."

"Must be a nice drive, that Vermont country, really pretty. They went coed, I understand. How's that working out?"

"I don't know, really."

"You don't know?"

"It happened around the time I was graduating."

"What did you major in?"

"I was a dance major, specializing in Labanotation. That's the way you write choreography."

"It's all electives, I gather. You don't have to take anything required, like sciences, for example." He didn't change tone as he said, "That was a terrible thing last night. I saw you watching. I guess a lot of us were watching. It was a really terrible thing."

She nodded dumbly. Fear came back.

"I understand the cops got him. Some nut, they don't even know why he killed her, or why he went charging into that bar. It was really an awful thing. I'd very much like to have dinner with you one night soon, if you're not attached."

"That would be all right."

"Maybe Wednesday. There's an Argentinian place I know. You might like it."

"That would be all right."

"Why don't you turn on the elevator, and we can go," he said, and smiled again. She did it, wondering why she had stopped the elevator in the first place.

On her third date with him, they had their first fight. It was at a party thrown by a director of television commercials. He lived on the ninth floor of their building. He had just done a series of spots for *Sesame Street* (the letters "U" for Underpass, "T" for Tunnel, lowercase "b" for boats, "c" for cars; the numbers 1 to 6 and the numbers 1 to 20; the words *light* and *dark*) and was celebrating his move from the arena of commercial tawdriness (and its attendant $75,000 a year) to the sweet fields of educational programming (and its accompanying descent into low-pay respectability). There was a logic in his joy Beth could not quite understand, and when she talked with him about it, in a far corner of the kitchen, his arguments didn't seem to parse. But he seemed happy, and his girlfriend, a long-legged ex-model from Philadelphia, continued to drift to him and away from him, like some exquisite undersea plant, touching his hair and kissing his neck, murmuring words of pride and barely submerged sexuality. Beth found it bewildering, though the celebrants were all bright and lively.

In the living room, Ray was sitting on the arm of the sofa, hustling a stewardess named Luanne. Beth could tell he was hustling; he was trying to look casual. When he *wasn't* hustling, he was always intense, about everything. She decided to ignore it, and wandered around the apartment, sipping at a Tanqueray and tonic.

There were framed prints of abstract shapes clipped from a calendar printed in Germany. They were in metal Bonniers frames.

In the dining room a huge door from a demolished building somewhere in the city had been handsomely stripped, teaked, and refinished. It was now the dinner table.

A Lightolier fixture attached to the wall over the bed swung out, levered up and down, tipped, and its burnished globe-head revolved a full three hundred and sixty degrees.

She was standing in the bedroom, looking out the window, when she realized *this* had been one of the rooms in which light had gone on, gone off; one of the rooms that had contained a silent watcher at the death of Leona Ciarelli.

When she returned to the living room, she looked around more carefully. With only three or four exceptions—the stewardess, a young married couple from the second floor, a stockbroker from Hemphill, Noyes—*everyone* at the party had been a witness to the slaying.

"I'd like to go," she told him.

"Why, aren't you having a good time?" asked the stewardess, a mocking smile crossing her perfect little face.

"Like all Bennington ladies," Ray said, answering for Beth, "she is enjoying herself most by not enjoying herself at all. It's a trait of the anal retentive. Being here in someone else's apartment, she can't empty ashtrays or rewind the toilet paper roll so it doesn't hang a tongue, and being tightassed, her nature demands we go.

"All right, Beth, let's say our goodbyes and take off. The Phantom Rectum strikes again."

She slapped him and the stewardess's eyes widened. But the smile remained frozen where it had appeared.

He grabbed her wrist before she could do it again. "Garbanzo beans, baby," he said, holding her wrist tighter than necessary.

They went back to her apartment, and after sparring silently with kitchen cabinet doors slammed and the television being tuned too loud, they got to her bed, and he tried to perpetuate the metaphor by fucking her in the ass. He had her on elbows and knees before she realized what he was doing; she struggled to turn over and he rode her bucking and tossing without a sound. And when it was clear to him that she would never permit it, he grabbed her breast from underneath and squeezed so hard she howled in pain. He dumped her on her back, rubbed himself between her legs a dozen times, and came on her stomach.

Beth lay with her eyes closed and an arm thrown across her face. She wanted to cry, but found she could not. Ray lay on her and said nothing. She wanted to rush to the bathroom and shower, but he did not move, till long after his semen had dried on their bodies.

"Who did you date at college?" he asked.

"I didn't date anyone very much." Sullen.

"No heavy makeouts with wealthy lads from Williams and Dartmouth . . . no Amherst intellectuals begging you to save them from creeping faggotry by permitting them to stick their carrots in your sticky little slit?"

"Stop it!"

"Come on, baby, it couldn't all have been knee socks and little round circle-pins. You don't expect me to believe you didn't get a little mouthful of cock from time to time. It's only, what? About fifteen miles to Williamstown? I'm sure the Williams werewolves were down burning the highway to your cunt on weekends; you can level with old Uncle Ray. . . ."

"*Why are you like this?!*" She started to move, to get away from him, and he grabbed her by the shoulder, forced her to lie down again. Then he rose up over her and said, "I'm like this because I'm a New Yorker, baby. Because I live in this fucking city every day. Because I have to play patty-cake with the ministers and other sanctified holy-joe assholes who want their goodness and lightness tracts published by the Blessed Sacrament Publishing and Storm Window Company of 277 Park Avenue, when what I *really* want to do is toss the stupid psalm-suckers out the thirty-seventh-floor window and listen to them quote chapter-and-worse all the way down. Because I've lived in this great big snapping dog of a city all my life and I'm mad as a mudfly, for chrissakes!"

She lay unable to move, breathing shallowly, filled with a sudden pity and affection for him. His face was white and strained, and she knew he was saying things to her that only a bit too much Almadén and exact timing would have let him say.

"What do you expect from me," he said, his voice softer now, but no less intense, "do you expect kindness and gentility and understanding and a hand on *your* hand when the smog burns your eyes? I can't do it, I haven't got it. No one has it in this cesspool of a city. Look around you; what do you think is happening here? They take rats and they put them in boxes and when there are too many of them, some of the little fuckers go out of their minds and start gnawing the rest to death. *It ain't no different here, baby!* It's rat time for everybody in this madhouse. You can't expect to jam as many people into this stone thing as we do, with buses and taxis and dogs shitting themselves scrawny and noise night and day and no money and not enough places to live and no place to go to have a decent think . . . you can't do it without making the time right for some godforsaken other kind of thing to be born! You can't hate everyone around you, and kick every beggar and nigger and *mestizo* shithead, you can't have cabbies stealing from you and taking tips they don't deserve, and then cursing you, you can't walk in the soot till your collar turns black, and your body stinks with the smell of flaking brick and decaying brains, you can't do it without calling up some kind of awful—"

He stopped.

His face bore the expression of a man who has just received brutal word of the death of a loved one. He suddenly lay down, rolled over, and turned off.

She lay beside him, trembling, trying desperately to remember where she had seen his face before.

He didn't call her again, after the night of the party. And when they met in the hall, he pointedly turned away, as though he had given her some obscure chance and she had refused to take it. Beth thought she understood: Though Ray Gleeson had not been her first affair, he had been the first to reject her so completely. The first to put her not only out of his bed and his life, but even out of his world. It was as though she were invisible, not even beneath contempt, simply not there.

She busied herself with other things.

She took on three new charting jobs for Guzman and a new group that had formed on Staten Island, of all places. She worked furiously and they gave her new assignments; they even paid her.

She tried to decorate the apartment with a less precise touch. Huge poster blowups of Merce Cunningham and Martha Graham replaced the Brueghel prints that had reminded her of the view looking down the hill toward Williams. The tiny balcony outside her window, the balcony she had steadfastly refused to stand upon since the night of the slaughter, the night of the fog with eyes, that balcony she swept and set about with little flower boxes in which she planted geraniums, petunias, dwarf zinnias, and other hardy perennials. Then, closing the window, she went to give herself, to involve herself in this city to which she had brought her ordered life.

And the city responded to her overtures:

Seeing off an old friend from Bennington, at Kennedy International, she stopped at the terminal coffee shop to have a sandwich. The counter—like a moat—surrounded a center service island that had huge advertising cubes rising above it on burnished poles. The cubes proclaimed the delights of Fun City. *New York Is a Summer Festival*, they said, and *Joseph Papp Presents Shakespeare in Central Park* and *Visit the Bronx Zoo* and *You'll Adore Our Contentious but Lovable Cabbies*. The food emerged from a window far down the service area and moved slowly on a conveyor belt through the hordes of screaming waitresses who slathered the counter with redolent washcloths. The lunchroom had all the charm and dignity of a steel-rolling mill, and approximately the same noise level. Beth ordered a cheeseburger that cost a dollar and a quarter, and a glass of milk.

When it came, it was cold, the cheese unmelted, and the patty of meat resembling nothing so much as a dirty scouring pad. The bun was cold and untoasted. There was no lettuce under the patty.

Beth managed to catch the waitress's eye. The girl approached with an annoyed look. "Please toast the bun and may I have a piece of lettuce?" Beth said.

"We dun' do that," the waitress said, turning half away, as though she would walk in a moment.

"You don't do what?"

"We dun' toass the bun here."

"Yes, but I *want* the bun toasted," Beth said firmly.

"An' you got to pay for extra lettuce."

"If I was asking for *extra* lettuce," Beth said, getting annoyed, "I would pay for it, but since there's *no* lettuce here, I don't think I should be charged extra for the first piece."

"We dun' do that."

The waitress started to walk away. "Hold it," Beth said, raising her voice just enough so the assembly line eaters on either side stared at her. "You mean to tell me I have to pay a dollar and a quarter, and I can't get a piece of lettuce or even get the bun toasted?"

"Ef you dun' like it . . ."

"Take it back."

"You gotta pay for it, you order it."

"I said take it back, I don't want the fucking thing!"

The waitress scratched it off the check. The milk cost 27¢ and tasted going-sour. It was the first time in her life that Beth had said *that* word aloud.

At the cashier's stand, Beth said to the sweating man with the felt-tip pens in his shirt pocket, "Just out of curiosity, are you interested in complaints?"

"No!" he said, snarling, quite literally snarling. He did not look up as he punched out seventy-three cents and it came rolling down the chute.

The city responded to her overtures:

It was raining again. She was trying to cross Second Avenue, with the light. She stepped off the curb and a car came sliding through the red and splashed her. "Hey!" she yelled.

"Eat shit, sister!" the driver yelled back, turning the corner.

Her boots, her legs and her overcoat were splattered with mud. She stood trembling on the curb.

The city responded to her overtures:

She emerged from the building at One Astor Place with her big briefcase full of Laban charts; she was adjusting her rain scarf about her head. A well-dressed man with an attaché case thrust the handle of his umbrella up between her legs from the rear. She gasped and dropped her case.

The city responded and responded and responded.

Her overtures altered quickly.

The old drunk with the stippled cheeks extended his hand and mumbled words. She cursed him and walked on up Broadway past the beaver film houses.

She crossed against the lights on Park Avenue, making hackies slam their brakes to avoid hitting her; she used *that* word frequently now.

When she found herself having a drink with a man who had elbowed up beside her in the singles' bar, she felt faint and knew she should go home.

But Vermont was so far away.

Nights later. She had come home from the Lincoln Center ballet and gone straight to bed. Lying half-asleep in her bedroom, she heard an alien sound. One room away, in the living room, in the dark, there was a sound. She slipped out of bed and went to the door between the rooms. She fumbled silently for the switch on the lamp just inside the living room, and found it, and clicked it on. A Black man in a leather car coat was trying to get *out* of the apartment. In that first flash of light filling the room she noticed the television set beside him on the floor as he struggled with the door, she noticed the police lock and bar had been broken in a new and clever manner *New York* magazine had not yet reported in a feature article on apartment ripoffs, she noticed that he had gotten his foot tangled in the telephone cord that she had requested be extra-long so she could carry the instrument into the bathroom, I don't want to miss any business calls when the shower is running; she noticed all things in perspective and one thing with sharpest clarity: the expression on the burglar's face.

There was something familiar in that expression.

He almost had the door open, but now he closed it, and slipped the police lock. He took a step toward her.

Beth went back, into the darkened bedroom.

The city responded to her overtures.

She backed against the wall at the head of the bed. Her hand fumbled in the shadows for the telephone. His shape filled the doorway, light, all light behind him.

In silhouette it should not have been possible to tell, but somehow she knew he was wearing gloves and the only marks he would leave would be deep bruises, very blue, almost black, with the tinge under them of blood that had been stopped in its course.

He came for her, arms hanging casually at his sides. She tried to climb over the bed, and he grabbed her from behind, ripping her nightgown. Then he had a hand around her neck, and he pulled her backward. She fell off the bed, landed at his feet and his hold was broken. She scuttled across the floor and for a moment she had the respite to feel terror. She was going to die, and she was frightened.

He trapped her in the corner between the closet and the bureau and kicked her. His foot caught her in the thigh as she folded tighter, smaller, drawing her legs up. She was cold.

Then he reached down with both hands and pulled her erect by her hair. He slammed her head against the wall. Everything slid up in her sight as though running off the edge of the world. He slammed her head against the wall again, and she felt something go soft over her right ear.

When he tried to slam her a third time she reached out blindly for his face and ripped down with her nails. He howled in pain, and she hurled herself forward, arms wrapping themselves around his waist. He stumbled backward and in a tangle of thrashing arms and legs they fell out onto the little balcony.

Beth landed on the bottom, feeling the window boxes jammed up against her spine and legs. She fought to get to her feet, and her nails hooked into his shirt under the open jacket, ripping. Then she was on her feet again and they struggled silently.

He whirled her around, bent her backward across the wrought-iron railing. Her face was turned outward.

They were standing in their windows, watching.

Through the fog she could see them watching. Through the fog she recognized their expressions. Through the fog she heard them breathing in unison, bellows breathing of expectation and wonder. Through the fog.

And the Black man punched her in the throat. She gagged and started to black out and could not draw air into her lungs. Back, back, he bent her farther back and she was looking up, straight up, toward the ninth floor and higher . . .

Up there: eyes.

The words Ray Gleeson had said in a moment filled with what he had become, with the utter hopelessness and finality of the choice the city had forced on him, the words came back. *You can't live in this city and survive unless you have protection . . . you can't live this way, like rats driven mad, without making the time right for some godforsaken other kind of thing to be born . . . you can't do it without calling up some kind of awful . . .*

God! A new God, an ancient God come again with the eyes and hunger of a child, a deranged blood God of fog and street violence. A God who needed worshippers and offered the choices of death as a victim or life as an eternal witness to the deaths of *other* chosen victims. A God to fit the times, a God of streets and of people.

She tried to shriek, to appeal to Ray, to the director in the bedroom window of his ninth-floor apartment with his long-legged Philadelphia model beside him and his fingers inside her as they worshipped in their holiest of ways, to the others who had been at the party that had been Ray's offer of a chance to join their congregation. She wanted to be saved from having to make that choice.

But the Black man had punched her in the throat, and now his hands were on her, one on her chest, the other in her face, the smell of leather filling her where the nausea could not. And she understood Ray had *cared*, had wanted her to take the chance offered; but she had come from a world of little white dormitories and Vermont countryside; it was not a real world. *This* was the real world and up there was the God who ruled this world, and she had rejected him, had said no to one of his priests and servitors. *Save me! Don't make me do it!*

She knew she had to call out, to make appeal, to try and win the approbation of that God. *I can't . . . save me!*

She struggled and made terrible little mewling sounds trying to summon the words to cry out, and suddenly she crossed a line, and screamed up into the echoing courtyard with a voice Leona Ciarelli had never known enough to use.

"Him! Take him! Not me! I'm yours, I love you, I'm yours! Take him, not me, please not me, take him, take him, I'm yours!"

And the Black man was suddenly lifted away, wrenched off her, and off the balcony, whirled straight up into the fog-thick air in the courtyard, as Beth sank to her knees on the ruined flower boxes.

She was half-conscious and could not be sure she saw it just that way, but up he went, end over end, whirling and spinning like a charred leaf.

And the form took firmer shape. Enormous paws with claws and shapes that no animal she had ever seen had ever possessed, and the burglar, Black, poor, terrified, whimpering like a whipped dog, was stripped of his flesh. His body was opened with a thin incision, and there was a rush as all the blood poured from him like a sudden cloudburst, and yet he was still alive, twitching with the involuntary horror of a frog's leg shocked with an electric current. Twitched, and twitched again as he was torn piece by piece to shreds. Pieces of flesh and bone and half a face with an eye blinking furiously, cascaded down past Beth, and hit the cement below with sodden thuds. And still he was alive, as his organs were squeezed and musculature and bile and shit and skin were rubbed, sandpapered together and let fall. It went on and on, as the death of Leona Ciarelli had gone on and on, and she understood with the blood-knowledge of survivors *at any cost* that the reason the witnesses to the death of Leona Ciarelli had done nothing was not that they had been frozen with horror, that they didn't want to get involved, or that they were inured to death by years of television slaughter.

They were worshippers at a black mass the city had demanded be staged; not once, but a thousand times a day in this insane asylum of steel and stone.

Now she was on her feet, standing half-naked in her ripped nightgown, her hands tightening on the wrought-iron railing, begging to see more, to drink deeper.

Now she was one of them, as the pieces of the night's sacrifice fell past her, bleeding and screaming.

Tomorrow the police would come again, and they would question her, and she would say how terrible it had been, that burglar, and how she had fought, afraid he would rape her and kill her, and how he had fallen, and she had no idea how he had been so hideously mangled and ripped apart, but a seven-story fall, after all . . .

Tomorrow she would not have to worry about walking in the streets, because no harm could come to her. Tomorrow she could even remove the police lock. Nothing in the city could do her any further evil, because she had made the only choice. She was now a dweller in the city, now wholly and richly a part of it. Now she was taken to the bosom of her God.

She felt Ray beside her, standing beside her, holding her, protecting her, his hand on her naked backside, and she watched the fog swirl up and fill the courtyard, fill the city, fill her eyes and her soul and her heart with its power. As Ray's naked body pressed tightly inside her, she drank deeply of the night, knowing whatever voices she heard from this moment forward would be the voices not of whipped dogs, but those of strong, meat-eating beasts.

At last she was unafraid, and it was so good, so very good *not* to be afraid.

> When inward life dries up, when feeling decreases and apathy increases, when one cannot affect or even genuinely touch another person, violence flares up as a daimonic necessity for contact, a mad drive forcing touch in the most direct way possible.
>
> **Rollo May**
> *Love and Will*

LOST SOULS

Jeffty Is Five

When I was five years old, there was a little kid I played with: Jeffty. His real name was Jeff Kinzer, and everyone who played with him called him Jeffty. We were five years old together, and we had good times playing together.

When I was five, a Clark Bar was as fat around as the gripping end of a Louisville Slugger, and pretty nearly six inches long, and they used real chocolate to coat it, and it crunched very nicely when you bit into the center, and the paper it came wrapped in smelled fresh and good when you peeled off one end to hold the bar so it wouldn't melt onto your fingers. Today, a Clark Bar is as thin as a credit card, they use something artificial and awful-tasting instead of pure chocolate, the thing is soft and soggy, it costs fifteen or twenty cents instead of a decent, correct nickel, and they wrap it so you think it's the same size it was twenty years ago, only it isn't; it's slim and ugly and nasty-tasting and not worth a penny, much less fifteen or twenty cents.

When I was that age, five years old, I was sent away to my Aunt Patricia's home in Buffalo, New York, for two years. My father was going through "bad times," and Aunt Patricia was very beautiful and had married a stockbroker. They took care of me for two years. When I was seven, I came back home and went to find Jeffty, so we could play together.

I was seven. Jeffty was still five. I didn't notice any difference. I didn't know: I was only seven.

When I was seven years old, I used to lie on my stomach in front of our Atwater Kent radio and listen to swell stuff. I had tied the ground wire to the radiator, and I would lie there with my coloring books and my Crayolas (when there were only sixteen colors in the big box), and listen to the NBC Red Network: Jack Benny on the *Jell-O Program*, *Amos 'n' Andy*, Edgar Bergen and Charlie McCarthy on the *Chase and Sanborn Program*, *One Man's Family*, *First Nighter*; the NBC Blue Network: *Easy Aces*, the *Jergens Journal* with Walter Winchell, *Information Please*, *Death Valley Days*; and best of all, the Mutual network with *The Green Hornet*, *The Lone Ranger*, *The Shadow* and *Quiet, Please*. Today, I turn on my car radio and go from one end of the dial to the other and all I get is 100-string orchestras, banal housewives, and insipid truckers discussing their kinky sex lives with arrogant talk show hosts, country and western drivel, and rock music so loud it hurts my ears.

When I was ten, my grandfather died of old age and I was "a troublesome kid," and they sent me off to military school, so I could be "taken in hand."

I came back when I was fourteen. Jeffty was still five.

When I was fourteen years old, I used to go to the movies on Saturday afternoons and a matinee was ten cents and they used real butter on the popcorn and I could always be sure of seeing a western like Lash LaRue, or Wild Bill Elliott as Red Ryder with Bobby Blake as Little Beaver, or Roy Rogers, or Johnny Mack Brown; a scary picture like *House of Horrors* with Rondo Hatton as Creeper, or *The Cat People*, or *The Mummy*, or *I Married a Witch* with Fredric March and Veronica Lake; plus an episode of a great serial like *The Shadow* with Victor Jory, or *Dick Tracy* or *Flash Gordon*; and three cartoons; and a James FitzPatrick Traveltalk; *Movietone News*; and a singalong. And if I stayed on till evening, Bingo or Keeno; and free dishes. Today, I go to movies and see Clint Eastwood blowing people's heads apart like ripe cantaloupes.

At eighteen, I went to college. Jeffty was still five. I came back during the summers, to work at my Uncle Joe's jewelry store. Jeffty hadn't changed. Now I knew there was something different about him, something wrong, something weird. Jeffty was still five years old, not a day older.

At twenty-two, I came home for keeps. To open a Sony television franchise in town, the first one. I saw Jeffty from time to time. He was five.

Things are better in a lot of ways. People don't die from some of the old diseases anymore. Cars go faster and get you there more quickly on better roads. Shirts are softer and silkier. We have paperback books, even though they cost as much as a good hardcover used to. When I'm running short in the bank, I can live off credit cards till things even out. But I still think we've lost a lot of good stuff. Did you know you can't buy linoleum anymore, only vinyl floor covering? There's no such thing as oilcloth anymore; you'll never again smell that special, sweet smell from your grandmother's kitchen. Furniture isn't made to last thirty years or longer because they took a survey and found that young homemakers like to throw their furniture out and bring in all new, color-coded borax every seven years. Records don't feel right; they're not thick and solid like the old ones, they're thin and you can bend them. That doesn't seem right to me. Restaurants don't serve cream in pitchers anymore, just that artificial glop in little plastic tubs, and one is never enough to get coffee the right color. You can make a dent in a car fender with only a sneaker. Everywhere you go, all the towns look the same with Burger Kings and McDonald's and 7-Elevens and Taco Bells and motels and shopping centers. Things may be better, but why do I keep thinking about the past?

What I mean by five years old is not that Jeffty was retarded. I don't think that's what it was. Smart as a whip for five years old; very bright, quick, cute, a funny kid.

But he was three feet tall, small for his age, and perfectly formed: no big head, no strange jaw, none of that. A nice, normal-looking five-year-old kid. Except that he was the same age as I was: twenty-two.

When he spoke, it was with the squeaking, soprano voice of a five-year-old; when he walked, it was with the little hops and shuffles of a five-year-old; when he talked to you, it was about the concerns of a five-year-old . . . comic books, playing soldier, using a clothes pin to attach a stiff piece of cardboard to the front fork of his bike so the sound it made when the spokes hit was like a motorboat, asking questions like *why does that thing do that like that,* how high is up, how old is old, why is grass green, what's an elephant look like? At twenty-two, he was five.

Jeffty's parents were a sad pair. Because I was still a friend of Jeffty's, still let him hang around with me, sometimes took him to the county fair or miniature golf or the movies, I wound up spending time with *them.* Not that I much cared for them, because they were so awfully depressing. But then, I suppose one couldn't expect much more from the poor devils. They had an alien thing in their home, a child who had grown no older than five in twenty-two years, who provided the treasure of that special childlike state indefinitely, but who also denied them the joys of watching the child grow into a normal adult.

Five is a wonderful time of life for a little kid . . . or it *can* be, if the child is relatively free of the monstrous beastliness other children indulge in. It is a time when the eyes are wide open and the patterns are not yet set; a time when one has not yet been hammered into accepting everything as immutable and hopeless; a time when the hands cannot do enough, the mind cannot learn enough, the world is infinite and colorful and filled with mysteries. Five is a special time before they take the questing, unquenchable, quixotic soul of the young dreamer and thrust it into dreary schoolroom boxes. A time before they take the trembling hands that want to hold everything, touch everything, figure everything out, and make them lie still on desktops. A time before people begin saying "act your age" and "grow up" or "you're behaving like a baby." It is a time when a child who acts adolescent is still cute and responsive and everyone's pet. A time of delight, of wonder, of innocence.

Jeffty had been stuck in that time, just five, just so.

But for his parents it was an ongoing nightmare from which no one—not social workers, not priests, not child psychologists, not teachers, not friends, not medical wizards, not psychiatrists, no one—could slap or shake them awake. For seventeen years their sorrow had grown through stages of parental dotage to concern, from concern to worry, from worry to fear, from fear to confusion, from confusion to anger, from anger to dislike, from dislike to naked hatred, and finally, from deepest loathing and revulsion to a stolid, depressive acceptance.

John Kinzer was a shift foreman at the Balder Tool & Die plant. He was a thirty-year man. To everyone but the man living it, his was a spectacularly uneventful life. In no way was he remarkable . . . save that he had fathered a twenty-two-year-old five-year-old.

John Kinzer was a small man; soft, with no sharp angles; with pale eyes that never seemed to hold mine for longer than a few seconds. He continually shifted in his chair during conversations and seemed to see things in the upper corners of the room, things no one else could see . . . or wanted to see. I suppose the word that best suited him was *haunted.* What his life had become . . . well, *haunted* suited him.

Leona Kinzer tried valiantly to compensate. No matter what hour of the day I visited, she always tried to foist food on me. And when Jeffty was in the house she was always at *him* about eating: "Honey, would you like an orange? A nice orange? Or a tangerine?

I have tangerines. I could peel a tangerine for you." But there was clearly such fear in her, fear of her own child, that the offers of sustenance always had a faintly ominous tone.

Leona Kinzer had been a tall woman, but the years had bent her. She seemed always to be seeking some area of wallpapered wall or storage niche into which she could fade, adopt some chintz or rose-patterned protective coloration and hide forever in plain sight of the child's big brown eyes, pass her a hundred times a day and never realize she was there, holding her breath, invisible. She always had an apron tied around her waist, and her hands were red from cleaning. As if by maintaining the environment immaculately she could pay off her imagined sin: having given birth to this strange creature.

Neither of them watched television very much. The house was usually dead silent, not even the sibilant whispering of water in the pipes, the creaking of timbers settling, the humming of the refrigerator. Awfully silent, as if time itself had taken a detour around that house.

As for Jeffty, he was inoffensive. He lived in that atmosphere of gentle dread and dulled loathing, and if he understood it, he never remarked in any way. He played, as a child plays, and seemed happy. But he must have sensed, in the way of a five-year-old, just how alien he was in their presence.

Alien. No, that wasn't right. He was *too* human, if anything. But out of phase, out of synch with the world around him, and resonating to a different vibration than his parents, god knows. Nor would other children play with him. As they grew past him, they found him at first childish, then uninteresting, then simply frightening as their perceptions of aging became clear and they could see he was not affected by time as they were. Even the little ones, his own age, who might wander into the neighborhood, quickly came to shy away from him like a dog in the street when a car backfires.

Thus, I remained his only friend. A friend of many years. Five years. Twenty-two years. I liked him; more than I can say. And never knew exactly why. But I did, without reserve.

But because we spent time together, I found I was also—polite society—spending time with John and Leona Kinzer. Dinner, Saturday afternoons sometimes, an hour or so when I'd bring Jeffty back from a movie. They were grateful: slavishly so. It relieved them of the embarrassing chore of going out with him, or having to pretend before the world that they were loving parents with a perfectly normal, happy, attractive child. And their gratitude extended to hosting me. Hideous, every moment of their depression, hideous.

I felt sorry for the poor devils, but I despised them for their inability to love Jeffty, who was eminently lovable.

I never let on, of course, even during the evenings in their company that were awkward beyond belief.

We would sit there in the darkening living room—*always* dark or darkening, as if kept in shadow to hold back what the light might reveal to the world outside through the bright eyes of the house—we would sit and silently stare at one another. They never knew what to say to me.

"So how are things down at the plant?" I'd say to John Kinzer.

He would shrug. Neither conversation nor life suited him with any ease or grace. "Fine, just fine," he would say, finally.

And we would sit in silence again.

"Would you like a nice piece of coffee cake?" Leona would say. "I made it fresh just this morning." Or deep-dish green apple pie. Or milk and tollhouse cookies. Or a brown betty pudding.

"No, no, thank you, Mrs. Kinzer; Jeffty and I grabbed a couple of cheeseburgers on the way home." And again, silence.

Then, when the stillness and the awkwardness became too much even for them (and who knew how long that total silence reigned when they were alone, with that thing they never talked about anymore, hanging between them), Leona Kinzer would say, "I think he's asleep."

John Kinzer would say, "I don't hear the radio playing."

Just so, it would go on like that, until I could politely find an excuse to bolt away on some flimsy pretext. Yes, that was the way it would go on, every time, just the same . . . except once.

"I don't know what to do any more," Leona said. She began crying. "There's no change, not one day of peace."

Her husband managed to drag himself out of the old easy chair and go to her. He bent and tried to soothe her, but it was clear from the graceless way in which he touched her graying hair that the ability to be compassionate had been stunned in him. "Shhh, Leona, it's all right. Shhh." But she continued crying. Her hands scraped gently at the antimacassars on the arms of the chair.

Then she said, "Sometimes I wish he had been stillborn."

John looked up into the corners of the room. For the nameless shadows that were always watching him? Was it God he was seeking in those spaces? "You don't mean that," he said to her, softly, pathetically, urging her with body tension and trembling in his voice to recant before God took notice of the terrible thought. But she meant it; she meant it very much.

I managed to get away quickly that evening. They didn't want witnesses to their shame. I was glad to go.

And for a week I stayed away. From them, from Jeffty, from their street, even from that end of town.

I had my own life. The store, accounts, suppliers' conferences, poker with friends, pretty women I took to well-lit restaurants, my own parents, putting antifreeze in the car, complaining to the laundry about too much starch in the collars and cuffs, working out at the gym, taxes, catching Jan or David (whichever one it was) stealing from the cash register. I had my own life.

But not even *that* evening could keep me from Jeffty. He called me at the store and asked me to take him to the rodeo. We chummed it up as best a twenty-two-year-old with other interests *could* . . . with a five-year-old. I never dwelled on what bound us together; I always thought it was simply the years. That, and affection for a kid who could have been the little brother I never had. (Except I *remembered* when we had played together, when we had both been the same age; I *remembered* that period, and Jeffty was still the same.)

And then, one Saturday afternoon, I came to take him to a double feature, and things I should have noticed so many times before, I first began to notice only that afternoon.

I came walking up to the Kinzer house, expecting Jeffty to be sitting on the front porch steps, or in the porch glider, waiting for me. But he was nowhere in sight.

Going inside, into that darkness and silence, in the midst of May sunshine, was unthinkable. I stood on the front walk for a few moments, then cupped my hands around my mouth and yelled, "Jeffty? Hey, Jeffty, come on out, let's go. We'll be late."

His voice came faintly, as if from under the ground.

"Here I am, Donny."

I could hear him, but I couldn't see him. It was Jeffty, no question about it: as Donald H. Horton, President and Sole Owner of The Horton TV & Sound Center, no one but Jeffty called me Donny. He had never called me anything else.

(Actually, it isn't a lie. I *am*, as far as the public is concerned, Sole Owner of the Center. The partnership with my Aunt Patricia is only to repay the loan she made me, to supplement the money I came into when I was twenty-one, left to me when I was ten by my grandfather. It wasn't a very big loan, only eighteen thousand, but I asked her to be a silent partner, because of when she had taken care of me as a child.)

"Where are you, Jeffty?"

"Under the porch in my secret place."

I walked around the side of the porch and stooped down and pulled away the wicker grating. Back in there, on the pressed dirt, Jeffty had built himself a secret place. He had comics in orange crates, he had a little table and some pillows, it was lit by big fat candles, and we used to hide there when we were both . . . five.

"What'cha up to?" I asked, crawling in and pulling the grate closed behind me. It was cool under the porch, and the dirt smelled comfortable, the candles smelled clubby and familiar. Any kid would feel at home in such a secret place: there's never been a kid who didn't spend the happiest, most productive, most deliciously mysterious times of his life in such a secret place.

"Playin'," he said. He was holding something golden and round. It filled the palm of his little hand.

"You forget we were going to the movies?"

"Nope. I was just waitin' for you here."

"Your mom and dad home?"

"Momma."

I understood why he was waiting under the porch. I didn't push it any further. "What've you got there?"

"Captain Midnight Secret Decoder Badge," he said, showing it to me on his flattened palm.

I realized I was looking at it without comprehending what it was for a long time. Then it dawned on me what a miracle Jeffty had in his hand. A miracle that simply could *not* exist.

"Jeffty," I said softly, with wonder in my voice, "where'd you get that?"

"Came in the mail today. I sent away for it."

"It must have cost a lot of money."

"Not so much. Ten cents an' two inner wax seals from two jars of Ovaltine."

"May I see it?" My voice was trembling, and so was the hand I extended. He gave it to me, and I held the miracle in the palm of my hand. It was *wonderful.*

You remember. *Captain Midnight* went on the radio nationwide in 1940. It was sponsored by Ovaltine. And every year they issued a Secret Squadron Decoder Badge. And every day at the end of the program, they would give you a clue to the next day's installment in a code that only kids with the official badge could decipher. They stopped making those wonderful Decoder Badges in 1949. I remember the one I had in 1945: it was beautiful. It had a magnifying glass in the center of the code dial. *Captain Midnight* went off the air in 1950, and though I understand it was a short-lived television series in the mid-Fifties, and though they issued Decoder Badges in 1955 and 1956, as far as the *real* badges were concerned, they never made one after 1949.

The Captain Midnight Code-O-Graph I held in my hand, the one Jeffty said he had gotten in the mail for ten cents (*ten cents!!!*) and two Ovaltine labels, was brand-new, shiny gold metal, not a dent or a spot of rust on it like the old ones you can find at exorbitant prices in collectible shoppes from time to time . . . it was a *new* Decoder. And the date on it was *this* year.

But *Captain Midnight* no longer existed. Nothing like it existed on the radio. I'd listened to the one or two weak imitations of old-time radio the networks were currently airing, and the stories were dull, the sound effects bland, the whole feel of it wrong, out of date, cornball. Yet I held a *new* Code-O-Graph.

"Jeffty, tell me about this," I said.

"Tell you what, Donny? It's my new Capt'n Midnight Secret Decoder Badge. I use it to figger out what's gonna happen tomorrow."

"Tomorrow how?"

"On the program."

"*What* program?!"

He stared at me as if I was being purposely stupid. "On Capt'n *Mid*night! Boy!" I was being dumb.

I still couldn't get it straight. It was right there, right out in the open, and I still didn't know what was happening. "You mean one of those records they made of the old-time radio programs? Is that what you mean, Jeffty?"

"What records?" he asked. He didn't know what *I* meant.

We stared at each other, there under the porch. And then I said, very slowly, almost afraid of the answer, "Jeffty, how do you hear *Captain Midnight*?"

"Every day. On the radio. On my radio. Every day at five-thirty."

News. Music, dumb music, and news. That's what was on the radio every day at 5:30. Not *Captain Midnight.* The Secret Squadron hadn't been on the air in twenty years.

"Can we hear it tonight?" I asked.

"Boy!" he said. I was being dumb. I knew it from the way he said it; but I didn't know *why.* Then it dawned on me: this was Saturday. *Captain Midnight* was on Monday through Friday. Not on Saturday or Sunday.

"We goin' to the movies?"

He had to repeat himself twice. My mind was somewhere else. Nothing definite. No conclusions. No wild assumptions leapt to. Just off somewhere trying to figure it out, and concluding—as *you* would have concluded, as *any*one would have concluded rather than accepting the truth, the impossible and wonderful truth—just finally concluding there was a simple explanation I didn't yet perceive. Something mundane and dull, like the passage of time that steals all good, old things from us, packratting trinkets and plastic in exchange. And all in the name of Progress.

"We goin' to the movies, Donny?"

"You bet your boots we are, kiddo," I said. And I smiled. And I handed him the Code-O-Graph. And he put it in his side pants pocket. And we crawled out from under the porch. And we went to the movies. And neither of us said anything about *Captain Midnight* all the rest of that day. And there wasn't a ten-minute stretch, all the rest of that day, that I didn't think about it.

It was inventory all that next week. I didn't see Jeffty till late Thursday. I confess I left the store in the hands of Jan and David, told them I had some errands to run, and left early. At 4:00. I got to the Kinzers' right around 4:45. Leona answered the door, looking exhausted and distant. "Is Jeffty around?" She said he was upstairs in his room . . .

. . . listening to the radio.

I climbed the stairs two at a time.

All right, I had finally made that impossible, illogical leap. Had the stretch of belief involved anyone but Jeffty, adult or child, I would have reasoned out more explicable answers. But it *was* Jeffty, clearly another kind of vessel of life, and what he might experience should not be expected to fit into the ordered scheme.

I admit it: I *wanted* to hear what I heard.

Even with the door closed, I recognized the program:

"There he goes, Tennessee! Get him!"

There was the heavy report of a squirrel rifle and the keening whine of the slug ricocheting, and then the same voice yelled triumphantly, *"Got him! D-e-a-a-a-a-d center!"*

He was listening to the American Broadcasting Company, 790 kilocycles, and he was hearing *Tennessee Jed*, one of my most favorite programs from the Forties, a western adventure I had not heard in twenty years, because it had not existed for twenty years.

I sat down on the top step of the stairs, there in the upstairs hall of the Kinzer home, and I listened to the show. It wasn't a rerun of an old program; I dimly remembered every one of *them* by heart. I had never missed an episode. And even more convincing evidence than childhood memory that this was a *new* installment were the occasional references during the commercials to current cultural and technological developments, and phrases that had not existed in common usage in the Forties: aerosol spray cans, laserasing of tattoos, Tanzania, the word "uptight."

I could not ignore the fact. Jeffty was listening to a *new* segment of *Tennessee Jed.*

I ran downstairs and out the front door to my car. Leona must have been in the kitchen. I turned the key and punched on the radio and spun the dial to 790 kilohertz. The ABC station. Rock music.

I sat there for a few moments, then ran the dial slowly from one end to the other. Music, news, talk shows. No *Tennessee Jed.* And it was a Blaupunkt, the best radio I could get. I wasn't missing some perimeter station. It simply was not there!

After a few moments I turned off the radio and the ignition and went back upstairs quietly. I sat down on the top step and listened to the entire program. It was *wonderful.*

Exciting, imaginative, filled with everything I remembered as being most innovative about radio drama. But it was modern. It wasn't an antique, rebroadcast to assuage the need of that dwindling listenership who longed for the old days. It was a new show, with all the old voices, but still young and bright. Even the commercials were for currently available products, but they weren't as loud or as insulting as the screamer ads one heard on radio these days.

And when *Tennessee Jed* went off at 5:00, I heard Jeffty spin the dial on his radio till I heard the familiar voice of the announcer Glenn Riggs proclaim, *"Presenting Hop Harrigan! America's ace of the airwaves!"* There was the sound of an airplane in flight. It was a prop plane, *not* a jet! Not the sound kids today have grown up with, but the sound *I* grew up with, the *real* sound of an airplane, the growling, revving, throaty sound of the kind of airplanes G-8 and His Battle Aces flew, the kind Captain Midnight flew, the kind Hop Harrigan flew. And then I heard Hop say, *"CX-4 calling control tower. CX-4 calling control tower. Standing by!"* A pause, then, *"Okay, this is Hop Harrigan . . . coming in!"*

And Jeffty, who had the same problem all of us kids had had in the Forties with programming that pitted equal favorites against one another on different stations, having paid his respects to Hop Harrigan and Tank Tinker, spun the dial and went back to ABC, where I heard the stroke of a gong, the wild cacophony of nonsense Chinese chatter, and the announcer yelled, *"T-e-e-e-rry and the Pirates!"*

I sat there on the top step and listened to Terry and Connie and Flip Corkin and, so help me god, Agnes Moorehead as The Dragon Lady, all of them in a new adventure that took place in a Red China that had not existed in the days of Milton Caniff's 1937 version of the Orient, with river pirates and Chiang Kai-shek and warlords and the naïve imperialism of American gunboat diplomacy.

Sat, and listened to the whole show, and sat even longer to hear *Superman* and part of *Jack Armstrong, the All-American Boy* and part of *Captain Midnight*, and John Kinzer came home and neither he nor Leona came upstairs to find out what had happened to me, or where Jeffty was, and sat longer, and found I had started crying, and could not stop, just sat there with tears running down my face, into the corners of my mouth, sitting and crying until Jeffty heard me and opened his door and saw me and came out and looked at me in childish confusion as I heard the station break for the Mutual Network and they began the theme music of *Tom Mix*, "When It's Round-up Time in Texas and the Bloom Is on the Sage," and Jeffty touched my shoulder and smiled at me, with his mouth and his big brown eyes, and said, "Hi, Donny. Wanna come in an' listen to the radio with me?"

Hume denied the existence of an absolute space, in which each thing has its place; Borges denies the existence of one single time, in which all events are linked.

Jeffty received radio programs from a place that could not, in logic, in the natural scheme of the space-time universe as conceived by Einstein, exist. But that wasn't all he received. He got mail-order premiums that no one was manufacturing. He read comic books that had been defunct for three decades. He saw movies with actors who had been dead for twenty years. He was the receiving terminal for endless joys and pleasures of the past that the world had dropped along the way. On its headlong suicidal flight toward New Tomorrows, the world had razed its treasure house of simple happinesses, had poured concrete over its playgrounds, had abandoned its elfin stragglers, and all of it was being impossibly, miraculously shunted back into the present through Jeffty. Revivified, updated, the traditions maintained but contemporaneous. Jeffty was the unbidding Aladdin whose very nature formed the magic lampness of his reality.

And he took me into his world with him.

Because he trusted me.

We had breakfast of Quaker Puffed Wheat Sparkies and warm Ovaltine we drank out of this year's Little Orphan Annie Shake-Up

Mugs. We went to the movies and while everyone else was seeing a comedy starring Goldie Hawn and Ryan O'Neal, Jeffty and I were enjoying Humphrey Bogart as the professional thief Parker in John Huston's brilliant adaptation of the Donald Westlake novel *Slayground*. The second feature was Spencer Tracy, Carole Lombard, and Laird Cregar in the Val Lewton–produced film of *Leiningen Versus the Ants*.

Twice a month we went down to the newsstand and bought the current pulp issues of *The Shadow*, *Doc Savage*, and *Startling Stories*. Jeffty and I sat together, and I read to him from the magazines. He particularly liked the new short novel by Henry Kuttner, *The Dreams of Achilles*, and the new Stanley G. Weinbaum series of short stories set in the subatomic particle universe of Redurna. In September we enjoyed the first installment of the new Robert E. Howard Conan novel, *Isle of the Black Ones*, in *Weird Tales*; and in August we were only mildly disappointed by Edgar Rice Burroughs's fourth novella in the Jupiter series featuring John Carter of Barsoom—"Corsairs of Jupiter." But the editor of *Argosy All-Story Weekly* promised there would be two more stories in the series, and it was such an unexpected revelation for Jeffty and me that it dimmed our disappointment at the lessened quality of the current story.

We read comics together, and Jeffty and I both decided—separately, before we came together to discuss it—that our favorite characters were Doll Man, Airboy, and The Heap. We also adored the George Carlson strips in *Jingle Jangle Comics*, particularly the Pie-Face Prince of Old Pretzleburg stories, which we read together and laughed over, even though I had to explain some of the esoteric puns to Jeffty, who was too young to have that kind of subtle wit.

How to explain it? I can't. I had enough physics in college to make some offhand guesses, but I'm more likely wrong than right. The laws of the conservation of energy occasionally break. These are laws that physicists call "weakly violated." Perhaps Jeffty was a catalyst for the weak violation of conservation laws we're only now beginning to realize exist. I tried doing some reading in the area—muon decay of the "forbidden" kind: gamma decay that doesn't include the muon neutrino among its products—but nothing I encountered, not even the latest readings from the Swiss Institute for Nuclear Research near Zurich, gave me an insight. I was thrown back on a vague acceptance of the philosophy that the real name for "science" is *magic.*

No explanations, but enormous good times.

The happiest time of my life.

I had the "real" world, the world of my store and my friends and my family, the world of profit&loss, of taxes and evenings with young women who talked about going shopping, or the United Nations, or the rising cost of coffee and microwave ovens. And I had Jeffty's world, in which I existed only when I was with him. The things of the past he knew as fresh and new, I could experience only when in his company. And the membrane between the two worlds grew ever thinner, more luminous and transparent. I had the best of both worlds. And knew, somehow, that I could carry nothing from one to the other.

Forgetting that, for just a moment, betraying Jeffty by forgetting, brought an end to it all.

Enjoying myself so much, I grew careless and failed to consider how fragile the relationship between Jeffty's world and my world really was. There is a reason why the Present begrudges the existence of the Past. I never really understood. Nowhere in the beast books, where survival is shown in battles between claw and fang, tentacle and poison sac, is there recognition of the ferocity the Present always brings to bear on the Past. Nowhere is there a detailed statement of how the Present lies in wait for What-Was, waiting for it to become Now-This-Moment so it can shred it with its merciless jaws.

Who could know such a thing . . . at any age . . . and certainly not at my age . . . who could understand such a thing?

I'm trying to exculpate myself. I can't. It was my fault.

It was another Saturday afternoon.

"What's playing today?" I asked him, in the car, on the way downtown.

He looked up at me from the other side of the front seat and smiled one of his best smiles. "Ken Maynard in *Bullwhip Justice* an' *The Demolished Man*." He kept smiling, as if he'd really put one over on me. I looked at him with disbelief.

"You're *kid*ding!" I said, delighted. "Bester's *The Demolished Man*?"

He nodded, delighted at my being delighted. He knew it was one of my favorite books. "Oh, that's super!"

"Super *duper*," he said.

"Who's in it?"

"Franchot Tone, Evelyn Keyes, Lionel Barrymore, and Elisha Cook, Jr." He was much more knowledgeable about movie actors than I'd ever been. He could name the character actors in any movie he'd ever seen. Even the crowd scenes.

"And cartoons?" I asked.

"Three of 'em: a *Little Lulu*, a *Donald Duck*, and a *Bugs Bunny*. An' a *Pete Smith Specialty* an' a *Lew Lehr Monkeys Is da C-r-r-raziest Peoples*."

"Oh boy!" I said. I was grinning from ear to ear. And then I looked down and saw the pad of purchase order forms on the seat. I'd forgotten to drop it off at the store.

"Gotta stop by the Center," I said. "Gotta drop off something. It'll only take a minute."

"Okay," Jeffty said. "But we won't be late, will we?"

"Not on your tintype, kiddo," I said.

When I pulled into the parking lot behind the Center, he decided to come in with me and we'd walk over to the theater. It's not a large town. There are only two movie houses, the Utopia and the Lyric. We were going to the Utopia, and it was only three blocks from the Center.

I walked into the store with the pad of forms, and it was bedlam. David and Jan were handling two customers each, and there were people standing around waiting to be helped. Jan turned a look on me and her face was a horror-mask of pleading. David was running from the stockroom to the showroom and all he could murmur as he whipped past was "Help!" and then he was gone.

"Jeffty," I said, crouching down, "listen, give me a few minutes. Jan and David are in trouble with all these people. We won't be late, I promise. Just let me get rid of a couple of these customers." He looked nervous but nodded okay.

I motioned to a chair and said, "Just sit down for a while and I'll be right with you."

He went to the chair, good as you please, though he knew what was happening, and he sat down.

I started taking care of people who wanted color television sets. This was the first really substantial batch of units we'd gotten in—color television was only now becoming reasonably priced, and this was Sony's first promotion—and it was bonanza time for me. I could see paying off the loan and being out in front for the first time with the Center. It was business.

In my world, good business comes first.

Jeffty sat there and stared at the wall. Let me tell you about the wall.

Stanchion and bracket designs had been rigged from floor to within two feet of the ceiling. Television sets had been stacked artfully on the wall. Thirty-three television sets. All playing at the same time. Black and white, color, little ones, big ones, all going at the same time.

Jeffty sat and watched thirty-three television sets, on a Saturday afternoon. We can pick up a total of thirteen channels, including the UHF educational stations. Golf was on one channel; baseball was on a second; celebrity bowling was on a third; the fourth channel was a religious seminar; a teenage dance show was on the fifth; the sixth was a rerun of a situation comedy; the seventh was a rerun of a police show; eighth was a nature program showing a man flycasting endlessly; ninth was news and conversation; tenth was a stock car race; eleventh was a man doing logarithms on a blackboard; twelfth was a woman in a leotard doing setting-up exercises; and on the thirteenth channel was a badly animated cartoon show in Spanish. All but six of the shows were repeated on three sets. Jeffty sat and watched that wall of television on a Saturday afternoon while I sold as fast and as hard as I could, to pay back my Aunt Patricia and stay in touch with my world. It was business.

I should have known better. I should have understood about the Present and the way it kills the Past. But I was selling with both hands. And when I finally glanced over at Jeffty, half an hour later, he looked like another child.

He was sweating. That terrible fever sweat when you have stomach flu. He was pale, as pasty and pale as a worm, and his little hands were gripping the arms of the chair so tightly I could see his knuckles in bold relief. I dashed over to him, excusing myself from the middle-aged couple looking at the new 21-inch Mediterranean model.

"Jeffty!"

He looked at me, but his eyes didn't track. He was in absolute terror. I pulled him out of the chair and started toward the front door with him, but the customers I'd deserted yelled at me, "Hey!" The middle-aged man said, "You wanna sell me this thing or don't you?"

I looked from him to Jeffty and back again. Jeffty was like a zombie. He had come where I'd pulled him. His legs were rubbery, and his feet dragged. The past, being eaten by the present, the sound of something in pain.

I clawed some money out of my pants pocket and jammed it into Jeffty's hand. "Kiddo . . . listen to me . . . get out of here right now!" He still couldn't focus properly. "*Jeffty*," I said as tightly as I could, "*listen* to me!" The middle-aged customer and his wife were walking toward us. "Listen, kiddo, get out of here right this minute. Walk over to the Utopia and buy the tickets. I'll be right behind you." The middle-aged man and his wife were almost on us. I shoved Jeffty through the door and watched him stumble away in the wrong direction, then stop as if gathering his wits, turn and go back past the front of the Center and in the direction of the Utopia. "Yes, sir," I said, straightening up and facing them, "yes, ma'am, that is one terrific set with some sen*sa*tional features! If you'll just step back here with me . . ."

There was a terrible sound of something hurting, but I couldn't tell from which channel, or from which set, it was coming.

Most of it I learned later, from the girl in the ticket booth, and from some people I knew who came to me to tell me what had happened. By the time I got to the Utopia, nearly twenty minutes later, Jeffty was already beaten to a pulp and had been taken to the manager's office.

"Did you see a very little boy, about five years old, with big brown eyes and straight brown hair . . . he was waiting for me?"

"Oh, I think that's the little boy those kids beat up?"

"What!?! *Where is he?*"

"They took him to the manager's office. No one knew who he was or where to find his parents—"

A young girl wearing an usher's uniform was kneeling down beside the couch, placing a wet paper towel on his face.

I took the towel away from her and ordered her out of the office.

She looked insulted and she snorted something rude, but she left. I sat on the edge of the couch and tried to swab away the blood from the lacerations without opening the wounds where the blood had caked. Both his eyes were swollen shut. His mouth was ripped badly. His hair was matted with dried blood.

He had been standing in line behind two kids in their teens. They started selling tickets at 12:30 and the show started at 1:00. The doors weren't opened till 12:45. He had been waiting, and the kids in front of him had had a portable radio. They were listening to the ball game. Jeffty had wanted to hear some program, god knows what it might have been, *Grand Central Station*, *Let's Pretend*, *The Land of the Lost*, god only knows which one it might have been.

He had asked if he could borrow their radio to hear the program for a minute, and it had been a commercial break or something, and the kids had given him the radio, probably out of some malicious kind of courtesy that would permit them to take offense and rag the little boy. He had changed the station . . . and they'd been unable to get it to go back to the ball game. It was locked into the past, on a station that was broadcasting a program that didn't exist for anyone but Jeffty.

They had beaten him badly . . . as everyone watched.

And then they had run away.

I had left him alone, left him to fight off the present without sufficient weaponry. I had betrayed him for the sale of a 21-inch

Mediterranean console television, and now his face was pulped meat. He moaned something inaudible and sobbed softly.

"Shhh, it's okay, kiddo, it's Donny. I'm here. I'll get you home, it'll be okay."

I should have taken him straight to the hospital. I don't know why I didn't. I should have. I should have done that.

When I carried him through the door, John and Leona Kinzer just stared at me. They didn't move to take him from my arms. One of his hands was hanging down. He was conscious, but just barely. They stared, there in the semi-darkness of a Saturday afternoon in the present. I looked at them. "A couple of kids beat him up at the theater." I raised him a few inches in my arms and extended him. They stared at me, at both of us, with nothing in their eyes, without movement. "Jesus Christ," I shouted, "he's been beaten! He's your son! Don't you even want to touch him? What the hell kind of people are you?!"

Then Leona moved toward me very slowly. She stood in front of us for a few seconds, and there was a leaden stoicism in her face that was terrible to see. It said, *I have been in this place before, many times, and I cannot bear to be in it again; but I am here now.*

So I gave him to her. God help me, I gave him over to her.

And she took him upstairs to bathe away his blood and his pain.

John Kinzer and I stood in our separate places in the dim living room of their home, and we stared at each other. He had nothing to say to me.

I shoved past him and fell into a chair. I was shaking.

I heard the bath water running upstairs.

After what seemed a very long time Leona came downstairs, wiping her hands on her apron. She sat down on the sofa and after a moment John sat down beside her. I heard the sound of rock music from upstairs.

"Would you like a piece of nice pound cake?" Leona said.

I didn't answer. I was listening to the sound of the music. Rock music. On the radio. There was a table lamp on the end table beside the sofa. It cast a dim and futile light in the shadowed living room. *Rock music from the present, on a radio upstairs?* I started to say something, and then *knew* . . . Oh, God . . . *no*!

I jumped up just as the sound of hideous crackling blotted out the music, and the table lamp dimmed and dimmed and flickered. I screamed something, I don't know what it was, and ran for the stairs.

Jeffty's parents did not move. They sat there with their hands folded, in that place they had been for so many years.

I fell twice rushing up the stairs.

There isn't much on television that can hold my interest. I bought an old cathedral-shaped Philco radio in a secondhand store, and I replaced all the burnt-out parts with the original tubes from old radios I could cannibalize that still worked. I don't use transistors or printed circuits. They wouldn't work. I've sat in front of that set for hours sometimes, running the dial back and forth as slowly as you can imagine, so slowly it doesn't look as if it's moving at all sometimes.

But I can't find *Captain Midnight* or *The Land of the Lost* or *The Shadow* or *Quiet, Please*.

So she did love him, still, a little bit, even after all those years. I can't hate them: they only wanted to live in the present world again. That isn't such a terrible thing.

It's a good world, all things considered. It's much better than it used to be, in a lot of ways. People don't die from the old diseases anymore. They die from new ones, but that's Progress, isn't it?

Isn't it?

Tell me.

Somebody please tell me.

Pretty Maggie Moneyeyes

With an eight hole card and a queen showing, with the dealer showing a four up, Kostner decided to let the house do the work. So he stood, and the dealer turned up. Six.

The dealer looked like something out of a 1935 George Raft film: Arctic diamond-chip eyes, manicured fingers long as a brain surgeon's, straight black hair slicked flat away from the pale forehead. He did not look up as he peeled them off. A three. Another three. Bam. A five. Bam. Twenty-one, and Kostner saw his last thirty dollars—six five-dollar chips—scraped on the edge of the cards, into the dealer's chip racks. Busted. Flat. Down and out in Las Vegas, Nevada. Playground of the Western World.

He slid off the comfortable stool-chair and turned his back on the blackjack table. The action was already starting again, like waves closing over a drowned man. He had been there, was gone, and no one had noticed. No one had seen a man blow the last tie with salvation. Kostner now had his choice: he could bum his way into Los Angeles and try to find something that resembled a new life . . . or he could go blow his brains out through the back of his head.

Neither choice showed much light or sense.

He thrust his hands deep into the pockets of his worn and dirty chinos and started away down the line of slot machines clanging and rattling on the other side of the aisle between blackjack tables.

He stopped. He felt something in his pocket. Beside him, but all-engrossed, a fiftyish matron in electric lavender capris, high heels, and Ship'n'Shore blouse was working two slots, loading and pulling one while waiting for the other to clock down. She was dumping quarters in a seemingly inexhaustible supply from a Dixie cup held in her left hand. There was a surrealistic presence to the woman. She was almost automated, not a flicker of expression on her face, the eyes fixed and unwavering. Only when the gong rang, someone down the line had pulled a jackpot, did she look up. And at that moment Kostner knew what was wrong and immoral and deadly about Vegas, about legalized gambling, about setting the traps all baited and open in front of the average human. The woman's face was gray with hatred, envy, lust, and dedication to the game—in that timeless instant when she heard another drugged soul down the line winning a minuscule jackpot. A jackpot that would only lull the player with words like *luck* and *ahead of the game.* The jackpot lure; the sparkling, bobbling many-colored wiggler in a sea of poor fish.

The thing in Kostner's pocket was a silver dollar.

He brought it out and looked at it.

The eagle was hysterical.

But Kostner pulled to an abrupt halt, only one half-footstep from the sign indicating the limits of Tap City. He was still with it. What the highrollers called the edge, the *vigorish*, that fine hole card. One buck. One cartwheel. Pulled out of the pocket not half as deep as the pit into which Kostner had just been about to plunge.

What the hell, he thought, and turned to the row of slot machines.

He had thought they'd all been pulled out of service, the silver dollar slots. A shortage of coinage, said the United States Mint. But right there, side by side with the nickel and quarter bandits, was one cartwheel machine. Two thousand dollar jackpot. Kostner grinned foolishly. If you're gonna go out, go out like a champ.

He thumbed the silver dollar into the coin slot and grabbed the heavy, oiled handle. Shining cast aluminum and pressed steel.

Big black plastic ball, angled for arm ease, pull it all day and you won't get weary.

Without a prayer in the universe, Kostner pulled the handle.

She had been born in Tucson, mother full-blooded Cherokee, father a bindlestiff on his way through. Mother had been working a truckers' stop, father had popped for spencer steak and sides. Mother had just gotten over a bad scene, indeterminate origins, unsatisfactory culminations. Mother had popped for bed. And sides. Margaret Annie Jessie had come nine months later; black of hair, fair of face, and born into a life of poverty. Twenty-three years later, a determined product of Miss Clairol and Berlitz, a dream-image formed by Vogue and intimate association with the rat race, Margaret Annie Jessie had become a contraction.

Maggie.

Long legs, trim and coltish; hips a trifle large, the kind that promote that specific thought in men, about getting their hands around them; belly flat, isometrics; waist cut to the bone, a waist that works in any style from dirndl to disco slacks; no breasts—all nipple, but no breast, like an expensive whore (the way O'Hara pinned it)—and no padding . . . forget the cans, baby, there's other, more important action; smooth, Michelangelo-sculpted neck, a pillar, proud; and all that face.

Outthrust chin, perhaps a tot too much belligerence, but if you'd walloped as many gropers, you too, sweetheart; narrow mouth, petulant lower lip, nice to chew on, a lower lip as though filled with honey, bursting, ready for things to happen; a nose that threw the right sort of shadow, flaring nostrils, the acceptable words—aquiline, patrician, classic, allathat; cheekbones as stark and promontory as a spit of land after ten years of open ocean; cheekbones holding darkness like narrow shadows, sooty beneath the taut-fleshed bone structure; amazing cheekbones, the whole face, really; an ancient kingdom's uptilted eyes, the touch of the Cherokee, eyes that looked out at you, as you looked in at them, like someone peering out of the keyhole as you peered in; actually, dirty eyes, they said you can get it.

Blonde hair, a great deal of it, wound and rolled and smoothed and flowing, in the old style, the pageboy thing men always admire; no tight little cap of slicked plastic; no ratted and teased Annapurna of bizarre coiffure; no ironed-flat discothèque hair like number 3 flat noodles. Hair, the way a man wants it, so he can dig his hands in at the base of the neck and pull all that face very close.

An operable woman, a working mechanism, a rigged and sudden machinery of softness and motivation.

Twenty-three, and determined as hell never to abide in that vale of poverty her mother had called purgatory for her entire life; snuffed out in a grease fire in the last trailer, somewhere in Arizona, thank God no more pleas for a little money from babygirl Maggie hustling drinks in a Los Angeles topless joint. (There ought to be some remorse in there somewhere, for a mommy gone where all the good grease-fire victims go. Look around, you'll find it.)

Maggie.

Genetic freak. Mommy's Cherokee uptilted eye-shape, and Polack quickscrewing Daddy WithoutaName's blue as innocence color.

Blue-eyed Maggie, dyed blonde, alla that face, alla that leg, fifty bucks a night can get it and it sounds like it's having a climax.

Irish-innocent blue-eyed-innocent French-legged-innocent Maggie. Polack. Cherokee. Irish. All-woman and going on the market for this month's rent on the stucco pad, eighty bucks' worth of groceries, a couple months' worth for a Mustang, three appointments with the specialist in Beverly Hills about that shortness of breath after a night on the hustle bump the sticky thigh the disco lurch the gotcha sweat: woman minutes. Increments under the meat; perspiration purchases, yeah it does.

Maggie, Maggie, Maggie, pretty Maggie Moneyeyes, who came from Tucson and trailers and rheumatic fever and a surge to live that was all kaleidoscope frenzy of clawing scrabbling no-nonsense. If it took lying on one's back and making sounds like a panther in the desert, then one did it, because nothing, but nothing *was as bad as being dirt-poor, itchy-skinned, soiled-underwear, scuff-toed, hairy and ashamed lousy with the no-gots. Nothing!*

Maggie. Hooker. Hustler. Grabber. Swinger. If there's a buck in it, there's rhythm and the onomatopoeia is Maggie Maggie Maggie.

She who puts out. For a price, whatever that might be.

Maggie was dating Nuncio. He was Sicilian. He had dark eyes and an alligator-grain wallet with slip-in pockets for credit cards. He was a spender, a sport, a high roller. They went to Vegas.

Maggie and the Sicilian. Her blue eyes and his slip-in pockets. But mostly her blue eyes.

The spinning reels behind the three long glass windows blurred, and Kostner knew there wasn't a chance. Two thousand dollar jackpot. Round and round, whirring. Three bells or two bells and a jackpot bar, get 18; three plums or two plums and a jackpot bar, get 14; three oranges or two oranges and a jac—

Ten, five, two bucks for a single cherry cluster in first position.

Something . . . I'm drowning . . . something . . .

The whirring . . .

Round and round . . .

As something happened that was not considered in the pit-boss manual.

The reels whipped and snapped to a stop, clank clank clank, tight in place.

Three bars looked up at Kostner. But they did not say JACKPOT. They were three bars from which stared three blue eyes. Very blue, very immediate, very JACKPOT!!

Twenty silver dollars clattered into the payoff trough at the bottom of the machine. An orange light popped on in the casino cashier's cage, bright orange on the jackpot board. And the gong began clanging overhead.

The slot machine floor manager nodded once to the pit boss, who pursed his lips and started toward the seedy-looking man still standing with his hand on the slot's handle.

The token payment—twenty silver dollars—lay untouched in the payoff trough. The balance of the jackpot—one thousand nine hundred and eighty dollars—would be paid manually by the casino cashier. And Kostner stood, dumbly, as the three blue eyes stared up at him.

There was a moment of idiotic disorientation, as Kostner stared back at the three blue eyes; a moment in which the slot machine's mechanisms registered to themselves; and the gong was clanging furiously.

All through the hotel's casino people turned from their games to stare. At the roulette tables the white-on-white players from Detroit and Cleveland pulled their watery eyes away from the clattering ball and stared down the line for a second, at the ratty-looking guy in front of the slot machine. From where they sat, they could not tell it was a two grand pot, and their rheumy eyes went back into billows of cigar smoke, and that little ball.

The blackjack hustlers turned momentarily, screwing around in their seats, and smiled. They were closer to the slot-players in temperament, but they knew the slots were a dodge to keep the old ladies busy, while the players worked toward their endless twenty-ones.

And the old dealer, who could no longer cut it at the fast-action boards, who had been put out to pasture by a grateful management, standing at the Wheel of Fortune near the entrance to the casino, even he paused in his zombie-murmuring ("Annnnother winner onna Wheel of Forchun!") to no one at all, and looked toward Kostner and that incredible gong-clanging. Then, in a moment, still with no players, he called *another* nonexistent winner.

Kostner heard the gong from far away. It had to mean he had won two thousand dollars, but that was impossible. He checked the payoff chart on the face of the machine. Three bars labeled JACKPOT meant JACKPOT. Two thousand dollars.

But these three bars did not say JACKPOT. They were three gray bars, rectangular in shape, with a blue eye directly in the center of each bar.

Blue eyes?

Somewhere, a connection was made, and electricity, a billion volts of electricity, shot through Kostner. His hair stood on end, his fingertips bled raw, his eyes turned to jelly, and every fiber in his musculature became radioactive. Somewhere, out there, in a place that was not this place, Kostner had been inextricably bound to—to someone. Blue eyes?

The gong had faded out of his head, the constant noise level of the casino, chips chittering, people mumbling, dealers calling plays, it had all gone, and he was embedded in silence.

Tied to that someone else, out there somewhere, through those three blue eyes.

Then in an instant, it had passed, and he was alone again, as though released by a giant hand, the breath crushed out of him. He staggered up against the slot machine.

"You all right, fellah?"

A hand gripped him by the arm, steadied him. The gong was still clanging overhead somewhere, and he was breathless from a journey he had just taken. His eyes focused and he found himself looking at the stocky pit boss who had been on duty while he had been playing blackjack.

"Yeah . . . I'm okay, just a little dizzy is all."

"Sounds like you got yourself a big jackpot, fellah." The pit boss grinned; it was a leathery grin; something composed of stretched muscles and conditioned reflexes, totally mirthless.

"Yeah . . . great . . ." Kostner tried to grin back. But he was still shaking from that electrical absorption that had kidnapped him.

"Let me check it out," the pit boss was saying, edging around Kostner, and staring at the face of the slot machine. "Yeah, three jackpot bars, all right. You're a winner."

Then it dawned on Kostner! Two thousand dollars! He looked down at the slot machine and saw—

Three bars with the word JACKPOT on them. No blue eyes, just words that meant money. Kostner looked around frantically, was he losing his mind? *From somewhere, not in the casino, he heard a tinkle of rhodium-plated laughter.*

He scooped up the twenty silver dollars. The pit boss dropped another cartwheel into the Chief and pulled the jackpot off. Then the pit boss walked him to the rear of the casino, talking to him in a muted, extremely polite tone of voice. At the cashier's window, the pit boss nodded to a weary-looking man at a huge Rolodex cardfile, checking credit ratings.

"Barney, jackpot on the cartwheel Chief; slot five-oh-oh-one-five." He grinned at Kostner, who tried to smile back. It was difficult. He felt stunned.

The cashier checked a payoff book for the correct amount to be drawn and leaned over the counter toward Kostner. "Check or cash, sir?"

Kostner felt buoyancy coming back to him. "Is the casino's check good?" They all three laughed at that. "A check's fine," Kostner said. The check was drawn, and the Check-Riter punched out the little bumps that said two thousand. "The twenty cartwheels are a gift," the cashier said, sliding the check through to Kostner.

He held it, looked at it, and still found it difficult to believe. Two grand, back on the golden road.

As he walked back through the casino with the pit boss, the stocky man asked pleasantly, "Well, what are you going to do with it?" Kostner had to think a moment. He didn't really have any plans. But then the sudden realization came to him: "I'm going to play that slot machine again." The pit boss smiled: a congenital sucker. He would put all twenty of those silver dollars back into the Chief, and then turn to the other games. Blackjack, roulette, faro, baccarat . . . in a few hours he would have redeposited the two grand with the hotel casino. It always happened.

He walked Kostner back to the slot machine and patted him on the shoulder. "Lotsa luck, fellah."

As he turned away, Kostner slipped a silver dollar into the machine and pulled the handle.

The pit boss had taken only five steps when he heard the incredible sound of the reels clicking to a stop, the clash of twenty token silver dollars hitting the payoff trough, and that goddamned gong went out of its mind again.

She had known that sonofabitch Nuncio was a perverted swine. A walking filth. A dungheap between his ears. Some kind of monster in nylon undershorts. There weren't many kinds of games Maggie hadn't played, but what that Sicilian de Sade wanted to do was outright vomity!

She nearly fainted when he suggested it. Her heart—which the Beverly Hills specialist had said she should not tax—began whumping frantically. "You pig!" she screamed. "You filthy dirty ugly pig you, Nuncio you pig!" She had bounded out of the bed and started to throw on clothes. She didn't even bother with a brassiere, pulling the poorboy sweater on over her thin breasts, still crimson with the touches and love-bites Nuncio had showered on them.

He sat up in the bed, a pathetic-looking little man, gray hair at the temples and no hair at all on top, and his eyes were moist. He was porcine, was indeed the swine she called him, but he was helpless before her. He was in love with his hooker, with the tart whom he was supporting. It had been the first time for the swine Nuncio, and he was helpless. Back in Detroit, had it been a floozy, a bimbo, a chippy broad, he would have gotten out of the double bed and rapped around pretty good. But this Maggie, she tied him in knots. He had suggested . . . that, *what they should do together . . . because he was so consumed with her. But* she *was furious with* him. *It wasn't* that *bizarre an idea!*

"Gimme a chanct'a talk t'ya, honey . . . Maggie . . ."

"You filthy pig, Nuncio! Give me some money, I'm going down to the casino, and I don't want to see your filthy pig face for the rest of the day, remember that!"

And she had gone in his wallet and pants, and taken eight hundred and sixteen dollars, while he watched. He was helpless before her. She was something stolen from a world he knew only as "class" and she could do what she wanted with him.

Genetic freak Maggie, blue-eyed posing mannequin Maggie, pretty Maggie Moneyeyes, who was one-half Cherokee and one-half a buncha other things, had absorbed her lessons well. She was the very model of a "class broad."

"Not for the rest of the day, do you understand?" She stared at him till he nodded; then she went downstairs, furious, to fret and gamble and wonder about nothing but years of herself.

Men stared after her as she walked. She carried herself like a challenge, the way a squire carried a pennon, the way a prize bitch carried herself in the judge's ring. Born to the blue. The wonders of mimicry and desire.

Maggie had no lust for gambling, none whatever. She merely wanted to taste the fury of her relationship with the swine Sicilian, her need for solidity in a life built on the edge of the slide area, the senselessness of being here in Las Vegas when she could be back in Beverly Hills. She grew angrier and more ill at the thought of Nuncio upstairs in the room, taking another shower. She bathed three times a day. But it was different with him. He knew she resented his smell; he had the soft odor of wet fur sometimes, and she had told him about it. Now he bathed constantly and hated it. He was a foreigner to the bath. His life had been marked by various kinds of filths, and baths for him now were more of an obscenity than dirt could ever have been. For her, bathing was different. It was a necessity. She had to keep the patina of the world off her, had to remain clean and smooth and white. A presentation, not an object of flesh and hair. A chromium instrument, something never pitted by rust and corrosion.

When she was touched by them, by any one of them, by the men, by all the Nuncios, they left little pitholes of bloody rust on her white, permanent flesh; cobwebs, sooty stains. She had *to bathe. Often.*

She strolled down between the tables and the slots, carrying eight hundred and sixteen dollars. Eight one hundred dollar bills and sixteen dollars in ones.

At the change booth she got cartwheels for the sixteen ones. The Chief waited. It was her baby. She played it to infuriate the Sicilian. He had told her to play the nickel slots, the quarter or dime slots, but she always infuriated him by blowing fifty or a hundred dollars in ten minutes, one coin after another, in the big Chief.

She faced the machine squarely and put in the first silver dollar. She pulled the handle that swine Nuncio. Another dollar, pulled the handle how long does this go on? The reels cycled and spun and whirled and whipped in a blurringspinning metalhumming overandoverandover as Maggie blue-eyed Maggie hated and hated and thought of hate and all the days and nights of swine behind her and ahead of her and if only she had all the money in this room in this casino in this hotel in this town right now this very instant just an instant thisinstant it would be enough to whirring and humming and spinning and overandoverandoverandoverandover and she would be free free free and all the world would never touch her body again the swine would never touch her white flesh again and then suddenly as dollarafterdollarafterdollar went aroundaroundaround hummmming in reels of cherries and bells and bars and plums and oranges there was suddenly painpainpain a SHARP *pain!pain!pain! in her chest, her heart, her center, a needle, a lancet, a burning, a pillar of flame that was purest pure purer* PAIN!

Maggie, pretty Maggie Moneyeyes, who wanted all that money in that cartwheel Chief slot machine, Maggie who had come from filth and rheumatic fever, who had come all the way to three baths a day and a specialist in Very Expensive Beverly Hills, that *Maggie suddenly had a seizure, a flutter, a slam of a coronary thrombosis and fell instantly dead on the floor of the casino. Dead.*

One instant she had been holding the handle of the slot machine, willing her entire being, all that hatred for all the swine she had ever rolled with, willing every fiber of every cell of every chromosome into that machine, wanting to suck out every silver vapor within its belly, and the next instant—so close they might have been the same—her heart exploded and killed her and she slipped to the floor . . . still touching the Chief.

On the floor.
Dead.
Struck dead.
Liar. All the lies that were her life.
Dead on a floor.

[A moment out of time ■ lights whirling and spinning in a cotton candy universe ■ down a bottomless funnel roundly sectioned like a goat's horn ■ a cornucopia that rose up cuculiform smooth and slick as a worm belly ■ endless nights that pealed ebony funeral bells ■ out of fog ■ out of weightlessness ■ suddenly total cellular knowledge ■ memory running backward ■ gibbering spastic blindness ■ a soundless owl of frenzy trapped in a cave of prisms ■ sand endlessly draining down ■ billows of forever ■ edges of the world as they splintered ■ foam rising drowning from inside ■ the smell of rust ■ rough green corners that burn ■ memory the gibbering spastic blind memory

■ seven rushing vacuums of nothing ■ yellow ■ pinpoints cast in amber straining and elongating running like live wax ■ chill fevers ■ overhead the odor of stop ■ this is the stopover before hell or heaven ■ this is limbo ■ trapped and doomed alone in a mist-eaten nowhere ■ a soundless screaming a soundless whirring a soundless spinning spinning spinning ■ spinning ■ spinning ■ spinning ■ spinninggggggggggggg]

Maggie had wanted all the silver in the machine. She had died, willing herself into the machine. Now, looking out from within, from inside the limbo that had become her own purgatory, Maggie was trapped, in the oiled and anodized interior of the silver dollar slot machine. The prison of her final desires, where she had wanted to be, completely trapped in that last instant of life between life/death. Maggie, gone inside, all soul now, trapped for all eternity in the cage soul of the machine. Limbo. Trapped. Trapped.

"I hope you don't mind if I call over one of the slot men," the slot machine floor manager was saying, from a far distance. He was in his late fifties, a velvet-voiced man whose eyes held nothing of light and certainly nothing of kindness. He had stopped the pit boss as the stocky man had turned in mid-step to return to Kostner and the jackpotted machine; he had taken the walk himself. "We have to make sure, you know how it is: somebody didn't fool with the slot, you know, maybe it's outta whack or something, you know."

He lifted his left hand and there was a clicker in it, the kind children use at Halloween. He clicked half a dozen times, like a rabid cricket, and there was a scurrying in the pit between the tables.

Kostner was only faintly aware of what was happening. Instead of being totally awake, feeling the surge of adrenaline through his veins, the feeling any gambler gets when he is ahead of the game, a kind of desperate urgency when he has hit it for a boodle, he was numb, partaking of the action around him only as much as a drinking glass involves itself in the alcoholic's drunken binge.

All color and sound had been leached out of him.

A tired-looking, resigned-weary man wearing a gray porter's jacket, as gray as his hair, as gray as his indoor skin, came to them, carrying a leather wrap-up of tools. The slot repairman studied the machine, turning the pressed steel body around on its stand, studying the back. He used a key on the back door and for an instant Kostner had a view of gears, springs, armatures, and the clock that ran the slot mechanism. The repairman nodded silently over it, closed and relocked it, turned it around again, and studied the face of the machine.

"Nobody's been spooning it," he said, and went away.

Kostner stared at the floor manager.

"Gaffing. That's what he meant. Spooning's another word for it. Some guys use a little piece of plastic, or a wire, shove it down through the escalator, it kicks the machine. Nobody thought that's what happened here, but you know, we have to make sure, two grand is a big payoff, and twicewell, you know, I'm sure you'll understand. If a guy was doing it with a boomerang—"

Kostner raised an eyebrow.

"—uh, yeah, a boomerang, it's another way to spoon the machine. But we just wanted to make a little check, and now everybody's satisfied, so if you'll just come back to the casino cashier with me—"

And they paid him off again.

So he went back to the slot machine, and stood before it for a long time, staring at it. The change girls and the dealers going off-duty; the little old ladies with their canvas work gloves worn to avoid calluses when pulling the slot handles; the men's room attendant on his way up front to get more matchbooks; the floral tourists, the idle observers, the hard drinkers, the sweepers, the busboys; the gamblers with poached-egg eyes who had been up all night; the showgirls with massive breasts and diminutive sugar daddies; all of them conjectured mentally about the beat-up walker who was staring at the silver dollar Chief. He did not move, merely stared at the machine . . . and they wondered.

The machine was staring back at Kostner.

Three blue eyes.

The electric current had sparked through him again, as the machine had clocked down and the eyes turned up a second time, as he had *won* a second time. But this time he knew there was something more than luck involved, for no one else had seen those three blue eyes.

So now he stood before the machine, waiting. It spoke to him. Inside his skull, where no one had ever lived but himself, now someone else moved and spoke to him. A girl. A beautiful girl. Her name was Maggie, and she spoke to him.

I've been waiting for you. A long time, I've been waiting for you, Kostner. Why do you think you hit the jackpot? Because I've been waiting for you, and I want you. You'll win all the jackpots. Because I want you, I need you. Love me, I'm Maggie, I'm so alone, love me.

Kostner had been staring at the slot machine for a very long time, and his weary brown eyes had seemed to be locked to the blue eyes on the jackpot bars. But he knew no one else could see the blue eyes, and no one else could hear the voice, and no one else knew about Maggie.

He was the universe to her. Everything to her.

He thumbed in another silver dollar, and the pit boss watched, the slot machine repairman watched, the slot machine floor manager watched, three change girls watched, and a pack of unidentified players watched, some from their seats.

The reels whirled, the handle snapped back, and in a second they flipped down to a halt, twenty silver dollars tokened themselves into the payoff trough and a woman at one of the crap tables belched a fragment of hysterical laughter.

And the gong went insane again.

The floor manager came over and said, very softly, "Mr. Kostner, it'll take us about fifteen minutes to pull this machine and check it out. I'm sure you understand." As two slot repairmen came out of the back, hauled the Chief off its stand, and took it into the repair room at the rear of the casino.

While they waited, the floor manager regaled Kostner with stories of spooners who had used intricate magnets inside their clothes, of boomerang men who had attached their plastic implements under their sleeves so they could be extended on spring-loaded clips, of cheaters who had come equipped with tiny electric drills in their hands and wires that slipped into the tiny drilled holes. And he kept saying he knew Kostner would understand.

But Kostner knew the floor manager would not understand.

When they brought the Chief back, one of the repairmen nodded assuredly. "Nothing wrong with it. Works perfectly. Nobody's been boomin' it."

But the blue eyes were gone on the jackpot bars.

Kostner knew they would return.

They paid him off again.

He returned and played again. And again. And again. They put a "spotter" on him. He won again. And again. And again. The crowd had grown to massive proportions. Word had spread like the silent communications of the telegraph vine, up and down the Strip, all the way to downtown Vegas and the sidewalk casinos where they played night and day every day of the year, and the crowd surged in a tide toward the hotel, and the casino, and the seedy-looking walker with his weary brown eyes. The crowd moved to him inexorably, drawn like lemmings by the odor of the luck that rose from him like musky electrical cracklings. And he won. Again and again. Thirty-eight thousand dollars. And the three blue eyes continued to stare up at him. Her lover was winning. Maggie and her Moneyeyes.

Finally, the casino decided to speak to Kostner. They pulled the Chief for fifteen minutes, for a supplemental check by experts from the slot machine company in downtown Vegas, and while they were checking it, they asked Kostner to come to the main office of the hotel.

The owner was there. His face seemed faintly familiar to Kostner. Had he seen it on television? The newspapers?

"Mr. Kostner, my name is Jules Hartshorn."

"I'm pleased to meet you."

"Quite a string of luck you're having out there."

"It's been a long time coming."

"You realize, this sort of luck is impossible."

"I'm compelled to believe it, Mr. Hartshorn."

"Um. As am I. It's happening to my casino. But we're thoroughly convinced of one of two possibilities, Mr. Kostner; one, either the machine is inoperable in a way we can't detect; or two, you are the cleverest spooner we've ever had in here."

"I'm not cheating."

"As you can see, Mr. Kostner, I'm smiling. The reason I'm smiling is at your naïveté in believing I would take your word for it. I'm perfectly happy to nod politely and say of course you aren't cheating. But no one can win thirty-eight thousand dollars on nineteen straight jackpots off one slot machine; it doesn't even have mathematical odds against its happening, Mr. Kostner. It's on a cosmic scale of improbability with three dark planets crashing into our sun within the next twenty minutes. It's on a par with the Pentagon, the Forbidden City, and the Kremlin, all three pushing the red button at the same microsecond. It's an impossibility, Mr. Kostner. An impossibility that's happening to me."

"I'm sorry."

"Not really."

"No, not really. I can use the money."

"For what, exactly, Mr. Kostner?"

"I hadn't thought about it, really."

"I see. Well, Mr. Kostner, let's look at it this way. I can't stop you from playing, and if you continue to win, I'll be required to pay off. And no stubble-chinned thugs will be waiting in an alley to jackroll you and take the money. The checks will be honored. The best I can hope for, Mr. Kostner, is the attendant publicity. Right now, every high roller in Vegas is in that casino, waiting for you to drop cartwheels into that machine. It won't make up for what I'm losing, if you continue the way you've been; but it'll help. Every sucker in town likes to rub up next to luck. All I ask is that you cooperate a little."

"The least I can do, considering your generosity."

"An attempt at humor."

"I'm sorry. What is it you'd like me to do?"

"Get about ten hours' sleep."

"While you pull the slot and have it worked over thoroughly?"

"Yes."

"If I wanted to keep winning, that might be a pretty stupid move on my part. You might change the thingamajig inside so I couldn't win if I put back every dollar of that thirty-eight grand."

"We're licensed by the state of Nevada, Mr. Kostner."

"I come from a good family, too, and take a look at me. I'm a bum with thirty-eight thousand dollars in my pocket."

"Nothing will be done to that slot machine, Kostner."

"Then why pull it for ten hours?"

"To work it over thoroughly in the shop. If something as undetectable as metal fatigue or a worn escalator tooth or—we want to make sure this doesn't happen with other machines. And the extra time will get the word around town; we can use the crowd. Some of those tourists will stick to our fingers, and it'll help defray the expense of having you break the bank at this casino—on a slot machine."

"I have to take your word."

"This hotel will be in business long after you're gone, Kostner."

"Not if I keep winning."

Hartshorn's smile was a stricture. "A good point."

"So it isn't much of an argument."

"It's the only one I have. If you want to get back out on that floor, I can't stop you."

"No Mafia hoods ventilate me later?"

"I beg your pardon?"

"I said: no Maf—"

"You have a picturesque manner of speaking. In point of fact, I haven't the faintest idea what you're talking about."

"I'm sure you haven't."

"You've got to stop reading *The National Enquirer.* This is a legally run business. I'm merely asking a favor."

"Okay, Mr. Hartshorn, I've been three days without any sleep. Ten hours will do me a world of good."

"I'll have the desk clerk find you a quiet room on the top floor. And thank you, Mr. Kostner."

"Think nothing of it."

"I'm afraid that will be impossible."

"A lot of impossible things are happening lately."

He turned to go, as Hartshorn lit a cigarette. "Oh, by the way, Mr. Kostner?"

Kostner stopped and half-turned. "Yes?"

His eyes were getting difficult to focus. There was a ringing in his ears. Hartshorn seemed to waver at the edge of his vision like heat lightning across a prairie. Like memories of things Kostner had come across the country to forget. Like the whimpering and pleading that kept tugging at the cells of his brain. The voice of Maggie. Still back in there, saying . . . things . . .

They'll try to keep you from me.

All he could think about was the ten hours of sleep he had been promised. Suddenly it was more important than the money, than forgetting, than anything. Hartshorn was talking, was saying things, but Kostner could not hear him. It was as if he had turned off the sound and saw only the silent rubbery movement of Hartshorn's lips. He shook his head trying to clear it.

There were half a dozen Hartshorns all melting into and out of one another. And the voice of Maggie.

I'm warm here, and alone. I could be good to you, if you can come to me. Please come, please hurry.

"Mr. Kostner?"

Hartshorn's voice came draining down through exhaustion, thick as velvet flocking. Kostner tried to focus again. His extremely weary brown eyes began to track.

"Did you know about that slot machine?" Hartshorn was saying. "A peculiar thing happened with it about six weeks ago."

"What was that?"

"A girl died playing it. She had a heart attack, a seizure while she was pulling the handle, and died right out there on the floor."

Kostner was silent for a moment. He wanted desperately to ask Hartshorn what color the dead girl's eyes had been, but he was afraid the owner would say blue.

He paused with his hand on the office door. "Seems as though you've had nothing but a streak of bad luck on that machine."

Hartshorn smiled an enigmatic smile. "It might not change for a while, either."

Kostner felt his jaw muscles tighten. "Meaning I might die, too, and wouldn't *that* be bad luck."

Hartshorn's smile became hieroglyphic, permanent, stamped on him forever. "Sleep tight, Mr. Kostner."

In a dream, she came to him. Long, smooth thighs and soft golden down on her arms; blue eyes deep as the past, misted with a fine scintillance like lavender spiderwebs; taut body that was the only body Woman had ever had, from the very first. Maggie came to him.

Hello, I've been traveling a long time.

"Who are you?" Kostner asked, wonderingly. He was standing on a chilly plain, or was it a plateau? The wind curled around them both, or was it only around him? She was exquisite, and he saw her clearly, or was it through a mist? Her voice was deep and resonant, or was it light and warm as night-blooming jasmine?

I'm Maggie. I love you. I've waited for you.

"You have blue eyes."

Yes. *With love.*

"You're very beautiful."

Thank you. *With female amusement.*

"But why me? Why let it happen to me? Are you the girl who—are you the one that was sick—the one who—?"

I'm Maggie. And you, I picked you, because you need me. You've needed someone for a long, long time.

Then it unrolled for Kostner. The past unrolled and he saw who he was. He saw himself alone. Always alone. As a child, born to kind and warm parents who hadn't the vaguest notion of who he was, what he wanted to be, where his talents lay. So he had run off, when he was in his teens, and alone always alone on the road. For years and months and days and hours, with no one. Casual friendships, based on food, or sex, or artificial similarities. But no one to whom he could cleave, and cling, and belong. It was that way till Susie, and with her he had found light. He had discovered the scents and aromas of a spring that was eternally one day away. He had laughed, really laughed, and known with her it would at last be all right. So he had poured all of himself into her, giving her everything; all his hopes, his secret thoughts, his tender dreams; and she had taken them, taken him, all of him, and he had known for the first time what it was to have a place to live, to have a home in someone's heart. It was all the silly and gentle things he laughed at in other people, but for him it was breathing deeply of wonder.

He had stayed with her for a long time, and had supported her, supported her son from the first marriage; the marriage Susie never talked about. And then one day, he had come back, as Susie had always known he would. He was a dark creature of ruthless habits and vicious nature, but she had been his woman, all along, and Kostner realized he had been used as a stopgap, as a bill-payer till her wandering terror came home to nest. Then she had asked him to leave. Broke, and tapped out in all the silent inner ways a man can be drained, he had left, without even a fight, for all the fight had been leached out of him. He had left, and wandered west, and finally come to Las Vegas, where he had hit bottom. And found Maggie. In a dream, with blue eyes, he had found Maggie.

I want you to belong to me. I love you. *Her truth was vibrant in Kostner's mind. She was his, at last someone who was special, was his.*

"Can I trust you? I've never been able to trust anyone before. Women, never. But I need someone. I really need someone."

It's me, always. Forever. You can trust me.

And she came to him, fully. Her body was a declaration of truth and trust such as no other Kostner had ever known before. She met him on a windswept plain of thought, and he made love to her more completely than he had known any passion before. She joined with him, entered him, mingled with his blood and his thought and his frustration, and he came away clean, filled with glory.

"Yes, I can trust you, I want you, I'm yours," he whispered to her, when they lay side by side in a dream nowhere of mist and soundlessness. "I'm yours."

She smiled, a woman's smile of belief in her man; a smile of trust and deliverance. And Kostner woke up.

The Chief was back on its stand, and the crowd had been penned back by velvet ropes. Several people had played the machine, but there had been no jackpots.

Now Kostner came into the casino, and the "spotters" got themselves ready. While Kostner had slept, they had gone through his clothes, searching for wires, for gaffs, for spoons or boomerangs. Nothing.

Now he walked straight to the Chief and stared at it.

Hartshorn was there. "You look tired," he said gently to Kostner, studying the man's weary brown eyes.

"I am a little," Kostner tried a smile; it didn't work. "I had a funny dream."

"Oh?"

"Yeah . . . about a girl . . ." He let it die off.

Hartshorn's smile was understanding. Pitying, empathetic, and understanding. "There are lots of girls in this town. You shouldn't have any trouble finding one with your winnings."

Kostner nodded and slipped his first silver dollar into the slot. He pulled the handle. The reels spun with a ferocity Kostner had not heard before, and suddenly everything went whipping slantwise as he felt a wrenching of pure flame in his stomach, as his head was snapped on its spindly neck, as the lining behind his eyes was burned out. There was a terrible shriek, of tortured metal, of an express train ripping the air with its passage, of a hundred small animals being gutted and torn to shreds, of incredible pain, of night winds that tore the tops off mountains of lava. And a keening whine of a voice that wailed and wailed and wailed as it went away from there in blinding light—

Free! Free! Heaven or Hell it doesn't matter! Free!

The sound of a soul released from an eternal prison, a genie freed from a dark bottle. And in that instant of damp soundless nothingness, Kostner saw the reels snap and clock down for the final time:

One, two, three. Blue eyes.

But he would never cash his checks.

The crowd screamed through one voice as he fell sidewise and lay on his face. The final loneliness . . .

The Chief was pulled. Bad luck. Too many gamblers resented its very presence in the casino. So it was pulled. And returned to the company, with explicit instructions it was to be melted down to slag. And not till it was in the hands of the ladle foreman, who was ready to dump it into the slag furnace, did anyone remark on the final tally the Chief had clocked.

"Look at that, ain't that weird," said the ladle foreman to his bucket man. He pointed to the three glass windows.

"Never saw jackpot bars like that before," the bucket man agreed. "Three eyes. Must be an old machine."

"Yeah, some of these old games go way back," the foreman said, hoisting the slot machine onto the conveyor track leading to the slag furnace.

"Three eyes, huh. How about that. Three brown eyes." And he threw the knife-switch that sent the Chief down the track, to puddle in the roaring inferno of the furnace.

Three brown *eyes.*

Three brown eyes that looked very very weary. That looked very very trapped. That looked very very betrayed. Some of these old games go way back.

SHATTERDAY

i: Someday

Not much later, but later nonetheless, he thought back on the sequence of what had happened and knew he had missed nothing. How it had gone, was this:

He had been abstracted, thinking about something else. It didn't matter what. He had gone to the telephone in the restaurant, to call Jamie, to find out where the hell she was already, to find out why she'd kept him sitting in the bloody bar for thirty-five minutes. He had been thinking about something else, nothing deep, just woolgathering, and it wasn't till the number was ringing that he realized he'd dialed his own apartment. He had done it other times, not often, but as many as anyone else, dialed a number by rote and not thought about it, and occasionally it was his own number, everyone does it (he thought later), everyone does it, it's a simple mistake.

He was about to hang up, get back his dime and dial Jamie, when the receiver was lifted at the other end.

He answered.

Himself.

He recognized his own voice at once. But didn't let it penetrate.

He had no little machine to take messages after the bleep, he had had his answering service temporarily disconnected (unsatisfactory service, they weren't catching his calls on the third ring as he'd *insisted*), there was no one guesting at his apartment, nothing. He was not at home, he was here, in the restaurant, calling his apartment, and *he* answered.

"Hello?"

He waited a moment. Then said, "Who's this?"

He answered, "Who're you calling?"

"Hold it," he said. "Who *is* this?"

His own voice, on the other end, getting annoyed, said, "Look, friend, what number do you want?"

"This is BEacon 3-6189, right?"

Warily: "Yeah?"

"Peter Novins's apartment?"

There was silence for a moment, then: "That's right."

He listened to the sounds from the restaurant's kitchen. "If this is Novins's apartment, who're you?"

On the other end, in his apartment, there was a deep breath. "This is Novins."

He stood in the phone booth, in the restaurant, in the night, the receiver to his ear, and listened to his own voice. He had dialed his own number by mistake, dialed an empty apartment . . . *and he had answered.*

Finally, he said, very tightly, "*This* is Novins."

"Where are you?"

"I'm at the High Tide, waiting for Jamie."

Across the line, with a terrible softness, he heard himself asking, "Is that you?"

A surge of fear pulsed through him, and he tried to get out of it with one last possibility. "If this is a gag . . . Freddy . . . is that you, man? Morrie? Art?"

Silence. Then, slowly, "I'm Novins. Honest to God."

His mouth was dry. "I'm out here. You can't be, I *can't* be in the apartment."

"Oh yeah? Well, I am."

"I'll have to call you back." Peter Novins hung up.

He went back to the bar and ordered a double Scotch, no ice, straight up, and threw it back in two swallows, letting it burn. He sat and stared at his hands, turning them over and over, studying them to make sure they were his own, not alien meat grafted onto his wrists when he was not looking.

Then he went back to the phone booth, closed the door and sat down, and dialed his own number. Very carefully.

It rang six times before *he* picked it up.

He knew why the voice on the other end had let it ring six times; he didn't want to pick up the snake and hear his own voice coming at him.

"Hello?" His voice on the other end was barely controlled.

"It's me," he said, closing his eyes.

"Jesus God," he murmured.

They sat there, in their separate places, without speaking. Then Novins said, "I'll call you Jay."

"That's okay," he answered from the other end. It was his middle name. He never used it, but it appeared on his insurance policy, his driver's license, and his social security card. Jay said, "Did Jamie get there?"

"No, she's late again." Jay took a deep breath and said, "We'd better talk about this, man."

"I suppose," Novins answered. "Not that I really want to. You're scaring the shit out of me."

"How do you think *I* feel about it?"

"Probably the same way I feel about it."

They thought about that for a long moment. Then Jay said, "Will we be feeling exactly the same way about things?"

Novins considered it, then said, "If you're really me then I suppose so. We ought to try and test that."

"You're taking this a lot calmer than I am, it seems to me," Jay said.

Novins was startled. "You really think so? I was just about to say I thought you were really terrific the way you're handling all this. I think you're *much* more together about it than I am. I'm really startled, I've got to tell you."

"So how'll we test it?" Jay asked.

Novins considered the problem, then said, "Why don't we compare likes and dislikes. That's a start. That sound okay to you?"

"It's as good a place as any, I suppose. Who goes first?"

"It's my dime," Novins said, and for the first time he smiled. "I like, uh, well-done prime rib, end cut if I can get it, Yorkshire pudding, smoking a pipe, Max Ernst's paintings, Robert Altman films, William Goldman's books, getting mail but not answering it, uh—"

He stopped. He had been selecting random items from memory, the ones that came to mind first. But as he had been speaking, he heard what he was saying, and it seemed stupid. "This isn't going to work," Novins said. "What the hell does it matter? Was there anything in that list you didn't like?"

Jay sighed. "No, they're all favorites. You're right. If I like it, you'll like it. This isn't going to answer any questions."

Novins said, "I don't even know what the questions *are*!"

"That's easy enough," Jay said. "There's only one question: Which of us is me, and how does *me* get rid of *him*?"

A chill spread out from Novins's shoulder blades and wrapped around his arms like a mantilla. "What's *that* supposed to mean? Get rid of *him*? What the hell's *that*?"

"Face it," Jay said—and Novins heard a tone in the voice he recognized, the tone *he* used when he was about to become a tough negotiator—"we can't *both* be Novins. One of us is going to get screwed."

"Hold it, friend," Novins said, adopting the tone. "That's pretty muddy logic. First of all, who's to say you're not going to vanish back where you came from as soon as I hang up . . ."

"Bullshit," Jay answered.

"Yeah, well, maybe; but even if you're here to stay, and I don't concede *that* craziness for a second, even if you *are* real—"

"Believe it, baby, I'm real," Jay said, with a soft chuckle. Novins was starting to hate him.

"—even if you *are* real," Novins continued, "there's no saying we can't both exist, and both lead happy, separate lives."

"You know something, Novins," Jay said, "you're really full of horse puckey. You can't lead a happy life by yourself, man, how the hell are you going to do it knowing I'm over here living your life, too?"

"What do you mean I can't lead a happy life? What do you know about it?" And he stopped; of course Jay knew about it. *All* about it.

"You'd better start facing reality, Novins. You'll be coming to it late in life, but you'd better learn how to do it. Maybe it'll make the end come easier."

Novins wanted to slam the receiver into its rack. He was at once furiously angry and frightened. He knew what the other Novins was saying was true; he *had* to know, without argument; it was, after all, himself saying it. "Only one of us is going to make it," he said, tightly. "And it's going to be me, old friend."

"How do you propose to do it, Novins? You're out there, locked out. I'm in here, in my home, safe where I'm supposed to be."

"How about we look at it *this* way," Novins said quickly, "you're trapped in there, locked away from the world in three-and-a-half rooms. I've got everywhere else to move in. You're limited. I'm free."

There was silence for a moment.

Then Jay said, "We've reached a bit of an impasse, haven't we? There's something to be said for being loose, and there's something to be said for being safe inside. The amazing thing is that we both have accepted this thing so quickly."

Novins didn't answer. He accepted it because he had no other choice; if he could accept that he was speaking to himself, then anything that followed had to be part of that acceptance. Now that Jay had said it bluntly, that only one of them could continue to exist, all that remained was finding a way to make sure it was he, Novins, who continued past this point.

"I've got to think about this," Novins said. "I've got to try to work some of this out better. You just stay celled in there, friend; I'm going to a hotel for the night. I'll call you tomorrow."

He started to hang up when Jay's voice stopped him. "What do I say if Jamie gets there and you're gone and she calls me?"

Novins laughed. "That's *your* problem, motherfucker."

He racked the receiver with nasty satisfaction.

ii: Moanday

He took special precautions. First the bank, to clean out the checking account. He thanked God he'd had his checkbook with him when he'd gone out to meet Jamie the night before. But the savings account passbook was in the apartment. That meant Jay had access to almost ten thousand dollars. The checking account was down to fifteen hundred, even with all outstanding bills paid, and the Banks for Cooperatives note came due in about thirty days and that meant . . . he used the back of a deposit slip to figure the interest . . . he'd be getting ten thousand four hundred and sixty-five dollars and seven cents deposited to his account. His *new* account, which he opened at another branch of the same bank, signing the identification cards with a variation of his signature sufficiently different to prevent Jay's trying to draw on the account. He was at least solvent. For the time being.

But all his work was in the apartment. All the public relations accounts he handled. Every bit of data and all the plans and phone numbers and charts, they were all there in the little apartment office. So he was quite effectively cut off from his career.

Yet in a way, that was a blessing. Jay would have to keep up with the work in his absence, would have to follow through on the important campaigns for Topper and McKenzie, would have to take all the moronic calls from Lippman and his insulting son, would have to answer all the mail, would have to keep popping Titralac all day just to stay ahead of the heartburn. He felt gloriously free and almost satanically happy that he was rid of the aggravation for a while, and that Jay was going to find out being Peter Jay Novins wasn't all fun and Jamies.

Back in his hotel room at the Americana he made a list of things he had to do. To survive. It was a new way of thinking, setting down one by one the everyday routine actions from which he was now cut off. He was all alone now, entirely and totally, for the first time in his life, cut off from everything. He could not depend on friends or associates or the authorities. It would be suicide to go to the police and say, "Listen, I hate to bother you, but I've split and one of me has assumed squatter's rights in my apartment; please go up there and arrest him." No, he was on his own, and he had to exorcise Jay from the world strictly by his own wits and cunning.

Bearing in mind, of course, that Jay had the same degree of wit and cunning.

He crossed half a dozen items off the list. There was no need to call Jamie, to find out what had happened to her the night before. Their relationship wasn't that binding in any case. Let Jay make the excuses. No need to cancel the credit cards, he had them with him. Let Jay pay the bills from the savings account. No need to contact any of his friends and warn them. He *couldn't* warn them, and if he did, what would he warn them against? Himself? But he did need clothes, fresh socks and underwear, a light jacket instead of his topcoat, a pair of gloves in case the weather turned. And he had to cancel out the delivery services to the apartment in a way that would prevent Jay from reinstating them: groceries, milk, dry cleaning, newspapers. He had to make it as difficult for him in there as possible. And so he called each tradesman and insulted him so grossly they would *never* serve him again. Unfortunately, the building provided heat and electricity and gas, and he *had* to leave the phone connected.

The phone was his tie-line to victory, to routing Jay out of there.

When he had it all attended to, by three o'clock in the afternoon, he returned to the hotel room, took off his shoes, propped the pillows up on the bed, lay down and dialed a 9 for the outside line, then dialed his own number.

As it rang, he stared out the forty-fifth-floor window of the hotel room, at the soulless pylons of the RCA and Grant buildings, the other dark-glass filing cabinets for people. It was a wonder *any*one managed to stay sane, stay whole in such surroundings! Living in cubicles, boxed and trapped and throttled, was it any surprise that people began to fall apart . . . even as *he* seemed to be falling apart? The wonder was that it all managed to hold together as well as it did. But the fractures were beginning to appear, culturally and now—as with Peter Novins, he mused—personally. The phone continued to ring. Clouds blocked out all light and the city was swamped by shadows. At three o'clock in the afternoon, the ominous threat of another night settled over Novins's hotel room.

The receiver was lifted at the other end. But Jay said nothing.

"It's me," Novins said. "How'd you enjoy your first day in my skin?"

"How did you enjoy your first day *out* of it?" he replied.

"Listen, I've got your act covered, friend, and your hours are numbered. The checking account is gone, don't try to find it; you're going to go out to get food and when you do I'll be waiting—"

"Terrific," Jay replied. "But just so you don't waste your time, I had the locks changed today. Your keys don't work. And I bought groceries. Remember the fifty bucks I put away in the jewelry box?"

Novins cursed himself silently. He hadn't thought of that.

"And I've been doing some figuring, Novins. Remember that old Jack London novel, *The Star Rover*? Remember how he used astral projection to get out of his body? I think that's what happened to me. I sent you out when I wasn't aware of it. So I've decided I'm me, and you're just a little piece that's wandered off. And I can get along just peachy-keen without that piece, so why don't you just go—"

"Hold it," Novins interrupted, "that's a sensational theory, but it's stuffed full of wild blueberry muffins, if you'll pardon my being so forward as to disagree with a smartass voice that's probably disembodied and doesn't have enough ectoplasm to take a healthy shit. Remember the weekend I went over to the lab with Kenny, and he took that Kirlian photograph of my aura? Well, my theory is that something happened, and the aura produced another me, or something . . ."

He slid down into silence. Neither theory was worth thinking about. He had no idea, *really*, what had happened. They hung there in silence for a long moment, then Jay said, "Mother called this morning."

Novins felt a hand squeeze his chest. "What did she say?"

"She said she knew you lied when you were down in Florida. She said she loved you and she forgave you and all she wants is for you to share your life with her."

Novins closed his eyes. He didn't want to think about it. His mother was in her eighties, very sick, and just recovering from her second serious heart attack in three years. The end was near and, combining a business trip to Miami with a visit to her, he had gone to Florida the month before. He had never had much in common with his mother, had been on his own since his early teens, and though he supported her in her declining years, he refused to allow her to impose on his existence. He seldom wrote letters, save to send the check, and during the two days he had spent in her apartment in Miami Beach he had thought he would go insane. He had wanted to bolt, and finally had lied to her that he was returning to New York a day earlier than his plans required. He had packed up and left her, checking into a hotel, and had spent the final day involved in business and that night had gone out with a secretary he dated occasionally when in Florida.

"How did she find out?" Novins asked.

"She called here, and the answering service told her you were still in Florida and hadn't returned. They gave her the number of the hotel and she called there and found out you were registered for that night."

Novins cursed himself. Why had he called the service to tell them where he was? He could have gotten away with one day of his business contacts not being able to reach him. "Swell," he said. "And I suppose you didn't do anything to make her feel better."

"On the contrary," Jay said, "I did what you never would have done. I made arrangements for her to come live here with me."

Novins heard himself moan with pain. "You did *what*!? Jesus Christ, you're out of your fucking mind. How the hell am I going to take care of that old woman in New York? I've got work to do, places I have to go, I have a life to lead. . . ."

"Not any more you don't, you guilty, selfish sonofabitch. Maybe *you* could live with the bad gut feelings about her, but not me. She'll be arriving in a week."

"You're crazy," Novins screamed. "You're fucking crazy!"

"Yeah," Jay said, softly, and added, "and you just lost your mother. Chew on *that* one, you creep."

And he hung up.

iii: Duesday

They decided between them that the one who *deserved* to be Peter Novins should take over the life. They had to make that decision; clearly, they could not go on as they had been; even two days had showed them half an existence was not possible. Both were fraying at the edges.

So Jay suggested they work their way through the pivot experiences of Novins's life, to see if he was really entitled to continue living.

"*Every*one's entitled to go on living," Novins said, vehemently. "That's why we live. To say no to death."

"You don't believe that for a second, Novins," Jay said. "You're a misanthrope. You hate people."

"That's not true; I just don't like some of the things people *do*."

"Like what, for instance? Like, for instance, you're always bitching about kids who wear ecology patches, who throw Dr Pepper cans in the bushes; like that, for instance?"

"That's good for starters," Novins said.

"You hypocritical bastard," Jay snarled back at him, "you have the audacity to beef about that and you took on the Cumberland account."

"That's another kind of thing!"

"My ass. You know damned well Cumberland's planning to strip-mine the guts out of that county, and they're going to get away with it with that publicity campaign you dreamed up. Oh, you're one hell of a good PR man, Novins, but you've got the ethics of a weasel."

Novins was fuming, but Jay was right. He had felt lousy about taking on Cumberland from the start, but they were big, they were international, and the billing for the account was handily in six figures. He had tackled the campaign with the same ferocity he brought to all his accounts, and the program was solid. "I have to make a living. Besides, if I didn't do it, someone else would. I'm only doing a job. They've got a terrific restoration program, don't forget that. They'll put that land back in shape."

Jay laughed. "That's what Eichmann said: 'We have a terrific restoration program, we'll put them Jews right back in shape, just a little gas to spiff 'em up.' He was just doing a job, too, Novins. Have I mentioned lately that you stink on ice?"

Novins was shouting again. "I suppose you'd have turned it down?"

"That's exactly what I did, old buddy," Jay said. "I called them today and told them to take their account and stuff it up their nose. I've got a call in to Nader right now, to see what he can do with all the data in the file."

Novins was speechless. He lay there, under the covers, the Tuesday snow drifting in enormous flakes past the forty-fifth-floor windows. Slowly, he let the receiver settle into the cradle. Only three days and his life was drifting apart inexorably; soon it would be impossible to knit it together.

His stomach ached. And all that day he had felt nauseated. Room service had sent up pot after pot of tea, but it hadn't helped. A throbbing headache was lodged just behind his left eye, and cold sweat covered his shoulders and chest.

He didn't know what to do, but he knew he was losing.

iv: Woundsday

On Wednesday Jay called Novins. He never told him how he'd located him, he just called. "How do you feel?" he asked. Novins could barely answer, the fever was close to immobilizing.

"I just called to talk about Jeanine and Patty and that girl in Denver," Jay said, and he launched into a long and stately recitation of Novins's affairs, and how they had ended. It was not as Novins remembered it.

"That isn't true," Novins managed to say, his voice deep and whispering, dry and nearly empty.

"It *is* true, Novins. That's what's so sad about it. That it *is* true, and you've never had the guts to admit it, that you go from woman to woman without giving anything, always taking, and when you leave them or they dump you—you've never learned a god damned thing. You've been married twice, divorced twice, you've been in and out of two dozen affairs and you haven't learned that you're one of those men who is simply no bloody good for a woman. So now you're forty-two years old and you're finally coming to the dim understanding that you're going to spend all the rest of the days and nights of your life alone, because you can't stand the company of another human being for more than a month without turning into a vicious prick."

"Not true," murmured Novins.

"True, Novins, true. Flat true. You set after Patty and got her to leave her old man, and when you'd pried her loose, her and the kid, you set her up in that apartment with three hundred a month rent, and then you took off and left her to work it out herself. It's true, old buddy. So don't try and con me with that 'I lead a happy life' bullshit."

Novins simply lay there with his eyes closed, shivering with the fever.

Then Jay said, "I saw Jamie last night. We talked about her future. It took some fast talking; she was really coming to hate you. But I think it'll work out if I go at it hard, and I *intend* to go at it hard. I don't intend to have any more years like I've had, Novins. From this point on it changes."

The bulk of the buildings outside the window seemed to tremble behind the falling snow. Novins felt terribly cold. He didn't answer.

"We'll name the first one after you, Peter," Jay said, and hung up.

That was Wednesday.

v: Thornsday

There were no phone calls that day. Novins lay there, the television set mindlessly playing and replaying the five-minute instruction film on the pay-movie preview channel, the ghost-image of a dark-haired girl in a gray suit showing him how to charge a first-run film to his hotel bill. After many hours he heard himself reciting the instructions along with her. He slept a great deal. He thought about Jeanine and Patty, the girl in Denver whose name he could not recall, and Jamie.

After many more hours, he thought about insects, but he didn't know what that meant. There were no phone calls that day. It was Thursday.

Shortly before midnight, the fever broke, and he cried himself back to sleep.

vi: Freeday

A key turned in the lock and the hotel room door opened. Novins was sitting in a mass-produced imitation of a Saarinen pedestal chair, its seat treated with Scotchgard. He had been staring out the window at the geometric irrelevancy of the glass-wall buildings. It was near dusk, and the city was gray as cardboard.

He turned at the sound of the door opening and was not surprised to see himself walk in.

Jay's nose and cheeks were still red from the cold outside. He unzipped his jacket and stuffed his kid gloves into a pocket, removed the jacket and threw it on the unmade bed. "Really cold out there," he said. He went into the bathroom and Novins heard the sound of water running.

Jay returned in a few minutes, rubbing his hands together. "That helps," he said. He sat down on the edge of the bed and looked at Novins.

"You look terrible, Peter," he said.

"I haven't been at all well," Novins answered dryly. "I don't seem to be myself these days."

Jay smiled briefly. "I see you're coming to terms with it. That ought to help."

Novins stood up. The thin light from the room-long window shone through him like white fire through milk glass. "You're looking well," he said.

"I'm getting better, Peter. It'll be a while, but I'm going to be okay."

Novins walked across the room and stood against the wall, hands clasped behind his back. He could barely be seen. "I remember the archetypes from Jung. Are you my shadow, my persona, my anima, or my animus?"

"What am I now, or what was I when I got loose?"

"Either way."

"I suppose I was your shadow. Now I'm the self."

"And I'm becoming the shadow."

"No, you're becoming a memory. A bad memory."

"That's pretty ungracious."

"I was sick for a long time, Peter. I don't know what the trigger was that broke us apart, but it happened and I can't be too sorry about it. If it hadn't happened I'd have been you till I died. It would have been a lousy life and a miserable death."

Novins shrugged. "Too late to worry about it now. Things working out with Jamie?"

Jay nodded. "Yeah. And Mom comes in Tuesday afternoon. I'm renting a car to pick her up at Kennedy. I talked to her doctors. They say she doesn't have too long. But for whatever she's got, I'm determined to make up for the last twenty-five years since Dad died."

Novins smiled and nodded. "That's good."

"Listen," Jay said slowly, with difficulty, "I just came over to ask if there was anything you wanted me to do . . . anything *you* would've done if . . . if it had been different."

Novins spread his hands and thought about it for a moment. "No, I don't think so, nothing special. You might try and get some money to Jeanine's mother, for Jeanine's care, maybe. That wouldn't hurt."

"I already took care of it. I figured that would be on your mind."

Novins smiled. "That's good. Thanks."

"Anything else . . . ?"

Novins shook his head. They stayed that way, hardly moving, till night had fallen outside the window. In the darkness, Jay could barely see Novins standing against the wall. Merely a faint glow.

Finally, Jay stood and put on his jacket, zipped up and put on his left glove. "I've got to go."

Novins spoke from the shadows. "Yeah. Well, take care of me, will you?"

Jay didn't answer. He walked to Novins and extended his right hand. The touch of Novins's hand in his was like the whisper of a cold wind; there was no pressure.

Then he left.

Novins walked back to the window and stared out. The last remaining daylight shone through him. Dimly.

vii: Shatterday

When the maid came in to make up the bed, she found the room empty. It was terribly cold in the room on the forty-fifth floor. When Peter Novins did not return that day, or the next, the management of the Americana marked him as a skip and turned it over to a collection agency.

In due course the bill was sent to Peter Novins's apartment on Manhattan's Upper East Side.

It was promptly paid, by Peter Jay Novins, with a brief, but *sincere* note of apology.

Mefisto in Onyx

Content warning: At the time in which this story was written, it was not uncommon for authors, especially Ellison, to use charged terminology when confronting the racism behind those words. Harlan believed that you cannot fight racism with velvet gloves and polite manners; it had to be called out plainly and punched in the mouth as hard as possible. Consequently, there are terms here that may cause offense. That was the intent, but time and an evolving culture have changed the target and the impact of those words, so reader discretion is advised.

Once. I only went to bed with her once. Friends for eleven years before and since—but it was just one of those things, just one of those crazy flings: the two of us alone on a New Year's Eve, watching rented Marx Brothers videos so we wouldn't have to go out with a bunch of idiots and make noise and pretend we were having a good time when all we'd be doing was getting drunk, whooping like morons, vomiting on slow-moving strangers, and spending more money than we had to waste. And we drank a little too much cheap champagne; and we fell off the sofa laughing at Harpo a few times too many; and we wound up on the floor at the same time; and next thing we knew we had our faces plastered together, and my hand up her skirt, and her hand down in my pants . . .

But it was just the *once*, fer chrissakes! Talk about imposing on a cheap sexual liaison! She *knew* I went mixing in other people's minds only when I absolutely had no other way to make a buck. Or I forgot myself and did it in a moment of human weakness.

It was always foul.

Slip into the thoughts of the best person who ever lived, even Saint Thomas Aquinas, for instance, just to pick an absolutely terrific person you'd think had a mind so clean you could eat off it (to paraphrase my mother), and when you come out—take my word for it—you'd want to take a long, intense shower in Lysol.

Trust me on this: I go into somebody's landscape when there's *nothing else* I can do, no other possible solution . . . or I forget and do it in a moment of human weakness. Such as, say, the IRS holds my feet to the fire; or I'm about to get myself mugged and robbed and maybe murdered; or I need to find out if some specific she that I'm dating has been using somebody else's dirty needle or has been sleeping around without she's taking some extra-heavy-duty AIDS precautions; or a co-worker's got it in his head to set me up so I make a mistake and look bad to the boss and I find myself in the unemployment line again; or . . .

I'm a wreck for weeks after.

Go jaunting through a landscape trying to pick up a little insider arbitrage bric-a-brac, and come away no better heeled, but all muddy with the guy's infidelities, and I can't look a decent woman in the eye for days. Get told by a motel desk clerk that they're all full up and he's sorry as hell but I'll just have to drive on for about another thirty miles to find the next vacancy, jaunt into his landscape and find him lit up with neon signs that got a lot of the word *nigger* in them, and I wind up hitting the sonofabitch so hard his grandmother has a bloody nose, and usually have to hide out for three or four weeks after. Just about to miss a bus, jaunt into the head of the driver to find his name so I can yell for him to hold it a minute Tom or George or Willie, and I get smacked in the mind with all the garlic he's been eating for the past month because his doctor told him it was good for his system, and I start to dry-heave, and I wrench out of the landscape, and not only have I missed the bus, but I'm so sick to my stomach I have to sit down on the filthy curb to get my gorge submerged. Jaunt into a potential employer, to see if he's trying to lowball me, and I learn he's part of a massive cover-up of industrial malfeasance that's caused hundreds of people to die when this or that cheaply made grommet or tappet or gimbal mounting underperforms and fails, sending the poor souls falling thousands of feet to shrieking destruction. Then just *try* to accept the job, even if you haven't paid your rent in a month. No way.

Absolutely: I listen in on the landscape *only* when my feet are being fried; when the shadow stalking me turns down alley after alley tracking me relentlessly; when the drywall guy I've hired to repair the damage done by my leaky shower presents me with a dopey smile and a bill three hundred and sixty bucks higher than the estimate. Or in a moment of human weakness.

But I'm a wreck for weeks after. For weeks.

Because you can't, you simply can't, you absolutely *cannot* know what people are truly and really like till you jaunt their landscape. If Aquinas had had my ability, he'd have very quickly gone off to be a hermit, only occasionally visiting the mind of a sheep or a hedgehog. In a moment of human weakness.

That's why in my whole life—and, as best I can remember back, I've been doing it since I was five or six years old, maybe even younger—there have only been eleven, maybe twelve people, of all those who know that I can "read minds," that I've permitted myself to get close to. Three of them never used it against me, or tried to exploit me, or tried to kill me when I wasn't looking. Two of those three were my mother and father, a pair of sweet old Black folks who'd adopted me, a late-in-life baby, and were now dead (but probably still worried about me, even on the Other Side), and whom I missed very very much, particularly in moments like this. The other eight, nine were either so turned off by the knowledge that they made sure I never came within a mile of them—one moved to another entire country just to be on the safe side, although her thoughts were a helluva lot more boring and innocent than she thought they were—or they tried to brain me with something heavy when I was distracted—I still have a shoulder separation that kills me for two days before it rains—or they tried to use me to make a buck for them. Not having the common sense to figure it out, that if I was *capable* of using the ability to make vast sums of money, why the hell was I living hand-to-mouth like some overaged grad student who was afraid to desert the university and go become an adult?

Now *they* was some dumb-ass muthuhfugguhs.

Of the three who never used it against me—my mom and dad—the last was Allison Roche. Who sat on the stool next to me, in the middle of May, in the middle of a Wednesday afternoon, in the middle of Clanton, Alabama, squeezing ketchup onto her All-American Burger, imposing on the memory of that one damned New Year's Eve sexual interlude, with Harpo and his sibs; the two of us all alone except for the fry-cook; and she waited for my reply.

"I'd sooner have a skunk spray my pants leg," I replied.

She pulled a napkin from the chrome dispenser and swabbed up the red that had overshot the sesame-seed bun and redecorated the Formica countertop. She looked at me from under thick, lustrous eyelashes; a look of impatience and violet eyes that must have been a killer when she unbottled it at some truculent witness for the defense. Allison Roche was a Chief Deputy District Attorney in and for Jefferson County, with her office in Birmingham, Alabama. Where near we sat, in Clanton, having a secret meeting, having All-American Burgers; three years after having had quite a bit of champagne, 1930s black-and-white video rental comedy, and black-and-white sex. One extremely stupid New Year's Eve.

Friends for eleven years. And once, just once; as a prime example of what happens in a moment of human weakness. Which is not to say that it wasn't terrific, because it was; absolutely terrific; but we never did it again; and we never brought it up again after the next morning when we opened our eyes and looked at each other the way you look at an exploding can of sardines, and both of us said *Oh Jeeezus* at the same time. Never brought it up again until this memorable afternoon at the greasy spoon where I'd joined Ally, driving up from Montgomery to meet her halfway, after her peculiar telephone invitation.

Can't say the fry-cook, Mr. All-American, was particularly happy at the pigmentation arrangement at his counter. But I stayed out of his head and let him think what he wanted. Times change on the outside, but the inner landscape remains polluted.

"All I'm asking you to do is go have a chat with him," she said. She gave me that look. I have a hard time with that look. It isn't entirely honest, neither is it entirely disingenuous. It plays on my remembrance of that one night we spent in bed. And is just *dis*honest enough to play on the part of that night we spent on the floor, on the sofa, on the coffee counter between the dining room and the kitchenette, in the bathtub, and about nineteen minutes crammed among her endless pairs of shoes in a walk-in clothes closet that smelled strongly of cedar and virginity. She gave me that look and wasted no part of the memory.

"I don't *want* to go have a chat with him. Apart from he's a piece of human shit, and I have better things to do with my time than to go on down to Atmore and take a jaunt through this crazy sonofabitch's diseased mind, may I remind you that of the hundred and sixty, seventy men who have died in that electric chair, including the original 'Yellow Mama' they scrapped in 1990, about a hundred and thirty of them were gentlemen of color, and I do not mean you to picture any color of a shade much lighter than that cuppa coffee you got sittin' by your left hand right this minute, which is to say that I, being an inordinately well-educated African-American who values the full measure of living negritude in his body, am not crazy enough to want to visit a racist '*co*-rectional center' like Holman Prison, thank you very much."

"Are you finished?" she asked, wiping her mouth.

"Yeah. I'm finished. Case closed. Find somebody else."

She didn't like that. "There *isn't* anybody else."

"There has to be. Somewhere. Go check the research files at Duke University. Call the Fortean Society. Mensa. *Jeopardy.* Some 900 number astrology psychic hotline. Ain't there some semi-senile senator with a full-time paid assistant who's been trying to get legislation through one of the statehouses for the last five years to fund this kind of bullshit research? What about the Russians . . . now that the Evil Empire's fallen, you ought to be able to get some word about their success with Kirlian auras or whatever those ass-holes were working at. Or you could—"

She screamed at the top of her lungs. *"Stop it, Rudy!"*

The fry-cook dropped the spatula he'd been using to scrape off the grill. He picked it up, looking at us, and his face (I didn't read his mind) said *If that white bitch makes one more noise, I'm callin' the cops.*

I gave him a look he didn't want, and he went back to his chores, getting ready for the after-work crowd. But the stretch of his back and angle of his head told me he wasn't going to let this pass.

I leaned in toward her, got as serious as I could, and just this quietly, just this softly, I said, "Ally, good pal, listen to me. You've been one of the few friends I could count on, for a long time now. We have history between us, and you've *never*, not once, made me feel like a freak. So okay, I trust you. I trust you with something about me that causes immeasurable goddam pain. A thing about me that could get me killed. You've never betrayed me, and you've never tried to use me.

"Till now. This is the first time. And you've got to admit that it's not even as rational as you maybe saying to me that you've gambled away every cent you've got, and you owe the mob a million bucks and would I mind taking a trip to Vegas or Atlantic City and taking a jaunt into the minds of some high-pocket poker players so I could win you enough to keep the goons from shooting you. Even *that*, as creepy as it would be if you said it to me, even *that* would be easier to understand than *this*!"

She looked forlorn. "There isn't anybody else, Rudy. *Please.*"

"What the hell is this all about? Come on, tell me. You're hiding something, or holding something back, or lying about—"

"I'm not lying!" For the second time she was suddenly, totally, extremely pissed at me. Her voice spattered off the white tile walls. The fry-cook spun around at the sound, took a step toward us, and I jaunted into his landscape, smoothed down the rippled Astro-Turf, drained away the storm clouds, and suggested in there that he go take a cigarette break out back. Fortunately, there were no other patrons at the elegant All-American Burger that late in the afternoon, and he went.

"Calm fer chrissakes down, will you?" I said.

She had squeezed the paper napkin into a ball.

She was lying, hiding, holding something back. Didn't have to be a telepath to figure *that* out. I waited, looking at her with a slow, careful distrust, and finally she sighed, and I thought, *Here it comes.*

"Are you reading my mind?" she asked.

"Don't insult me. We know each other too long."

She looked chagrined. The violet of her eyes deepened. "Sorry."

But she didn't go on. I wasn't going to be outflanked. I waited.

After a while she said, softly, very softly, "I think I'm in love with him. I *know* I believe him when he says he's innocent."

I never expected that. I couldn't even reply.

It was unbelievable. Unfuckingbelievable. She was the Chief Deputy D.A. who had prosecuted Henry Lake Spanning for murder. Not just one murder, one random slaying, a heat of the moment Saturday night killing regretted deeply on Sunday morning but punishable by electrocution in the Sovereign State of Alabama nonetheless, but a string of the vilest, most sickening serial slaughters in Alabama history, in the history of the Glorious South, in the history of the United States. Maybe even in the history of the entire wretched human universe that went wading hip-deep in the wasted spilled blood of innocent men, women, and children.

Henry Lake Spanning was a monster, an ambulatory disease, a killing machine without conscience or any discernible resemblance to a thing we might call decently human. Henry Lake Spanning had butchered his way across a half-dozen states; and they had caught up to him in Huntsville, in a garbage dumpster behind a supermarket, doing something so vile and inhuman to what was left of a sixty-five-year-old cleaning woman that not even the tabloids would get more explicit than *unspeakable*; and somehow he got away from the cops; and somehow he evaded their dragnet; and somehow he found out where the police lieutenant in charge of the manhunt lived; and somehow he slipped into that neighborhood when the lieutenant was out creating roadblocks—and he gutted the man's wife and two kids. Also the family cat. And then he killed a couple of more times in Birmingham and Decatur, and by then had gone so completely out of his mind that they got him again, and the second time they hung onto him, and they brought him to trial. And Ally had prosecuted this bottom-feeding monstrosity.

And oh, what a circus it had been. Though he'd been *caught*, the second time, and this time for keeps, in Jefferson County, scene of three of his most sickening jobs, he'd murdered (with such a disgustingly similar m.o. that it was obvious he was the perp) in twenty-two of the sixty-seven counties; and every last one of them wanted him to stand trial in that venue. Then there were the other five states in which he had butchered, to a total body count of fifty-six. Each of *them* wanted him extradited.

So, here's how smart and quick and smooth an attorney Ally is: she somehow managed to cozy up to the attorney general, and somehow managed to unleash those violet eyes on him, and somehow managed to get and keep his ear long enough to con him into setting a legal precedent. Attorney General of the State of Alabama allowed Allison Roche to consolidate, to secure a multiple bill of indictment that forced Spanning to stand trial on all twenty-nine Alabama murder counts at once. She meticulously documented to the state's highest courts that Henry Lake Spanning presented such a clear and present danger to society that the prosecution was willing to take a chance (big chance!) of trying in a winner-take-all consolidation of venues. Then she managed to smooth the feathers of all those other vote-hungry prosecutors in those twenty-one other counties, and she put on a case that dazzled everyone, including Spanning's defense attorney, who had screamed about the legality of the multiple bill from the moment she'd suggested it.

And she won a fast jury verdict on all twenty-nine counts. Then she got *really* fancy in the penalty phase after the jury verdict and proved up the *other* twenty-seven murders with their flagrantly identical trademarks, from those other five states, and there was nothing left but to sentence Spanning—essentially for all fifty-six—to the replacement for the "Yellow Mama."

Even as pols and power brokers throughout the state were murmuring Ally's name for higher office, Spanning was slated to sit in that new electric chair in Holman Prison, built by the Fred A. Leuchter Associates of Boston, Massachusetts, that delivers 2,640 volts of pure sparklin' death in 1/240th of a second, six times faster than the 1/40th of a second that it takes for the brain to sense it, which is—if you ask me—much too humane an exit line, more than three times the 700 volt jolt lethal dose that destroys a brain, for a pus-bag like Henry Lake Spanning.

But if we were lucky—and the scheduled day of departure was very nearly upon us—if we were lucky, if there was a God and Justice and Natural Order and all that good stuff, then Henry Lake Spanning, this foulness, this corruption, this thing that lived only to ruin . . . would end up as a pile of fucking ashes somebody might use to sprinkle over a flower garden, thereby providing this ghoul with his single opportunity to be of some use to the human race.

That was the guy that my pal Allison Roche wanted me to go and "chat" with, down to Holman Prison, in Atmore, Alabama. There, sitting on Death Row, waiting to get his demented head tonsured, his pants legs slit, his tongue fried black as the inside of a sheep's belly . . . down there at Holman my pal Allison wanted me to go "chat" with one of the most awful creatures made for killing this side of a hammerhead shark, which creature had an infinitely greater measure of human decency than Henry Lake Spanning had ever demonstrated. Go chit-chat, and enter his landscape, and read his mind, Mr. Telepath, and use the marvelous mythic power of extra-sensory perception: this nifty swell ability that has made me a bum all my life, well, not *exactly* a bum: I do have a decent apartment, and I do earn a decent, if sporadic, living; and I try to follow Nelson Algren's warning never to get involved with a woman whose troubles are bigger than my own; and sometimes I even have a car of my own, even though at that moment such was not the case, the Camaro having been repo'd, and not by Harry

Dean Stanton or Emilio Estevez, lemme tell you; but a bum in the sense of—how does Ally put it?—oh yeah—I don't "realize my full and forceful potential"—a bum in the sense that I can't hold a job, and I get rotten breaks, and all of this despite a Rhodes scholarly education so far above what a poor nigrah-lad such as myself could expect that even Rhodes hisownself would've been chest-out proud as hell of me. A bum, mostly, despite an *outstanding* Rhodes scholar education and a pair of kind, smart, loving parents—even for foster parents—shit, *especially* for being foster parents—who died knowing the certain sadness that their only child would spend his life as a wandering freak unable to make a comfortable living or consummate a normal marriage or raise children without the fear of passing on this special personal horror . . . this astonishing ability fabled in song and story that I possess . . . that no one else seems to possess, though I know there must have been others, somewhere, sometime, somehow! Go, Mr. Wonder of Wonders, shining Black Cagliostro of the modern world, go with this super nifty swell ability that gullible idiots and flying saucer assholes have been trying to prove exists for at least fifty years, that no one has been able to isolate the way I, me, the only one has been isolated, let me tell you about *isolation*, my brothers; and here I was, here was I, Rudy Pairis . . . just a guy, making a buck every now and then with nifty swell impossible ESP, resident of thirteen states and twice that many cities so far in his mere thirty years of landscape-jaunting life, here was I, Rudy Pairis, Mr. I-Can-Read-Your-Mind, being asked to go and walk through the mind of a killer who scared half the people in the world. Being asked by the only living person, probably, to whom I could not say no. And, oh, take me at my word here: I *wanted* to say no. *Was*, in fact, saying no at every breath. What's that? Will I do it? Sure, yeah sure, I'll go on down to Holman and jaunt through this sick bastard's mind landscape. Sure I will. You got two chances: slim, and none.

All of this was going on in the space of one greasy double cheeseburger and two cups of coffee.

The worst part of it was that Ally had somehow gotten involved with him. *Ally!* Not some bimbo bitch . . . but *Ally.* I couldn't believe it.

Not that it was unusual for women to become mixed up with guys in the joint, to fall under their "magic spell," and to start corresponding with them, visiting them, taking them candy and cigarettes, having conjugal visits, playing mule for them and smuggling in dope where the tampon never shine, writing them letters that got steadily more exotic, steadily more intimate, steamier and increasingly dependent emotionally. It wasn't that big a deal; there exist entire psychiatric treatises on the phenomenon; right alongside the papers about women who go stud-crazy for cops. No big deal indeed: hundreds of women every year find themselves writing to these guys, visiting these guys, building dream castles with these guys, fucking these guys, pretending that even the worst of these guys, rapists and woman-beaters and child molesters, repeat pedophiles of the lowest pustule sort, and murderers and stickup punks who crush old ladies' skulls for food stamps, and terrorists and bunco barons . . . that one sunny might-be, gonna-happen pink cloud day these demented creeps will emerge from behind the walls, get back in the wind, become upstanding nine-to-five Brooks Bros. Galahads. Every year hundreds of women marry these guys, finding themselves in a hot second snookered by the wily, duplicitous, motherfuckin' lying greaseball addictive behavior of guys who had spent their sporadic years, their intermittent freedom on the outside, doing *just that*: roping people in, ripping people off, bleeding people dry, conning them into being tools, taking them for their every last cent, their happy home, their sanity, their ability to trust or love ever again.

But this wasn't some poor illiterate naïve woman-child. This was *Ally.* She had damned near pulled off a legal impossibility, come *that* close to Bizarro Jurisprudence by putting the attorneys general of five other states in a maybe frame of mind where she'd have been able to consolidate a multiple bill of indictment *across state lines*! Never been done; and now, probably, never ever would be. But she could have possibly pulled off such a thing. Unless you're a stone court-bird, you can't know what a mountaintop that is!

So, now, here's Ally, saying this shit to me. Ally, my best pal, stood up for me a hundred times; not some dip, but the steely-eyed Sheriff of Suicide Gulch, the over-forty, past the age of innocence, no-nonsense woman who had seen it all and come away tough but not cynical, hard but not mean.

"I think I'm in love with him." She had said.

"I *know* I believe him when he says he's innocent." She had said.

I looked at her. No time had passed. It was still the moment the universe decided to lie down and die. And I said, "So if you're certain this paragon of the virtues *isn't* responsible for fifty-six murders—that we *know* about—and who the hell knows how many more we *don't* know about, since he's apparently been at it since he was twelve years old—remember the couple of nights we sat up and you *told* me all this shit about him, and you said it with your skin crawling, *remember*?—then if you're so damned positive the guy you spent eleven weeks in court sending to the chair is innocent of butchering half the population of the planet—then why do you need me to go to Holman, drive all the way to Atmore, just to take a jaunt in this sweet peach of a guy?

"Doesn't your 'woman's intuition' tell you he's squeaky clean? Don't 'true love' walk yo' sweet young ass down the primrose path with sufficient surefootedness?"

"Don't be a smartass!" she said.

"Say again?" I replied, with disfuckingbelief.

"I said: don't be such a high-verbal goddamned smart aleck!"

Now *I* was steamed. "No, I shouldn't be a smartass: I should be your pony, your show dog, your little trick bag mind-reader freak! Take a drive over to Holman, Pairis; go right on into Rednecks from Hell; sit your ass down on Death Row with the rest of the niggers and have a chat with the one white boy who's been in a cell up there for the past three years or so; sit down nicely with the king of the fucking vampires, and slide inside his garbage dump of a brain—and what a joy *that's* gonna be, I can't believe you'd ask me to do this—and read whatever piece of boiled shit in there he calls a brain, and see if he's jerking you around. *That's* what I ought to do, am I correct? Instead of being a smartass. Have I got it right? Do I properly pierce your meaning, pal?"

She stood up. She didn't even say *Screw you, Pairis!*

She just slapped me as hard as she could.

She hit me a good one straight across the mouth.

I felt my upper teeth bite my lower lip. I tasted the blood. My head rang like a church bell. I thought I'd fall off the goddam stool.

When I could focus, she was just standing there, looking ashamed of herself, and disappointed, and mad as hell, and worried that she'd brained me. All of that, all at the same time. Plus, she looked as if I'd broken her choo-choo train.

"Okay," I said wearily, and ended the word with a sigh that reached all the way back into my hip pocket. "Okay, calm down. I'll see him. I'll do it. Take it easy."

She didn't sit down. "Did I hurt you?"

"No, of course not," I said, unable to form the smile I was trying to put on my face. "How could you possibly hurt someone by knocking his brains into his lap?"

She stood over me as I clung precariously to the counter, turned halfway around on the stool by the blow. Stood over me, the balled-up paper napkin in her fist, a look on her face that said she was nobody's fool, that we'd known each other a long time, that she hadn't asked this kind of favor before, that if we were buddies and I loved her, that I would see she was in deep pain, that she was conflicted, that she needed to know, *really* needed to know without a doubt, and in the name of God—in which she believed, though I didn't, but either way what the hell—that I do this thing for her, that I just *do it* and not give her any more crap about it.

So I shrugged, and spread my hands like a man with no place to go, and I said, "How'd you get into this?"

She told me the first fifteen minutes of her tragic, heartwarming, never-to-be-ridiculed story still standing. After fifteen minutes I said, "Fer chrissakes, Ally, at least *sit down*! You look like a damned fool standing there with a greasy napkin in your mitt."

A couple of teenagers had come in. The four-star chef had finished his cigarette out back and was reassuringly in place, walking the duckboards and dishing up All-American arterial cloggage.

She picked up her elegant attaché case and without a word, with only a nod that said let's get as far from them as we can, she and I moved to a double against the window to resume our discussion of the varieties of social suicide available to an unwary and foolhardy gentleman of the colored persuasion if he allowed himself to be swayed by a cagey and cogent, clever and concupiscent female of another color entirely.

See, what it is, is this:

Look at that attaché case. You want to know what kind of an Ally this Allison Roche is? Pay heed, now.

In New York, when some wannabe junior ad exec has smooched enough butt to get tossed a bone account, and he wants to walk his colors, has a need to signify, has got to demonstrate to everyone that he's got the juice, first thing he does, he hies his ass downtown to Barneys, West 17th and Seventh, buys hisself a Burberry, loops the belt casually *behind*, leaving the coat open to suh*wing*, and he circumnavigates the office.

In Dallas, when the wife of the CEO has those six or eight upper-management husbands and wives over for an *intime*, *faux*-casual dinner, sans placecards, sans *entrée* fork, *sans cérémonie*, and we're talking the kind of woman who flies Virgin Air instead of the Concorde, she's so in charge she don't got to use the Orrefors, she can put out the Kosta Boda and say *give a fuck*.

What it is, kind of person so in charge, so easy with they own self, they don't *have* to laugh at your poor dumb struttin' Armani suit, or your bedroom done in Laura Ashley, or that you got a gig writing articles for *TV Guide*. You see what I'm sayin' here? The sort of person Ally Roche is, you take a look at that attaché case, and it'll tell you everything you need to know about how strong she is, because it's an Atlas. Not a Hartmann. Understand: she could *afford* a Hartmann, that gorgeous imported Canadian belting leather, top of the line, somewhere around nine hundred and fifty bucks maybe, equivalent of Orrefors, a Burberry, breast of guinea hen and Mouton Rothschild 1492 or 1066 or whatever year is the most expensive, drive a Rolls instead of a Bentley and the only difference is the grille . . . but she doesn't *need* to signify, doesn't *need* to suh*wing*, so she gets herself this Atlas. Not some dumb chickenshit Louis Vuitton or Mark Cross all the divorcée real estate ladies carry, but an Atlas. Irish hand leather. Custom tanned cowhide. Hand tanned in Ireland by out of work IRA bombers. Very classy. Just a state understated. See that attaché case? That tell you why I said I'd do it?

She picked it up from where she'd stashed it, right up against the counter wall by her feet, and we went to the double over by the window, away from the chef and the teenagers, and she stared at me till she was sure I was in a right frame of mind, and she picked up where she'd left off.

The next twenty-three minutes by the big greasy clock on the wall she related from a sitting position. Actually, a series of sitting positions. She kept shifting in her chair like someone who didn't appreciate the view of the world from that window, someone hoping for a sweeter horizon. The story started with a gang rape at the age of thirteen, and moved right along: two broken foster-home families, a little casual fondling by surrogate poppas, intense studying for perfect school grades as a substitute for happiness, working her way through John Jay College of Law, a truncated attempt at wedded bliss in her late twenties, and the long miserable road of legal success that had brought her to Alabama. There could have been worse places.

I'd known Ally for a long time, and we'd spent totals of weeks and months in each other's company. Not to mention the New Year's Eve of the Marx Brothers. But I hadn't heard much of this. Not much at all.

Funny how that goes. Eleven years. You'd think I'd've guessed or suspected or *something.* What the hell makes us think we're friends with *any*body, when we don't know the first thing about them, not really?

What are we, walking around in a dream? That is to say: What the fuck are we *thinking*!?!

And there might never have been a reason to hear *any* of it, all this Ally that was the real Ally, but now she was asking me to go somewhere I didn't want to go, to do something that scared the shit out of me; and she wanted me to be as fully informed as possible.

It dawned on me that those same eleven years between us hadn't really given her a full, laser-clean insight into the why and wherefore of Rudy Pairis, either. I hated myself for it. The concealing, the holding-back, the giving up only fragments, the evil misuse of charm when honesty would have hurt. I was facile, and a very quick study; and I had buried all the equivalents to Ally's pains and travails. I could've matched her, in spades; or Blacks, or just plain nigras. But I remained frightened of losing her friendship. I've never been able to believe in the myth of unqualified friendship. Too much like standing hip-high in a fast-running, freezing river. Standing on slippery stones.

Her story came forward to the point at which she had prosecuted Spanning; had amassed and winnowed and categorized the evidence so thoroughly, so deliberately, so flawlessly; had orchestrated the case so brilliantly; that the jury had come in with guilty on all twenty-nine, soon—in the penalty phase—fifty-six. Murder in the first. Premeditated murder in the first. Premeditated murder with special ugly circumstances in the first. On each and every of the twenty-nine. Less than an hour it took them. There wasn't even time for a lunch break. Fifty-one minutes it took them to come back with the verdict guilty on all charges. Less than a minute per killing. Ally had done that.

His attorney had argued that no direct link had been established between the fifty-sixth killing (actually, only his 29th in Alabama) and Henry Lake Spanning. No, they had not caught him down on his knees eviscerating the shredded body of his final victim—ten-year-old Gunilla Ascher, a parochial school girl who had missed her bus and been picked up by Spanning just about a mile from her home in Decatur—no, not down on his knees with the can opener still in his sticky red hands, but the m.o. was the same, and he was there in Decatur, on the run from what he had done in Huntsville, what they had *caught* him doing in Huntsville, in that dumpster, to that old woman. So they *couldn't* place him with his smooth, slim hands inside dead Gunilla Ascher's still-steaming body. So what? They could not have been surer he was the serial killer, the monster, the ravaging nightmare whose methods were so vile the newspapers hadn't even *tried* to cobble up some smart-aleck name for him like The Strangler or The Backyard Butcher. The jury had come back in fifty-one minutes, looking sick, looking as if they'd try and try to get everything they'd seen and heard out of their minds, but knew they never would, and wishing to god they could've managed to get out of their civic duty on this one.

They came shuffling back in and told the numbed court: hey, put this slimy excuse for a maggot in the chair and cook his ass till he's fit only to be served for breakfast on cinnamon toast. This was the guy my friend Ally told me she had fallen in love with. The guy she now believed to be innocent.

This was seriously crazy stuff.

"So how did you get, er, uh, how did you . . . ?"

"How did I fall in love with him?"

"Yeah. That."

She closed her eyes for a moment, and pursed her lips as if she had lost a flock of wayward words and didn't know where to find them. I'd always known she was a private person, kept the really important history to herself—hell, until now I'd never known about the rape, the ice mountain between her mother and father, the specifics of the seven-month marriage—I'd known there'd been a husband briefly; but not what had happened; and I'd known about the foster homes; but again, not how lousy it had been for her—even so, getting *this* slice of steaming craziness out of her was like using your teeth to pry the spikes out of Jesus's wrists.

Finally, she said, "I took over the case when Charlie Whilborg had his stroke. . . ."

"I remember."

"He was the best litigator in the office, and if he hadn't gone down two days before they caught . . ." she paused, had trouble with the name, went on, ". . . before they caught Spanning in Decatur, and if Morgan County hadn't been so worried about a case this size, and bound Spanning over to us in Birmingham . . . all of it so fast nobody really had a chance to talk to him . . . I was the first one even got *near* him, everyone was so damned scared of him, of what they *thought* he was . . ."

"Hallucinating, were they?" I said, being a smartass.

"Shut up.

"The office did most of the donkeywork after that first interview I had with him. It was a big break for me in the office; and I got obsessed by it. So after the first interview, I never spent much actual time with Spanky, never got too close, to see what kind of a man he *really* . . ."

I said: "Spanky? Who the hell's 'Spanky'?"

She blushed. It started from the sides of her nostrils and went out both ways toward her ears, then climbed to the hairline. I'd seen that happen only a couple of times in eleven years, and one of those times had been when she'd farted at the opera. *Lucia di Lammermoor.*

I said it again: "Spanky? You're putting me on, right? You call him *Spanky*?" The blush deepened. "Like the fat kid in *The Little Rascals* . . . c'mon, I don't fuckin' *believe* this!"

She just glared at me.

I felt the laughter coming.

My face started twitching.

She stood up again. "Forget it. Just forget it, okay?" She took two steps away from the table, toward the street exit. I grabbed her hand and pulled her back, trying not to fall apart with laughter, and I said, "Okay okay okay . . . I'm *sorry* . . . I'm really and truly, honest to goodness, may I be struck by a falling space lab no kidding one hundred percent absolutely sorry . . . but you gotta admit . . . catching me unawares like that . . . I mean, come *on*, Ally . . . *Spanky*!?! You call this guy who murdered at least fifty-six people Spanky? Why not Mickey, or Froggy, or Alfalfa . . . ? I can understand not calling him Buckwheat, you can save that one for me, but *Spanky*???"

And in a moment *her* face started to twitch; and in another moment she was starting to smile, fighting it every micron of the way; and in another moment she was laughing and swatting at me with her free hand; and then she pulled her hand loose and stood there falling apart with laughter; and in about a minute she was sitting down again. She threw the balled-up napkin at me.

"It's from when he was a kid," she said. "He was a fat kid, and they made fun of him. You know the way kids are . . . they corrupted Spanning into 'Spanky' because *The Little Rascals* were on television and . . . oh, shut *up*, Rudy!"

I finally quieted down and made conciliatory gestures.

She watched me with an exasperated wariness till she was sure I wasn't going to run any more dumb gags on her, and then she resumed. "After Judge Fay sentenced him, I handled Spa . . . *Henry's* case from our office, all the way up to the appeals stage. I was the one who did the pleading against clemency when Henry's lawyers took their appeal to the Eleventh Circuit in Atlanta.

"When he was denied a stay by the appellate, three-to-nothing, I helped prepare the brief when Henry's counsel went to the Alabama Supreme Court; then when the Supreme Court refused to hear his appeal, I thought it was all over. I knew they'd run out of moves for him, except maybe the governor; but that wasn't ever going to happen. So I thought: *that's that.*

"When the Supreme Court wouldn't hear it three weeks ago, I got a letter from him. He'd been set for execution next Saturday, and I couldn't figure out why he wanted to see *me.*"

I asked, "The letter . . . it got to you how?"

"One of his attorneys."

"I thought they'd given up on him."

"So did I. The evidence was so overwhelming; half a dozen counselors found ways to get themselves excused; it wasn't the kind of case that would bring any litigator good publicity. Just the number of eyewitnesses in the parking lot of that Winn-Dixie in Huntsville . . . must have been fifty of them, Rudy. And they all saw the same thing, and they all identified Henry in lineup after lineup, twenty, thirty, could have been fifty of them if we'd needed that long a parade. And all the rest of it . . ."

I held up a hand. *I know*, the flat hand against the air said. She had told me all of this. Every grisly detail, till I wanted to puke. It was as if I'd done it all myself, she was so vivid in her telling. Made my jaunting nausea pleasurable by comparison. Made me so sick I couldn't even think about it. Not even in a moment of human weakness.

"So the letter comes to you from the attorney . . ."

"I think you know this lawyer. Larry Borlan; used to be with the ACLU; before that he was senior counsel for the Alabama Legislature down to Montgomery; stood up, what was it, twice, three times, before the Supreme Court? Excellent guy. And not easily fooled."

"And what's *he* think about all this?"

"He thinks Henry's absolutely innocent."

"Of all of it?"

"Of everything."

"But there were fifty disinterested random eyewitnesses at one of those slaughters. Fifty, you just said it. Fifty, you could've had a parade. All of them nailed him cold, without a doubt. Same kind of kill as all the other fifty-five, including that schoolkid in Decatur when they finally got him. And Larry Borlan thinks he's not the guy, right?"

She nodded. Made one of those sort of comic pursings of the lips, shrugged, and nodded. "Not the guy."

"So the killer's still out there?"

"That's what Borlan thinks."

"And what do *you* think?"

"I agree with him."

"Oh, jeezus, Ally, my aching boots and saddle! You got to be workin' some kind of off-time! The killer is still out here in the mix, but there hasn't been a killing like those Spanning slaughters for the three years that he's been in the joint. Now *what* do that say to you?"

"It says whoever the guy *is*, the one who killed all those people, he's *days* smarter than all the rest of us, and he set up the perfect freefloater to take the fall for him, and he's either long far gone in some other state, working his way, or he's sitting quietly right here in Alabama, waiting and watching. And smiling." Her face seemed to sag with misery. She started to tear up, and said, "In four days he can stop smiling."

Saturday night.

"Okay, take it easy. Go on, tell me the rest of it. Borlan comes to you, and he begs you to read Spanning's letter and . . . ?"

"He didn't beg. He just gave me the letter, told me he had no idea what Henry had written, but he said he'd known me a long time, that he thought I was a decent, fair-minded person, and he'd appreciate it in the name of our friendship if I'd read it."

"So you read it."

"I read it."

"Friendship. Sounds like you an' him was *good* friends. Like maybe you and I were good friends?"

She looked at me with astonishment.

I think *I* looked at me with astonishment.

"Where the hell did *that* come from?" I said.

"Yeah, really," she said, right back at me, "where the hell *did* that come from?" My ears were hot, and I almost started to say something about how if it was okay for *her* to use our Marx Brothers indiscretion for a lever, why wasn't it okay for me to get cranky about it? But I kept my mouth shut; and for once knew enough to move along. "Must've been *some* letter," I said.

There was a long moment of silence during which she weighed the degree of shit she'd put me through for my stupid remark, after all this was settled; and having struck a balance in her head, she told me about the letter.

It was perfect. It was the only sort of come-on that could lure the avenger who'd put you in the chair to pay attention. The letter had said that fifty-six was not the magic number of deaths. That there were many, *many* more unsolved cases, in many, *many* different states; lost children, runaways, unexplained disappearances, old people, college students hitchhiking to Sarasota for spring break, shopkeepers who'd carried their day's take to the night deposit drawer and never gone home for dinner, hookers left in pieces in Hefty bags all over town, and death death death unnumbered and unnamed. Fifty-six, the letter had said, was just the start. And if she, her, no one else, Allison Roche, my pal Ally, would come on down to Holman, and talk to him, Henry Lake Spanning would help her close all those open files. National rep. Avenger of the unsolved. Big time mysteries revealed. "So you read the letter, and you went . . ."

"Not at first. Not immediately. I was sure he was guilty, and I was pretty certain at that moment, three years and more, dealing with the case, I was pretty sure if he said he could fill in all the blank spaces, that he could do it. But I just didn't like the idea. In court, I was always twitchy when I got near him at the defense table. His eyes, he never took them off me. They're blue, Rudy, did I tell you that . . . ?"

"Maybe. I don't remember. Go on."

"Bluest blue you've ever seen . . . well, to tell the truth, he just plain *scared* me. I wanted to win that case so badly, Rudy, you can never know . . . not just for me or the career or for the idea of justice or to avenge all those people he'd killed, but just the thought of him out there on the street, with those blue eyes, so blue, never stopped looking at me from the moment the trial began . . . the *thought* of him on the loose drove me to whip that case like a howling dog. I *had* to put him away!"

"But you overcame your fear."

She didn't like the edge of ridicule on the blade of that remark. "That's right. I finally 'overcame my fear' and I agreed to go see him."

"And you saw him."

"Yes."

"And he didn't know shit about no other killings, right?"

"Yes."

"But he talked a good talk. And his eyes was blue, so blue."

"Yes, you asshole."

I chuckled. Everybody is somebody's fool.

"Now let me ask you this—very carefully—you don't hit me again: the moment you discovered he'd been shuckin' you, lyin', that he *didn't* have this long, unsolved crime roster to tick off, why didn't you get up, load your attaché case, and hit the bricks?"

Her answer was simple. "He begged me to stay a while."

"That's it? He *begged* you?"

"Rudy, he has no one. He's *never* had anyone." She looked at me as if I were made of stone, some basalt thing, an onyx statue, a figure carved out of melanite, soot and ashes fused into a monolith. She feared she could not, in no way, no matter how piteously or bravely she phrased it, penetrate my rocky surface.

Then she said a thing that I never wanted to hear.

"Rudy . . ."

Then she said a thing I could never have imagined she'd say. Never in a million years.

"Rudy . . ."

Then she said the most awful thing she could say to me, even more awful than that she was in love with a serial killer.

"Rudy . . . go inside . . . read my mind . . . I need you to know, I need you to understand . . . Rudy . . ."

The look on her face killed my heart.

I tried to say no, oh god no, not that, please, no, not that, don't ask me to do that, please *please* I don't want to go inside, we mean so much to each other, I don't *want* to know your landscape. Don't make me feel filthy, I'm no Peeping Tom, I've *never* spied on you, never stolen a look when you were coming out of the shower, or undressing, or when you were being sexy . . . I never invaded your privacy, I wouldn't *do* a thing like that . . . we're friends, I don't need to know it all, I don't *want* to go in there. I can go inside anyone, and it's always awful . . . please don't make me see things in there I might not like, you're my friend, please don't steal that from me . . .

"Rudy, *please.* Do it."

Oh jeezusjeezusjeezus, again, she said it again!

We sat there. And we sat there. And we sat there longer. I said, hoarsely, in fear, "Can't you just . . . just *tell* me?"

Her eyes looked at stone. A man of stone. And she tempted me to do what I could do casually, tempted me the way Faust was tempted by Mefisto, Mephistopheles, Mefistofele, Mephostopilis. Black rock Dr. Faustus, possessor of magical mind-reading powers, tempted by thick, lustrous eyelashes and violet eyes and a break in the voice and an imploring movement of hand to face and a tilt of the head that was pitiable and the begging word *please* and all the guilt that lay between us that was mine alone. The seven chief demons. Of whom Mefisto was the one "not loving the light."

I knew it was the end of our friendship. But she left me nowhere to run. Mefisto in onyx.

So I jaunted into her landscape.

I stayed in there less than ten seconds. I didn't want to know everything I could know; and I definitely wanted to know *nothing* about how she really thought of me. I couldn't have borne seeing a caricature of a bug-eyed, shuffling, thick-lipped darkie in there. Mandingo man. Steppin Porchmonkey Rudy Pair—

Oh god, what was I thinking!

Nothing in there like that. Nothing! Ally wouldn't *have* anything like that in there. I was going nuts, going absolutely fucking crazy, in there, back out in less than ten seconds. I want to block it, kill it, void it, waste it, empty it, reject it, squeeze it, darken it, obscure it, wipe it, do away with it like it never happened. Like the moment you walk in on your momma and poppa and catch them fucking, and you want never to have known that.

But at least I understood.

In there, in Allison Roche's landscape, I saw how her heart had responded to this man she called Spanky, not Henry Lake Spanning. She did not call him, in there, by the name of a monster; she called him a honey's name. I didn't know if he was innocent or not, but *she* knew he was innocent. At first she had responded to just talking with him, about being brought up in an orphanage, and she was able to relate to his stories of being used and treated like chattel, and how they had stripped him of his dignity, and made him afraid all the time. She knew what that was like. And how he'd always been on his own. The running-away. The being captured like a wild thing and put in this home or that lockup or the orphanage "for his own good." Washing stone steps with a tin bucket full of gray water, with a horsehair brush and a bar of lye soap, till the tender folds of skin between the fingers were furiously red and hurt so much you couldn't make a fist.

She tried to tell me how her heart had responded, with a language that has never been invented to do the job. I saw as much as I needed, there in that secret landscape, to know that Spanning had led a miserable life, but that somehow he'd managed to become a decent human being. And it showed through enough when she was face to face with him, talking to him without the witness box between them, without the adversarial thing, without the tension of the courtroom and the gallery and those parasite creeps from the tabloids sneaking around taking pictures of him, that she identified with his pain. Hers had been not the same, but similar; of a kind, if not of identical intensity.

She came to know him a little.

And came back to see him again. Human compassion. In a moment of human weakness.

Until, finally, she began examining everything she had worked up as evidence, trying to see it from *his* point of view, using *his* explanations of circumstantiality. And there were inconsistencies. Now she saw them. Now she did not turn her prosecuting attorney's mind from them, recasting them in a way that would railroad Spanning; now she gave him just the barest possibility of truth. And the case did not seem as incontestable.

By that time, she had to admit to herself, she had fallen in love with him. The gentle quality could not be faked; she'd known fraudulent kindness in her time.

I left her mind gratefully. But at least I understood.

"Now?" she asked.

Yes, now. Now I understood. And the fractured glass in her voice told me. Her face told me. The way she parted her lips in expectation, waiting for me to reveal what my magic journey had conveyed by way of truth. Her palm against her cheek. All that told me. And I said, "Yes."

Then, silence between us.

After a while she said, "I didn't feel anything."

I shrugged. "Nothing to feel. I was in for a few seconds, that's all."

"You didn't see everything?"

"No."

"Because you didn't want to?"

"Because . . ."

She smiled. "I understand, Rudy."

Oh, do you? Do you really? That's just fine. And I heard me say, "You made it with him yet?"

I could have torn off her arm; it would've hurt less.

"That's the second time today you've asked me that kind of question. I didn't like it much the first time, and I like it less *this* time."

"You're the one wanted me to go into your head. I didn't buy no ticket for the trip."

"Well, you were in there. Didn't you look around enough to find out?"

"I didn't look for that."

"What a chickenshit, wheedling, lousy and *cowardly* . . ."

"I haven't heard an answer, Counselor. Kindly restrict your answers to a simple yes or no."

"Don't be ridiculous! He's on Death Row!"

"There are ways."

"How would *you* know?"

"I had a friend. Up at San Rafael. What they call Tamal. Across the bridge from Richmond, a little north of San Francisco."

"That's San Quentin."

"That's what it is, all right."

"I thought that *friend* of yours was at Pelican Bay?"

"Different friend."

"You seem to have a lot of old chums in the joint in California."

"It's a racist nation."

"I've heard that."

"But Q ain't Pelican Bay. Two different states of being. As hard time as they pull at Tamal, it's worse up to Crescent City. In the Shoe."

"You never mentioned 'a friend' at San Quentin."

"I never mentioned a lotta shit. That don't mean I don't know it. I am large, I contain multitudes."

We sat silently, the three of us: me, her, and Walt Whitman. *We're fighting*, I thought. Not make-believe, dissin' some movie we'd seen and disagreed about; this was nasty. Bone nasty and memorable. No one ever forgets this kind of fight. Can turn dirty in a second, say some trash you can never take back, never forgive, put a canker on the rose of friendship for all time, never be the same look again.

I waited. She didn't say anything more; and I got no straight answer; but I was pretty sure Henry Lake Spanning had gone all the way with her. I felt a twinge of emotion I didn't even want to look at, much less analyze, dissect, and name. *Let it be*, I thought. Eleven years. Once, just once. *Let it just lie there and get old and withered and die a proper death like all ugly thoughts.*

"Okay. So I go on down to Atmore," I said. "I suppose you mean in the very near future, since he's supposed to bake in four days. Sometime very soon: like today."

She nodded.

I said, "And how do I get in? Law student? Reporter? Tag along as Larry Borlan's new law clerk? Or do I go in with you? What am I, friend of the family, representative of the Alabama State Department of Corrections; maybe you could set me up as an inmate's rep from Project Hope."

"I can do better than that," she said. The smile. "Much."

"Yeah, I'll just bet you can. Why does that worry me?"

Still with the smile, she hoisted the Atlas onto her lap. She unlocked it, took out a small manila envelope, unsealed but clasped, and slid it across the table to me. I pried open the clasp and shook out the contents.

Clever. Very clever. And already made up, with my photo where necessary, admission dates stamped for tomorrow morning, Thursday, absolutely authentic and foolproof.

"Let me guess," I said, "Thursday mornings, the inmates of Death Row have access to their attorneys?"

"On Death Row, family visitation Monday and Friday. Henry has no family. Attorney visitations Wednesdays and Thursdays, but I couldn't count on today. It took me a couple of days to get through to you . . ."

"I've been busy."

". . . but inmates consult with their counsel on Wednesday and Thursday mornings."

I tapped the papers and plastic cards. "This is very sharp. I notice my name and my handsome visage already here, already sealed in plastic. How long have you had these ready?"

"Couple of days."

"What if I'd continued to say no?"

She didn't answer. She just got that look again.

"One last thing," I said. And I leaned in very close, so she would make no mistake that I was dead serious. "Time grows short. Today's Wednesday. Tomorrow's Thursday. They throw those computer-controlled twin switches Saturday night midnight. What if I jaunt into him and find out you're right, that he's absolutely innocent? What then? They going to listen to me? Fiercely high-verbal Black boy with the magic mind-read power?

"I don't think so. Then what happens, Ally?"

"Leave that to me." Her face was hard. "As you said: there are ways. There are roads and routes and even lightning bolts, if you know where to shop. The power of the judiciary. An election year coming up. Favors to be called in."

I said, "And secrets to be wafted under sensitive noses?"

"You just come back and tell me Spanky's telling the truth," and she smiled as I started to laugh, "and I'll worry about the world one minute after midnight Sunday morning."

I got up and slid the papers back into the envelope and put the envelope under my arm. I looked down at her and I smiled as gently as I could, and I said, "Assure me that you haven't stacked the deck by telling Spanning I can read minds."

"I wouldn't do that."

"Tell me."

"I haven't told him you can read minds."

"You're lying."

"Did you . . . ?"

"Didn't have to. I can see it in your face, Ally."

"Would it matter if he knew?"

"Not a bit. I can read the sonofabitch cold or hot, with or without. Three seconds inside and I'll know if he did it all, if he did part of it, if he did none of it."

"I think I love him, Rudy."

"You told me that."

"But I wouldn't set you up. I need to know . . . that's why I'm asking you to do it."

I didn't answer. I just smiled at her. She'd told him. He'd know I was coming. But that was terrific. If she hadn't alerted him, I'd have asked her to call and let him know. The more aware he'd be, the easier to scorch his landscape.

I'm a fast study, king of the quick learners: vulgate Latin in a week; standard apothecary's pharmacopoeia in three days; Fender bass on a weekend; Atlanta Falcons' play book in an hour; and, in a moment of human weakness, what it feels like to have a very crampy, heavy-flow menstrual period, two minutes flat.

So fast, in fact, that the more somebody tries to hide the boiling pits of guilt and the crucified bodies of shame, the faster I adapt to their landscape. Like a man taking a polygraph test gets nervous, starts to sweat, ups the galvanic skin response, tries to duck and dodge, gets himself hinky and more hinky and hinkyer till his upper lip could water a truck garden, the more he tries to hide from me . . . the more he reveals . . . the deeper inside I can go.

There is an African saying: *Death comes without the thumping of drums.*

I have no idea why that one came back to me just then.

Last thing you expect from a prison administration is a fine sense of humor. But they got one at the Holman facility.

They had the bloody monster dressed like a virgin.

White duck pants, white short sleeve shirt buttoned up to the neck, white socks. Pair of brown ankle-high brogans with crepe soles, probably neoprene, but they didn't clash with the pale, virginal apparition that came through the security door with a large Black brother in Alabama Prison Authority uniform holding on to his right elbow.

Didn't clash, those work shoes, and didn't make much of a tap on the white tile floor. It was as if he floated. Oh yes, I said to myself, oh yes indeed: I could see how this messianic figure could wow even as tough a cookie as Ally. *Oh my, yes.*

Fortunately, it was raining outside.

Otherwise, sunlight streaming through the glass, he'd no doubt have a halo. I'd have lost it. Right there, a laughing jag would *not* have ceased. Fortunately, it was raining like a sonofabitch.

Which hadn't made the drive down from Clanton a possible entry on any deathbed list of Greatest Terrific Moments in My Life. Sheets of aluminum water, thick as misery, like a never-ending shower curtain that I could drive through for an eternity and never really penetrate. I went into the ditch off the I-65 half a dozen times. Why I never plowed down and buried myself up to the axles in the sucking goo running those furrows, never be something I'll understand.

But each time I skidded off the Interstate, even the twice I did a complete three-sixty and nearly rolled the old Fairlane I'd borrowed from John the C Hepworth, even then I just kept digging, slewed like an epileptic seizure, went sideways and climbed right up the slippery grass and weeds and running, sucking red Alabama goo, right back onto that long black anvil pounded by rain as hard as roofing nails. I took it then, as I take it now, to be a sign that Destiny was determined the mere heavens and earth would not be permitted to fuck me around. I had a date to keep, and Destiny was on top of things.

Even so, even living charmed, which was clear to me, even so: when I got about five miles north of Atmore, I took the 57 exit off the I-65 and a left onto 21, and pulled in at the Best Western. It wasn't my intention to stay overnight that far south—though I knew a young woman with excellent teeth down in Mobile—but the rain was just hammering and all I wanted was to get this thing done and go fall asleep. A drive that long, humping something as lame as that Fairlane, hunched forward to scope the rain . . . with Spanning in front of me . . . all I desired was surcease. A touch of the old oblivion.

I checked in, stood under the shower for half an hour, changed into the three-piece suit I'd brought along, and phoned the front desk for directions to the Holman facility.

Driving there, a sweet moment happened for me. It was the last sweet moment for a long time thereafter, and I remember it now as if it were still happening. I cling to it.

In May, and on into early June, the Yellow Lady's Slipper blossoms. In the forests and the woodland bogs, and often on some otherwise undistinguished slope or hillside, the yellow-and-purple orchids suddenly appear.

I was driving. There was a brief stop in the rain. Like the eye of the hurricane. One moment sheets of water, and the next, absolute silence before the crickets and frogs and birds started complaining; and darkness on all sides, just the idiot staring beams of my headlights poking into nothingness; and cool as a well between the drops of rain; and I was driving. And suddenly, the window rolled down so I wouldn't fall asleep, so I could stick my head out when my eyes started to close, suddenly I smelled the delicate perfume of the sweet May-blossoming Lady's Slipper. Off to my left, off in the dark somewhere on a patch of hilly ground, or deep in a stand of invisible trees, *Cypripedium calceolus* was making the night world beautiful with its fragrance.

I neither slowed, nor tried to hold back the tears.

I just drove, feeling sorry for myself; for no good reason I could name.

Way, way down—almost to the corner of the Florida Panhandle, about three hours south of the last truly imperial barbeque in that part of the world, in Birmingham—I made my way to Holman. If you've never been inside the joint, what I'm about to say will resonate about as clearly as Chaucer to one of the gentle Tasaday.

The stones call out.

That institution for the betterment of the human race, the Organized Church, has a name for it. From the fine folks at Catholicism, Lutheranism, Baptism, Judaism, Islamism, Druidism . . .

Ismism . . . the ones who brought you Torquemada, several spicy varieties of Inquisition, original sin, holy war, sectarian violence, and something called "pro-lifers" who bomb and maim and kill . . . comes the catchy phrase Damned Places.

Rolls off the tongue like *God's On Our Side*, don't it?

Damned Places.

As we say in Latin, the *situs* of malevolent shit. The *venue* of evil happenings. *Locations* forever existing under a black cloud, like residing in a rooming house run by Jesse Helms or Strom Thurmond. The big slams are like that. Joliet, Dannemora, Attica, Rahway State in Jersey, that hellhole down in Louisiana called Angola, old Folsom—not the new one, the old Folsom—Q, and Ossining. Only people who read about it call it "Sing Sing." Inside, the cons call it Ossining. The Ohio State pen in Columbus. Leavenworth, Kansas. The ones they talk about among themselves when they talk about doing hard time. The Shoe at Pelican Bay State Prison. In there, in those ancient structures mortared with guilt and depravity and no respect for human life and just plain meanness on both sides, cons and screws, in there where the walls and floors have absorbed all the pain and loneliness of a million men and women for decades . . . in there, the stones call out.

Damned places. You can feel it when you walk through the gates and go through the metal detectors and empty your pockets on counters and open your briefcase so that thick fingers can rumple the papers. You feel it. The moaning and thrashing, and men biting holes in their own wrists so they'll bleed to death.

And I felt it worse than anyone else.

I blocked out as much as I could. I tried to hold on to the memory of the scent of orchids in the night. The last thing I wanted was to jaunt into somebody's landscape at random. Go inside and find out what he had done, what had *really* put him here, not just what they'd got him for. And I'm not talking about Spanning; I'm talking about every one of them. Every guy who had kicked to death his girlfriend because she brought him bratwurst instead of spicy Cajun sausage. Every pale, wormy Bible-reciting psycho who had stolen, buttfucked, and sliced up an altar boy in the name of secret voices that "tole him to g'wan *do* it!" Every amoral druggie who'd shot a pensioner for her food stamps. If I let down for a second, if I didn't keep that shield up, I'd be tempted to send out a scintilla and touch one of them. In a moment of human weakness.

So I followed the trusty to the warden's office, where his secretary checked my papers, and the little plastic cards with my face encased in them, and she kept looking down at the face, and up at my face, and down at my face, and up at the face in front of her, and when she couldn't restrain herself a second longer she said, "We've been expecting you, Mr. Pairis. Uh. Do you *really* work for the president of the United States?"

I smiled at her. "We go bowling together."

She took that highly and offered to walk me to the conference room where I'd meet Henry Lake Spanning. I thanked her the way a well-mannered gentleman of color thanks a civil servant who can make life easier or more difficult, and I followed her along corridors and in and out of guarded steel-riveted doorways, through Administration and the segregation room and the main hall to the brown-paneled, stained walnut, white tile over cement floored, roll-out security windowed, white draperied, drop ceiling with two-inch acoustical Celotex squared conference room, where a security officer met us. She bid me fond adieu, not yet fully satisfied that such a one as I had come, that morning, on Air Force One, straight from a 7-10 split with the president of the United States.

It was a big room.

I sat down at the conference table; about twelve feet long and four feet wide; highly polished walnut, maybe oak. Straight back chairs: metal tubing with a light-yellow upholstered cushion. Everything quiet, except for the sound of matrimonial rice being dumped on a connubial tin roof. The rain had not slacked off. Out there on the I-65 some luck-lost bastard was being sucked down into red death.

"He'll be here," the security officer said.

"That's good," I replied. I had no idea why he'd tell me that, seeing as how it was the reason I was there in the first place. I imagined him to be the kind of guy you dread sitting in front of, at the movies, because he always explains everything to his date. Like a *bracero* laborer with a valid green card interpreting a Woody Allen movie line-by-line to his illegal-alien cousin Humberto, three weeks under the wire from Matamoros. Like one of a pair of Beltone-wearing octogenarians on the loose from a rest home for a wild Saturday afternoon at the mall, plonked down in the third-level multiplex, one of them describing whose ass Clint Eastwood is about to kick, and why. All at the top of her voice.

"Seen any good movies lately?" I asked him.

He didn't get a chance to answer, and I didn't jaunt inside to find out, because at that moment the steel door at the far end of the conference room opened, and another security officer poked his head in and called across to Officer Let-Me-State-the-Obvious, "Dead man walking!"

Officer Self-Evident nodded to him, the other head poked back out, the door slammed, and my companion said, "When we bring one down from Death Row, he's gotta walk through the Ad Building and Segregation and the Main Hall. So everything's locked down. Every man's inside. It takes some time, y'know."

I thanked him.

"Is it true you work for the president, yeah?" He asked it so politely, I decided to give him a straight answer; and to hell with all the phony credentials Ally had worked up. "Yeah," I said, "we're on the same *bocce* ball team."

"Izzat so?" he said, fascinated by sports stats.

I was on the verge of explaining that the president was, in actuality, of Italian descent, when I heard the sound of the key turning in the security door, and it opened outward, and in came this messianic apparition in white, being led by a guard who was seven feet in any direction.

Henry Lake Spanning, sans halo, hands and feet shackled, with the chains cold-welded into a wide anodized steel belt, shuffled toward me; and his neoprene soles made no disturbing cacophony on the white tiles.

I watched him come the long way across the room, and he watched me right back. I thought to myself, *Yeah, she told him I can read minds. Well, let's see which method you use to try and keep me out of the landscape.* But I couldn't tell from the outside of him, not just by the way he shuffled and looked, if he had fucked Ally. But I knew it had to've been. Somehow. Even in the big lockup. Even here.

He stopped right across from me, with his hands on the back of the chair, and he didn't say a word, just gave me the nicest smile I'd ever gotten from anyone, even my momma. *Oh, yes,* I thought, *oh my goodness, yes.* Henry Lake Spanning was either the most masterfully charismatic person I'd ever met, or so good at the charm con that he could sell a slashed throat to a stranger.

"You can leave him," I said to the great Black behemoth brother.

"Can't do that, sir."

"I'll take full responsibility."

"Sorry, sir; I was told someone had to be right here in the room with you and him, all the time."

I looked at the one who had waited with me. "That mean you, too?"

He shook his head. "Just one of us, I guess."

I frowned. "I need absolute privacy. What would happen if I were this man's attorney of record? Wouldn't you have to leave us alone? Privileged communication, right?"

They looked at each other, this pair of security officers, and they looked back at me, and they said nothing. All of a sudden Mr. Plain-as-the-Nose-on-Your-Face had nothing valuable to offer; and the sequoia with biceps "had his orders."

"They tell you who I work for? They tell you who it was sent me here to talk to this man?" Recourse to authority often works. They mumbled yessir yessir a couple of times each, but their faces stayed right on the mark of *sorry, sir, but we're not supposed to leave anybody alone with this man.* It wouldn't have mattered if they'd believed I'd flown in on Jehovah One.

So I said to myself *fuckit* I said to myself, and I slipped into their thoughts, and it didn't take much rearranging to get the phone wires restrung and the underground cables rerouted and the pressure on their bladders something fierce.

"On the other hand . . ." the first one said.

"I suppose we could . . ." the giant said.

And in a matter of maybe a minute and a half one of them was entirely gone, and the great one was standing outside the steel door, his back filling the double-pane chickenwire-imbedded security window. He effectively sealed off the one entrance or exit to or from the conference room; like the three hundred Spartans facing the tens of thousands of Xerxes's army at the Hot Gates.

Henry Lake Spanning stood silently watching me.

"Sit down," I said. "Make yourself comfortable."

He pulled out the chair, came around, and sat down.

"Pull it closer to the table," I said.

He had some difficulty, hands shackled that way, but he grabbed the leading edge of the seat and scraped forward till his stomach was touching the table.

He was a handsome guy, even for a white man. Nice nose, strong cheekbones, eyes the color of that water in your toilet when you toss in a tablet of 2000 Flushes. Very nice-looking man. He gave me the creeps.

If Dracula had looked like Shirley Temple, no one would've driven a stake through his heart. If Harry Truman had looked like Freddy Krueger, he would never have beaten Tom Dewey at the polls. Joe Stalin and Saddam Hussein looked like sweet, avuncular friends of the family, really nice-looking, kindly guys—who just incidentally happened to slaughter millions of men, women, and children. Abe Lincoln looked like an axe murderer, but he had a heart as big as Guatemala.

Henry Lake Spanning had the sort of face you'd trust immediately if you saw it in a TV commercial. Men would like to go fishing with him, women would like to squeeze his buns. Grannies would hug him on sight, kids would follow him straight into the mouth of an open oven. If he could play the piccolo, rats would gavotte around his shoes.

What saps we are. Beauty is only skin deep. You can't judge a book by its cover. Cleanliness is next to godliness. Dress for success. What saps we are.

So what did that make my pal Allison Roche?

And why the hell didn't I just slip into his thoughts and check out the landscape? Why was I stalling?

Because I was scared of him.

This was fifty-six verified, gruesome, disgusting murders sitting forty-eight inches away from me, looking straight at me with blue eyes and soft, gently blond hair. Neither Harry nor Dewey would've had a prayer.

So why was I scared of him? Because; that's why.

This was damned foolishness. I had all the weaponry, he was shackled, and I didn't for a second believe he was what Ally *thought* he was: innocent. Hell, they'd caught him, literally, redhanded. Bloody to the armpits, fer chrissakes. Innocent, my ass! *Okay,*

Rudy, I thought, *get in there and take a look around.* But I didn't. I waited for him to say something.

He smiled tentatively, a gentle and nervous little smile, and he said, "Ally asked me to see you. Thank you for coming."

I looked *at* him, but not *into* him.

He seemed upset that he'd inconvenienced me. "But I don't think you can do me any good, not in just three days."

"You scared, Spanning?"

His lips trembled. "Yes, I am, Mr. Pairis. I'm about as scared as a man can be." His eyes were moist.

"Probably gives you some insight into how your victims felt, whaddaya think?"

He didn't answer. His eyes were moist.

After a moment just looking at me, he scraped back his chair and stood up. "Thank you for coming, sir. I'm sorry Ally imposed on your time." He turned and started to walk away. I jaunted into his landscape.

Oh my god, I thought. He was innocent.

Never done any of it. None of it. Absolutely no doubt, not a shadow of a doubt. Ally had been right. I saw every bit of that landscape in there, every fold and crease; every bolt hole and rat run; every gully and arroyo; all of his past, back and back and back to his birth in Lewistown, Montana, near Great Falls, thirty-six years ago; every day of his life right up to the minute they arrested him leaning over that disemboweled cleaning woman the real killer had tossed into the dumpster.

I saw every second of his landscape; and I saw him coming out of the Winn-Dixie in Huntsville; pushing a cart filled with grocery bags of food for the weekend. And I saw him wheeling it around the parking lot toward the dumpster area overflowing with broken-down cardboard boxes and fruit crates. And I heard the cry for help from one of those dumpsters; and I saw Henry Lake

Spanning stop and look around, not sure he'd heard anything at all. Then I saw him start to go to his car, parked right there at the edge of the lot beside the wall because it was a Friday evening and everyone was stocking up for the weekend, and there weren't any spaces out front; and the cry for help, weaker this time, as pathetic as a crippled kitten; and Henry Lake Spanning stopped cold, and he looked around; and we *both* saw the bloody hand raise itself above the level of the open dumpster's filthy green steel side. And I saw him desert his groceries without a thought to their cost, or that someone might run off with them if he left them unattended, or that he only had eleven dollars left in his checking account, so if those groceries were snagged by someone he wouldn't be eating for the next few days . . . and I watched him rush to the dumpster and look into the crap filling it . . . and I felt his nausea at the sight of that poor old woman, what was left of her . . . and I was with him as he crawled up onto the dumpster and dropped inside to do what he could for that mass of shredded and pulped flesh.

And I cried with him as she gasped, with a bubble of blood that burst in the open ruin of her throat, and she died. But though *I* heard the scream of someone coming around the corner, Spanning did not; and so he was still there, holding the poor mass of stripped skin and black bloody clothing, when the cops screeched into the parking lot. And only *then*, innocent of anything but decency and rare human compassion, did Henry Lake Spanning begin to understand what it must look like to middle-aged *hausfraus*, sneaking around dumpsters to pilfer cardboard boxes, who see what they think is a man murdering an old woman.

I was with him, there in that landscape within his mind, as he ran and ran and dodged and dodged. Until they caught him in Decatur, seven miles from the body of Gunilla Ascher. But they had him, and they had positive identification, from the dumpster in Huntsville; and all the rest of it was circumstantial, gussied up by bedridden, recovering Charlie Whilborg and the staff in Ally's office. It looked good on paper—so good that Ally had brought him down on twenty-nine-cum-fifty-six counts of murder in the vilest extreme.

But it was all bullshit.

The killer was still out there.

Henry Lake Spanning, who looked like a nice, decent guy, was exactly that. A nice, decent, goodhearted, but most of all *innocent* guy.

You could fool juries and polygraphs and judges and social workers and psychiatrists and your mommy and your daddy, but you could *not* fool Rudy Pairis, who travels regularly to the place of dark where you can go but not return.

They were going to burn an innocent man in three days.

I had to do something about it.

Not just for Ally, though that was reason enough; but for this man who thought he was doomed, and was frightened, but didn't have to take no shit from a wiseguy like me.

"Mr. Spanning," I called after him.

He didn't stop.

"Please," I said. He stopped shuffling, the chains making their little charm bracelet sounds, but he didn't turn around.

"I believe Ally is right, sir," I said. "I believe they caught the wrong man; and I believe all the time you've served is wrong; and I believe you ought not die."

Then he turned slowly, and stared at me with the look of a dog that has been taunted with a bone. His voice was barely a whisper. "And why is that, Mr. Pairis? Why is it that you believe me when nobody else but Ally and my attorney believed me?"

I didn't say what I was thinking. What I was thinking was that I'd been *in* there, and I *knew* he was innocent. And more than that, I knew that he truly loved my pal Allison Roche.

And there wasn't much I wouldn't do for Ally.

So what I said was: "I know you're innocent, because I know who's guilty."

His lips parted. It wasn't one of those big moves where someone's mouth flops open in astonishment; it was just a parting of the lips. But he was startled; I knew that as I knew the poor sonofabitch had suffered too long already.

He came shuffling back to me and sat down.

"Don't make fun, Mr. Pairis. Please. I'm what you said, I'm scared. I don't want to die, and I surely don't want to die with the world thinking I did those . . . those things."

"Makin' no fun, captain. I know who ought to burn for all those murders. Not six states, but eleven. Not fifty-six dead, but an even seventy. Three of them little girls in a day nursery, and the woman watching them, too."

He stared at me. There was horror on his face. I know that look real good. I've seen it at least seventy times.

"I know you're innocent, cap'n because *I'm* the man they want. *I'm* the guy who put your ass in here."

In a moment of human weakness. I saw it all. What I had packed off to live in that place of dark where you can go but not return. The wall-safe in my drawing-room. The four-foot-thick walled crypt encased in concrete and sunk a mile deep into solid granite. The vault whose composite laminate walls of judiciously sloped extremely thick blends of steel and plastic, the equivalent of six hundred to seven hundred millimeters of homogenous depth protection approached the maximum toughness and hardness of crystaliron, that iron grown with perfect crystal structure and carefully controlled quantities of impurities that in a modern combat tank can shrug off a hollow charge warhead like a spaniel shaking himself dry. The Chinese puzzle box. The hidden chamber. The labyrinth. The maze of the mind where I'd sent all seventy to die, over and over and over, so I wouldn't hear their screams, or see the ropes of bloody tendon, or stare into the pulped sockets where their pleading eyes had been.

When I had walked into that prison, I'd been buttoned up totally. I was safe and secure, I knew nothing, remembered nothing, suspected nothing.

But when I walked into Henry Lake Spanning's landscape, and I could not lie to myself that he was the one, I felt the earth crack. I felt the tremors and the upheavals, and the fissures started at my feet and ran to the horizon; and the lava boiled up and began to flow. And the steel walls melted, and the concrete turned to dust, and the barriers dissolved; and I looked at the face of the monster.

No wonder I had such nausea when Ally had told me about this or that slaughter ostensibly perpetrated by Henry Lake Spanning, the man she was prosecuting on twenty-nine counts of murders I had committed. No wonder I could picture all the details when she would talk to me about the barest description of the murder site. No wonder I fought so hard against coming to Holman.

In there, in his mind, his landscape open to me, I saw the love he had for Allison Roche, for my pal and buddy with whom I had once, just once . . .

Don't try tellin' me that the Power of Love can open the fissures. I don't want to hear that shit. I'm telling *you* that it was a combination, a buncha things that split me open, and possibly maybe one of those things was what I saw between them.

I don't know that much. I'm a quick study, but this was in an instant. A crack of fate. A moment of human weakness. That's what I told myself in the part of me that ventured to the place of dark: that I'd done what I'd done in moments of human weakness.

And it was those moments, not my "gift," and not my blackness, that had made me the loser, the monster, the liar that I am.

In the first moment of realization, I couldn't believe it. Not me, not good old Rudy. Not likeable Rudy Pairis never done no one but hisself wrong his whole life.

In the next second, I went wild with anger, furious at the disgusting thing that lived on one side of my split brain. Wanted to tear a hole through my face and yank the killing thing out, wet and putrescent, and squeeze it into pulp.

In the next second, I was nauseated, actually wanted to fall down and puke, seeing every moment of what I had done, unshaded, unhidden, naked to this Rudy Pairis who was decent and reasonable and law-abiding, even if such a Rudy was little better than a well-educated fuckup. But not a killer . . . I wanted to puke.

Then, finally, I accepted what I could not deny.

For me, never again would I slide through the night with the scent of the blossoming Yellow Lady's Slipper. I recognized that perfume now.

It was the odor that rises from a human body cut wide open, like a mouth making a big, dark yawn.

The other Rudy Pairis had come home at last.

They didn't have half a minute's worry. I sat down at a little wooden writing table in an interrogation room in the Jefferson County D.A.'s offices, and I made up a graph with the names and dates and locations. Names of as many of the seventy as I actually knew. (A lot of them had just been on the road, or in a men's toilet, or taking a bath, or lounging in the back row of a movie, or getting some cash from an ATM, or just sitting around doing nothing but waiting for me to come along and open them up, and maybe have a drink off them, or maybe just something to snack on . . . down the road.) Dates were easy, because I've got a good memory for dates. And the places where they'd find the ones they didn't know about, the fourteen with exactly the same m.o. as the other fifty-six, not to mention the old-style rip-and-pull can opener I'd used on that little Catholic bead-counter Gunilla Whatsername, who did Hail Mary this and Sweet Blessed Jesus that all the time I was opening her up, even at the last, when I held up parts of her insides for her to look at, and tried to get her to lick them, but she died first. Not half a minute's worry for the State of Alabama. All in one swell foop they corrected a tragic miscarriage of justice, nobbled a maniac killer, solved fourteen more murders than they'd counted on (in five additional states, which made the police departments of those five additional states extremely pleased with the law enforcement agencies of the Sovereign State of Alabama), and made first spot on the evening news on all three major networks, not to mention CNN, for the better part of a week. Knocked the Middle East right out of the box. Neither Harry Truman nor Tom Dewey would've had a prayer.

Ally went into seclusion, of course. Took off and went somewhere down on the Florida coast, I heard. But after the trial, and the verdict, and Spanning being released, and me going inside, and all like that, well, oo-poppa-dow as they used to say, it was all reordered properly. *Sat cito si sat bene*, in Latin. "It is done quickly enough if it is done well." A favorite saying of Cato. The Elder Cato.

And all I asked, all I begged for, was that Ally and Henry Lake Spanning, who loved each other and deserved each other, and whom I had almost fucked up royally, that the two of them would be there when they jammed my weary black butt into that new electric chair at Holman.

Please come, I begged them.

Don't let me die alone. Not even a shit like me. Don't make me cross over into that place of dark, where you can go, but not return—without the face of a friend. Even a former friend. And as for you, captain, well, hell didn't I save your life so you could enjoy the company of the woman you love? Least you can do. Come on now; be there or be square!

I don't know if Spanning talked her into accepting the invite, or if it was the other way around; but one day about a week prior to the event of cooking up a mess of fried Rudy Pairis, the warden stopped by my commodious accommodations on Death Row and gave me to understand that it would be SRO for the barbeque, which meant Ally, my pal, and her boyfriend, the former resident of the Row where now I dwelt in durance vile.

The things a guy'll do for love.

Yeah, that was the key. Why would a very smart operator who had gotten away with it, all the way free and clear, why would such a smart operator suddenly pull one of those hokey courtroom "I did it, I did it!" routines, and as good as strap himself into the electric chair?

Once. I only went to bed with her once.

The things a guy'll do for love.

When they brought me into the death chamber from the holding cell where I'd spent the night before and all that day, where I'd had my last meal (which had been a hot roast beef sandwich, double meat, on white toast, with very crisp french fries, and hot brown country gravy poured over the whole thing, apple sauce, and a bowl of Concord grapes), where a representative of the Holy Roman Empire had tried to make amends for destroying most of the gods, beliefs, and cultures of my black forebears, they held me between security officers, neither one of whom had been in attendance when I'd visited Henry Lake Spanning at this very same correctional facility slightly more than a year before.

It hadn't been a bad year. Lots of rest; caught up on my reading, finally got around to Proust and Langston Hughes, I'm ashamed to admit, so late in the game; lost some weight; worked out regularly; gave up cheese and dropped my cholesterol count. Ain't nothin' to it, just to do it.

Even took a jaunt or two or ten, every now and awhile. It didn't matter none. I wasn't going anywhere, neither were they. I'd done worse than the worst of them; hadn't I confessed to it? So there wasn't a lot that could ice me, after I'd copped to it and released all seventy of them out of my unconscious, where they'd been rotting in shallow graves for years. No big thang, Cuz.

Brought me in, strapped me in, plugged me in.

I looked through the glass at the witnesses.

There sat Ally and Spanning, front row center. Best seats in the house. All eyes and crying, watching, not believing everything had come to this, trying to figure out when and how and in what way it had all gone down without her knowing anything at all about it. And Henry Lake Spanning sitting close beside her, their hands locked in her lap. True love.

I locked eyes with Spanning.

I jaunted into his landscape.

No, I *didn't.*

I *tried* to and couldn't squirm through. Thirty years, or less, since I was five or six, I'd been doing it; without hindrance, all alone in the world the only person who could do this listen in on the landscape trick; and for the first time I was stopped. Absolutely no fuckin' entrance. I went wild! I tried running at it full-tilt, and hit something khaki-colored, like beach sand, and only slightly giving, not hard, but resilient. Exactly like being inside a ten-foot-high, fifty-foot-diameter paper bag, like a big shopping bag from a supermarket, that stiff butcher's paper kind of bag, and that color, like being inside a bag that size, running straight at it, thinking you're going to bust through . . . and being thrown back. Not hard, not like bouncing on a trampoline, just shunted aside like the fuzz from a dandelion hitting a glass door. Unimportant. Khaki-colored and not particularly bothered.

I tried hitting it with a bolt of pure blue lightning mental power, like someone out of a Marvel comic, but that wasn't how mixing in other people's minds works. You don't think yourself in with a psychic battering ram. That's the kind of arrant foolishness you hear spouted by unattractive people on public access cable channels, talking about The Power of Love and The Power of the Mind and the ever-popular toe-tapping Power of a Positive Thought. Bullshit; I don't be home to *that* folly!

I tried picturing myself in there, but that didn't work, either. I tried blanking my mind and drifting across, but it was pointless. And at that moment it occurred to me that I didn't really know *how* I jaunted. I just . . . did it. One moment I was snug in the privacy of my own head, and the next I was over there in someone else's landscape. It was instantaneous, like teleportation, which also is an impossibility, like telepathy.

But now, strapped into the chair, and them getting ready to put the leather mask over my face so the witnesses wouldn't have to see the smoke coming out of my eye sockets and the little sparks as my nose hairs burned, when it was urgent that I get into the thoughts and landscape of Henry Lake Spanning, I was shut out completely. And right *then*, that moment, I was scared!

Presto, without my even opening up to him, there he was: inside my head.

He had jaunted into *my* landscape.

"You had a nice roast beef sandwich, I see."

His voice was a lot stronger than it had been when I'd come down to see him a year ago. A *lot* stronger inside my mind.

"Yes, Rudy, I'm what you knew probably existed somewhere. Another one. A shrike." He paused. "I see you call it 'jaunting in the landscape.' I just called myself a shrike. A butcherbird. One name's as good as another. Strange, isn't it; all these years; and we never met anyone else? There *must* be others, but I think—now I can't prove this, I have no real data, it's just a wild idea I've had for years and years—I think they don't know they can do it."

He stared at me across the landscape, those wonderful blue eyes of his, the ones Ally had fallen in love with, hardly blinking.

"Why didn't you let me know before this?"

He smiled sadly. "Ah, Rudy. Rudy, Rudy, Rudy; you poor benighted pickaninny.

"Because I needed to suck you in, kid. I needed to put out a bear trap, and let it snap closed on your scrawny leg, and send you over. Here, let me clear the atmosphere in here . . ." And he wiped away all the manipulation he had worked on me, way back a year ago, when he had so easily covered his own true thoughts, his past, his life, the real panorama of what went on inside his landscape—like bypassing a surveillance camera with a continuous-loop tape that continues to show a placid scene while the joint is being actively burgled—and when he convinced me not only that he was innocent, but that the real killer was someone who had blocked the hideous slaughters from his conscious mind and had lived an otherwise exemplary life. He wandered around my landscape—and all of this in a second or two, because time has no duration in the landscape, like the hours you can spend in a dream that are just thirty seconds long in the real world, just before you wake up—and he swept away all the false memories and suggestions, the logical structure of sequential events that he had planted that would dovetail with my actual existence, my true memories, altered and warped and rearranged so I would believe that I had done all seventy of those ghastly murders . . . so that I'd believe, in a moment of horrible realization, that I was the demented psychopath who had ranged state to state to state, leaving piles of ripped flesh at every stop. Blocked it all, submerged it all, sublimated it all, me.

Good old Rudy Pairis, who never killed anybody. I'd been the patsy he was waiting for.

"There, now, kiddo. See what it's really like?

"You didn't do a thing.

"Pure as the driven snow, nigger. That's the truth. And what a find you were. Never even suspected there was another like me, till Ally came to interview me after Decatur. But there you were, big and Black as a Great White Hope, right there in her mind. Isn't she fine, Pairis? Isn't she something to take a knife to? Something to split open like a nice piece of fruit warmed in a summer sunshine field, let all the steam rise off her . . . maybe have a picnic . . ."

He stopped.

"I wanted her right from the first moment I saw her.

"Now, you know, I could've done it sloppy, just been a shrike to Ally, that first time she came to the holding cell to interview me; just jump into her, that was my plan. But what a noise that Spanning in the cell would've made, yelling it wasn't a man, it was a woman, not Spanning, but Deputy D.A. Allison Roche . . . too much noise, too many complications. But I *could* have done it, jumped into her. Or a guard, and then slice her at my leisure, stalk her, find her, let her steam . . .

"You look distressed, Mr. Rudy Pairis. Why's that? Because you're going to die in my place? Because I could have taken you over at any time, and didn't? Because after all this time of your miserable, wasted, lousy life you finally find someone like you, and we don't even have the convenience of a chat? Well, that's sad, that's really sad, kiddo. But you didn't have a chance."

"You're stronger than me, you kept me out," I said. He chuckled.

"Stronger? Is that all you think it is? Stronger? You still don't get it, do you?" His face, then, grew terrible. "You don't even understand now, right now that I've cleaned it all away and you can *see* what I did to you, do you?

"Do you think I stayed in a jail cell, and went through that trial, all of that, because I couldn't do anything about it? You poor jig slob. I could have jumped like a shrike any time I wanted to. But the first time I met your Ally, I saw *you*."

I cringed. "And you waited . . . ? For me, you spent all that time in prison, just to get to me . . . ?"

"At the moment when you couldn't do anything about it, at the moment you couldn't shout 'I've been taken over by someone else, I'm Rudy Pairis here inside this Henry Lake Spanning body, help me, help me!' Why stir up noise when all I had to do was bide my time, wait a bit, wait for Ally, and let Ally go for you."

I felt like a drowning turkey, standing idiotically in the rain, head tilted up, mouth open, water pouring in. "You can . . . leave the mind . . . leave the body . . . go out . . . jaunt, jump permanently . . ."

Spanning sniggered like a schoolyard bully.

"You stayed in jail three years just to get *me*?"

He smirked. Smarter than thou.

"Three years? You think that's some big deal to me? You don't think I could have someone like you running around, do you? Someone who can 'jaunt' as I do? The only other shrike I've ever encountered. You think I wouldn't sit in here and wait for you to come to me?"

"But three *years* . . ."

"You're what, Rudy . . . thirty-one, is it? Yes, I can see that. Thirty-one. You've never jumped like a shrike. You've just entered, jaunted, gone into the landscapes, and never understood that it's more than reading minds. You can change domiciles, Black boy. You can move out of a house in a bad neighborhood—such as strapped into the electric chair—and take up residence in a brand, spanking, new housing complex of million-and-a-half-buck condos, like Ally."

"But you have to have a place for the other one to go, don't you?" I said it just flat, no tone, no color to it at all. I didn't even think of the place of dark, where you can go . . .

"Who do you think I am, Rudy? Just who the hell do you think I was when I started, when I learned to shrike, how to jaunt, what I'm telling you now about changing residences? You wouldn't know my first address. I go a long way back.

"But I can give you a few of my more famous addresses. Gilles de Rais, France, 1440; Vlad Tepes, Romania, 1462; Elizabeth Bathory, Hungary, 1611; Catherine DeShayes, France, 1680; Jack the Ripper, London, 1888; Henri Désiré Landru, France, 1915; Albert Fish, New York City, 1934; Ed Gein, Plainfield, Wisconsin, 1954; Myra Hindley, Manchester, 1963; Albert DeSalvo, Boston, 1964; Charles Manson, Los Angeles, 1969; John Wayne Gacy, Norwood Park Township, Illinois, 1977.

"Oh, but how I do go on. And on. And on and on and on, Rudy, my little porch monkey. That's what I do. I go on. And on and on. Shrike will nest where it chooses. If not in your beloved Allison Roche, then in the cheesy fucked-up Black boy, Rudy Pairis. But don't you think that's a waste, kiddo? Spending however much time I might have to spend in your socially unacceptable body, when Henry Lake Spanning is such a handsome devil? Why should I have just switched with you when Ally lured you to me, because all it would've done is get you screeching and howling that you weren't Spanning, you were this nigger son who'd had his head stolen . . . and then you might have manipulated some guards or the warden . . .

"Well, you see what I mean, don't you?

"But now that the mask is securely in place, and now that the electrodes are attached to your head and your left leg, and now that the warden has his hand on the switch, well, you'd better get ready to do a lot of drooling."

And he turned around to jaunt back out of me, and I closed the perimeter. He tried to jaunt, tried to leap back to his own mind, but I had him in a fist. Just that easy. Materialized a fist and turned him to face me.

"Fuck you, Jack the Ripper. And fuck you twice, Bluebeard. And on and on and on fuck you, Manson and Boston Strangler and any other dipshit warped piece of sick crap you been in your years. You sure got some muddy-shoes credentials there, boy.

"What I care about all those names, Spanky, my brother? You really think I don't know those names? I'm an educated fellah, Mistuh Rippuh, Mistuh Mad Bomber. You missed a few. Were you also, did you inhabit, hast thou possessed Winnie Ruth Judd and Charlie Starkweather and Mad Dog Coll and Richard Speck and Sirhan Sirhan and Jeffrey Dahmer? You the boogieman responsible for *every* bad number the human race ever played? You ruin Sodom and Gomorrah, burned the Great Library of Alexandria, orchestrated the Reign of Terror *dans Paree*, set up the Inquisition, stoned and drowned the Salem witches, slaughtered unarmed women and kids at Wounded Knee, bumped off John Kennedy?

"I don't think so.

"I don't even think you got so close as to share a pint with Jack the Ripper. And even if you did, even if you *were* all those maniacs, you were small potatoes, Spanky. The least of us human beings outdoes you, three times a day. How many lynch ropes you pulled tight, M'sieur Landru?

"What colossal egotism you got, makes you blind, makes you think you're the only one, even when you find out there's someone else, you can't get past it. What makes you think I didn't know what you can do? What makes you think I didn't let you do it, and sit here waiting for you like you sat there waiting for me, till this moment when you can't do shit about it?

"You so goddam stuck on yourself, Spankyhead, you never give it the barest that someone else is a faster draw than you.

"Know what your trouble is, captain? You're old, you're *real* old, maybe hundreds of years who gives a damn old. That don't count for shit, old man. You're old, but you never got smart. You're just mediocre at what you do.

"You moved from address to address. You didn't have to be Son of Sam or Cain slayin' Abel, or whoever the fuck you been . . . you could've been Moses or Galileo or George Washington Carver or Harriet Tubman or Sojourner Truth or Mark Twain or Joe Louis. You could've been Alexander Hamilton and helped found the Manumission Society in New York. You could've discovered radium, carved Mount Rushmore, carried a baby out of a burning building. But you got old real fast, and you never got any smarter. You didn't need to, did you, Spanky? You had it all to yourself, all this 'shrike' shit, just jaunt here and jaunt there, and bite off someone's hand or face like the old, tired, boring, repetitious, no-imagination stupid shit that you are.

"Yeah, you got me good when I came here to see your landscape. You got Ally wired up good. And she suckered me in, probably not even knowing she was doing it . . . you must've looked in her head and found just the right technique to get her to make me come within reach. Good, m'man; you were excellent. But I had a year to torture myself. A year to sit here and think about it. About how many people I'd killed, and how sick it made me, and little by little I found my way through it.

"Because . . . and here's the big difference 'tween us, dummy:

"I unraveled what was going on . . . it took time, but I learned. Understand, asshole? *I* learn! *You* don't.

"There's an old Japanese saying—I got lots of these, Henry m'man—I read a whole lot—and what it says is, 'Do not fall into the error of the artisan who boasts of twenty years experience in his craft while in fact he has had only one year of experience—twenty times.'" Then I grinned back at him.

"Fuck you, sucker," I said, just as the warden threw the switch and I jaunted out of there and into the landscape and mind of Henry Lake Spanning.

I sat there getting oriented for a second; it was the first time I'd done more than a jaunt . . . this was . . . *shrike*; but then Ally beside me gave a little sob for her old pal, Rudy Pairis, who was baking like a Maine lobster, smoke coming out from under the black cloth that covered my, his, face; and I heard the vestigial scream of what had been Henry Lake Spanning and thousands of other monsters, all of them burning, out there on the far horizon of my new landscape; and I put my arm around her, and drew her close, and put my face into her shoulder and hugged her to me; and I heard the scream go on and on for the longest time, I think it was a long time, and finally it was just wind . . . and then gone . . . and I came up from Ally's shoulder, and I could barely speak.

"Shhh, honey, it's okay," I murmured. "He's gone where he can make right for his mistakes. No pain. Quiet, a real quiet place; and all alone forever. And cool there. And dark."

I was ready to stop failing at everything and blaming everything. Having fessed up to love, having decided it was time to grow up and be an adult—not just a very quick study who learned fast, extremely fast, a lot faster than anybody could imagine an orphan like me could learn, than *anybody* could imagine—I hugged her with the intention that Henry Lake Spanning would love Allison Roche more powerfully, more responsibly, than anyone had ever loved anyone in the history of the world. I was ready to stop failing at everything.

And it would be just a whole lot easier as a white boy with great big blue eyes.

HARLAN ELLISON

Because—get on this now—all my wasted years didn't have as much to do with Blackness or racism or being overqualified or being unlucky or being high-verbal or even the curse of my "gift" of jaunting, as they did with one single truth I learned waiting in there, inside my own landscape, waiting for Spanning to come and gloat:

I have always been one of those miserable guys who couldn't get out of his own way.

Which meant I could, at last, stop feeling sorry for that poor nigger Rudy Pairis. Except, maybe, in a moment of human weakness.

On the Downhill Side

In love, there is always one who kisses and one who offers the cheek.

—French Proverb

I knew she was a virgin because she was able to ruffle the silken mane of my unicorn. Named Lizette, she was a Grecian temple in which no sacrifice had ever been made. A Vestal virgin of New Orleans found walking without shadow in the thankgod coolness of cockroach-crawling Louisiana night. My unicorn whinnied, inclined his head, and she stroked the ivory spiral of his horn.

Much of this took place in what is called the Irish Channel, a strip of street in old New Orleans where the lace curtain micks had settled decades before; now the Irish were gone, and the Cubans had taken over the Channel. Now the Cubans were sleeping, recovering from the muggy today that held within its hours the *déjà vu* of muggy yesterday, the *déjà rêvé* of intolerable tomorrow. Now the crippled bricks of side streets off Magazine had given up their nightly ghosts, and one such phantom had come to me, calling my unicorn to her—thus, clearly, a virgin—and I stood waiting.

Had it been Sutton Place, had it been a Manhattan evening, and had we met, she would have kneeled to pet my dog. And I would have waited. Had it been Puerto Vallarta, had it been 200 36′ N, 1050 13′ W, and had we met, she would have crouched to run her fingertips over the oil-slick hide of my iguana. And I would have waited. Meeting in streets requires ritual. One must wait and not breathe too loudly, if one is to enjoy the congress of the nightly ghosts.

She looked across the fine head of my unicorn and smiled at me. Her eyes were a shade of gray between onyx and miscalculation. "Is it a bit chilly for you?" I asked.

"When I was thirteen," she said, linking my arm, taking a tentative two steps that led me with her, up the street, "or perhaps I was twelve, well, no matter, when I was that approximate age, I had a marvelous shawl of Belgian lace. I could look through it and see the mysteries of the sun and the other stars unriddled. I'm sure someone important and very nice has purchased that shawl from an antique dealer, and paid handsomely for it."

It seemed not a terribly responsive reply to a simple question.

"A queen of the Mardi Gras Ball doesn't get chilly," she added, unasked. I walked along beside her, the cool evasiveness of her arm binding us, my mind a welter of answer choices, none satisfactory.

Behind us, my unicorn followed silently. Well, not entirely silently. His platinum hoofs clattered on the bricks. I'm afraid I felt a straight pin of jealousy. Perfection does that to me.

"When were you queen of the Ball?"

The date she gave me was one hundred and thirteen years before.

It must have been brutally cold down there in the stones.

There is a little book they sell, a guide to manners and dining in New Orleans: I've looked: nowhere in the book do they indicate the proper responses to a ghost: But then, it says nothing about the wonderful cemeteries of New Orleans's West Bank, or Metairie. Or the gourmet dining at such locations. One seeks, in vain, through the mutable, mercurial universe, for the compleat guide. To everything. And, failing in the search, one makes do the best one can. And suffers the frustration, suffers the ennui.

Perfection does that to me.

We walked for some time, and grew to know each other, as best we'd allow. These are some of the high points. They lack continuity. I don't apologize, I merely point it out, adding with some truth, I feel, that *most* liaisons lack continuity. We find ourselves in odd places at various times, and for a brief span we link our lives to others—even as Lizette had linked her arm with mine—and then, our time elapsed, we move apart. Through a haze of pain occasionally; usually through a veil of memory that clings, then passes; sometimes as though we have never touched.

"My name is Paul Ordahl," I told her. "And the most awful thing that ever happened to me was my first wife, Bernice. I don't know how else to put it—even if it sounds melodramatic, it's simply what happened—she went insane, and I divorced her, and her mother had her committed to a private mental home."

"When I was eighteen," Lizette said, "my family gave me my coming-out party. We were living in the Garden District, on Prytania Street. The house was a lovely white Plantation—they call them antebellum now—with Grecian pillars. We had a persimmon-green gazebo in the rear gardens, directly beside a weeping willow. It was six-sided. Octagonal. Or is that hexagonal? It was the loveliest party. And while it was going on, I sneaked away with a boy . . . I don't remember his name . . . and we went into the gazebo, and I let him touch my breasts. I don't remember his name."

We were on Decatur Street, walking toward the French Quarter; the Mississippi was on our right, dark but making its presence known.

"Her mother was the one had her committed, you see. I only heard from them twice after the divorce. It had been four stinking years and I really didn't want any more of it. Once, after I'd started making some money, the mother called and said Bernice had to be put in the state asylum. There wasn't enough money to pay for the private home anymore. I sent a little; not much. I suppose I could have sent more, but I was remarried, there was a child from her previous marriage. I didn't want to send any more. I told the mother not to call me again. There was only once after that . . . it was the most terrible thing that ever happened to me."

We walked around Jackson Square, looking in at the very black grass, reading the plaques bolted to the spear-topped fence, plaques telling how New Orleans had once belonged to the French. We sat on one of the benches in the street. The street had been closed to traffic, and we sat on one of the benches.

"Our name was Charbonnet. Can you say that?"

I said it, with a good accent.

"I married a very wealthy man. He was in real estate. At one time he owned the entire block where the *Vieux Carré* now stands, on Bourbon Street. He admired me greatly. He came and sought my hand, and my *maman* had to strike the bargain because my father was too weak to do it; he drank. I can admit that now. But it didn't matter, I'd already found out how my suitor was set financially. He wasn't common, but he wasn't quality, either. But he was wealthy, and I married him. He gave me presents. I did what I had to do. But I refused to let him make love to me after he became friends with that awful Jew who built the Metairie Cemetery over the racetrack because they wouldn't let him race his Jew horses. My husband's name was Dunbar. Claude Dunbar, you may have heard the name? Our parties were *de rigueur*."

"Would you like some coffee and *beignets* at du Monde?"

She stared at me for a moment, as though she wanted me to say something more, then she nodded and smiled.

We walked around the Square. My unicorn was waiting at the curb. I scratched his rainbow flank, and he struck a spark off the cobblestones with his right front hoof. "I know," I said to him, "we'll soon start the downhill side. But not just yet. Be patient. I won't forget you."

Lizette and I went inside the Café du Monde, and I ordered two coffees with warm milk and two orders of *beignets* from a waiter who was originally from New Jersey but had lived most of his life only a few miles from College Station, Texas.

There was a coolness coming off the levee.

"I was in New York," I said. "I was receiving an award at an architects' convention—did I mention I was an architect—yes, that's what I was at the time, an architect—and I did a television interview. The mother saw me on the program, and checked the newspapers to find out what hotel we were using for the convention, and she got my room number and called me. I had been out quite late after the banquet where I'd gotten my award, quite late. I was sitting on the side of the bed, taking off my shoes, my tuxedo tie hanging from my unbuttoned collar, getting ready just to throw clothes on the floor and sink away, when the phone rang. It was the mother. She was a terrible person, one of the worst I ever knew, a shrike, a terrible, just a terrible person. She started telling me about Bernice in the asylum. How they had her in this little room and how she stared out the window most of the time. She'd reverted to childhood, and most of the time she couldn't even recognize the mother; but when she did, she'd say something like, 'Don't let them hurt me, Mommy, don't let them hurt me.' So I asked her what she wanted me to do, did she want money for Bernice or what . . . did she want me to go see her since I was in New York . . . and she said God no. And then she did an awful thing to me. She said the last time she'd been to see Bernice, my ex-wife had turned around and put her finger to her lips and said, 'Shhh, we have to be very quiet. Paul is working.' And I swear, a snake uncoiled in my stomach. It was the most terrible thing I'd ever heard. No matter how secure you are that you honest to God had *not* sent someone to a madhouse, there's always that little core of doubt, and saying what she'd said just burned out my head. I couldn't even think about it, couldn't even really *hear* it, or it would have collapsed me. So down came these iron walls and I just kept on talking, and after a while she hung up.

"It wasn't till two years later that I allowed myself to think about it, and then I cried; it had been a long time since I'd cried. Oh, not because I believed that nonsense about a man isn't supposed to cry, but just because I guess there hadn't been anything that important to cry *about.* But when I let myself hear what she'd said, I started crying, and just went on and on till I finally went in and looked into the bathroom mirror and I asked myself, face-to-face, if I'd done that, if I'd ever made her be quiet so I could work on blueprints or drawings . . .

"And after a while I saw myself shaking my head no, and it was easier. That was perhaps three years before I died."

She licked the powdered sugar from the *beignets* off her fingers and launched into a long story about a lover she had taken. She didn't remember his name.

It was sometime after midnight. I'd thought midnight would signal the start of the downhill side, but the hour had passed, and we were still together, and she didn't seem ready to vanish. We left the Café du Monde and walked into the Quarter.

I despise Bourbon Street. The strip joints, with the pasties over nipples, the smell of need, the dwarfed souls of men attuned only to flesh. The noise.

We walked through it like art connoisseurs at a showing of motel room paintings. She continued to talk about her life, about the men she had known, about the way they had loved her, the ways in which she had spumed them, and about the trivia of her past existence. I continued to talk about my loves, about all the women I had held dear in my heart for however long each had been linked with me. We talked across each other, our conversation at right angles, only meeting in the intersections of silence at story's end.

She wanted a julep, and I took her to the Royal Orleans Hotel and we sat in silence as she drank. I watched her, studying that phantom face, seeking for even the smallest flicker of light off the ice in her eyes, hoping for an indication that glacial melting could be forthcoming. But there was nothing, and I burned to say correct words that might cause heat. She drank and reminisced about evenings with young men in similar hotels, a hundred years before.

We went to a nightclub where a flamenco dancer and his two-woman troupe performed on a stage of unpolished woods, their star-shining black shoes setting up resonances in me that I chose to ignore.

Then I realized there were only three couples in the club, and that the extremely pretty flamenco dancer was playing to Lizette. He gripped the lapels of his bolero jacket and clattered his heels against the stage like a man driving nails. She watched him, and her tongue made a wholly obvious flirtatious trip around the rim of her liquor glass. There was a two-drink minimum, and as I have never liked the taste of alcohol, she was more than willing to prevent waste by drinking mine as well as her own. Whether she was getting drunk or simply indulging herself, I do not know. It didn't matter. I became blind with jealousy, and dragons took possession of my eyes.

When the dancer was finished, when his half hour show was concluded, he came to our table. His suit was skintight and the color of Arctic lakes. His hair was curly and moist from his exertions, and his prettiness infuriated me. There was a scene. He asked her name, I interposed a comment, he tried to be polite, sensing my ugly mood, she overrode my comment, he tried again in Castilian, *th*-ing his *esses*, she answered, I rose and shoved him, there was a scuffle. We were asked to leave.

Once outside, she walked away from me.

My unicorn was at the curb, eating from a porcelain *Sèvres* soup plate filled with *flan.* I watched her walk unsteadily up the street toward Jackson Square. I scratched my unicorn's neck, and he stopped eating the egg custard. He looked at me for a long moment. Ice crystals were sparkling in his mane.

We were on the downhill side.

"Soon, old friend," I said.

He dipped his elegant head toward the plate. "I see you've been to the Las Americas. When you return the plate, give my best to *Señor* Pena."

I followed her up the street. She was walking rapidly toward the Square. I called to her, but she wouldn't stop. She began dragging her left hand along the steel bars of the fence enclosing the Square. Her fingertips thudded softly from bar to bar, and once I heard the chitinous *clak* of a manicured nail.

"Lizette!"

She walked faster, dragging her hand across the dark metal bars.

"Lizette! Damn it!"

I was reluctant to run after her; it was somehow terribly demeaning. But she was getting farther and farther away. There were bums in the Square, sitting slouched on the benches, their arms out along the backs. Itinerants, kids with beards and knapsacks. I was suddenly frightened for her. Impossible. She had been dead for a hundred years. There was no reason for it . . . I was afraid for her!

I started running, the sound of my footsteps echoing up and around the Square. I caught her at the corner and dragged her around. She tried to slap me, and I caught her hand. She kept trying to hit me, to scratch my face with the manicured nails. I held her and swung her away from me, swung her around, and around, dizzyingly, trying to keep her off-balance. She swung wildly, crying out and saying things inarticulately. Finally, she stumbled, and I pulled her in to me and held her tight against my body.

"Stop it! Stop, Lizette! I . . . *stop it*!" She went limp against me, and I felt her crying against my chest. I took her into the shadows and my unicorn came down Decatur Street and stood under a streetlamp, waiting.

The chimera winds rose. I heard them, and knew we were well on the downhill side, that time was growing short. I held her close and smelled the woodsmoke scent of her hair. "Listen to me," I said, softly, close to her. "Listen to me, Lizette. Our time's almost gone. This is our last chance. You've lived in stone for a hundred years; I've heard you cry. I've come there, to that place, night after night, and I've heard you cry. You've paid enough, God knows. So have I. We can *do* it. We've got one more chance, and we can make it, if you'll try. That's all I ask. Try."

She pushed away from me, tossing her head so the auburn hair swirled away from her face. Her eyes were dry. Ghosts can do that. Cry without making tears. Tears are denied us. Other things; I won't talk of them here.

"I lied to you," she said.

I touched the side of her face. The high cheekbone just at the hairline. "I know. My unicorn would never have let you touch him if you weren't pure. I'm not, but he has no choice with me. He was assigned to me. He's my familiar and he puts up with me. We're friends."

"No. Other lies. My life was a lie. I've told them all to you. We can't make it. You have to let me go."

I didn't know exactly where, but I knew how it would happen. I argued with her, trying to convince her there was a way for us. But she couldn't believe it, hadn't the strength or the will or the faith. Finally, I let her go.

She put her arms around my neck, and drew my face down to hers, and she held me that way for a few moments. Then the winds rose, and there were sounds in the night, the sounds of calling, and she left me there, in the shadows.

I sat down on the curb and thought about the years since I'd died. Years without much music. Light leached out. Wandering. Nothing to pace me but memories and the unicorn. How sad I was for *him*; assigned to me till I got my chance. And now it had come and I'd taken my best go, and failed.

Lizette and I were the two sides of the same coin; devalued and impossible to spend. Legal tender of nations long since vanished, no longer even names on the cracked papyrus of cartographers' maps. We had been snatched away from final rest, had been set adrift to roam for our crimes, and only once between death and eternity would we receive a chance. This night . . . this nothing-special night . . . this was our chance.

My unicorn came to me, then, and brushed his muzzle against my shoulder. I reached up and scratched around the base of his spiral horn, his favorite place. He gave a long, silvery sigh, and in that sound I heard the sentence I was serving on him, as well as myself. We had been linked, too. Assigned to one another by the One who had ordained this night's chance. But if I lost out, so did my unicorn; he who had wandered with me through all the soundless, lightless years.

I stood up. I was by no means ready to do battle, but at least I could stay in for the full ride . . . all the way on the downhill side. "Do you know where they are?"

My unicorn started off down the street.

I followed, hopelessness warring with frustration. Dusk to dawn is the full ride, the final chance. After midnight is the downhill side. Time was short, and when time ran out there would be nothing for Lizette or me or my unicorn *but* time. Forever.

When we passed the Royal Orleans Hotel I knew where we were going. The sound of the Quarter had already faded. It was getting on toward dawn. The human lice had finally crawled into their flesh-mounds to sleep off the night of revelry. Though I had never experienced directly the New Orleans in which Lizette had grown up, I longed for the power to blot out the cancerous blight that Bourbon Street and the Quarter had become, with its tourist filth and screaming neon, to restore it to the colorful yet healthy state in which it had thrived a hundred years before. But I was only a ghost, not one of the gods with such powers, and at that moment I was almost at the end of the line held by one of those gods.

My unicorn turned down dark streets, heading always in the same general direction, and when I saw the first black shapes of the tombstones against the night sky, the *lightening* night sky, I knew I'd been correct in my assumption of destination.

The Saint Louis Cemetery.

Oh, how I sorrow for anyone who has never seen the world-famous Saint Louis Cemetery in New Orleans. It is the perfect graveyard, the complete graveyard, the finest graveyard in the universe. (There is a perfection in some designs that informs the function totally. There are Danish chairs that could be nothing *but* chairs, are so totally and completely *chair* that if the world as we know it ended, and a billion years from now the New Orleans horsy cockroaches became the dominant species, and they dug down through the alluvial layers, and found one of those chairs, even if they themselves did not use chairs, were not constructed physically for the use of chairs, had never seen a chair, *still* they would know it for what it had been made to be: a chair. Because it would be the essence of *chairness.* And from it, they could reconstruct the human race in replica. *That* is the kind of graveyard one means when one refers to the world-famous Saint Louis Cemetery.)

The Saint Louis Cemetery is ancient. It sighs with shadows and the comfortable bones and their afterimages of deaths that became great merely because those who died went to be interred in the Saint Louis Cemetery. The water table lies just eighteen inches below New Orleans—there are no graves in the earth for that reason. Bodies are entombed aboveground in crypts, in sepulchers, vaults, mausoleums. The gravestones are all different, no two alike, each one a testament to the stonecutter's art. Only secondarily testaments to those who lie beneath the markers.

We had reached the moment of final nightness. That ultimate moment before day began. Dawn had yet to fill the eastern sky, yet there was a warming of tone to the night; it was the last of the downhill side of my chance. Of Lizette's chance.

We approached the cemetery, my unicorn and I. From deep in the center of the skyline of stones beyond the fence I could see the ice-chill glow of a pulsing blue light. The light one finds in a refrigerator, cold and flat and brittle.

I mounted my unicorn, leaned close along his neck, clinging to his mane with both hands, knees tight to his silken sides, now rippling with light and color, and I gave a little hiss of approval, a little sound of go.

My unicorn sailed over the fence, into the world-famous Saint Louis Cemetery.

I dismounted and thanked him. We began threading our way between the tombstones, the sepulchers, the crypts.

The blue glow grew more distinct. And now I could hear the chimera winds rising, whirling, coming in off alien seas. The pulsing of the light, the wail of the winds, the night dying. My unicorn stayed close. Even we of the spirit world know when to be afraid.

After all, I was only operating off a chance; I was under no god's protection. Naked, even in death.

There is no fog in New Orleans.

Mist began to form around us.

Except sometimes in the winter, there is no fog in New Orleans.

I remembered the daybreak of the night I'd died. There had been mist. I had been a suicide.

My third wife had left me. She had gone away during the night, while I'd been at a business meeting with a client; I had been engaged to design a church in Baton Rouge. All that day I'd steamed the old wallpaper off the apartment we'd rented. It was to have been our first home together, paid for by the commission. I'd done the steaming myself, with a tall ladder and a steam condenser and two flat pans with steam holes. Up near the ceiling the heat had been so awful I'd almost fainted. She'd brought me lemonade, freshly squeezed. Then I'd showered and changed and gone to my meeting. When I'd returned, she was gone. No note.

Lizette and I were two sides of the same coin, cast off after death for the opposite extremes of the same crime. She had never loved. I had loved too much. Overindulgence in something as delicate as love is to be found monstrously offensive in the eyes of the God of Love. And some of us—who have never understood the salvation in the Golden Mean—some of us are cast adrift with but one chance. It can happen.

Mist formed around us, and my unicorn crept close to me, somehow smaller, almost timid. We were moving into realms he did not understand, where his limited magics were useless. These were realms of potency so utterly beyond even the limbo creatures—such as my unicorn—so completely alien to even the intermediary zone wanderers—Lizette and myself—that we were as helpless and without understanding as those who live. We had only one advantage over living, breathing, as yet undead humans: we *knew* for certain that the realms on the other side existed.

Above, beyond, deeper: where the gods live. Where the One who had given me my chance, had given Lizette *her* chance, where He lived. Undoubtedly watching.

The mist swirled up around us, as chill and final as the dust of pharaohs' tombs.

We moved through it, toward the pulsing heart of blue light. And as we came into the penultimate circle, we stopped. We were in the outer ring of potency, and we saw the claiming things that had come for Lizette. She lay out on an altar of crystal, naked and trembling. They stood around her, enormously tall and transparent. Man shapes without faces. Within their transparent forms a strange, silvery fog swirled, like smoke from holy censers. Where eyes should have been on a man or a ghost, there were only dull flickering firefly glowings, inside, hanging in the smoke, moving, changing shape and position. No eyes at all. And tall, very tall, towering over Lizette and the altar.

For me, overcommitted to love, when dawn came without salvation, there was only an eternity of wandering, with my unicorn as sole companion. Ghost forevermore. Incense chimera viewed as dust-devil on the horizon, chilling as I passed in city streets, forever gone, invisible, lost, empty, helpless, wandering.

But for her, empty vessel, the fate was something else entirely. The God of Love had allowed her the time of wandering, trapped by day in stones, freed at night to wander. He had allowed her the final chance. And having failed to take it, her fate was with these claiming creatures, gods themselves . . . of another order . . . higher or lower I had no idea. But terrible.

"Lagniappe!" I screamed the word. The old Creole word they use in New Orleans when they want a little extra; a bonus of *croissants*, a few additional carrots dumped into the shopping bag, a baker's dozen, a larger portion of clams or crabs or shrimp. "*Lagniappe!* Lizette, take a little more! Try for the extra! Try . . . demand it . . . there's time . . . you have it coming to you . . . you've paid . . . I've paid . . . it's ours . . . *try*!"

She sat up, her naked body lit by lambent fires of chill blue cold from the other side. She sat up and looked across the inner circle to me, and I stood there with my arms out, trying desperately to break through the outer circle to her.

But it was solid, and I could not pass. Only virgins could pass.

And they would not let her go. They had been promised a feed, and they were there to claim. I began to cry, as I had cried when I finally heard what the mother had said, when I finally came home to the empty apartment and knew I had spent my life loving too much, demanding too much, myself a feeder at a board that *could* be depleted and emptied and serve up no more. She wanted to come to me, I could *see* she wanted to come to me. But they would have their meal.

Then I felt the muzzle of my unicorn at my neck, and in a step he had moved through the barrier that was impenetrable to me, and he moved across the circle and stood waiting. Lizette leaped from the altar and ran to me.

It all happened at the same time. I felt Lizette's body anchor into mine, and *we* saw my unicorn standing over there on the other side, and for a moment *we* could not summon up the necessary reactions, the correct sounds. *We* knew for the first time in either our lives or our deaths what it was to be paralyzed. Then reactions began washing over me, *we,* us; in wave after wave: cascading joy that Lizette had come to . . . us; utter love for this Paul ghost creature; realization that instinctively part of us was falling into the same pattern again; fear that that part would love too much at this mystic juncture; resolve to temper our love; and then anguish at the sight of our unicorn standing there, waiting to be claimed . . .

We called to him . . . using his secret name, one *we* had never spoken aloud. *We* could barely speak. Weight pulled at his throat, our throats. "Old friend . . ." *We* took a step toward him but could not pass the barrier. Lizette clung to me, Paul held me tight as I trembled with terror and the cold of that inner circle still frosting my flesh.

The great transparent claimers stood silently, watching, waiting, as if content to allow us our moments of final decision. But their impatience could be felt in the air, a soft purring, like the death rattle always in the throat of a cat. "Come back! Not for me . . . don't do it for me . . . it's not fair!"

Paul's unicorn turned his head and looked at us.

My friend of starless nights, when we had gone sailing together through the darkness. My friend who had walked with me on endless tours of empty places. My friend of gentle nature and constant companionship. Until Lizette, my friend, my only friend, my familiar assigned to an onerous task, who had come to love me and to whom I had belonged, even as he had belonged to me.

I could not bear the hurt that grew in my chest, in my stomach; my head was on fire, my eyes burned with tears first for Paul, and now for the sweetest creature a god had ever sent to temper a man's anguish . . . and for myself. I could not bear the thought of never knowing—as Paul had known it—the silent company of that gentle, magical beast.

But he turned back, and moved to them, and they took that as final decision, and the great transparent claimers moved in around him, and their quickglass hands reached down to touch him, and for an instant they seemed to hesitate, and I called out, "Don't be afraid . . ." and my unicorn turned his head to look across the mist of potency for the last time, and I saw he *was* afraid, but not as much as he would have been if *we* had not been there.

Then the first of them touched his smooth, silvery flank and he gave a trembling sigh of pain. A ripple ran down his hide. Not the quick flesh movement of ridding himself of a fly, but a completely alien, unnatural tremor, containing in its swiftness all the agony and loss of eternities. A sigh went out from Paul's unicorn, though he had not uttered it.

We could feel the pain, the loneliness. My unicorn with no time left to him. Ending. All was now a final ending; he had stayed with me, walked with me, and had grown to care for me until that time when he would be released from his duty by that special god; but now freedom was to be denied him; an ending.

The great transparent claimers all touched him, their ice fingers caressing his warm hide as we watched, helpless, Lizette's face buried in Paul's chest. Colors surged across my unicorn's body, as if by becoming more intense the chill touch of the claimers could be beaten off. Pulsing waves of rainbow color that lived in his hide for moments, then dimmed, brightened again and were bled off. Then the colors leaked away one by one, chroma weakening: purple-blue, manganese violet, discord, cobalt blue, doubt, affection, chrome green, chrome yellow, raw sienna, contemplation, alizarin crimson, irony, silver, severity, compassion, cadmium red, white.

They emptied him . . . he did not fight them . . . going colder and colder . . . flickers of yellow, a whisper of blue, pale as white . . . the tremors blending into one constant shudder . . . the wonderful golden eyes rolled in torment, went flat, brightness dulled, flat metal . . . the platinum hoofs caked with rust . . . and he stood, did not try to escape, gave himself for us . . . and he was emptied. Of everything. Then, like the claimers, we could see through him. Vapors swirled within the transparent husk, a fogged glass, shimmering . . . then nothing. And then they absorbed even the husk.

The chill blue light faded, and the claimers grew indistinct in our sight. The smoke within them seemed thicker, moved more slowly, horribly, as though they had fed and were sluggish and would go away, back across the line to that dark place where they waited, always waited, till their hunger was aroused again. And my unicorn was gone. I was alone with Lizette. I was alone with Paul. The mist died away, and the claimers were gone, and once more it was merely a cemetery as the first rays of the morning sun came easing through the tumble and disarray of headstones.

We stood together as one, her naked body white and virginal in my weary arms; and as the light of the sun struck us *we* began to fade, to merge, to mingle our bodies and our wandering spirits one into the other, forming one spirit that would neither love too much, nor too little, having taken our chance on the downhill side.

We faded and were lifted invisibly on the scented breath of that good god who had owned us, and were taken away from there. To be born again as one spirit, in some other human form, man or woman we did not know which. Nor would we remember. Nor did it matter.

This time, love would not destroy us. This time out, we would have luck.

The luck of silken mane and rainbow colors, platinum hoofs, and spiral horn.

THE PASSAGE OF TIME

Paladin of the Lost Hour

This was an old man. Not an incredibly old man: obsolete, spavined; not as worn as the sway-backed stone steps ascending the Pyramid of the Sun to an ancient temple; not yet a relic. But even so, a *very* old man, this old man perched on an antique shooting stick, its handles opened to form a seat, its spike thrust at an angle into the soft ground and trimmed grass of the cemetery. Gray, thin rain misted down at almost the same angle as that at which the spike pierced the ground. The winter-barren trees lay flat and black against an aluminum sky, unmoving in the chill wind. An old man sitting at the foot of a grave mound whose headstone had tilted slightly when the earth had settled; sitting in the rain and speaking to someone below.

"They tore it down, Minna.

"I tell you, they must have bought off a councilman.

"Came in with bulldozers at six o'clock in the morning, and you *know* that's not legal. There's a Municipal Code. Supposed to hold off till at least seven on weekdays, eight on the weekend; but there they were at six, even *before* six, barely light for godsakes. Thought they'd sneak in and do it before the neighborhood got wind of it and called the landmarks committee. Sneaks: they come on *holidays*, can you imagine!

"But I was out there waiting for them, and I told them, 'You can't do it, that's Code number 91.3002, sub-section E,' and they lied and said they had special permission, so I said to the big mucky-muck in charge, 'Let's see your waiver permit,' and he said the Code didn't apply in this case because it was supposed to be only for grading, and since they were demolishing and not grading, they could start whenever they felt like it. So I told him I'd call the police, then, because it came under the heading of Disturbing the Peace, and he said . . . well, I know you hate that kind of language, old girl, so I won't tell you what he said, but you can imagine.

"So I called the police, and gave them my name, and of course they didn't get there till almost quarter after seven (which is what makes me think they bought off a councilman), and by then those 'dozers had leveled most of it. Doesn't take long, you know that.

"And I don't suppose it's as great a loss as, maybe, say, the Great Library of Alexandria, but it was the last of the authentic Deco design drive-ins, and the carhops still served you on roller skates, and it was a landmark, and just about the only place left in the city where you could still get a decent grilled cheese sandwich pressed very flat on the grill by one of those weights they used to use, made with real cheese and not that rancid plastic they cut into squares and call it 'cheese food.'

"Gone, old dear, gone and mourned. And I understand they plan to put up another one of those mini-malls on the site, just ten blocks away from one that's already there, and you know what's going to happen: this new one will drain off the traffic from the older one, and then that one will fail the way they all do when the next one gets built, you'd think they'd see some history in it; but no, they never learn. And you should have seen the crowd by seven-thirty. All ages, even some of those kids painted like aborigines, with torn leather clothing. Even they came to protest. Terrible language, but at least they were concerned. And nothing could stop it. They just whammed it, and down it went.

"I do so miss you today, Minna. No more good grilled cheese." Said the *very* old man to the ground. And now he was crying softly, and now the wind rose, and the mist rain stippled his overcoat.

Nearby, yet at a distance, Billy Kinetta stared down at another grave. He could see the old man over there off to his left, but he took no further notice. The wind whipped the vent of his trenchcoat. His collar was up but rain trickled down his neck. This was a younger man, not yet thirty-five. Unlike the old man, Billy Kinetta neither cried nor spoke to memories of someone who had once listened. He might have been a geomancer, so silently did he stand, eyes toward the ground.

One of these men was Black; the other was white.

Beyond the high, spiked-iron fence surrounding the cemetery two boys crouched, staring through the bars, through the rain; at the men absorbed by grave matters, by matters of graves. These were not really boys. They were legally young men. One was nineteen, the other two months beyond twenty. Both were legally old enough to vote, to drink alcoholic beverages, to drive a car. Neither would reach the age of Billy Kinetta.

One of them said, "Let's take the old man."

The other responded, "You think the guy in the trenchcoat'll get in the way?"

The first one smiled; and a mean little laugh. "I sure as shit hope so." He wore, on his right hand, a leather carnaby glove with the fingers cut off, small round metal studs in a pattern along the line of his knuckles. He made a fist, flexed, did it again.

They went under the spiked fence at a point where erosion had created a shallow gully. "Sonofabitch!" one of them said, as he slid through on his stomach. It was muddy. The front of his sateen roadie jacket was filthy. "Sonofabitch!" He was speaking in general of the fence, the sliding under, the muddy ground, the universe in total. And the old man, who would now *really* get the crap kicked out of him for making this fine sateen roadie jacket filthy.

They sneaked up on him from the left, as far from the young guy in the trenchcoat as they could. The first one kicked out the shooting stick with a short, sharp, downward movement he had learned in his tae kwon do class. It was called the *yup-chagi*. The old man went over backward.

Then they were on him, the one with the filthy sonofabitch sateen roadie jacket punching at the old man's neck and the side of his face as he dragged him around by the collar of the overcoat. The other one began ransacking the coat pockets, ripping the fabric to get his hand inside.

The old man commenced to scream. "Protect me! You've got to protect me . . . it's necessary to protect me!"

The one pillaging pockets froze momentarily. What the hell kind of thing is that for this old fucker to be saying? Who the hell does he think'll protect him? Is he asking *us* to protect him? I'll protect you, scumbag! I'll kick in your fuckin' lung! "Shut 'im up!" he whispered urgently to his friend. "Stick a fist in his mouth!" Then his hand, wedged in an inside jacket pocket, closed over something. He tried to get his hand loose, but the jacket and coat and the old man's body had wound around his wrist. "C'mon loose, motherfuckah!" he said to the very old man, who was still screaming for protection. The other young man was making huffing sounds, as dark as mud, as he slapped at the rain-soaked hair of his victim. "I can't . . . he's all twisted 'round . . . getcher hand outta there so's I can . . ." Screaming, the old man had doubled under, locking their hands on his person.

And then the pillager's fist came loose, and he was clutching—for an instant—a gorgeous pocket watch.

What used to be called a turnip watch.

The dial face was *cloisonné*, exquisite beyond the telling.

The case was of silver, so bright it seemed blue.

The hands, cast as arrows of time, were gold. They formed a shallow V at precisely eleven o'clock. This was happening at 3:45 in the afternoon, with rain and wind.

The timepiece made no sound, no sound at all.

Then: there was space all around the watch, and in that space in the palm of the hand, there was heat. Intense heat for just a moment, just long enough for the hand to open.

The watch glided out of the boy's palm and levitated.

"Help me! You *must* protect me!"

Billy Kinetta heard the shrieking but did not see the pocket watch floating in the air above the astonished young man. It was silver, and it was end-on toward him, and the rain was silver and slanting; and he did not see the watch hanging free in the air, even when the furious young man disentangled himself and leaped for it. Billy did not see the watch rise just so much, out of reach of the mugger.

Billy Kinetta saw two boys, two young men of ratpack age, beating someone much older; and he went for them. Pow, like that!

Thrashing his legs, the old man twisted around—over, under—as the boy holding him by the collar tried to land a punch to put him away. Who would have thought the old man to have had so much battle in him?

A flapping shape, screaming something unintelligible, hit the center of the group at full speed. The carnaby-gloved hand reaching for the watch grasped at empty air one moment, and the next was buried under its owner as the boy was struck a crackback block that threw him face-first into the soggy ground. He tried to rise, but something stomped him at the base of his spine; something kicked him twice in the kidneys; something rolled over him like a flash flood.

Twisting, twisting, the very old man put his thumb in the right eye of the boy clutching his collar.

The great trenchcoated mælstrom that was Billy Kinetta whirled into the boy as he let loose of the old man on the ground and, howling, slapped a palm against his stinging eye. Billy locked his fingers and delivered a roundhouse wallop that sent the boy reeling backward to fall over Minna's tilted headstone.

Billy's back was to the old man. He did not see the miraculous pocket watch smoothly descend through rain that did not touch it, to hover in front of the old man. He did not see the old man reach up, did not see the timepiece snuggle into an arthritic hand, did not see the old man return the turnip to an inside jacket pocket.

Wind, rain, and Billy Kinetta pummeled two young men of a legal age that made them accountable for their actions. There was no thought of the knife stuck down in one boot, no chance to reach it, no moment when the wild thing let them rise. So they crawled. They scrabbled across the muddy ground, the slippery grass, over graves, and out of his reach. They ran; falling, rising, falling again; away, without looking back.

Billy Kinetta, breathing heavily, knees trembling, turned to help the old man to his feet; and found him standing, brushing dirt from his overcoat, snorting in anger and mumbling to himself.

"Are you all right?"

For a moment the old man's recitation of annoyance continued, then he snapped his chin down sharply as if marking the end to the situation, and looked at his cavalry to the rescue. "That was very good, young fella. Considerable style you've got there."

Billy Kinetta stared at him wide-eyed. "Are you sure you're okay?" He reached over and flicked several blades of wet grass from the shoulder of the old man's overcoat.

"I'm fine. I'm fine but I'm wet and I'm cranky. Let's go somewhere and have a nice cup of Earl Grey."

There had been a look on Billy Kinetta's face as he stood with lowered eyes, staring at the grave he had come to visit. The emergency had removed that look. Now it returned.

"No, thanks. If you're okay, I've got to do some things."

The old man felt himself all over, meticulously, as he replied, "I'm only superficially bruised. Now if I were an old woman, instead of a spunky old man, same age, though, I'd have lost considerable of the calcium in my bones, and those two would have done me some mischief. Did you know that women lose a considerable part of their calcium when they reach my age? I read a report." Then he paused, and said shyly, "Come on, why don't you and I sit and chew the fat over a nice cup of tea?"

Billy shook his head with bemusement, smiling despite himself. "You're something else, Dad. I don't even know you."

"I like that."

"What: that I don't know you?"

"No, that you called me 'Dad' and not 'Pop.' I *hate* 'Pop.' Always makes me think the wise-apple wants to snap off my cap with a bottle opener. Now *Dad* has a ring of respect to it. I like that right down to the ground. Yes, I believe we should find someplace warm and quiet to sit and get to know each other. After all, you saved my life. And you know what that means in the Orient."

Billy was smiling continuously now. "In the first place, I doubt very much I saved your life. Your wallet, maybe. And in the second place, I don't even know your name; what would we have to talk about?"

"Gaspar," he said, extending his hand. "That's a first name. Gaspar. Know what it means?"

Billy shook his head.

"See, already we have something to talk about."

So Billy, still smiling, began walking Gaspar out of the cemetery. "Where do you live? I'll take you home."

They were on the street, approaching Billy Kinetta's 1979 Cutlass. "Where I live is too far for now. I'm beginning to feel a bit peaky. I'd like to lie down for a minute. We can just go on over to your place, if that doesn't bother you. For a few minutes. A cup of tea. Is that all right?"

He was standing beside the Cutlass, looking at Billy with an old man's expectant smile, waiting for him to unlock the door and hold it for him till he'd placed his still-calcium-rich but nonetheless old bones in the passenger seat. Billy stared at him, trying to figure out what was at risk if he unlocked that door. Then he snorted a tiny laugh, unlocked the door, held it for Gaspar as he seated himself, slammed it, and went around to unlock the other side and get in. Gaspar reached across and thumbed up the door lock knob. And they drove off together in the rain.

Through all of this the timepiece made no sound, no sound at all.

Like Gaspar, Billy Kinetta was alone in the world.

His three-room apartment was the vacuum in which he existed. It was furnished, but if one stepped out into the hallway and, for all the money in all the numbered accounts in all the banks in Switzerland, one were asked to describe those furnishings, one would come away no richer than before. The apartment was charisma poor. It was a place to come to when all other possibilities had been expended. Nothing green, nothing alive, existed in those boxes. No eyes looked back from the walls. Neither warmth nor chill marked those spaces. It was a place to wait.

Gaspar leaned his closed shooting stick, now a walking stick with handles, against the bookcase. He studied the titles of the paperbacks stacked haphazardly on the shelves.

From the kitchenette came the sound of water running into a metal pan. Then tin on cast iron. Then the hiss of gas and the flaring of a match as it was struck; and the pop of the gas being lit.

"Many years ago," Gaspar said, taking out a copy of Moravia's *Two Adolescents* and thumbing it as he spoke, "I had a library of books, oh, thousands of books—never could bear to toss one out, not even the bad ones—and when folks would come to the house to visit they'd look around at all the nooks and crannies stuffed with books; and if they were the sort of folks who don't snuggle with books, they'd always ask the same dumb question." He waited a moment for a response and when none was forthcoming (the sound of china cups on sink tile), he said, "Guess what the question was."

From the kitchen, without much interest: "No idea."

"They'd always ask it with the kind of voice people use in the presence of large sculptures in museums. They'd ask me, 'Have you read all these books?'" He waited again, but Billy Kinetta was not playing the game. "Well, young fella, after a while the same dumb question gets asked a million times, you get sorta snappish about it. And it came to annoy me more than a little bit. Till I finally figured out the right answer.

"And you know what that answer was? Go ahead, take a guess."

Billy appeared in the kitchenette doorway. "I suppose you told them you'd read a lot of them but not all of them."

Gaspar waved the guess away with a flapping hand. "Now, what good would that have done? They wouldn't know they'd asked a dumb question, but I didn't want to insult them, either. So when they'd ask if I'd read all those books, I'd say, 'Hell no. Who wants a library full of books you've already read?'"

Billy laughed despite himself. He scratched at his hair with idle pleasure and shook his head at the old man's verve. "Gaspar, you are a wild old man. You retired?"

The old man walked carefully to the most comfortable chair in the room, an overstuffed Thirties-style lounge that had been reupholstered many times before Billy Kinetta had purchased it at the American Cancer Society Thrift Shop. He sank into it with a sigh. "No, sir, I am not by any means retired. Still very active."

"Doing what, if I'm not prying?"

"Doing ombudsman."

"You mean, like a consumer advocate? Like Ralph Nader?"

"Exactly. I watch out for things. I listen, I pay some attention; and if I do it right, sometimes I can even make a little difference. Yes, like Mr. Nader. A very fine man."

"And you were at the cemetery to see a relative?"

Gaspar's face settled into an expression of loss. "My dear old girl. My wife, Minna. She's been gone, well, it was twenty years in January." He sat silently staring inward for a while, then: "She was everything to me. The nice part was that I knew how important we were to each other; we discussed, well, just *everything*. I miss that the most, telling her what's going on.

"I go to see her every other day.

"I used to go every day. But. It. Hurt. Too much."

They had tea. Gaspar sipped and said it was very nice, but had Billy ever tried Earl Grey? Billy said he didn't know what that was, and Gaspar said he would bring him a tin, that it was splendid. And they chatted. Finally, Gaspar asked, "And who were you visiting?"

Billy pressed his lips together. "Just a friend." And would say no more. Then he sighed and said, "Well, listen, I have to go to work."

"Oh? What do you do?"

The answer came slowly. As if Billy Kinetta wanted to be able to say that he was in computers, or owned his own business, or held a position of import. "I'm night manager at a 7-Eleven."

"I'll bet you meet some fascinating people coming in late for milk or one of those slushies," Gaspar said gently. He seemed to understand.

Billy smiled. He took the kindness as it was intended. "Yeah, the cream of high society. That is, when they're not threatening to shoot me through the head if I don't open the safe."

"Let me ask you a favor," Gaspar said. "I'd like a little sanctuary, if you think it's all right. Just a little rest. I could lie down on the sofa for a bit. Would that be all right? You trust me to stay here while you're gone, young fella?"

Billy hesitated only a moment. The very old man seemed okay, not a crazy, certainly not a thief. And what was there to steal? Some tea that wasn't even Earl Grey?

"Sure. That'll be okay. But I won't be coming back till two a.m. So just close the door behind you when you go; it'll lock automatically."

They shook hands, Billy shrugged into his still-wet trench-coat, and he went to the door. He paused to look back at Gaspar sitting in the lengthening shadows as evening came on. "It was nice getting to know you, Gaspar."

"You can make that a mutual pleasure, Billy. You're a nice young fella."

And Billy went to work, alone as always.

When he came home at two, prepared to open a can of Hormel chili, he found the table set for dinner; with the scent of an elegant beef stew enriching the apartment. There were new potatoes and stir-fried carrots and zucchini that had been lightly battered to delicate crispness. And cupcakes. White cake with chocolate frosting. From a bakery.

And in that way, as gently as that, Gaspar insinuated himself into Billy Kinetta's apartment and his life.

As they sat with tea and cupcakes, Billy said, "You don't have any place to go, do you?"

The old man smiled and made one of those deprecating movements of the head. "Well, I'm not the sort of fella who can bear to be homeless, but at the moment I'm what vaudevillians used to call 'at liberty.'"

"If you want to stay on a time, that would be okay," Billy said. "It's not very roomy here, but we seem to get on all right."

"That's strongly kind of you, Billy. Yes, I'd like to be your roommate for a while. Won't be too long, though. My doctor tells me I'm not long for this world." He paused, looked into the teacup and said softly, "I have to confess . . . I'm a little frightened. To go. Having someone to talk to would be a great comfort."

And Billy said, without preparation, "I was visiting the grave of a man who was in my rifle company in Vietnam. I go there sometimes." But there was such pain in his words that Gaspar did not press him for details.

So the hours passed, as they will with or without permission, and when Gaspar asked Billy if they could watch the television, to catch an early newscast, and Billy tuned in the old set just in time to pick up dire reports of another aborted disarmament talk, and Billy shook his head and observed that it wasn't only Gaspar who was frightened of something like death, Gaspar chuckled, patted Billy on the knee and said, with unassailable assurance, "Take my word for it, Billy . . . it isn't going to happen. No nuclear holocaust. Trust me, when I tell you this: it'll never happen. Never, never, not ever."

Billy smiled wanly. "And why not? What makes *you* so sure . . . got some special inside information?"

And Gaspar pulled out the magnificent timepiece, which Billy was seeing for the first time, and he said, "It's not going to happen because it's only eleven o'clock."

Billy stared at the watch, which read 11:00 precisely. He consulted his wristwatch. "Hate to tell you this, but your watch has stopped. It's almost five-thirty."

Gaspar smiled his own certain smile. "No, it's eleven." And they made up the sofa for the very old man, who placed his pocket change and his fountain pen and the sumptuous turnip watch on the now-silent television set, and they went to sleep.

One day Billy went off while Gaspar was washing the lunch dishes, and when he came back, he had a large paper bag from Toys R Us.

Gaspar came out of the kitchenette rubbing a plate with a souvenir dish towel from Niagara Falls, New York. He stared at Billy and the bag. "What's in the bag?" Billy inclined his head, and indicated the very old man should join him in the middle of the room. Then he sat down cross-legged on the floor and dumped the contents of the bag. Gaspar stared with startlement and sat down beside him.

So for two hours they played with tiny cars that turned into robots when the sections were unfolded.

Gaspar was excellent at figuring out all the permutations of the Transformers, Starriors, and GoBots. He played well.

Then they went for a walk. "I'll treat you to a matinee," Gaspar said. "But no films with Karen Black, Sandy Dennis, or Meryl Streep. They're always crying. Their noses are always red. I can't stand that."

They started to cross the avenue. Stopped at the light was this year's Cadillac Brougham, vanity license plates, ten coats of acrylic lacquer and two coats of clear (with a little retarder in the final "color coat" for a slow dry) of a magenta hue so rich that it approximated the shade of light shining through a decanter filled with Château Lafite-Rothschild 1945.

The man driving the Cadillac had no neck. His head sat thumped down hard on the shoulders. He stared straight ahead, took one last deep pull on the cigar, and threw it out the window. The still-smoking butt landed directly in front of Gaspar as he passed the car. The old man stopped, stared down at this coprolitic metaphor, and then stared at the driver. The eyes behind the wheel, the eyes of a macaque, did not waver from the stoplight's red circle. Just outside the window, someone was looking in, but the eyes of the rhesus were on the red circle.

A line of cars stopped behind the Brougham.

Gaspar continued to stare at the man in the Cadillac for a moment, and then, with creaking difficulty, he bent and picked up the smoldering butt of stogie.

The old man walked the two steps to the car—as Billy watched in confusion—thrust his face forward till it was mere inches from the driver's profile, and said with extreme sweetness, "I think you dropped this in our living room."

And as the glazed simian eyes turned to stare directly into the pedestrian's face, nearly nose-to-nose, Gaspar casually flipped the butt with its red glowing tip, into the back seat of the Cadillac, where it began to burn a hole in the fine Corinthian leather.

Three things happened simultaneously:

The driver let out a howl, tried to see the butt in his rearview mirror, could not get the angle, tried to look over his shoulder into the back seat but without a neck could not perform that feat of agility, put the car into neutral, opened his door and stormed into the street trying to grab Gaspar. "You fuckin' bastid, whaddaya think you're doin' tuh my car you asshole bastid, I'll kill ya . . ."

Billy's hair stood on end as he saw what Gaspar was doing; he rushed back the short distance in the crosswalk to grab the old man; Gaspar would not be dragged away, stood smiling with unconcealed pleasure at the mad bull rampaging and screaming of the hysterical driver. Billy yanked as hard as he could and Gaspar began to move away, around the front of the Cadillac, toward the far curb. Still grinning with octo-generic charm.

The light changed.

These three things happened in the space of five seconds, abetted by the impatient honking of the cars behind the Brougham; as the light turned green.

Screaming, dragging, honking, as the driver found he could not do three things at once: he could not go after Gaspar while the traffic was clanging at him; could not let go of the car door to crawl into the back seat from which now came the stench of charring leather that could not be rectified by an inexpensive Tijuana tuck'n'roll; could not save his back seat and at the same time stave off the hostility of a dozen drivers cursing and honking. He trembled there, torn three ways, doing nothing.

Billy dragged Gaspar.

Out of the crosswalk. Out of the street. Onto the curb. Up the side street. Into the alley. Through a backyard.

To the next street over away from the avenue.

Puffing with the exertion, Billy stopped at last, five houses up the street. Gaspar was still grinning, chuckling softly with unconcealed pleasure at his puckish ways. Billy turned on him with wild gesticulations and babble.

"You're *nuts*!"

"How about that?" the old man said, giving Billy an affectionate poke in the bicep.

"Nuts! Looney! That guy would've torn off your head! What the hell's wrong with you, old man? Are you out of your boots?"

"I'm not crazy. I'm responsible."

"Responsible!?! Res*pon*sible, fer chrissakes? For what? For all the butts every yotz throws into the street?"

The old man nodded. "For butts, and trash, and pollution, and toxic waste dumping in the dead of night; for bushes, and cactus, and the baobab tree; for pippin apples and even lima beans, which I despise. You show me someone who'll eat lima beans without being at gunpoint, I'll show you a pervert!"

Billy was screaming. "What the hell are you talking about?"

"I'm also responsible for dogs and cats and guppies and cockroaches and the president of the United States and Jonas Salk and your mother and the entire chorus line at the Sands Hotel in Las Vegas. Also their choreographer."

"Who do your think you are? God?"

"Don't be sacrilegious. I'm too old to wash your mouth out with laundry soap. Of course I'm not God. I'm just an old man. *But I'm responsible.*"

Gaspar started to walk away, toward the corner and the avenue, and a resumption of their route. Billy stood where the old man's words had pinned him.

"Come on, young fella," Gaspar said, walking backward to speak to him, "we'll miss the beginning of the movie. I hate that."

Billy had finished eating, and they were sitting in the dimness of the apartment, only the lamp in the corner lit. The old man had gone to the County Art Museum and had bought inexpensive prints—Max Ernst, Gérôme, Richard Dadd, a subtle Feininger—which he had mounted in Insta-Frames. They sat in silence for a time, relaxing; then murmuring trivialities in a pleasant undertone.

Finally, Gaspar said, "I've been thinking a lot about my dying. I like what Woody Allen said."

Billy slid to a more comfortable position in the lounger. "What was that?"

"He said: I don't mind dying, I just don't want to be there when it happens."

Billy snickered.

"I feel something like that, Billy. I'm not afraid to go, but I don't want to leave Minna entirely. The times I spend with her, talking to her, well, it gives me the feeling we're still in touch. When I go, that's the end of Minna. She'll be well and truly dead. We never had any children, almost everyone who knew us is gone, no relatives. And we never did anything important that anyone would put in a record book, so that's the end of us. For me, I don't mind; but I wish there was someone who knew about Minna . . . she was a remarkable person."

So Billy said, "Tell me. I'll remember for you."

Memories in no particular order. Some as strong as ropes that could pull the ocean ashore. Some that shimmered and swayed in the faintest breeze like spiderwebs. The entire person, all the little movements, that dimple that appeared when she was amused at something foolish he had said. Their youth together, their love, the procession of their days toward middle age. The small cheers and the pain of dreams never realized. So much about him as he spoke of her. His voice soft and warm and filled with a longing so deep and true that he had to stop frequently because the words broke and would not come out till he had thought away some of the passion. He thought of her and was glad. He had gathered her together, all her dowry of love and taking care of him, her clothes and the way she wore them, her favorite knickknacks, a few clever remarks: and he packed it all up and delivered it to a new repository.

The very old man gave Minna to Billy Kinetta for safekeeping.

Dawn had come. The light filtering in through the blinds was saffron. "Thank you, Dad," Billy said. He could not name the feeling that had taken him hours earlier. But he said this: "I've never had to be responsible for anything, or anyone, in my whole life. I never belonged to anybody . . . I don't know why. It didn't bother me, because I didn't know any other way to be."

Then his position changed, there in the lounger. He sat up in a way that Gaspar thought was important. As if Billy were about to open the secret box buried at his center. And Billy spoke so softly the old man had to strain to hear him.

"I didn't even know him.

"We were defending the airfield at Da Nang. Did I tell you we were 1st Battalion, 9th Marines? Charlie was massing for a big push out of Quang Ngai province, south of us. Looked as if they were going to try to take the provincial capital. My rifle company was assigned to protect the perimeter. They kept sending in patrols to bite us. Every day we'd lose some poor bastard who scratched his head when he shouldn't of. It was June, late in June, cold and a lot of rain. The foxholes were hip-deep in water.

"Flares first. Our howitzers started firing. Then the sky was full of tracers, and I started to turn toward the bushes when I heard something coming, and these two main-force regulars in dark blue uniforms came toward me. I could see them so clearly. Long black hair. All crouched over. And they started firing. And that goddam carbine seized up, wouldn't fire; and I pulled out the banana clip, tried to slap in another, but they saw me and just turned a couple of AK-47s on me . . . god, I remember everything slowed down . . . I looked at those things, seven-point-six-two-millimeter assault rifles they were . . . I got crazy for a second, tried to figure out in my own mind if they were Russian-made, or Chinese, or Czech, or North Korean. And it was so bright from the flares I could see them starting to squeeze off the rounds, and then from out of nowhere this lance corporal jumped out at them and yelled somedamnthing like, 'Hey, you VC fucks, looka here!' except it wasn't that . . . I never could recall what he said actually . . . and they turned to brace him . . . and they opened him up like a Baggie full of blood . . . and he was all over me, and the bushes, and oh god there was pieces of him floating on the water I was standing in . . ."

Billy was heaving breath with impossible weight. His hands moved in the air before his face without pattern or goal. He kept looking into far corners of the dawn-lit room as if special facts might present themselves to fill out the reasons behind what he was saying.

"Aw, geezus, he was *floating* on the water . . . aw, christ, *he got in my boots*!" Then a wail of pain so loud it blotted out the sound of traffic beyond the apartment; and he began to moan, but not cry; and the moaning kept on; and Gaspar came from the sofa and held him and said such words as *it's all right*, but they might not have been those words, or *any* words.

And pressed against the old man's shoulder, Billy Kinetta ran on only half sane: "He wasn't my friend, I never knew him, I'd never talked to him, but I'd seen him, he was just this guy, and there wasn't any reason to do that, he didn't know whether I was a good guy or a shit or anything, so why did he do that? He didn't need to do that. They wouldn't of seen him. He was dead before I killed them. He was gone already. I never got to say thank you or thank you or . . . *anything*!

"Now he's in that grave, so I came here to live, so I can go there, but I try and try to say thank you, and he's dead, and he can't hear me, he can't hear nothin', he's just down there, down in the ground, and I can't say thank you . . . oh, geezus, geezus, why don't you hear me, I just want to say thanks . . ."

Billy Kinetta wanted to assume the responsibility for saying thanks, but that was possible only on a night that would never come again; and this was the day.

Gaspar took him to the bedroom and put him down to sleep in exactly the same way he would soothe an old, sick dog.

Then he went to his sofa, and because it was the only thing he could imagine saying, he murmured, "He'll be all right, Minna. Really, he will."

When Billy left for the 7-Eleven the next evening, Gaspar was gone. It was an alternate day, and that meant he was out at the cemetery. Billy fretted that he shouldn't be there alone, but the old man had a way of taking care of himself. Billy was not smiling as he thought of his friend, and the word *friend* echoed as he realized that, yes, this was his friend, truly and really his friend. He wondered how old Gaspar was, and how soon Billy Kinetta would be once again what he had always been: alone.

When he returned to the apartment at two-thirty, Gaspar was asleep, cocooned in his blanket on the sofa. Billy went in and tried to sleep, but hours later, when sleep would not come, when thoughts of murky water and calcium night light on dark foliage kept him staring at the bedroom ceiling, he came out of the room for a drink of water. He wandered around the living room, not wanting to be by himself even if the only companionship in this sleepless night was breathing heavily, himself in sleep.

He stared out the window. Clouds in chiffon strips across the sky. The squealing of tires from the street.

Sighing, idle in his movement around the room, he saw the old man's pocket watch lying on the coffee table beside the sofa. He walked to the table. If the watch was still stopped at eleven o'clock, perhaps he would borrow it and have it repaired. It would be a nice thing to do for Gaspar. The old man loved that beautiful timepiece.

Billy bent to pick it up.

The watch, stopped at the V of eleven precisely, levitated at an angle, floating away from him.

Billy Kinetta felt a shiver travel down his back to burrow in at the base of his spine. He reached for the watch hanging in air before him. It floated away just enough that his fingers massaged empty space. He tried to catch it. The watch eluded him, lazily turning away like an opponent who knows he is in no danger of being struck from behind.

Then Billy realized Gaspar was awake. Turned away from the sofa, nonetheless he knew the old man was observing him. And the blissful floating watch.

He looked at Gaspar.

They did not speak for a long time.

Then: "I'm going back to sleep," Billy said. Quietly.

"I think you have some questions," Gaspar replied.

"Questions? No, of course not, Dad. Why in the world would I have questions? I'm still asleep." But that was not the truth, because he had not been asleep that night.

"Do you know what 'Gaspar' means? Do you remember the three wise men of the Bible, the Magi?"

"I don't want any frankincense and myrrh. I'm going back to bed. I'm going now. You see, I'm going right now."

"'Gaspar' means master of the treasure, keeper of the secrets, paladin of the palace." Billy was staring at him, not walking into the bedroom; just staring at him. As the elegant timepiece floated to the old man, who extended his hand palm-up to receive it. The watch nestled in his hand, unmoving, and it made no sound, no sound at all.

"You go back to bed. But will you go out to the cemetery with me tomorrow? It's important."

"Why?"

"Because I believe I'll be dying tomorrow."

It was a nice day, cool and clear. Not at all a day for dying, but neither had been many such days in Southeast Asia, and death had not been deterred.

They stood at Minna's gravesite, and Gaspar opened his shooting stick to form a seat; and he thrust the spike into the ground; and he settled onto it, and sighed, and said to Billy Kinetta, "I'm growing cold as that stone."

"Do you want my jacket?"

"No, I'm cold inside." He looked around at the sky, at the grass, at the rows of markers. "I've been responsible, for all of this, and more."

"You've said that before."

"Young fella, are you by any chance familiar, in your reading, with an old novel by James Hilton called *Lost Horizon*? Perhaps you saw the movie. It was a wonderful movie. It was a wonderful movie, actually much better than the book. Mr. Capra's greatest achievement. A human testament. Ronald Colman was superb. Do you know the story?"

"Yes."

"Do you remember the High Lama, played by Sam Jaffe? His name was Father Perrault?"

"Yes."

"Do you remember how he passed on the caretakership of that magical hidden world, Shangri-La, to Ronald Colman?"

"Yes, I remember that." Billy paused. "Then he died. He was very old, and he died."

Gaspar smiled up at him. "Very good, Billy. I knew you were a good boy. So now, if you remember all that, may I tell you a story? It's not a very long story."

Billy nodded, smiling at his friend.

"In 1582 Pope Gregory XIII decreed that the civilized world would no longer observe the Julian calendar. October 4th, 1582, was followed, the next day, by October 15th. Eleven days vanished from the world. One hundred and seventy years later, the British Parliament followed suit, and September 2nd, 1752, was followed, the next day, by September 14th. Why did he do that, the pope?"

Billy was bewildered by the conversation. "Because he was bringing it into synch with the real world. The solstices and equinoxes. When to plant, when to harvest."

Gaspar waggled a finger at him with pleasure. "Excellent, young fella. And you're correct when you say Gregory abolished the Julian calendar because its error of one day in every one hundred and twenty-eight years had moved the vernal equinox to March 11th. That's what the history books say. It's what *every* history book says. But what if?"

"What if *what*? I don't know what you're talking about."

"What if: Pope Gregory had the knowledge revealed to him that he *must* readjust time in the minds of men? What if: the excess time in 1582 was eleven days and one hour? What if: he accounted for those eleven days, vanished those eleven days, but that one hour slipped free, was left loose to bounce through eternity? A very special hour . . . an hour that must *never* be used . . . an hour that must never toll. What if?"

Billy spread his hands. "What if, what if, what if! It's all just philosophy. It doesn't mean anything. Hours aren't real, time isn't something that you can bottle up. So what if there *is* an hour out there somewhere that . . ."

And he stopped.

He grew tense and leaned down to the old man. "The watch. Your watch. It doesn't work. It's stopped."

Gaspar nodded, "At eleven o'clock. My watch works; it keeps very special time, for one very special hour."

Billy touched Gaspar's shoulder. Carefully he asked, "Who are you, Dad?"

The old man did not smile as he said. "Gaspar. Keeper. Paladin. Guardian."

"Father Perrault was hundreds of years old."

Gaspar shook his head with a wistful expression on his old face. "I'm eighty-six years old, Billy. You asked me if I thought I was God. Not God, not Father Perrault, not an immortal, just an old man who will die too soon. Are you Ronald Colman?"

Billy nervously touched his lower lip with a finger. He looked at Gaspar as long as he could, then turned away. He walked off a few paces, stared at the barren trees. It seemed suddenly much chillier here in this place of entombed remembrances. From a distance he said, "But it's only . . . what? A chronological convenience. Like daylight saving time; Spring forward, Fall back. We don't actually *lose* an hour; we get it back."

Gaspar stared at Minna's grave. "At the end of April I lost an hour. If I die now, I'll die an hour short in my life. I'll have been cheated out of one hour I want, Billy." He swayed toward all he had left of Minna. "One last hour I could have with my old girl.

That's what I'm afraid of, Billy. I have that hour in my possession. I'm afraid I'll use it, god help me, I want so much to use it."

Billy came to him. Tense, and chilled, he said, "Why must that hour never toll?"

Gaspar drew a deep breath and tore his eyes away from the grave. His gaze locked with Billy's. And he told him.

The years, all the days and hours, exist. As solid and as real as mountains and oceans and men and women and the baobab tree. Look, he said, at the lines in my face and deny that time is real. Consider these dead weeds that were once alive and try to believe it's all just vapor or the mutual agreement of popes and caesars and young men like you.

"The lost hour must never come, Billy, for in that hour it all ends. The light, the wind, the stars, this magnificent open place we call the universe. It all ends, and in its place—waiting, always waiting—is eternal darkness. No new beginnings, no world without end, just the infinite emptiness."

And he opened his hand, which had been lying in his lap, and there, in his palm, rested the watch, making no sound at all, and stopped dead at eleven o'clock. "Should it strike twelve, Billy, eternal night falls; from which there is no recall."

There he sat, this very old man, just a perfectly normal old man. The most recent in the endless chain of keepers of the lost hour, descended in possession from Caesar and Pope Gregory XIII, down through the centuries of men and women who had served as caretakers of the excellent timepiece. And now he was dying, and now he wanted to cling to life as every man and woman clings to life no matter how awful or painful or empty, even if it is for one more hour. The suicide, falling from the bridge, at the final instant, tries to fly, tries to climb back up the sky. This weary old man, who only wanted to stay one brief hour more with Minna. Who was afraid that his love would cost the universe.

He looked at Billy, and he extended his hand with the watch waiting for its next paladin. So softly Billy could barely hear him, knowing that he was denying himself what he most wanted at this last place in his life, he whispered, "If I die without passing it on . . . it will begin to tick."

"Not me," Billy said. "Why did you pick me? I'm no one special. I'm not someone like you. I run an all-night service mart. There's nothing special about me the way there is about you! I'm *not* Ronald Colman! I don't want to be responsible, I've *never* been responsible!"

Gaspar smiled gently. "You've been responsible for me."

Billy's rage vanished. He looked wounded.

"Look at us, Billy. Look at what color you are; and look at what color I am. You took me in as a friend. I think of you as worthy, Billy. Worthy."

They remained there that way, in silence, as the wind rose. And finally, in a timeless time, Billy nodded.

Then the young man said, "You won't be losing Minna, Dad. Now you'll go to the place where she's been waiting for you, just as she was when you first met her. There's a place where we find everything we've ever lost through the years."

"That's good, Billy, that you tell me that. I'd like to believe it, too. But I'm a pragmatist. I believe in what exists . . . like rain and Minna's grave and the hours that pass that we can't see, but they *are*. I'm afraid, Billy. I'm afraid this will be the last time I can speak to her. So I ask a favor. As payment, in return for my life spent protecting the watch.

"I ask for one minute of the hour, Billy. One minute to call her back so we can stand face-to-face and I can touch her and say goodbye. You'll be the new protector of this watch, Billy, so I ask you please, just let me steal one minute."

Billy could not speak. The look on Gaspar's face was without horizon, empty as tundra, bottomless. The child left alone in darkness; the pain of eternal waiting. He knew he could never deny this old man, no matter what he asked, and in the silence he heard a voice say: *"No!"* And it was his own.

He had spoken without conscious volition. Strong and determined, and without the slightest room for reversal. If a part of his heart had been swayed by compassion, that part had been instantly overridden. No. A final, unshakeable no.

For an instant Gaspar looked crestfallen. His eyes clouded with tears; and Billy felt something twist and break within himself at the sight. He knew he had hurt the old man. Quickly, but softly, he said urgently, "You know that would be wrong, Dad. We mustn't . . ."

Gaspar said nothing. Then he reached out with his free hand and took Billy's. It was an affectionate touch.

"That was the last test, young fella. Oh, you know I've been testing you, don't you? This important item couldn't go to just anyone.

"And you passed the test, my friend: my last, best friend. When I said I could bring her back from where she's gone, here in this place we've both come to so often, to talk to someone lost to us, I knew you would understand that *anyone* could be brought back in that stolen minute. I knew you wouldn't use it for yourself, no matter how much you wanted it; but I wasn't sure that as much as you like me, it might not sway you. But you wouldn't even give it to *me*, Billy."

He smiled up at him, his eyes now clear and steady.

"I'm content, Billy. You needn't have worried. Minna and I don't need that minute. But if you're to carry on for me, I think you *do* need it. You're in pain, and that's no good for someone who carries this watch. You've got to heal, Billy.

"So I give you something you would never take for yourself. I give you a going-away present . . ."

And he started the watch, whose ticking was as loud and as clear as a baby's first sound; and the sweep-second hand began to move away from eleven o'clock.

Then the wind rose, and the sky seemed to cloud over, and it grew colder, with a remarkable silver-blue mist that rolled across the cemetery; and though he did not see it emerge from that grave at a distance far to the right, Billy Kinetta saw a shape move toward him. A soldier in the uniform of a day past, and his rank was lance corporal. He came toward Billy Kinetta, and Billy went to meet him as Gaspar watched.

They stood together and Billy spoke to him. And the man whose name Billy had never known when he was alive, answered. And then he faded, as the seconds ticked away. Faded, and faded, and was gone. And the silver-blue mist rolled through them, and past them, and was gone; and the soldier was gone.

Billy stood alone.

When he turned back to look across the grounds to his friend, he saw that Gaspar had fallen from the shooting-stick. He lay on the ground. Billy rushed to him and fell to his knees and lifted him onto his lap. Gaspar was still.

"Oh, god, Dad, you should have heard what he said. Oh, geez, he let me go. He let me go so I didn't even have to say I was sorry. He told me he didn't even *see* me in that foxhole. He never knew he'd saved my life. I said thank you and he said no, thank *you*, that he hadn't died for nothing. Oh, please, Dad, please don't be dead yet. I want to tell you . . ."

And, as it sometimes happens, rarely but wonderfully, sometimes they come back for a moment, for an instant before they go, the old man, this very old man, opened his eyes, just before going on his way, and he looked through the dimming light at his friend, and he said, "May I remember you to my old girl, Billy?"

And his eyes closed again, after only a moment; and his caretakership was at an end; as his hand opened and the most excellent timepiece, now stopped again at one minute past eleven, floated from his palm and waited till Billy Kinetta extended his hand; and then it floated down and lay there silently, making no sound, no sound at all. Safe. Protected.

There in the place where all lost things returned, the young man sat on the cold ground, rocking the body of his friend. And he was in no hurry to leave. There was time.

A blessing of the 18th Egyptian Dynasty:

God be between you and harm
in all the empty places you walk.

The author gratefully acknowledges the importance of a discussion with Ms. Ellie Grossman in the creation of this work of fiction.

The Beast That Shouted Love at the Heart of the World

After an idle discussion with the pest control man who came once a month to spray around the outside of his home in the Ruxton section of Baltimore, William Sterog stole a canister of malathion, a deadly insecticide poison, from the man's truck, and went out early one morning, following the route of the neighborhood milkman, and spooned medium-large quantities into each bottle left on the rear doorstep of seventy homes. Within six hours of Bill Sterog's activities, two hundred men, women, and children died in convulsive agony.

Learning that an aunt who had lived in Buffalo was dying of cancer of the lymph glands, William Sterog hastily helped his mother pack three bags and took her to Friendship Airport, where he put her on an Eastern Airlines jet with a simple but efficient time bomb made from a Westclox Travalarm and four sticks of dynamite in her three-suiter. The jet exploded somewhere over Harrisburg, Pennsylvania. Ninety-three people—including Bill Sterog's mother—were killed in the explosion, and flaming wreckage added seven to the toll by cascading down on a public swimming pool.

On a Sunday in November, William Sterog made his way to Babe Ruth Plaza on 33rd Street where he became one of 54,000 fans jamming Memorial Stadium to see the Baltimore Colts play the Green Bay Packers. He was dressed warmly in gray flannel slacks, a navy blue turtleneck pullover, and a heavy hand-knitted Irish wool sweater under his parka. With three minutes and thirteen seconds of the fourth quarter remaining to be played, and Baltimore trailing seventeen to sixteen on Green Bay's eighteen yard line, Bill Sterog found his way up the aisle to the exit above the mezzanine seats and fumbled under his parka for the U.S. Army surplus M-3 submachine gun he had bought for $49.95 from a mail order armaments dealer in Alexandria, Virginia. Even as 53,999 screaming fans leaped to their feet—making his range of fire that much better—as the ball was snapped to the quarterback, holding for the defensive tackle most able to kick a successful field goal, Bill Sterog opened fire on the massed backs of the fans below him. Before the mob could bring him down, he had killed forty-four people.

When the first Expeditionary Force to the elliptical galaxy in Sculptor descended on the second planet of a fourth magnitude star the Force had designated Flammarion Theta, they found a thirty-seven-foot-high statue of a hitherto-unknown blue-white substance—not quite stone, something like metal—in the shape of a man. The figure was barefoot, draped in a garment that vaguely resembled a toga, the head encased in a skull-tight cap, and holding in its left hand a peculiar ring-and-ball device of another substance altogether. The statue's face was curiously beatific. It had high cheekbones; deep-set eyes; a tiny, almost alien mouth; and a broad, large-nostriled nose. The statue loomed enormous among the pitted and blasted curvilinear structures of some forgotten architect. The members of the Expeditionary Force commented on the peculiar expression each noted on the face of the statue. None of these men, standing under a gorgeous brass moon that shared an evening sky with a descending sun quite dissimilar in color to the one that now shone wanly on an Earth unthinkably distant in time and space, had ever heard of William Sterog. And so none of them was able to say that the expression on the giant statue was the same as the one Bill Sterog had shown as he told the final appeals judge who was about to sentence him to death in the lethal gas chamber, "I love everyone in the world. I do. So help me God, I love you, all of you!" He was shouting.

Crosswhen, through interstices of thought called time, through reflective images called space; another then, another now. This place, over *there*. Beyond concepts, the transmogrification of simplicity finally labeled *if*. Forty and more steps sidewise but later, much later. There, in that ultimate center, with everything radiating outward, becoming infinitely more complex, the enigma of symmetry, harmony, apportionment singing with fine-tuned order in *this* place, where it all began, begins, will always begin. The center. Crosswhen.

Or: a hundred million years in the future. And: a hundred million parsecs beyond the farthest edge of measurable space. And: parallax warpages beyond counting across the universes of parallel existences. Finally: an infinitude of mind-triggered leaps beyond human thought.

There: Crosswhen.

On the mauve level, crouched down in deeper magenta washings that concealed his arched form, the maniac waited. He was a dragon, squat and round in the torso, tapered ropey tail tucked under his body; the small, thick osseous shields rising perpendicularly from the arched back, running down to the end of the tail, tips pointing upward; his taloned shorter arms folded across his massive chest. He had the seven-headed dog faces of an ancient Cerberus. Each head watched, waiting, hungry, insane.

He saw the bright yellow wedge of light as it moved in random patterns through the mauve, always getting closer. He knew he could not run, the movement would betray him, the specter light finding him instantly. Fear choked the maniac. The specter light had pursued him through innocence and humility and nine other emotional obfuscations he had tried. He had to do something, get them off his scent. But he was alone on this level. It had been closed down some time before, to purge it of residue emotions. Had he not been so terribly confused after the killings, had he not been drowning in disorientation, he would never have trapped himself on a closed level.

Now that he was here, there was nowhere to hide, nowhere to escape the specter light that would systematically hunt him down. Then they would purge *him*.

The maniac took the one final chance; he closed down his mind, all seven brains, even as the mauve level was closed down. He shut off all thought, banked the fires of emotion, broke the neural circuits that fed power to his mind. Like a great machine phasing down from peak efficiency, his thoughts slackened and wilted and grew pale. Then there was a blank where he had been. Seven dog-heads slept.

The dragon had ceased to exist in terms of thought, and the specter light washed past him, finding nothing there to home in on. But those who sought the maniac were sane, not deranged as he was: their sanity was ordered, and in order they considered every exigency. The specter light was followed by heat-seeking beams, by mass-tallying sensors, by trackers that could hunt out the spoor of foreign matter on a closed-down level.

They found the maniac. Shut down like a sun gone cold, they located him, and transferred him; he was unaware of the movement; he was locked away in his own silent skulls.

But when he chose to open his thoughts again, in the timeless disorientation that follows a total shutdown, he found himself locked in stasis in a drainage ward on the 3rd Red Active Level. Then, from seven throats, he screamed.

The sound, of course, was lost in the throat baffles they had inserted, before he had turned himself back on. The emptiness of the sound terrified him even more.

He was imbedded in an amber substance that fit around him comfortably; had it been a much earlier era, on another world, in another continuum, it would have been simply a hospital bed with restraining straps. But the dragon was locked in stasis on a red level, crosswhen. His hospital bed was anti-grav, weightless, totally relaxing, feeding nutrients through his leathery hide along with depressants and toners. He was waiting to be drained.

Linah drifted into the ward, followed by Semph. Semph, the discoverer of the drain. And his most eloquent nemesis, Linah, who sought Public Elevation to the position of Proctor. They drifted down the rows of amber-encased patients: the toads, the tambour-lidded crystal cubes, the exoskeletals, the pseudopodal changers, and the seven-headed dragon. They paused directly in front and slightly above the maniac. He was able to look up at them; images seven times seen; but he was not able to make sound.

"If I needed a conclusive reason, here's one of the best," Linah said, inclining his head toward the maniac.

Semph dipped an analysis rod into the amber substance, withdrew it and made a hasty reading of the patient's condition. "If you needed a greater *warning*," Semph said quietly, "this would be one of the best."

"Science bends to the will of the masses," Linah said.

"I'd hate to have to believe that," Semph responded quickly. There was a tone in his voice that could not be named, but it undershadowed the aggressiveness of his words.

"I'm going to see to it, Semph; *believe it*. I'm going to have the Concord pass the resolution."

"Linah, how long have we known each other?"

"Since your third flux. My second."

"That's about right. Have I ever told you a lie, have I ever asked you to do something that would harm you?"

"No. Not that I can recall."

"Then why won't you listen to me *this* time?"

"Because I think you're wrong. I'm not a fanatic, Semph. I'm not making political hay with this. I feel very strongly that it's the best chance we've ever had."

"But disaster for everyone and everywhere else, all the way back, and God only knows how far across the parallax. We stop fouling our own nest, at the expense of all the other nests that ever were."

Linah spread his hands in futility. "Survival."

Semph shook his head slowly, with a weariness that was mirrored in his expression. "I wish I could drain *that*, too."

"Can't you?"

Semph shrugged. "I can drain *any*thing. But what we'd have left wouldn't be worth having."

The amber substance changed hue. It glowed deep within itself with a blue intensity. "The patient is ready," Semph said. "Linah, one more time. I'll beg if it'll do any good. Please. Stall till the next session. The Concord needn't do it *now*. Let me run some further tests, let me see how far back this garbage spews, how much damage it can cause. Let me prepare some reports."

Linah was firm. He shook his head in finality. "May I watch the draining with you?"

Semph let out a long sigh. He was beaten and knew it. "Yes, all right."

The amber substance carrying its silent burden began to rise. It reached the level of the two men and slid smoothly through the air between them. They drifted after the smooth container with the dog-headed dragon imbedded in it, and Semph seemed as though he wanted to say something else. But there was nothing to say.

The amber chrysalloid cradle faded and vanished, and the men became insubstantial and were no more. They all reappeared in the drainage chamber. The beaming stage was empty. The amber cradle settled down on it without sound, and the substance flowed away, vanishing as it uncovered the dragon.

The maniac tried desperately to move, to heave himself up. Seven heads twitched futilely. The madness in him overcame the depressants and he was consumed with frenzy, fury, crimson hate. But he could not move. It was all he could do to hold his shape.

Semph turned the band on his left wrist. It glowed from within, a deep gold. The sound of air rushing to fill a vacuum filled the chamber. The beaming stage was drenched in silver light that seemed to spring out of the air itself, from an unknown source. The dragon was washed by the silver light, and the seven great mouths opened once, exposing rings of fangs. Then his double-lidded eyes closed.

The pain within his heads was monstrous. A fearful wrenching that became the sucking of a million mouths. His very brains were pulled upon, pressured, compressed, and then purged.

Semph and Linah looked away from the pulsing body of the dragon to the drainage tank across the chamber. It was filling from the bottom as they watched. Filling with a nearly colorless roiling cloud of smokiness, shot through with sparks. "Here it comes," Semph said, needlessly.

Linah dragged his eyes away from the tank. The dragon with seven dog heads was rippling. As though seen through shallow water, the maniac was beginning to alter. As the tank filled, the maniac found it more and more difficult to maintain his shape. The denser grew the cloud of sparkling matter in the tank, the less constant was the shape of the creature on the beaming stage.

Finally, it was impossible, and the maniac gave in. The tank filled more rapidly, and the shape quavered and altered and shrank and then there was a superimposition of the form of a man, over that of the seven-headed dragon. Then the tank reached three-quarters filled and the dragon became an underlying shadow, a hint, a suggestion of what had been there when the drainage began. Now the man-form was becoming more dominant by the second.

Finally, the tank was filled, and a normal man lay on the beaming stage, breathing heavily, eyes closed, muscles jumping involuntarily.

"He's drained," Semph said.

"Is it all in the tank?" Linah asked softly.

"No, none of it."

"Then . . . ?"

"This is the residue. Harmless. Reagents purged from a group of sensitives will neutralize it. The dangerous essences, the degenerate force-lines that make up the field . . . they're gone. Drained off already."

Linah looked disturbed, for the first time. "Where did it go?"

"Do you love your fellow man, tell me?"

"Please, Semph! I asked where it went . . . when it went?"

"And I asked if you cared at all about anyone else?"

"You know my answer . . . you know *me*! I want to know, tell me, at least what you know. Where . . . when . . . ?"

"Then you'll forgive me, Linah, because I love my fellow man, too. Whenever he was, wherever he is; I have to, I work in an inhuman field, and I have to cling to that. So . . . you'll forgive me . . ."

"What are you going to . . ."

In Indonesia they have a phrase for it: Djam Karet—*the hour that stretches.*

In the Vatican's Stanza of Heliodorus, the second of the great rooms he designed for Pope Julius II, Raphael painted (and his pupils completed) a magnificent fresco representation of the historic meeting between Pope Leo I and Attila the Hun, in the year 452.

In this painting is mirrored the belief of Christians everywhere that the spiritual authority of Rome protected her in that desperate hour when the Hun came to sack and burn the Holy City. Raphael has painted in Saint Peter and Saint Paul, descending from Heaven to reinforce Pope Leo's intervention. His interpretation was an elaboration on the original legend, in which only the Apostle Peter was mentioned—standing behind Leo with a drawn sword. And the legend was an elaboration of what little facts have come down through antiquity relatively undistorted: Leo had no cardinals with him, and certainly no wraith Apostles. He was one of three in the deputation. The other two were secular dignitaries of the Roman state. The meeting did not take place—as legend would have us believe—just outside the gates of Rome, but in northern Italy, not far from what is today Peschiera.

Nothing more than this is known of the confrontation. Yet Attila, who had never been stopped, did not raze Rome. He turned back.

Djam Karet. The force-line field spewed out from a parallax center crosswhen, a field that had pulsed through time and space and the minds of men for twice ten thousand years. Then cut out suddenly, inexplicably, and Attila the Hun clapped his hands to his head, his mind twisting like rope within his skull. His eyes glazed, then cleared, and he breathed from deep in his chest. Then he signaled his army to turn back. Leo the Great thanked God and the living memory of Christ the Savior. Legend added Saint Peter. Raphael added Saint Paul.

For twice ten thousand years—*Djam Karet*—the field had pulsed, and for a brief moment that could have been instants or years or millennia, it was cut off.

Legend does not tell the truth. More specifically, it does not tell *all* of the truth: forty years before Attila raided Italy, Rome had been taken and sacked by Alaric the Goth. *Djam Karet.* Three years after the retreat of Attila Rome was once more taken and sacked, by Gaiseric, king of all the Vandals.

There was a reason the garbage of insanity had ceased to flow through everywhere and everywhen from the drained mind of a seven-headed dragon . . .

Semph, traitor to his race, hovered before the Concord. His friend, the man who now sought his final flux, Linah, proctored the hearing. He spoke softly, but eloquently, of what the great scientist had done.

"The tank was draining; he said to me, 'Forgive me, because I love my fellow man. Whenever he was, wherever he is; I have to, I work in an inhuman field, and I have to cling to that. So you'll forgive me.' Then he interposed himself."

The sixty members of the Concord, a representative from each race that existed in the center, bird-creatures and blue things and large-headed men and orange scents with cilia shuddering . . . all of them looked at Semph where he hovered. His body and head were crumpled like a brown paper bag. All hair was gone. His eyes were dim and watery. Naked, shimmering, he drifted slightly to one side, then a vagrant breeze in the wall-less chamber sent him back. He had drained himself.

"I ask for this Concord to affix sentence of final flux on this man. Though his interposition only lasted a few moments, we have no way of knowing what damage or unnaturalness it may have caused crosswhen. I submit that his intent was to overload the drain and thereby render it inoperative. This act, the act of a beast who would condemn the sixty races of the center to a future in which insanity still prevailed, is an act that can only be punished by termination."

The Concord blanked and meditated. A timeless time later they re-linked, and the proctor's charges were upheld; his demand of sentence was fulfilled.

On the hushed shores of a thought, the papyrus man was carried in the arms of his friend, his executioner, the proctor. There in the dusting quiet of an approaching night, Linah laid Semph down in the shadow of a sigh.

"Why did you stop me?" the wrinkle with a mouth asked.

Linah looked away across the rushing dark.

"Why?"

"Because here, in the center, there is a chance."

"And for them, all of them out there . . . no chance ever?"

Linah sat down slowly, digging his hands into the golden mist, letting it sift over his wrists and back into the waiting flesh of the world. "If we can begin it here, if we can pursue our boundaries outward, then perhaps one day, sometime, we can reach to the ends of time with that little chance. Until then, it is better to have one center where there is no madness."

Semph hurried his words. The end was rapidly striding for him. "You have sentenced them all. Insanity is a living vapor. A force. It can be bottled. The most potent genie in the most easily uncorked bottle. And you have condemned them to live with it always. In the name of love."

Linah made a sound that was not quite a word, but called it back. Semph touched his wrist with a tremble that had been a hand. Fingers melting into softness and warmth. "I'm sorry for you, Linah. Your curse is to be a true man. The world is made for strugglers. You never learned how to do that."

Linah did not reply. He thought only of the drainage that was eternal now. Set in motion and kept in motion by its necessity.

"Will you do a memorial for me?" Semph asked.

Linah nodded. "It's traditional."

Semph smiled softly. "Then do it for them; not for me. I'm the one who devised the vessel of their death, and I don't need it. But choose one of them; not a very important one, but one that will mean everything to them if they find it and understand. Erect the memorial in my name to that one. Will you?"

Linah nodded.

"Will you?" Semph asked. His eyes were closed, and he could not see the nod.

"Yes. I will," Linah said. But Semph could not hear. The flux began and ended, and Linah was alone in the cupped silence of loneliness.

The statue was placed on a far planet of a far star in a time that was ancient while yet never having been born. It existed in the minds of men who would come later. Or never.

But if they did, they would know that hell was with them, that there was a Heaven that men called Heaven, and in it there was a center from which all madness flowed; and once within that center, there was peace.

In the remains of a blasted building that had been a shirt factory, in what had been Stuttgart, Friedrich Drucker found a many-colored box. Maddened by hunger and the memory of having eaten human flesh for weeks, the man tore at the lid of the box with the bloodied stubs of his fingers. As the box flew open, pressed at a certain point, cyclones rushed out past the terrified face of Friedrich Drucker. Cyclones and dark, winged, faceless shapes that streaked away into the night, followed by a last wisp of purple smoke smelling strongly of decayed gardenias.

But Friedrich Drucker had little time to ponder the meaning of the purple smoke, for the next day, World War IV broke out.

I'm Looking for Kadak

You'll pardon me but my name is Evsise and I'm standing here in the middle of sand, talking to a butterfly, and if I sound like I'm talking to myself, again you'll pardon but what can I tell you? A grown person standing talking to a butterfly. In sand.

So *nu*? What else can you expect? There are times you got to make adjustments, you got to let be a little. Just to get along. I'm not all that happy about this, if you want the specific truth. I've learned, God knows I've learned. I'm a Jew, and if there is a thing Jews have learned in a *bissel* more than six thousand years, it's that you got to compromise if you want to make it to seven thousand. So, let be. I'll talk to this butterfly, hey, you butterfly, and I'll pray for the best.

You don't understand. You got that look.

Listen: I read once in a book that they found a tribe of Jewish Indians, somewhere deep in the heart of South America. That was on the Earth. The Earth, *shtumie*! It's been in all the papers.

So. Jewish Indians. What a thing! And everyone wondered and yelled and made such a *mishegoss* that they had to send historians and sociologists and anthropologists and all manner of very learned types to establish if this was a true thing or maybe somebody was just lying.

And what they found was that maybe what had happened was that some *galus* from Spain, fleeing the Inquisition, got on board with Cortés and came to the New World, *kayn-ahora*, and when no one was looking, he ran away. So then he got *farblondjet* and wound up in some little place full of very suggestible native types, and being something of a *tummeler* he started teaching them about being Jewish—just to keep busy, you know what I mean? because

Jews have never been missionaries, none of that "converting" crap *other*, I shouldn't name names, religions need to keep going, unlike Judaism which does very cute thank you on its own—and by the time all the smart-alecks found the tribe, they were keeping kosher, and having *brises* when the sons were born, and observing the High Holy Days, and not doing any fishing on the *Shabbes*, and it was a very nice thing altogether.

So it shouldn't surprise anyone that there are Jews here on Zsouchmuhn. Zoochhhhhh-moooohn. With a *chhhhh*, not a *kuh*. You got a no-accent like a Litvak.

It shouldn't even surprise that I'm a Jew and I'm blue and I have eleven arms thereby defying the Law of Bilateral Symmetry and I am squat and round and move very close to the ground by a series of caterpillar feet set around the rim of ball joints and sockets on either side of my *tuchis* which *obeys* the Law of Bilateral Symmetry and when I've wound the feet tight I have to jump off the ground so they can unwind and then I move forward again which makes my movement very peculiar I'm told by tourists without very much class.

In the Universal Ephemeris I am referred to as a native of Theta 996:VI, Cluster Messier 3 in Canes Venatici. The VI is Zsouchmuhn. A Baedeker from some publisher in the Crab came here a few turns ago and wrote a travel pamphlet on Zsouchmuhn; he kept calling me a Zsouchmoid; he should grow in the ground, headfirst like a turnip. I am a Jew.

I don't know what a turnip is.

Now I'm raving. What it'll do to you, talking to a butterfly. I have a mission, and it's making me crazy, giving me *shpilkess*, you could die from a mission like this. I'm looking for Kadak.

Hey, you butterfly! A blink, a flutter, a movement it wouldn't hurt, you should make an indication you can hear me, I shouldn't stand like a *schlemiel* telling you all this.

Nothing. You wouldn't give me a break.

Listen: if it wasn't for that *oysvorf*, that bum, Snodle, I wouldn't be here. I would be with my family and my lust-nest concubines on Theta 996:III, what the Ephemeris calls Bromios, what we Jews call Kasrilevka. There is historical precedent for our naming Bromios another name, Kasrilevka. You'll read Sholom Aleichem, you'll understand. A planet for *schlimazels*. I don't want to discuss it. That's where they're moving us. Everyone went. A few crazy ones stayed, there are always a few. But mostly, everyone went: who would want to stay? They're moving Zsouchmuhn. God knows where. Every time you look around they're dragging a place off and putting it somewhere else. I don't want to go into that. Terrible people, they got no hearts in them.

So we were sitting in the *yeshiva*, the last ten of us, a proper *minyan*, getting ready to sit *shivah* for the whole planet, for the last days we would be here, when that *oysvorf* Snodle had a seizure and up and died. Oh, a look: a question, maybe? Why were we sitting *shivah* in the rabbinical college when everybody else was running like a thief to get off the planet before those *gonifs* from the Relocation Center came with their skyhooks, a *glitch* if ever I saw one, shady, disreputable, to give a yank and drag a place out of orbit and give a shove and jam in big *meshiginah* magnets to float around where a nice, cute world was, just to keep the Cluster running smooth, when they pull out a world everything shouldn't go bump together . . . ? Why, you ask me. So, I'll tell you why.

Because, Mr. I-Won't-Talk-Or-Even-Flap-My-Wings Butterfly, *shivah* is the holiest of the holies. Because the Talmud says when you mourn the dead you get ten Jewish men who come to the home of the deceased, not eight or seven or four, but *ten* men, and you sit and you pray, and you hold services, and you light the *yorzeit* candles, and you recite the *Kaddish* which as every intelligent life-form in the Cluster except maybe a nut butterfly knows, is the prayer for the dead, in honor and praise of God and the deceased.

And why do we want to sit *shivah* for a world that was such a good home for us for so many turns? Because, and it strikes me foolishness to expect a *farchachdah* butterfly to grasp what I'm trying to say here, because God has been good to us here, and we've property (which now is gone) and we've got families (which now are gone) and we've got our health (which, if I continue talking to you I'll be losing shortly) and God's name can be hallowed by word of mouth only in the presence of others—the community of worshippers—the congregation—the *minyan* of ten, and *that's* why.

You know, even for a butterfly, you don't *look* Jewish.

So *nu*, now you understand a little, maybe? Zsouchmuhn was the *goldeneh medina* for us, the golden country; it was good here, we were happy here, now we have to move to Kasrilevka, a world for *schlimazels*. Not even a Red Sea to be parted, it isn't slavery, it's just a world that's not enough, you know what I mean? So we wanted to pay last respects. It's not so crazy. And everyone went, and only the ten of us left to sit the seven turns till we went away and Zsouchmuhn was *goniffed* out of the sky to go God-knows-where. It would have been fine, except for that Snodle, that crazy. Who seized up and died on us.

So where would we get a tenth man for the *minyan*?

There were only nine Jews on the whole planet.

Then Snodle said, "There's always Kadak."

"Shut up, you're dead," Reb Jeshaia said, but it didn't do any good. Snodle kept suggesting Kadak.

You should understand, one of the drawbacks of my species, which maybe a butterfly wouldn't know, is that when we die, and pass on, there's still talking. *Nuhdzhing*. Oh. You want to know how that can be. How a dead Jew can talk, through the veil, from the other side. What am I, a science authority, I should know how that works? I wouldn't lie on you: I don't know. Always it's been the same. One of us seizes up and dies, and the body squats there and doesn't decay the way the tourists' do when they get *shikker* in a blind pig bar in downtown Houmitz and stagger out in the gutter and get knocked over by a tumbrel on the way to the casinos.

But the voice starts up. *Nuhdzhing!*

It probably has something to do with the soul, but I wouldn't put a bet on that; all I can say is thank God we don't worship ancestors here on Zsouchmuhn, because we'd have such a sky full of *nuhdzhing* old farts telling us how to run our lives, it wouldn't be worth it to keep on this side of the veil. Bless the name of Abraham, after a while they shut up and go off somewhere.

Probably to *nuhdz* each other, they should rest in peace already and stop talking.

But Snodle wasn't going away. He died, and now he was demanding we not only sit *shivah* out of courtesy for having lived here so prosperously, but we should also, you shouldn't take it as an imposition, sit *shiva* for *him*! An *oysvorf*, that Snodle.

"There's always Kadak," he said. His voice came from a nowhere spot in the air about a foot above his body, which was dumped upside down on a table in the *yeshiva*.

"Snodle, if you don't mind," said Shmuel with the one good antenna, "would you kindly shut your face and let us handle this?" Then seeing, I suppose for the first time, that Snodle was upside down, he added, but softly he shouldn't speak ill of the dead, "I always said he talked through his *tuchis*."

"I'll turn him over," said Chaim with the defective unwind in his hop.

"Let be," said Shmuel. "I like this end better than the other."

"This is getting us nowhere," said Yitzchak. "The *gonifs* come in a little while to take away the planet, we can't stay, we can't go, and I have lust-nest concubines lubricating and lactating on Bromios this very minute."

"Kasrilevka," said Avram.

"Kasrilevka," Yitzchak agreed, his prop-arm, the one in the back, curling an ungrammatical apology.

"A planet of ten million Snodles," said Yankel.

"There's always Kadak," said Snodle.

"Who is this Kadak the *oysvorf*'s babbling about?" asked Meyer Kahaha. The rest of us rolled our eyes at the remark. Ninety-six *tsuris*-filled eyes rolled. Meyer Kahaha was always the town *schlemiel*; if there was a bigger *oysvorf* than Snodle, it was Meyer Kahaha.

Yankel stuck the tip of his pointing arm in Meyer Kahaha's ninth eye, the one with the cataract. "Quiet!"

We sat and stared at each other. Finally, Moishe said, "He's right. It's another tragedy we can mourn on *Tisha B'ab* (if they have enough turns on Kasrilevka for *Tisha B'ab* to fall in the right month), but the *oysvorf* and the *schlemiel* are right. Our only hope is Kadak, lightning shouldn't strike me for saying it."

"Someone will have to go find him," said Avram.

"Not me," said Yankel. "A mission for a fool."

Then Reb Jeshaia, who was the wisest of all the blue Jews on Zsouchmuhn, even *before* the great exodus, one or two of them it wouldn't have hurt if they'd stayed behind to give a little help so we shouldn't find out too late we were in this miserable state of things because Snodle seized up and died, Reb Jeshaia nodded that it was a mission for a fool and he said, "We'll send Evsise."

"Thanks a lot for that," I said.

He looked at me with the six eyes on the front, and he said, "Evsise. Should we send Shmuel with one good antenna? Should we send Chaim with a defective hop? Should we send Yitzchak who is so crippled with lust he gets cramps? Maybe we should send Yankel who is older than even Snodle and would die from the journey then we'd have to find *two* Jews? Moishe? Moishe argues with everyone. Some cooperation *he'd* get."

"What about Avram?" I asked. Avram looked away.

"You want I should talk about Avram's problem here in front of an open Talmud, here in front of the dead, right here in front of God and everyone?" Reb Jeshaia looked stern.

"Forget it. I'm sorry I mentioned," I said.

"Maybe I should go myself, the rabbi should go? Or maybe you'd prefer we sent Meyer Kahaha?"

"You made your point," I said. "I'll go. I'm far from a happy person about this, and you should know it before I go. But I'll do it. You'll never see me again, I'll die out there looking for that Kadak, but I'll go."

I started for the burrow exit of the *yeshiva*. I passed Yitzchak, who looked sheepish. "Cramps," I muttered. "It should only wither up and fall off like a dead leaf."

Then I rolled, hopped, and unwound my way up the tunnel to the street, and went looking for Kadak.

The last time I saw Kadak was seventeen years ago. He was squatting in the synagogue during Purim, and suddenly he rolled into the aisle, tore off his *yarmulkah*, his *tallis*, and his *t'fillin*, all at once with his top three arms on each side, threw them into the aisle, yelled he had had it with Judaism, and was converting to the Church of the Apostates.

That was the last any of us saw of him. Good riddance to bad rubbish, you ask me. Kadak, to begin with, was never my favorite person, if you want the truth. He snuffled.

Oh, that isn't such an *averah*, I can see you think I'm making a big something out of a big nothing. Listen, Mr. Terrific-I-Flap-My-Wings-And-You-Should-Notice-Me, I'm a person who says what's on his mind, I don't make no moofky-foofky with anyone. You want someone who beats around the bushes you should talk to that Avram. Me, I'll tell you I couldn't stand that Kadak's snuffling, all the time snuffling. You sit in the *shul* and right in the middle of the *Shema*, right in the direct absolute center of "Hear O Israel, the Lord, Our God, the Lord is One," comes a snuffle that sounds like a double-snouted peggalomer in a mud-wallow.

He had a snuffle made you want to go take a bath.

A terrible snuffle, if you'll listen to me for a minute. He was the kind, that Kadak, he wouldn't care *when* he'd snuffle. When you were sleeping, eating, *shtupping*, making a ka-ka, he didn't care . . . would come a blast, a snort, a rotten snuffle could make you want to get rid of your last three or four meals. And forget talking to him: How can you talk to a person who punctuates with a snuffle?

So when he went off to convert to the Apostates, sure there was a scandal . . . there weren't that many Jews on Zsouchmuhn . . . *anything* was a scandal . . . but to be absolutely frank with you, I'll speak my mind no matter what, we were very relieved. To be free of that snuffle was already a *naches*, like getting one free. Or seven for five.

So now I had to go all over there and back, looking for that terrible snuffle. It was an ugliness I could live without, you should pardon my frankness.

But I went through downtown Houmitz and went over to the Holy Cathedral of the Church of the Apostates. The city was in a very bad way. When everyone had gone to Kasrilevka, they took everything that wasn't bolted down. They also took everything that *was* bolted down. They also took the bolts. Not to mention a lot of the soil it was all bolted down into. Big holes, everywhere. Zsouchmuhn was not, at this point in time I'm telling you about, such a cute little world anymore. It looked like an old man with a *krenk*. Like a *pisher* with acne. Very unpleasant, it wasn't a trip I care to talk about.

But there was a little left of that crazy *farchachdah* cathedral still standing. Why shouldn't they let it stand: How much does it cost to make a new one? String. The dummies, they make a holy place from string and spit and bits of dried crap off the streets and their bodies, I don't even want to think about what a sacrilege.

I rolled inside. The smell, you could die from the smell. On Zsouchmuhn here, we got a groundworm, this filthy little segmented thing everyone calls a pincercrusher. *Lumbricus rubellus Venaticus* my Uncle Beppo, the lunatic zoologist, calls it. It isn't at all peculiar why I remember a foreign name like that—Latin is what it is, I'm a *bissel* scholar, too, you know, not such a dummy as you might think, and it's no wonder Reb Jeshaia sent me on this it-could-kill-a-lesser-Jew mission to find Kadak. I remember because once I had one of them bite me in the *tuchis* when I went swimming, and you learn these things, believe you me, you learn them. This rotten little worm, it's got pinching things in the front and on the sides, and it lies in wait for a juicy *tuchis* and when you're just ready to relax in a swim, or maybe to take a nap on a picnic, *chomp!*, it goes right for the *tuchis*. And it hangs on with those triple-damned the entire species should go straight to Gehenna pinch-things, and it makes me sick to remember, but it sucks the blood right out of you, right through your *tuchis*. And you couldn't get one off, medical science as hootsy-tootsy as it is, you could *varf* from the size of a doctor's bill, even the hootsie-tootsies can't get one off you. The only thing that does it, is you get a musician and he bangs together a pair of cymbals, and it falls off. All bloated up with your blood, leaving a bunch of little pinch-marks on your *tuchis* you're ashamed to let your lust-mates see it. And don't ask why the doctors don't carry cymbals with them for such occasions. You wouldn't be*lieve* the union problems here on Zsouchmuhm, which includes musicians and doctors both, so you'd better be near a band and not a hospital when a pincercrusher bites you in the *tuchis*, otherwise forget it. And when the terrible thing falls off, it goes *pop!* And it bursts, and all the awful crap it had in it makes a stink you shouldn't even think about it, the eyes, all twelve of them could roll up in your head, with the smell of all that *feh!* And blood and crap.

Inside the Cathedral of the Church of the Apostates, the smell. Like a million popped pincercrushers. I almost went over on my face from that smell.

It took three hands to hold all of my nose, a little whiff shouldn't slip through.

I started reeling around, hitting the strings they called walls. Fortunately, I rolled around near the entrance, and I stretched my nose a couple of feet outside, and I took a *very* deep breath, and snapped my nose back, and held it, and looked around.

There were still half a dozen of them who hadn't run off to Kasrilevka, all down on their stomachs, their feet winding up and unwinding, very fast, their faces down in the mud and crap in front of the altar, doing what I suppose they call praying. To that idol of theirs, Seymour, or Simon, or Shtumie, whatever they call it. I should know the name of a heathen idol, you bet your life never, better I should know the Latin name of a miserable worm that stinks first, let me tell you.

So there they were, and let me assure you it pained me in several more than a couple of ways to have to go over to them, but . . . I'm looking for Kadak.

"Hey," I said to one of them. A terrific look at his *tuchis* I got. Such a perfect *tuchis*, if ever there was one, for a pincercrusher to come and *chomp!*

Nothing. "Hey!" I yelled it a second time. No attention. Crazy with their faces down in the crap. "Listen, hey!" I yelled at the top of my voice, which isn't such a soft niceness when I'm suffocating holding my nose with three hands and I want to get out of that place already.

So I gave him a *zetz* in the *tuchis*. I wound up every foot on the left side, and I let it unwind right where a pinchercrusher would have brunch.

Then the dummy looked up.

A sight you could become very ill with. A nose covered with crap from the floor, a bunch of eyes filled with blue jelly, a mouth from out of which could only come heathen hosannahs to a dummy idol called Shaygets or something.

"You kicked me," he said.

"All by yourself you figured that out, eh?"

He looked at me with six, and blinked, and started to fall over on his *punim* again, and I started to wind up I'd give him such a *zetz* I'd kick him into a better life.

"We don't accept violence," he said.

"That's a terrific saying," I told him. "Meanwhile, I don't accept an unobstructed view up your *tuchis*. So if you want I should go away and stop kicking you, so you can go root around in the *dreck* some more, what you'd better do is come up here a minute and talk to me."

He kept looking. I wound up tighter. You could hear my sockets creaking. I'm not such a young one anymore. He got up.

"What do you want? I'm worshipping to Seymool."

Seymool. That's a name for a God. I wouldn't even *hire* something called a Seymool.

"You'll worship later. That *bubbie* isn't going anywhere."

"But Zsouchmuhn *is*."

"Very correct. Which is the same reason I got to talk to you now. Time is a thing I got very little of, if you catch my meaning here."

"Well, what is it you want, precisely?"

Oy, a Talmudic scholar, no less. *Precisely.* "Well, Mr. Precisely, I'll tell you what it is *precisely* I want. You know where it is I can find a no-good snuffler called Kadak?"

He stared at me with six, then blinked rapidly, in sequence—two and four, three and five, one and six—then went back in reverse order. "You have a nauseating sense of humor. May Seymool forgive you."

Then he fell back on his face, his legs up winding and unwinding, his nose deep in *dreck.* "I say Kadak, he says Seymool. I'll give you a Seymool!"

I started to wind up for a kick would put that *momzer* in the next time zone, when a voice stopped me. From over the side of that stinking cathedral—and you can bet I was turning yellow from not breathing—a woman said, "Come outside. I'll tell you about your friend Kadak."

I turned to look, and there was this *shikseh*, all dolled up in such a pile of colored *shmatehs* and baubles and bangles and crap from the floor, I thought to myself, *Gevalt! This turn I should never have crawled out of the burrow.*

So anyhow I followed her outside, thank God, and let my nose extend to its full length and breathed such a deep one my cheek-sacs puffed up like I had a pair of *bialies* stuffed in. So now this *bummerkeh*, this floozie, this painted hussy says to me, "What do you want with Kadak?"

"Wait a minute," I said, "I'll get upwind from you, meaning no offense, lady, but you smell like your church." I rolled around her and got a little away, and when it was possible to breathe like a person, I said, "What I *want* is to go join my lust-mates on Kas—, on Bromios, but what I *got* to do, is I *got* to find Kadak. We need him for a very sacred religious service, you'll excuse me for saying this, dear lady, but you being Gentile, you wouldn't understand what it is."

She batted four eyelids and flapped phony eyelashes on three of them. Oy, a *nafkeh*, a lady of easy virtue, a courtesan of the byways, a *bummerkeh*. "Would you contribute to a worthy charity to find this Kadak?"

I knew it. I knew somewhere on that damned looking for Kadak it would cost me a little something out of pocket. She was looking directly at my pouch. "You'll take a couple of coins, is that right?"

"It isn't exactly what I was thinking of," she said, still looking at my pouch, and I suddenly realized with what I'll tell you honestly was a chill, that she was cross-eyed in four of her front six. She was staring at my *pupik*. What? I'm trying to tell you, butterfly, that she wasn't staring at my pouch which was hanging to the left side of my stomach. She was staring with that cockeye four at my cute little *pupik*. What? You'll forgive me, Mr. Silent-Butterfly-with-the-Very-Dumb-Expression, I should know that butterflies don't have *pupiks*? A navel. A belly button. Now you understand what it is a *pupik*? What? Maybe I should get gross and explain to a butterfly that *shtups* flowers, that we have sex through our *pupiks*. The female puts her long middle finger of the bottom arm on the right side, straight into the *pupik* and goes moofky-foofky, and that's how we *shtup*. You needed that, is that right? You needed to know how we do it. A filth you are, butterfly; a very dirty mind.

But not as dirty as that *nafkeh*, that saucy baggage, that whore of Babylon. "Listen," I said, "meaning no offense, lady, but I'm not that kind of a person. I'm saving myself for my lust-mates. I'm sure you'll understand. Besides, meaning no offense, I don't *shtup* with strangers. It wouldn't be such a good thing for you, either, believe me. *Every*body says Evsise is a rotten *shtup*. I got very little feeling in my *pupik*, you wouldn't like it, not even a little. Why don't I give you a few nice coins, you could use them on Kasri—on Bromios.

You could maybe set yourself up in business there, a pretty lady such as yourself." God shouldn't strike me down with a bolt of lightning in the *tuchis* for telling this filthy-mind cockeye heathen *nafkeh* what a cutie she was.

"You want to find this Kadak?" she asked, staring straight at two things at the same time.

"Please, lady," I said. My nose started running.

"Don't cry," she said. "Seymool is my God, I trust in Seymool."

"What the hell has that got to do with anything?"

"We are the last of the Faithful of the Church. We plan to stay on Zsouchmuhn when they relocate it. Seymool has decreed it. I have no hope of living through it. I understand cataclysms are commonplace when they pull a planet out of orbit."

"So run," I said. "What kind of dummies are you?"

"We are the Faithful."

It gave me pause. Even Gentiles, even nut cases like these worshippers of Shmoe-ool, whoever, even *they* got to believe. It was nice. In a very dumb way.

"So what has all that got to do in even the slightest way with me, lady?"

"I'm horny."

"Well, why not go in your cathedral there and *shtup* one of your playmates?"

"They're worshipping."

"To that statue that looks like a big bug picking its nose, with the *dreck* and crap and mud all over it?"

"Don't speak disrespectfully of Seymool."

"I'll cut out my tongue."

"That isn't necessary, just stick out your navel."

"Lady, you got a dirty mouth."

"You want to know where Kadak is?"

I won't tell what nasty indignities came next. It makes me very ashamed even to think about it. She had a dirty fingernail.

So I'll tell you only that when she was done ravaging my *pupik* and left me lying there against a mud-wall of a building, the pink *shmootz* running down my stomach, I knew that Kadak had been as lousy an Apostate as he had been a Jew. One afternoon, just like in the synagogue years before, he ran amuck and started biting the statue of that bug-God they got. Before they could pry him off, he had bitten off the kneecap of Shmoogle. So they threw him out of the Church. This *nafkeh* knew what had happened to him, because he had used her services, you could *brechh* from such a thought, and he still owed her some coins. So she'd followed him around, trying to get him to pay, and she'd seen he'd bounced from religion to religion until they accepted him as a Slave of the Rock.

So I got up and went to a fountain and washed myself the best way I could, and said a couple of quick prayers that I wouldn't get knocked up from that dirty finger, and I went looking for the Slaves of the Rock, still looking for that damned Kadak. I walked with an uneven roll, hop, unwind. You would, too, if you'd been ravished, butterfly.

Just a second you'd think on it, how would you feel if a flower grabbed you by the *tuchis* and stuck a pistil and stamen in *your pupik*? What? Oh, terrific. Butterflies don't have *pupiks*.

Talking to you, standing here in sand, is not necessarily the most sensational thing I've ever done, you want to know.

The Slaves of the Rock were all gathered in a valley just outside the city limits of Houmitz. The Governors wouldn't let them inside the city. Who can blame them. If you think those Apostates were pukers, you should only see the Rocks. Such cuties. It is to *varf*!

Big rocks they turned themselves into. With tongues like string, six or seven feet long, all rolled up inside. And when a krendl or a znigh or a buck-fly goes whizzing past, *slurp!* Out comes that ugly tongue like a shot and snags it and wraps around and comes whipping back and smashes the bug all over the rock, and then the rock gets soft and spongy like a piece rotten fruit and absorbs all the *dreck* and crap and awfulness squished there. Oh, such terrifics, those Rocks. Just the kind of thing I would expect a Kadak to be when he couldn't stand being himself no more. Thank you oh so very greatly, Reb Jeshaia, for this looking mission.

So I found the head Rock and I stood there in that valley, all surrounded by Rocks going *slurp!* And *squish!* And sucking up bug food. This was not the best part of my life I'm telling you about.

"How do you do?"

I figured it was the most polite way to talk to a rock. "How did you know I was the chief Slave?" the Rock said.

"You had the longest tongue."

Slurp! A znigh on the wing, cruising by humming a tune, minding its own business, got it right in the *punim*, a tongue like a wet noodle, splat right in the *punim*, and a quick overhead twist and *squish!* All over the Rock. It splattered on me, gooey and altogether puke-making. Definitely not the kind of individual to have a terrific dinner out with. The *guderim* was all over me.

"Excuse the mess," said the chief Slave. He really sounded sorry.

"Think nothing," I said. "That was a very cute little overhand twist you gave it there at the last minute."

He seemed flattered. "You noticed that, did you?"

"How could I help? Such a class move."

"You know, you're the first one who's ever noticed that. There have been lots of studies made, by all kinds of foreigners, from other worlds, other galaxies, even, but never once did one of them notice that move. What did you say your name was?"

The bug ooze was dripping down my stomach. "My name is Evsise, and I'm looking for a person who used to be a person named Kadak. I was given to understand that he'd become a Rock a few years ago. I have a great need to find this Kadak rock, he should drop dead already such a rotten time he's been making for me."

"Listen," said the chief Slave (as the remains of the znigh oozed down through the spongy surface), "I like you. Have you ever thought of converting?"

"Forget it."

"No, really, I'm serious. To Worship the Rock is such an enriching experience, it really isn't smart to dismiss it without giving it a try. What do you say?"

I figured I had to be a little smartsy then, just a little. "Say, I wish I could. You got no *idea* what a nice proposition that is you're making to me. And in a quick second I'd take you up on it, but I got this one *bissel* tot of a problem."

"Would you like to talk about it?"

A psychiatrist rock yet. I really needed this.

"I'm afraid from bugs," I said.

He didn't say anything for a moment. Then, "I see your point. Bugs are a very big part of our religion."

"I can see that."

"Ah, well. I'm sorry for you. But let's see if I can help you. What did you say his name was?"

"Kadak."

"Oh, yeah, I remember now. What a creep."

"That's him."

"Let me see now," said the Rock. "If I recall correctly, we threw him out of the order for being a disruptive influence, oh, it must have been fifteen years ago. He used to make the ugliest noises I've ever heard out of a Rock."

"Snuffling."

"I beg your pardon?"

"Snuffling is what he did. A terrible snort noise, all wet and cloggy, it could make you sick to be near it."

"Yes, that was it."

"So what happened to him, I'm afraid to ask."

"He reconstituted his atoms and became just like you again."

"Not like me, please."

"Well, I mean the same species."

"And he went off?"

"Yes. He said he was going to try the Fleshists."

"I wish you hadn't told me that."

"I'm sorry."

I sat down. Settled my *tuchis* right down between my rims, drew up my legs, and dropped my head into a half dozen of my hands. I was very glum.

"Would you like to sit on me?" the Rock asked.

It was a nice offer. "Thanks," I said politely, looking at the last slimy ooze of the znigh on the Rock, "but I'm too miserable to be comfortable."

"What do you need him for?" he asked.

So I explained the best I could—this was, after all, to a rock, a piece of stone, even if it *could* talk—about the *minyan* of ten. The chief Slave asked me why ten.

So I said, "On the Earth, a long time ago . . . you know about the Earth, right? Right. Well, on the Earth, a long time ago, God was going to give a terrific *zetz* to a place called Sodom. What it was, this Sodom, was a whole city *full* of Fleshists. Not a nice place."

"I can't conceive of an entire *city* of Fleshists," the Rock said. "That's rather an ugly thought."

"That's the way God looked at it."

We were both quiet for a while, thinking about that.

"So, anyhow," I said, "Abraham, blessed be his name, who was this very holy Jew even if he wasn't blue, you shouldn't hold that against him—"

"I won't."

"—uh. Yes. Right. Well, Abraham pleaded with God to save Sodom."

"Why did he do that . . . a city *full* of Fleshists. Yechh."

"How do *I* know? He was holy, that's all. So God must have thought that was a little *meshugge* . . . a little crazy . . . also, you know God is no dummy . . . and he told Abraham he'd spare Sodom if Abraham could find fifty righteous men living there . . ."

"Just men? What about women?"

"There isn't scripture on that one."

"Sounds like your God is a sexist."

"At least, you'll pardon my frankness now, but at least he isn't a thing that lies in a valley for birds to make ka-ka on."

"That's rather rude of you."

"I'm terribly sorry, but it isn't nice to call the one true God a rotten name."

"I was only asking."

"Well, it isn't too classy for a rock to ask them kinds of questions. Now do you want to hear this or don't you?"

"Yes, sure. But—"

"But *what*!?"

"Why did this God haggle with this Abraham? Why didn't he just tell him he was going to do it, and then do it?"

I was getting pretty upset, you know what I mean? "It was because Abraham was a *mensch*, a real terrific person, a snappy dresser, *that's* why, okay?"

The rock didn't answer. I guess he was sulking. So okay, let him sulk. "Then Abraham said, okay, what if I can only find *forty* righteous men? And God said, okay, let be forty. So Abraham said what if only thirty, and God said, *nu*, let be *thirty* already, and then Abraham said what if only twenty, and God started yelling all right stop *nuhdzhing* me, let be *twenty* . . ."

"Let me guess," the rock said, "Abraham said ten, and your God got really mad and said ten was it, and no further, and that's how you came up with ten men for the congregation."

"You've heard it," I said.

The rock was silent again.

Finally, he said, "Listen, I like your idea of religion. I'm not altogether happy being a Slave of the Rock, even if I am the *chief* Rock. How about if *I* converted and came back with you, and made the tenth for the *minyan*?"

I thought about that for a while. "Well," I said slowly, "the Talmud *does* say, 'Nine free men and a slave may be reckoned together for a quorum,' but against that is quoted that Rabbi Eliezer went into a synagogue and didn't find ten there, so he freed his slave and with him completed the number, but if there had only been seven and he had freed *two* slaves, it wouldn't have been *kosher*. But with one freed slave and the rabbi it made ten. So, clearly, as all agree, eight freemen and two slaves would *not* answer the purpose. But, if you just put yourself in my place for a moment, you're not, even remotely speaking, *my* slave. You're the Slave of the Rock. And besides, it takes a long time to convert. Can you speak Hebrew? Even a little?"

"What's Hebrew?"

"Forget it. How about keeping *kosher*?"

"What are they? I'll keep them if it's part of the program. After all, when you've been a Rock, eating bugs all your life, keeping some kind of pet doesn't sound too difficult."

It was hopeless. For a minute there I gave it a maybe, you know what I mean. But the more I thought about it, even if I could summon up the *chutzpah* to go back to Reb Jeshaia with a rock, not with a Kadak, it wouldn't work. This Rock was a nice enough fellow, you know what I mean, but even as I sat there pondering, he shot out that ick tongue of his, and snared a buck-fly and whipped it in that move he thought was such a sensational thing, and splatted it all over the place, and started eating it. And clearly, very clearly, Genesis 9:4 forbade animal blood to all the seed of Noah, so how could I bring a Rock back and say, here, I freed this Slave of the Rock, and he'll be the tenth man, and then right in the middle of *Adonai*, out would come that crummy tongue and eat a bug off the wall. Forget it.

"Listen," I said, as gentle as I could, I didn't want to hurt his feelings, "it's a strictly great offer you've made, and under other circumstances I'd take you up on that, you know what I'm saying? But right now I'm really pressed for time and it would take too long for you to learn Hebrew, so let's let it sit for a while. I'll get back to you."

He wasn't happy about that, I could tell. But he was a real *mensch*. He told me he understood, and he wished me good luck with the Fleshists, and he let me roll away fast. I could see his point, though, and I was very sorry about his not being a possible. I mean, how would *you* like it to sit all day baking in the sun, with birds making pish in your face, and the best you got to look forward to is a juicy bug.

And if I'd known what I had coming, what *tsuris*, I'd have gladly only, happily yet, you can believe it, taken that Rock back with me, bug *dreck* and all. Believe me, there are worse things than a rock that eats bugs.

I'll make a long story short. I followed the trail of that *putz* Kadak from the pit of the Fleshists (where I lost the use of my *pupik*, all my coin, the sight of one eye in the back, the second arm on the left side, and my *yarmulkah*), to the embarkation dock at the spaceport where the sect called the Denigrators were getting on board ships for that Bromios (where I got beat up so bad I crawled away), to the lava beds where the True Believers of Suffering were doing their last rites before leaving (where I suffered first degree miserable and such a pain you wouldn't ac*cept* over half my poor body), to the Tabernacle of the Mouth (where some big deal prophet that was all teeth bit off the tip of one antenna. God knows why, maybe out of pique at being left behind), to the Caucus Race of the Malforms (where I fit right in, as crapped up and bloody as I was), to the Lair of the Blessed Profundity of the Unspeakable Trihll (which I could not, even if I had *several* mouths, pronounce . . . but they punched and kicked me anyhow, really sensational people), to the Archdruid of Nothingness, always following that miserable creep Kadak from religion to religion—and let me tell you, *no one* has a good word for that *schmuck*, not even the worst of those heathens—and it was there, *kayn-ahora*, that the Archdruid told me the last he'd seen of Kadak was ten years earlier, when he had changed him into a butterfly, and sent him out into the desert, it should be sincerely hoped he would drop dead in the heat.

Which is why, finally, I'm standing here talking to you, dumb creep butterfly. So now I've told it all, and you see what a puke condition I'm in, don't for a minute think that Avram or those others will respect me for what I did, they'll only *nuhdz* me about how long it took, and that's why you got to come back with me.

Not a word. Not a sound through all this. Not a flap or a flitter or a how are you, Evsise. Nothing.

Look. I'm not going to *tummel* with you, Mr. I-Can't-Make-Up-My-Mind-What-Kind-of-Religion-I-Want-To-Be butterfly.

You think I stood here all this time, sinking in up to my rims in sand, just to tell you a cute story? I *know* you're Kadak! And how do I know?

Go ahead, snuffle like that again and ask me how I know!

Come on. You'll come either by yourself or I'll drag you by your wings, you know for a butterfly you're not even a nice *looking* butterfly? You're an ugly, is what you are. And as for being a Jew, only that by birth, such a disgrace to the entire blue Jews on Zsouchmuhn.

As you can see, I'm getting angry. You've gotten me raped, crapped on, burned, maimed, crippled, blinded, insulted, run around, exposed to heathens, robbed, sunburned, covered with bug *schmutz*, altogether miserable and unhappy, and I'll tell you, very frankly, you'll come with me, Mr. Kadak, or I'll choke you dead right here in this *farblondjet* desert!

Now what do you say?

I thought that's what you'd say.

"Here he is."

Yankel didn't believe it. Chaim laughed. Shmuel started to cry, his nose running green. Snodle coughed. And Reb Jeshaia hung his head. "I should have sent Avram," he said.

Avram looked away. Like a dead leaf it should fall off.

"Here he is, is what I said, and here he is, is what it is," I said. "This is your Kadak, may he rot in his cocoon."

Then I told them the whole story.

At least they had the grace to be amazed.

"*This* is what makes the *minyan*?" Moishe said. "This?"

"Make him change back, and that's him," I said. "I wash my hands of it." I went over in a corner of the *shul* and settled down. It was their problem now.

For hours they went at him. They tried everything. They threatened him, they begged him, they implored him, they intimidated him, they cajoled him, they *shmacheled* him, they insulted him, they slugged him, they chased his *tuchis* all over the *shul* . . .

Sure. Of course. Wouldn't you know. That rotten Kadak wouldn't change back. At last, he found a thing he wanted to be. A dumb creep butterfly.

With a snuffle. Still with a rotten snuffle. Did you ever know how much *worse* a butterfly snuffles than a person?

You could *plotz* from it.

And finally, when they couldn't get him to change back—and if you want to know the truth, I don't think he *could* change back after that weirdnik *bubbie* Archdruid changed him—they held him down and Reb Jeshaia made the rabbinical decision that his *presence* was enough, in this great emergency. So Meyer Kahaha sat on him, and we started to sit *shivah*, finally, for Zsouchmuhn and for Snodle.

And then Reb Jeshaia got a terrible look on his face, and he said, "Oh my God!"

"What? What what!?" I yelled. "What now, what?"

Very softly, Reb Jeshaia asked me, "Evsise, how long ago did the Archdruid say he changed Kadak into this thing?"

"Ten years ago," I said, "but what—"

And I stopped. And I sat down again. And knew we had lost, and we would still be there when the *gonifs* came to rip the planet out of orbit, and we would die, along with the crazies in the Apostate Cathedral and the *nafkeh*, and the Rock and the Archdruid and everyone else who was too nuts to get safely away the way they were supposed to.

"What's the matter?" asked Meyer Kahaha, the *oysvorf*. "What's wrong? Why does it matter he's been a butterfly for ten years?"

"*Only* ten years," said Shmuel.

"Not thirteen, *schmuck*, only ten," said Yankel, sticking his pointing arm in Meyer Kahaha's ninth eye.

We looked at Meyer Kahaha till the light dawned, even for him. "Oh my God," he said, and rolled over on his side. The butterfly, that miserable Kadak, fluttered up and flew around the *shul.* No one paid any attention to him. It had all been in vain.

Scripture says, very clearly there should be no mistake, that all ten of the participants of a *minyan* have to be over thirteen years old. At thirteen, for a Jew, a boy becomes a man. "Today I am a man," it's an old gag. Ha ha. Very funny. It's the reason for the *Bar Mitzvah*. Thirteen. Not ten.

Kadak wasn't old enough.

Still dead, still lying on his face, Snodle began weeping.

Reb Jeshaia and the other seven, the last blue Jews on Zsouchmuhn, now doomed to die without ever again gumming their lust-nest concubines, they all slumped into seats and waited for destruction.

I felt worse than them. I hurt in more places.

Then I looked up and began to smile. I smiled so wide and so loud, everyone turned to look at me.

"He's gone crazy," said Chaim.

"It's better that way," said Shmuel. "He won't feel the pain."

"Poor Evsise," said Yitzchak.

"Dummies!" I shouted, leaping up and rolling and hopping and unwinding like a *tummeler*. "Dummies! Dummies! Even you, Reb Jeshaia, you're a dummy, we're *all* dummies!"

"Is that a way to talk to a rabbi?" said Reb Jeshaia.

"Sure it is," I yowled, reeling and rocking, "sure it is, sure it is, sure it is, sure it is . . ."

Meyer Kahaha came and sat on me.

"Get off me, you *schlemiel*! I know how to save us, it's been here all the time, we *never* needed that creep snuffle butterfly Kadak!"

So he got off me, and I looked at them with great pleasure because I was about to demonstrate that I was a *folks-mensh* of the first water, and I said, "Under a ruling in Tractate *Berakhot*, nine Jews and the holy ark of the law containing the Torah may, *together*, hey *nu*, *nu*, do you get what I'm saying, may *together* be considered for congregational worship!"

And Reb Jeshaia kissed me.

"Evsise, Evsise, how do you remember such a thing? You're not a Talmudic scholar, how did you remember such a wonderful thing?" Reb Jeshaia hugged and kissed and babbled in my face at me.

"*I* didn't," I said, "Kadak did."

And they all looked up, as I'd looked up, and there was that not-such-an-altogether-worthless-after-all Kadak, sitting up on top of the Holy Ark, the *Aronha-Kodesh*, the sacred cabinet holding the sacred scrolls of the Lord. Sitting up there, a butterfly, always to remain a butterfly, sitting and beating his wings frantically, trying to let someone know what *he* knew, something even a rabbi had forgotten.

And when he came down to perch on Reb Jeshaia's shoulder, we all sat down and rested for a minute, and then Reb Jeshaia said, "Now we will sit *shivah*. Nine men, the Holy Ark, and one butterfly make a *minyan*."

And for the last time on Zsouchmuhn (which means look for me) we said the holy words, this last time for the home we had had, the home we would leave. And all through the prayers, there sat Kadak, flapping his dumb wings.

And you want to know a thing? Even *that* was a *mechaieh* (which means a terrific pleasure).

How Interesting: A Tiny Man

I created a tiny man. It was very hard work. It took me a long time. But I did it, finally: he was five inches tall. Tiny; he was very tiny. And creating him, the creating of him, it seemed an awfully good idea at the time.

I can't remember why I wanted to do it, not at the very beginning, when I first got the idea to create this extremely tiny man. I know I *had* a most excellent reason, or at least an excellent *conception*, but I'll be darned if I can now, at this moment, remember what it was. Now, of course, it is much later than that moment of conception.

But it was, as I recall, a very *good* reason. At the time.

When I showed him to everyone else in the lab at Eleanor Roosevelt Tech, they thought it was interesting. "How interesting," some of them said. I thought that was a proper way of looking at it, the way of looking at a tiny man who didn't really *do* anything except stand around looking up in wonder and amusement at all the tall things above and around him.

He was no trouble. Getting clothes tailored for him was not a problem. I went to the couture class. I had made the acquaintance of a young woman, a very nice young woman, named Jennifer Cuffee, we had gone out a few times, nothing very much came of it—I don't think we were suited to each other—but we were casual friends. And I asked her if she would make a few different outfits for the tiny man.

"Well, he's too short to fit into ready-mades, say, the wardrobe of Barbie's boyfriend, Ken. And action figure clothing would just be too twee. But I think I can whip you up an ensemble or two. It won't be 'bespoke,' but he'll look nice enough. What sort of thing did you have in mind?"

"I think suits," I said. "He probably won't be doing much traveling, or sports activities . . . yes, why don't we stick to just a couple of suits. Nice shirts, perhaps a tie or two."

And that worked out splendidly. He always looked well-turned-out, fastidious, perky but quite serious in appearance. Not stuffy, like an attorney all puffed up with himself, but with an unassuming gravitas. In fact, my attorney, Charles, said of him, "There is a quotidian elegance about him." Usually, he merely stood around, one hand in his pants pocket, his jacket buttoned, his tie snugly abutting the top of his collar, staring with pleasure at everything around him. Sometimes, when I would carry him out to see more of the world, he would lean forward peering over the top seam of *my* suit jacket pocket, arms folded atop the edge to prevent his slipping sidewise, and he would hum in an odd tenor.

He never had a name. I cannot really summon a reason for that. Names seemed a bit too cute for someone that singular and, well, suppose I had called him say, Charles, like my attorney. Eventually someone would have called him "Charlie" or even "Chuck," and nicknames are what come to be imploded from names. Nicknames for him would have been insipidly unthinkable. Don't you think?

He spoke, of course. He was a fully formed tiny man. It took him a few hours after I created him for his speech to become fluent and accomplished. We did it by prolonged exposure (more than two hours) to thesauri, encyclopedias, dictionaries, word histories, and other such references. I pronounced right along with him, when he had a problem. We used books only, nothing on a screen. I don't think he much cared for all of the electronic substitutes. He remarked once that his favorite phrase was *vade mecum*, and so I tried not to let him be exposed to computers or televisions or any of the hand-held repugnancies. His word, not mine.

He had an excellent memory, particularly for languages. For instance, *vade mecum*, which is a well-known Latin phrase for a handy little reference book one can use on a moment's notice. It means, literally, "go with me." Well, he heard and read it and then used it absolutely correctly. So when he said "repugnancies," he meant nothing milder. (I confess, from time to time, when my mind froze up trying to recall a certain word that had slipped behind the gauze of forgetting, I could tilt my head a trifle, and my pocket-size little man became *my* "vade mecum." Function follows form.)

Everywhere we went, the overwhelming impact was, "How interesting, a tiny man." Well, *ignorantia legis neminem excusat.* I should have understood human nature better. I should have known every such beautiful arcade must have a boiler room in which rats and worms and grubs and darkness rule.

I was asked to come, with the tiny man that I had created, to a sort of Sunday morning intellectual conversational television show. I was reluctant, because he had no affinity for the medium; but I was assured the cameras would be swathed in black cloth and the monitors turned away from him. So, in essence, it was merely another get-together of interesting spirits trying to fathom the ethical structure of the universe. The tiny man had a relishment for such potlatches.

It was a pleasant outing.

Nothing untoward.

We were thanked all around, and we went away, and no one—certainly not I—thought another thing about it.

It took less than twelve hours.

When it comes to human nature, I should have known better. But I didn't and *ignorantia legis neminem excusat* if there are truly any "laws" to human nature. Rats, worms, grubs, and an inexplicable darkness of the soul. A great philosopher named Isabella, last name not first, once pointed out, "Hell hath no fury like that of the uninvolved." In less than twelve hours I learned the spike-in-the-heart relevance of that aphorism: to me, and to him.

A woman I didn't know started it. I didn't understand why she would do such a thing. It didn't have anything to do with her. Perhaps she was as mean-spirited as everyone but her slavish audience said. Her name was Franco. Something Franco. She was very thin, as if she couldn't keep down solids. And her hair was a bright yellow. She was not a bad-looking woman as facial standards go, but there was something feral in the lines of her mien, and her smile was the smile of the ferret, her eyes clinkingly cold.

She called him a monstrosity. Other words, some of which I had never heard before: abnormity, perversion of nature, a vile derision of what God had created first, a hideous crime of unnatural science. She said, I was told, "This thing would make Jesus himself vomit!"

Then there were commentators. And news anchors. And hand-held cameras and tripods and long-distance lenses. There were men with uncombed hair and stubble on their faces who found ways to confront us that were heroic. There were awful newspapers one can apparently buy alongside decks of playing cards and various kinds of chewing gum at the check-out in the Rite Aid where I bought him his eyewash.

There was much talk of God and "natural this" and "unnatural that," most of which seemed very silly to me. But this Franco woman would not stop. She appeared everywhere and said it was clearly an attempt by Godless atheists and some people she called the cultural elite and "limousine liberals" to pervert God's Will and God's Way. I was deemed "Dr. Frankenstein" and men with unruly hair and shadowy cheeks found their way into the lab at Eleanor Roosevelt Tech, seeking busbars and galvanic coils and Van de Graaff generators. But, of course, there were no such things in the lab. Not even the creche in which I'd created the tiny man.

It grew worse and worse.

In the halls, no one would speak to me. I had to carry him in my inside pocket, out of fear. Even Jennifer Cuffee was frightened and became opposed to me and to him. She demanded I return his clothing. I did so, of a certainty, but I thought it was, as the tiny man put it, "Rather craven for someone who used to be so nice."

There were threats. A great many threats. Some of them curiously misspelled—its, rather than it's—and suchlike. Once, someone threw a cracked glass door off an old phone booth through my window. The tiny man hid but didn't seem too frightened by this sudden upheaval of a once-kindly world. People who had nothing to do with me or my work or the tiny man, people who were not hurt or affected in any way, became vocal and menacing and so fervid one could see the steam rising off them. If there had been a resemblance between my tiny man and the race of men, all such similarity was gone. He seemed virtually, well, godlike in comparison.

And then I was told we had to go.

"Where?" I said to them.

"We don't care," they answered, and they had narrow mouths.

I resisted. I had created this tiny man, and I was there to protect him. There is such a thing as individual responsibility. It is the nature of grandeur in us. To deny it is to become a beast of the fields. No way. Not I.

And so, with my tiny man—who now mostly wore Kleenex—but who was making excellent progress with Urdu and Quechua, and needlework—we took to the hills. As students at Eleanor Roosevelt put it, we "got in the wind."

I know how to drive, and I have a car. Though there are those who call me geezer and ask if I use two Dixie Cups and a waxed string to call my friends, if my affection for Ginastera and Stravinsky gets in the way of my appreciation of Black Sabbath and Kanye West, I am a man of today. And as with individual responsibility for myself, and my deeds, I take the world on sum identically. I choose and reject. That, I really and truly believe, is the way a responsible individual acts.

And so, I have a car. I use raw sugar instead of aspartame, my pants do not sag around my shoetops, and I drive a perfectly utilitarian car. The make and year do not matter for this disquisition. The fate of the tiny man does.

We fled, "got in the wind."

But, as Isabella has said, "Hell hath no fury like that of the uninvolved," and everywhere we went, at some small moment, my face would be recognized by a bagger in a Walmart, or a counterserf in a Taco Bell, and the next thing I would know, there would be (at minimum) a jackal-faced blonde girl with a hand-microphone, or some young man with unruly shark hair and the look of someone who didn't stand close enough to his razor that morning, or even a police officer. I had done nothing, my good friend the tiny man had done nothing, but what they all said to us, in one way or another, was something I think Alan Ladd said to Lee Van Cleef: "Don't let the sun go down on you in this town, boy."

We tried West Virginia. It was an unpleasant place.

Oklahoma. The world there was dry, but the people were wet with sweat at our presence.

Even towns that were dying, Detroit, Cleveland, Las Vegas, none of them would have us, not even for a moment.

And then, all because of this terrible blonde woman Franco, who had nothing better to do with her time or her anger, a warrant was sworn out for us. A Federal warrant. We tried to hide, but both of us had to eat. And neither of us, as clever as he had become, as agile as I had become, were adepts at "being on the dodge." And in a Super 8 motel in Aberdeen, South Dakota, the Feds cornered us.

The tiny man stood complacently on the desk blotter, and we looked honestly at each other. He knew, as I knew. I felt a little like God himself. I had created this tiny man, who had harmed no one, who at prime point should have elicited no more serious a view than, "How interesting: a tiny man."

But I had been ignorant of the laws of human nature, and we both knew it was all my responsibility. The beginning, the term of the adventure, and now, the ending:

The First Ending

I held the Aberdeen, South Dakota telephone book in my hands, raised it above my head and, in the moment before I brought it smashing down as ferociously as I could, the tiny man looked up at me, wistful, resolved, and said, "Mother."

The Second Ending

I stood staring down at him and could barely see through my tears. He looked up at me with compassion and understanding and said, "Yes, it would always have had to come to this," and then, being god, he destroyed the world, leaving only the two of us, and now, because he is a compassionate deity, he will destroy me, an even tinier man.

THE LIGHTER SIDE

Djinn, No Chaser

"Who the hell ever heard of Turkish Period?" Danny Squires said. He said it at the top of his voice, on a city street.

"Danny! People are staring at us; lower your voice!" Connie Squires punched his bicep. They stood on the street, in front of the furniture store. Danny was determined not to enter.

"Come on, Connie," he said, "let's get away from these junk shops and go see some inexpensive modern stuff. You know perfectly well I don't make enough to start filling the apartment with expensive antiques."

Connie furtively looked up and down the street—she was more concerned with a "scene" than with the argument itself—and then moved in toward Danny with a determined air. "Now listen up, Squires. *Did* you or did you *not* marry me four days ago, and promise to love, honor, and cherish and all that other good jive?"

Danny's blue eyes rolled toward Heaven; he knew he was losing ground. Instinctively defensive, he answered, "Well, sure, Connie, but—"

"Well, then, I am your wife, and you have not taken me on a honeymoon—"

"I can't *afford* one!"

"—have not taken me on a honeymoon," Connie repeated with inflexibility. "Consequently, we will buy a little furniture for that rabbit warren you laughingly call our little love nest. And *little* is hardly the term: that vale of tears was criminally undersized when Barbara Fritchie hung out her flag.

"So to make my life *bearable*, for the next few weeks, till we can talk Mr. Upjohn into giving you a raise—"

"Upjohn!" Danny fairly screamed. "You've got to stay away from the boss, Connie. Don't screw around. He won't give me a raise, and I'd rather you stayed away from him—"

"Until then," she went on relentlessly, "we will decorate our apartment in the style I've wanted for years."

"Turkish Period?"

"Turkish Period."

Danny flipped his hands in the air. What was the use? He had known Connie was strong-willed when he'd married her.

It had seemed an attractive quality at the time; now he wasn't so sure. But he was strong-willed too: he was sure he could outlast her. Probably.

"Okay," he said finally, "I suppose Turkish Period it'll be. What the hell *is* Turkish Period?"

She took his arm lovingly and turned him around to look in the store window. "Well, honey, it's not *actually* Turkish. It's more Mesopotamian. You know, teak and silk and . . ."

"Sounds hideous."

"So you're starting up again!" She dropped his arm, her eyes flashing, her mouth a tight little line. "I'm really ashamed of you, depriving me of the few little pleasures I need to make my life a blub, sniff, hoo-hoo . . ."

The edge was hers.

"Connie . . . Connie . . ." She knocked away his comforting hand, saying, "You beast." That was too much for him. The words were so obviously put-on, he was suddenly infuriated:

"Now, goddammit!"

Her tears came faster. Danny stood there, furious, helpless, outmaneuvered, hoping desperately that no cop would come along and say, "This guy botherin' ya, lady?"

"Connie, okay, okay, we'll *have* Turkish Period. Come on, come on. It doesn't matter what it costs, I can scrape up the money somehow."

It was not one of the glass-brick and onyx emporia where sensible furniture might be found (if one searched hard enough and paid high enough and retained one's senses long enough as they were trying to palm off modernistic nightmares in which no comfortable position might be found); no, it was not even one of those. This was an antique shop.

They looked at beds that had canopies and ornate metalwork on the bedposts. They looked at rugs that were littered with pillows, so visitors could sit on the floors. They looked at tables built six inches off the deck, for low banquets. They inspected incense burners and hookahs and coffers and giant vases until Danny's head swam with visions of the courts of long-dead caliphs.

Yet, despite her determination, Connie chose very few items; and those she did select were moderately priced and quite handsome . . . for what they were. And as the hours passed, and as they moved around town from one dismal junk emporium to another, Danny's respect for his wife's taste grew. She was selecting an apartment full of furniture that wasn't bad at all.

They were finished by six o'clock and had bills of sale that totaled just under two hundred dollars. Exactly thirty dollars less than Danny had decided could be spent to furnish the new household . . . and still survive on his salary. He had taken the money from his spavined savings account and had known he must eventually start buying on credit, or they would not be able to get enough furniture to start living properly.

He was tired, but content. She'd shopped wisely. They were in a shabby section of town. How had they gotten here? They walked past an empty lot sandwiched in between two tenements—wet-wash slapping on lines between them. The lot was weed-overgrown and garbage-strewn.

"May I call your attention to the depressing surroundings and my exhaustion?" Danny said. "Let's get a cab and go back to the apartment. I want to collapse."

They turned around to look for a cab, and the empty lot was gone.

In its place, sandwiched between the two tenements, was a little shop. It was a one-story affair, with a dingy façade, and its front window completely grayed-over with dust. A hand-painted line of elaborate script on the glass-panel of the door, also opaque with grime, proclaimed:

Mohanadus Mukhar, Curios.

A little man in a flowing robe, wearing a fez, plunged out the front door, skidded to a stop, whirled, and slapped a huge sign on the window. He swiped at it four times with a big paste-brush, sticking it to the glass, and whirled back inside, slamming the door.

"No," Danny said.

Connie's mouth was making peculiar sounds.

"There's no insanity in my family," Danny said firmly. "We come from very good stock."

"We've made a visual error," Connie said.

"Simply didn't notice it," Danny said. His usually baritone voice was much nearer soprano.

"If there's crazy, we've both got it," Connie said.

"Must be, if you see the same thing I see."

Connie was silent a moment, then said, "Large seagoing vessel, three stacks, maybe the *Titanic*. Flamingo on the bridge, flying the flag of Liechtenstein?"

"Don't play with me, woman," Danny whimpered. "I think I'm losing it."

She nodded soberly. "Right. Empty lot?"

He nodded back, "Empty lot. Clothesline, weeds, garbage."

"Right."

He pointed at the little store. "Little store?"

"Right."

"Man in a fez, name of Mukhar?"

She rolled her eyes. "Right."

"So why are we walking toward it?"

"Isn't this what always happens in stories where weird shops suddenly appear out of nowhere? Something inexorable draws the innocent bystanders into its grip?"

They stood in front of the grungy little shop. They read the sign. It said:

BIG SALE! HURRY! NOW! QUICK!

"The word *unnatural* comes to mind," Danny said.

"Nervously," Connie said, "she turned the knob and opened the door."

A tiny bell went tinkle-tinkle, and they stepped across the threshold into the gloaming of Mohanadus Mukhar's shop.

"Probably not the smartest move we've ever made," Danny said softly. The door closed behind them without any assistance.

It was cool and musty in the shop, and strange fragrances chased one another past their noses.

They looked around carefully. The shop was loaded with junk. From floor to ceiling, wall to wall, on tables and in heaps, the place was filled with oddities and bric-a-brac. Piles of things tumbled over one another on the floor; heaps of things leaned against the walls. There was barely room to walk down the aisle between the stacks and mounds of things. Things in all shapes, things in all sizes and colors. Things. They tried to separate the individual items from the jumble of the place, but all they could perceive was stuff . . . things! Stuff and flotsam and bits and junk.

"Curios, effendi," a voice said, by way of explanation.

Connie leaped in the air and came down on Danny's foot.

Mukhar was standing beside such a pile of tumbled miscellany that for a moment they could not separate him from the stuff, junk, things he sold.

"We saw your sign," Connie said.

But Danny was more blunt, more direct. "There was an empty lot here; then a minute later, this shop. How come?"

The little man stepped out from the mounds of dust-collectors and his little nut-brown, wrinkled face burst into a million-creased smile. "A fortuitous accident, my children. A slight worn spot in the fabric of the cosmos, and I have been set down here for . . . how long I do not know. But it never hurts to try and stimulate business while I'm here."

"Uh, yeah," Danny said. He looked at Connie. Her expression was as blank as his own.

"Oh!" Connie cried, and went dashing off into one of the side-corridors lined with curios. "This is perfect! Just what we need for the end table. Oh, Danny, it's a dream! It's absolutely the *ne plus ultra*!"

Danny walked over to her, but in the dimness of the aisle between the curios he could barely make out what it was she was holding. He drew her into the light near the door. It had to be:

Aladdin's lamp.

Well, perhaps not that *particular* person's lamp, but one of the ancient, vile-smelling oil burning jobs: long thin spout; round-bottom body; wide, flaring handle.

It was algae-green with tarnish, brown with rust, and completely covered by the soot and debris of centuries. There was no contesting its antiquity; nothing so time-corrupted could fail to be authentic. "What the hell do you want with that old thing, Connie?"

"But Danny, it's so *per*-fect. If we just shine it up a bit. As soon as we put a little work into this lamp, it'll be a beauty." Danny knew he was defeated . . . and she'd probably be right, too. It probably would be very handsome when shined and brassed-up.

"How much?" he asked Mukhar. He didn't want to seem anxious; old camel traders were merciless at bargaining when they knew the item in question was hotly desired.

"Fifty drachmae, eh?" the old man said. His tone was one of malicious humor. "At current exchange rates, taking into account the fall of the Ottoman Empire, thirty dollars."

Danny's lips thinned. "Put it down, Connie; let's get out of here."

He started toward the door, dragging his wife behind him. But she still clutched the lamp; and Mukhar's voice halted them. "All right, noble sir. You are a cunning shopper, I can see that. You know a bargain when you spy it. But I am unfamiliar in this time frame with your dollars and your strange fast-food native customs, having been set down here only once before; and since I am more at ease with the drachma than the dollar, with the shekel than the cent, I will cut my own throat, slash both my wrists, and offer you this magnificent antiquity for . . . uh . . . twenty dollars?" His voice was querulous, his tone one of wonder and hope.

"Jesse James at least had a horse!" Danny snarled, once again moving toward the door.

"Fifteen!" Mukhar yowled. "And may all your children need corrective lenses from too much TV-time!"

"Five; and may a hundred thousand syphilitic camels puke into your couscous," Danny screamed back over his shoulder.

"Not bad," said Mukhar.

"Thanks," said Danny, stifling a smile. Now he waited.

"Bloodsucker! Heartless trafficker in cheapness! Pimple on the fundament of decency! Graffito on the subway car of life! Thirteen; my last offer; and may the gods of ITT and the Bank of America turn a blind eye to your venality!" But *his* eyes held the golden gleam of the born haggler, at last, blessedly, in his element.

"Seven, not a penny more, you Arabic anathema! And may a weighty object drop from a great height, flattening you to the niggardly thickness of your soul." Connie stared at him with open awe and admiration.

"Eleven! Eleven dollars, a pittance, an outright theft we're talking about. Call the security guards, get a consumer advocate, gimme a break here!"

"My shadow will vanish from before the evil gleam of your rapacious gaze before I pay a penny more than six bucks, and let the word go out to every wadi and oasis across the limitless desert, that Mohanadus Mukhar steals maggots from diseased meat, flies from horse dung, and the hard-earned drachmae of honest laborers. Six, fuckface, and that's it!"

"My death is about to become a reality," the Arab bellowed, tearing at the strands of white hair showing under the fez. "Rob me, go ahead, rob me: drink my life's blood! Ten! A twenty-dollar loss I'll take."

"Okay, okay." Danny turned around and produced his wallet. He pulled out one of the three ten dollar bills still inside and, turning to Connie, said, "You sure you want this ugly, dirty piece of crap?" She nodded, and he held the bill naked in the vicinity of the little merchant. For the first time Danny realized Mukhar was wearing pointed slippers that curled up; there was hair growing from his ears.

"Ten bucks."

The little man moved with the agility of a ferret, and whisked the tenner from Danny's outstretched hand before he could draw it back. "Sold!" Mukhar chuckled.

He spun around once, and when he faced them again, the ten dollars was out of sight. "And a steal, though Allah be the wiser; a hot deal, a veritable steal, blessed sir!"

Danny abruptly realized he had been taken. The lamp had probably been picked up in a junkyard and was worthless. He started to ask if it was a genuine antique, but the piles of junk had begun to waver and shimmer and coruscate with light. "Hey!" Danny said, alarmed, "What's this now?"

The little man's wrinkled face drew up in panic. "Out! Get out, quick! The time frame is sucking back together! Out! Get out now if you don't want to roam the eternities with me and this shop . . . and I can't afford any help! Out!"

He shoved them forward, and Connie slipped and fell, flailing into a pile of glassware. None of it broke. Her hand went out to protect herself and went right through the glass. Danny dragged her to her feet, panic sweeping over him . . . as the shop continued to waver and grow more indistinct around them.

"Out! Out! Out!" Mukhar kept yelling.

Then they were at the door, and he was kicking them—literally planting his curl-slippered foot in Danny's backside and shoving—from the store. They landed in a heap on the sidewalk. The lamp bounced from Connie's hand and went into the gutter with a clang. The little man stood there grinning in the doorway, and as the shop faded and disappeared, they heard him mumble happily, "A clear nine-seventy-five profit. What a lemon! You got an Edsel, kid, a real lame piece of goods. But I gotta give it to you; the syphilitic camel bit was inspired."

Then the shop was gone, and they got to their feet in front of an empty, weed-overgrown lot.

A lame piece of goods?

"Are you asleep?"

"Yes."

"How come you're answering me?"

"I was raised polite."

"Danny, talk to me . . . come on!"

"The answer is no. I'm not going to talk about it."

"We have to!"

"Not only don't we *have* to, I don't *want* to, ain't *going* to, and shut up so I can go to sleep."

"We've been lying here almost an hour. Neither of us can sleep. We *have* to discuss it, Danny."

The light went on over his side of the bed. The single pool of illumination spread from the hand-me-down daybed they had gotten from Danny's brother in New Jersey, faintly limning the few packing crates full of dishes and linens, the three Cuisinarts they'd gotten as wedding gifts, the straightback chairs from Connie's Aunt Medora, the entire bare and depressing reality of their first home together.

It would be better when the furniture they'd bought today was delivered. Later, it would be better. Now, it was the sort of urban landscape that drove divorcées and aging bachelors to jump down the airshaft at Christmastime.

"I'm going to talk about it, Squires."

"So talk. I have my thumbs in my ears."

"I think we should rub it."

"I can't hear you. It never happened. I deny the evidence of my senses. It never happened. I have these thumbs in my ears so I cannot hear a syllable of this craziness."

"For god's sake, Squires, I was *there* with you today. I saw it happen, the same as you. I saw that weird little old man and I saw his funky shop come and go like a big burp. Now, neither of us can deny it!"

"If I could hear you, I'd agree; and then I'd deny the evidence of my senses and tell you . . ." He took his thumbs from his ears, looking distressed. ". . . tell you with all my heart that I love you, that I have loved you since the moment I saw you in the typing pool at Upjohn, that if I live to be a hundred thousand years old I'll never love any one or any thing as much as I love you this very moment; and then I would tell you to piss off and forget it, and let me go to sleep so that tomorrow I can con myself into believing it never happened the way I know it happened.

"Okay?"

She threw back the covers and got out of bed. She was naked. They had not been married that long.

"Where are you going?"

"You know where I'm going."

He sat up in the daybed. His voice had no lightness in it. "Connie!"

She stopped and stared at him, there in the light.

He spoke softly. "Don't. I'm scared. Please don't."

She said nothing. She looked at him for a time. Then, naked, she sat down cross-legged on the floor at the foot of the daybed. She looked around at what little they had, and she answered him gently. "I have to, Danny. I just have to . . . if there's a chance; I have to."

They sat that way, reaching across the abyss with silent imperatives, until—finally—Danny nodded, exhaled heavily, and got out of the daybed. He walked to one of the cartons, pulled out a dustrag, shook it clean over the box, and handed it to her. He walked over to the window ledge where the tarnished and rusted oil lamp sat, and he brought it to her.

"Shine the damned thing, Squires. Who knows, maybe we actually got ourselves a twenty-four-karat genie. Shine on, oh mistress of my Mesopotamian mansion."

She held the lamp in one hand, the rag in the other. For a few minutes she did not bring them together. "I'm scared, too," she said, held her breath, and briskly rubbed the belly of the lamp.

Under her flying fingers the rust and tarnish began to come away in spots. "We'll need brass polish to do this right," she said; but suddenly the ruin covering the lamp melted away, and she was rubbing the bright skin of the lamp itself.

"Oh, Danny, look how nice it is, underneath all the crud!" And at that precise instant the lamp jumped from her hand, emitted a sharp, gray puff of smoke, and a monstrous voice bellowed in the apartment:

AH-HA! It screamed, louder than a subway train. AH-HA!

FREE AT LAST! FREE—AS FREE AS *I'LL* EVER BE—AFTER TEN THOUSAND YEARS! FREE TO SPEAK AND ACT, MY WILL TO BE KNOWN!

Danny went over backward. The sound was as mind-throttling as being at ground zero. The window glass blew out. Every light bulb in the apartment shattered. From the carton containing their meager chinaware came the distinct sound of hailstones as every plate and cup dissolved into shards. Dogs and cats blocks away began to howl. Connie screamed—though it could not be heard over the foghorn thunder of the voice—and was knocked head over ankles into a corner, still clutching the dustrag. Plaster showered in the little apartment. The window shades rolled up.

Danny recovered first. He crawled over a chair and stared at the lamp with horror. Connie sat up in the corner, face white, eyes huge, hands over her ears. Danny stood and looked down at the seemingly innocuous lamp.

"Knock off that noise! You want to lose us the lease?"

CERTAINLY, OFFSPRING OF A WORM!

"I said: stop that goddam bellowing!"

THIS WHISPER? THIS IS NAUGHT TO THE HURRICANE I SHALL LOOSE, SPAWN OF PARAMECIUM!

"That's it," Danny yelled. "I'm not getting kicked out of the only apartment in the city of New York I can afford just because of some loudmouthed genie in a jug . . ."

He stopped. He looked at Connie. Connie looked back at him.

"Oh, my god," she said.

"It's real," he said.

They got to their knees and crawled over. The lamp lay on its side on the floor at the foot of the daybed.

"Are you really in there?" Connie asked.

WHERE ELSE WOULD I BE, SLUT!

"Hey, you can't talk to my wife that way—"

Connie shushed him. "If he's a genie, he can talk any way he likes. Sticks and stones; name-calling is better than poverty."

"Yeah? Well, *nobody* talks to my—"

"Put a lid on it, Squires. I can take care of myself. If what's in this lamp is even half the size of the genie in that movie you took me to the Thalia to see . . ."

"*The Thief of Bagdad* . . . 1939 version . . . but Rex Ingram was just an actor, they only made him *look* big."

"Even so. As big as he was, if this genie is only *half* that big, playing macho overprotective chauvinist hubby—"

So humans continue to prattle like monkeys even after ten thousand years! Will nothing cleanse the earth of this raucous plague of insects?

"We're going to get thrown right out of here," Danny said. His face screwed up in a horrible expression of discomfort.

"If the cops don't beat the other tenants to it."

"Please, genie," Danny said, leaning down almost to the lamp. "Just tone it down a little, willya?"

Offspring of a million stinks! Suffer!

"You're no genie," Connie said smugly. Danny looked at her with disbelief.

"He's no genie? Then what the hell do you *think* he is?"

She swatted him. Then put her finger to her lips.

That is what I am, whore of degeneracy!

"No, you're not."

I am.

"Am not."

Am.

"Am not."

Am so, charnel house harlot! Why say you nay?

"A genie has a lot of power; a genie doesn't need to shout like that to make himself heard. You're no genie, or you'd speak softly. You *can't* speak at a decent level, because you're a fraud."

Caution, trollop!

"Foo, you don't scare me. If you were as powerful as you make out, you'd tone it way down."

is this better? are you convinced?

"Yes," Connie said, "I think that's more convincing. Can you keep it up, though? That's the question."

forever, if need be.

"And you can grant wishes?" Danny was back in the conversation.

naturally, but not to you, disgusting grub of humanity.

"Hey, listen," Danny replied angrily, "I don't give a damn what or *who* you are! You can't talk to me that way." Then a thought dawned on him. "After all, I'm your master!"

ah! correction, filth of primordial seas. there are some djinn who are mastered by their owners, but unfortunately for you i am not one of them, for i am not free to leave this metal prison. i was imprisoned in this accursed vessel many ages ago by a besotted sorcerer who knew nothing of molecular compression and even less of the binding forces of the universe. he put me into this thrice-cursed lamp, far too small for me, and i have been wedged within ever since. over the ages my good nature has rotted away. i am powerful, but trapped. those who own me cannot request anything and hope to realize their boon. i am unhappy, and an unhappy djinn is an evil djinn. were i free, i might be your slave; but as i am now, i will visit unhappiness on you in a thousand forms!

Danny chuckled. "The hell you will. I'll toss you in the incinerator."

ah! but you cannot. once you have bought the lamp, you cannot lose it, destroy it, or give it away, only sell it. i am with you forever, for who would buy such a miserable lamp?

And thunder rolled in the sky.

"What are you going to do?" Connie asked.

do? just ask me for something, and you shall see!

"Not me," Danny said, "you're too cranky."

wouldn't you like a billfold full of money?

There was sincerity in the voice from the lamp.

"Well, sure, I want money, but—"

The djinn's laughter was gigantic, and suddenly cut off by the rain of frogs that fell from a point one inch below the ceiling, clobbering Danny and Connie with small, reeking, wriggling green bodies. Connie screamed and dove for the clothes closet. She came out a second later, her hair full of them; they were falling in the closet, as well. The rain of frogs continued and when Danny opened the front door to try and escape them, they fell in the hall. He slammed the door—he realized he was still naked—and covered his head with his hands. The frogs fell, writhing, stinking, and then they were knee-deep in them, with little filthy, warty bodies jumping up at their faces.

what a lousy disposition i've got! the djinn said, and then he laughed. And he laughed again, a clangorous peal that was silenced only when the frogs stopped, disappeared, and the flood of blood began.

It went on for a week.

They could not get away from him, no matter where they went. They were also slowly starving: they could not go out to buy groceries without the earth opening under their feet, or a herd of elephants chasing them down the street, or hundreds of people getting violently ill and vomiting on them. So they stayed in and ate what canned goods they had stored up in the first four days of their marriage. But who could eat with locusts filling the apartment from top to bottom, or snakes that were intent on gobbling them up like little white rats?

First came the frogs, then the flood of blood, then the whirling dust storm, then the spiders and gnats, then the snakes and then the locusts and then the tiger that had them backed against a wall and ate the chair they used to ward him off. Then came the bats and the leprosy and the hailstones and then the floor dissolved under them, and they clung to the wall fixtures while their furniture—which had been quickly delivered (the moving men had brought it during the hailstones)—fell through, nearly killing the little old lady who lived beneath them.

Then the walls turned red hot and melted, and then the lightning burned everything black, and finally Danny had had enough. He cracked, and went gibbering around the room, tripping over the man-eating vines that were growing out of the light sockets and the floorboards. He finally sat down in a huge puddle of monkey urine and cried till his face grew puffy and his eyes flame-red and his nose swelled to three times normal size.

"I've got to get *away* from all this!" he screamed hysterically, drumming his heels, trying to eat his pants' cuffs.

you can divorce her, and that means you are voided out of the purchase contract: she wanted the lamp, not you, the djinn suggested.

Danny looked up (just in time to get a ripe Black Angus meadow muffin in his face) and yelled, "I won't! You can't make me. We've only been married a week and four days and I won't leave her!"

Connie, covered with running sores, stumbled to Danny and hugged him, though he had turned to tapioca pudding and was melting. But three days later, when ghost images of people he had feared all his life came to haunt him, he broke completely and allowed Connie to call the rest home on the boa constrictor that had once been the phone. "You can come and get me when this is over," he cried pitifully, kissing her poison ivy lips. "Maybe if we split up, he'll have some mercy." But they both doubted it.

When the downstairs buzzer rang, the men from the Home for the Mentally Absent came into the debacle that had been their apartment and saw Connie pulling her feet out of the swamp slime only with difficulty; she was crying in unison with Danny as they bundled him into the white ambulance. Unearthly laughter rolled around the sky like thunder as her husband was driven away.

Connie was left alone. She went back upstairs; she had nowhere else to go.

She slumped into the pool of molten slag, and tried to think while ants ate at her flesh and rabid rats gnawed off the wallpaper.

i'm just getting warmed up, the djinn said from the lamp.

Less than three days after he had been admitted to the Asylum for the Temporarily Twitchy, Connie came to get Danny. She came into his room; the shades were drawn, the sheets were very white; when he saw her his teeth began to chatter.

She smiled at him gently. "If I didn't know better, I'd swear you weren't simply overjoyed to see me, Squires."

He slid under the sheets till only his eyes were showing. His voice came through the covers. "If I break out in boils, it will definitely cause a relapse, and the day nurse hates mess."

"Where's my macho protective husband now?"

"I've been unwell."

"Yeah, well, that's all over. You're fit as a fiddle, so bestir your buns and let's get out of here."

Danny Squires' brow furrowed. This was not the tone of a woman with frogs in her hair. "I've been contemplating divorce or suicide."

She yanked the covers down, exposing his naked legs sticking out from the hem of the hospital gown. "Forget it, little chum. There are at least a hundred and ten positions we haven't tried yet before I consider dissolution. Now will you get out of that bed and *come on*?"

"But . . ."

". . . a thing I'll kick, if you don't move it."

Bewildered, he moved it.

Outside, the Rolls-Royce waited with its motor running. As they came through the front doors of the Institute for the Neurologically Flaccid, and Connie helped Danny from the discharge wheelchair, the liveried chauffeur leaped out and opened the door for them. They got in the back seat, and Connie said, "To the house, Mark." The chauffeur nodded, trotted briskly around and climbed behind the wheel. They took off to the muted roar of twin mufflers.

Danny's voice was a querulous squeak. "Can we afford a rented limo?"

Connie did not answer, merely smiled, and snuggled closer to him.

After a moment Danny asked, "What house?"

Connie pressed a button on the console in the armrest and the glass partition between front and back seats slid silently closed. "Do me a favor, will you," she said, "just hold the twenty questions till we get home? It's been a tough three days and all I ask is that you hold it together for another hour."

Danny nodded reluctantly. Then he noticed she was dressed in extremely expensive clothes. "I'd better not ask about your mink-trimmed jacket, either, right?"

"It would help."

He settled into silence, uneasy and juggling more than just twenty unasked questions. And he remained silent until he realized they were not taking the expressway into New York. He sat up sharply, looked out the rear window, snapped his head right and left trying to ascertain their location, and Connie said, "We're not going to Manhattan. We're going to Darien, Connecticut."

"Darien? Who the hell do we know in Darien?"

"Well, Upjohn, for one, lives in Darien."

"Upjohn!?! Ohmigod, he's fired me and sent the car to bring me to him so he can have me executed! I *knew* it!"

"Squires," she said, "Daniel, my love, Danny heart of my heart, will you just kindly close the tap on it for a while! Upjohn has nothing to do with us anymore. Nothing at all."

"But . . . but we live in New York!"

"Not no more we don't."

Twenty minutes later they turned into the most expensive section in Darien and sped down a private road.

They drove an eighth of a mile down the private road lined with Etruscan pines, beautifully maintained, and pulled into a winding driveway. Five hundred yards farther, and the drive spiraled in to wind around the front of a huge, luxurious, completely tasteful Victorian mansion. "Go on," Connie said. "Look at your house."

"Who lives here?" Danny asked.

"I just told you: *we* do."

"I thought that's what you said. Let me out here, I'll walk back to the nuthouse."

The Rolls pulled up before the mansion, and a butler ran down to open the car door for them. They got out and the servant bowed low to Connie. Then he turned to Danny. "Good to have you home, Mr. Squires," he said. Danny was too unnerved to reply.

"Thank you, Penzler," Connie said. Then, to the chauffeur, "Take the car to the garage, Mark; we won't be needing it again this afternoon. But have the Porsche fueled and ready; we may drive out later to look at the grounds."

"Very good, Mrs. Squires," Mark said. Then he drove away.

Danny was somnambulistic. He allowed himself to be led into the house, where he was further stunned by the expensive fittings, the magnificent halls, the deep-pile rugs, the spectacular furniture, the communications complex set into an entire wall, the Art Deco bar that rose out of the floor at the touch of a button, the servants who bowed and smiled at him, as if he belonged there. He was boggled by the huge kitchen, fitted with every latest appliance; and the French chef who saluted with a huge ladle as Connie entered.

"Wh-where did all this *come* from?" He finally gasped out the question as Connie led him upstairs on the escalator.

"Come on, Danny; you know where it all came from."

"The limo, the house, the grounds, the mink-trimmed jacket, the servants, the Vermeer in the front hall, the cobalt-glass Art Deco bar, the entertainment center with the beam television set, the screening room, the bowling alley, the polo field, the Neptune swimming pool, the escalator, and six-strand necklace of black pearls I now notice you are wearing around your throat . . . all of it came from the genie?"

"Sorta takes your breath away, don't it?" Connie said, ingenuously.

"I'm having a little trouble with this."

"What you're having trouble with, champ, is that Mas'úd gave you a hard time, you couldn't handle it, you crapped out, and somehow I've managed to pull it all out of the swamp."

"I'm thinking of divorce again."

They were walking down a long hall lined with works of modern Japanese illustration by Yamazaki, Kobayashi, Takahiko Li, Kenzo Tanii, and Orai. Connie stopped and put both her hands on Danny's trembling shoulders.

"What we've got here, Squires, is a bad case of identity reevaluation. Nobody gets through *all* the battles. We've been married less than two weeks, but we've known each other for three years. You don't know how many times I folded before that time, and I don't know how many times you triumphed before that time.

"What I've known of you for three years made it okay for me to marry you; to think 'This guy will be able to handle it the times I can't: That's a lot of what marriage is, to my way of thinking. I don't have to score every time, and neither do you. As long as the unit maintains. This time it was my score. Next time it'll be yours. Maybe."

Danny smiled weakly. "I'm not thinking of divorce."

Movement out of the corner of his eye made him look over his shoulder.

An eleven-foot-tall Black man, physically perfect in every way, with chiseled features like an obsidian Adonis, dressed in an impeccably tailored three-piece Savile Row suit, silk tie knotted precisely, stood just in the hallway, having emerged from open fifteen-foot-high doors of a room at the juncture of corridors.

"Uh . . ." Danny said.

Connie looked over her shoulder. "Hi, Mas'úd. Squires, I would like you to meet Mas'úd Jan bin Jan, a Mazikeen djinn of the ifrit, by the grace of Sulaymin, master of *all* the jinni, though Allah be the wiser. Our benefactor. My friend."

"How *good* a friend?" Danny whispered, seeing the totem of sexual perfection looming eleven feet high before him.

"We haven't known each other carnally, if that's what I perceive your squalid little remark to mean," she replied. And a bit wistfully she added, "I'm not his type. I think he's got it for Lena Horne." At Danny's semi-annoyed look, she added, "For god's sake, stop being so bloody suspicious!"

Mas'úd stepped forward, two steps bringing him the fifteen feet intervening, and proffered his greeting in the traditional Islamic head-and-heart salute, flowing outward, a smile on his matinee idol face. "Welcome home, Master. I await your smallest request."

Danny looked from the djinn to Connie, amazement and copelessness rendering him almost speechless. "But . . . you were stuck in the lamp . . . bad-tempered, oh boy were you bad-tempered . . . how did you . . . how did she . . ."

Connie laughed, and with great dignity the djinn joined in.

"You were in the lamp . . . you gave us all this . . . but you said you'd give us nothing but aggravation! Why?"

In deep, mellifluous tones Danny had come to associate with a voice that could knock high-flying fowl from the air, the djinn smiled warmly at them and replied, "Your good wife freed me. After ten thousand years cramped over in pain with an eternal bellyache, in that most miserable of dungeons, Mistress Connie set me loose. For the first time in a hundred times ten thousand years of cruel and venal master after master, I have been delivered into the hands of one who treats me with respect. We are friends. I look forward to extending that friendship to you, Master Squires." He seemed to be warming to his explanation, expansive and effusive. "Free now, permitted to exist among humans in a time where my kind are thought a legend, and thus able to live an interesting, new life, my gratitude knows no bounds, as my hatred and anger knew no bounds. Now I need no longer act as a Kako-daemon, now I can be the sort of ifrit Rabbi Jeremiah bin Eliazar spoke of in Psalm XLI.

"I have seen much of this world in the last three days as humans judge time. I find it most pleasing in my view. The speed, the shine, the light. The incomparable Lena Horne. Do you like basketball?"

"But how? How did you *do* it, Connie? How? No one could get him out . . ."

She took him by the hand, leading him toward the fifteen-foot-high doors. "May we come into your apartment, Mas'úd?"

The djinn made a sweeping gesture of invitation, bowing so low his head was at Danny's waist as he and Connie walked past.

They stepped inside the djinn's suite, and it was as if they had stepped back in time to ancient Basra and the Thousand Nights and a Night. Or into a Cornel Wilde costume epic.

But amid all the silks and hangings and pillows and tapers and coffers and brassware, there in the center of the foyer, in a Lucite case atop an onyx pedestal, lit from an unknown source by a single glowing spot of light, was a single icon.

"Occasionally magic has to bow to technology," Connie said. Danny moved forward. He could not make out what the item lying on the black velvet pillow was. "And sometimes ancient anger has to bow to common sense."

Danny was close enough to see it now.

Simple. It had been so simple. But no one had thought of it before. Probably because the last time it had been needed, by the lamp's previous owner, it had not existed.

"A can opener," Danny said. "A can opener!?! A simple, stupid, everyday can opener!?! That's all it took? I had a nervous breakdown, and you figured out a can opener?"

"Can do," Connie said, winking at Mas'úd.

"Not cute, Squires," Danny said. But he was thinking of the diamond as big as the Ritz.

How's the Night Life on Cissalda?

When they unscrewed the time capsule, preparatory to helping temponaut Enoch Mirren to disembark, they found him doing a disgusting thing with a disgusting thing.

Every head turned away. The word that sprang to mind first was, *"Feh!"*

They wouldn't tell Enoch Mirren's wife he was back. They evaded the question when Enoch Mirren's mother demanded to know the state of her son's health after his having taken the very first journey into another time/universe. The new president was given dissembling answers. No one bothered to call San Clemente. The chiefs of staff were kept in the dark. Inquiries from the CIA and the FBI were met with responses in pig Latin and the bureaus were subtly diverted into investigating each other. Walter Cronkite found out, but after all, there are even limits to how tight security can get.

Their gorges buoyant, everyone of them, the rescue crew and the medical team and the chrono-experts at TimeSep Central did their best but found it impossible to pry temponaut Enoch Mirren's penis from the (presumably) warm confines of the disgusting thing's (presumed) sexual orifice.

A cadre of alien morphologists was assigned to make an evaluation: to decide if the disgusting thing was male or female. After a sleepless week they gave up. The head of the group made a good case for his team's failure. "It'd be a damned sight easier to decide if we could get that clown out of her . . . him . . . it . . . that thing.'"

They tried cajoling, they tried threatening, they tried rational argument, they tried inductive logic, they tried deductive logic, they tried salary incentives, they tried profit sharing, they tried tickling his risibilities, they tried tickling his feet, they tried punching him, they tried shocking him, they tried arresting him, they tried crowbars, they tried hosing him down with cold water, then hot water, then seltzer water, they tried suction devices, they tried sensory deprivation, they tried doping him into unconsciousness. They tried shackling him to a team of Percherons pulling north and the disgusting thing to a team of Clydesdales pulling south. They gave up after three and a half weeks.

The word somehow leaked out that the capsule had come back from time/universe $Earth_2$, and the Russians rattled swords—suggesting that the decadent American filth had brought back a decimating plague that was even now oozing toward Minsk. (TimeSep Central quarantined anyone even remotely privy to the truth.) The OPEC nations announced that the Americans, in league with Zionist Technocrats, had found a way to siphon off crude oil from the time/universe next to our own, and promptly raised the price of gasoline another forty-one cents a gallon. (TimeSep Central moved Enoch Mirren and the disgusting thing to its supersecret bunker headquarters sunk beneath the Painted Desert.) The Pentagon demanded the results of the debriefing and threatened to cut throats; Congress demanded the results and threatened to cut appropriations. (TimeSep Central bit the bullet—they had no other choice, there had been no debriefing—and they stonewalled: *we cannot relay the requested data at this time*.)

Temponaut Enoch Mirren continued coitusing.

The expert from Johns Hopkins, a tall, gray gentleman who wore three-piece suits, and whose security clearance was so stratospherically high the president called him on the red phone, sequestered himself with the temponaut and the disgusting thing for three days. When he emerged, he called in the TimeSep Central officials and said, "Ladies and gentlemen, quite simply put, Enoch

Mirren has brought back from Earth$_2$ the most perfect fuck in the universe."

After they had revived one of the women and four of the men, the expert from Johns Hopkins, a serious, pale gentleman who wore wing-tip shoes, continued. "As best I can estimate, this creature—clearly an alien life-form from some other planet in that alternate time/universe—has an erotic capacity that, once engaged, cannot be neutralized. Once having begun to enjoy its, uh, favors . . . a man either cannot or *will not* stop having relations."

"But that's impossible!" said one of the women. "Men simply cannot hold an erection that long." She looked around at several of her male compatriots with disdain.

"Apparently the thing secretes some sort of stimulant, a jelly, perhaps, that re-engorges the male member," said the expert from Johns Hopkins.

"But is it male or female?" asked one of the men, an administrative assistant who had let it slip in one of their regular encounter sessions that he was concerned about his own sexual preferences.

"It's both, and neither," said the expert from Johns Hopkins. "It seems equipped to handle anything up to and including chickens or kangaroos with double vaginas." He smiled a thin, controlled smile, saying, "You folks have a problem," and then he presented them with a staggering bill for his services. And then he departed, still smiling.

They were little better off than they had been before.

But the women seemed interested.

Two months later, having fed temponaut Enoch Mirren intravenously when they noticed that his weight had been dropping alarmingly, they found an answer to the problem of separating the man and the sex object. By setting up a random sequence sound wave system, pole to pole, with Mirren and his paramour between, they were able to disrupt the flow of energy in the disgusting thing's metabolism. Mirren opened his eyes, blinked several times, murmured, "Oh, that was *good*!" and they pried him loose.

The disgusting thing instantly rolled into a ball and went to sleep.

They immediately hustled Enoch Mirren into an elevator and dropped with him to the deepest, most tightly secured level of the supersecret underground TimeSep Central complex, where a debriefing interrogation cell waited to claim him. It was 10′ × 10′ × 20′, heavily padded in black Naugahyde, and was honeycombed with sensors and microphones. No lights.

They put him in the cell, let him stew for twelve hours, then fed him, and began the debriefing.

"Mirren, what the hell *is* that disgusting thing?"

The voice came from the ceiling. In the darkness Enoch Mirren belched lightly from the quenelles of red snapper they had served him, and scooted around on the floor where he was sitting, trying to locate the source of the annoyed voice.

"It's a terrific little person from Cissalda," he said.

"Cissalda?" Another voice; a woman's voice.

"A planet in another star system of that other time/universe," he replied politely. "They call it Cissalda."

"It can talk?" A third voice, more studious.

"Telepathically. Mind-to-mind. When we're making love."

"All right, knock it off, Mirren!" the first voice said.

Enoch Mirren sat in darkness, smiling.

"Then there's life in that other universe, apart from that disgusting thing, is that right?" The third voice.

"Oh, sure," Enoch Mirren said, playing with his toes. He had discovered he was naked.

"How's the night life on Cissalda?" asked the woman's voice, not really seriously.

"Well, there's not much activity during the week," he answered, "but Saturday nights are dynamite, I'm told."

"I said knock it off, Mirren!"

"Yes, sir."

The third voice, as if reading from a list of prepared questions, asked, "Describe time/universe Earth$_2$ as fully as you can, will you do that, please?"

"I didn't see that much, to be perfectly frank with you, but it's really nice over there. It's warm and very bright, even when the frenzel smelches. Every nolnek there's a vit, when the cosmish isn't drendeling. But *I* found . . ."

"*Hold it, Mirren!*" the first voice screamed.

There was a gentle click, as if the speakers were cut off while the interrogation team talked things over. Enoch scooted around till he found the soft wall, and sat up against it, whistling happily. He whistled "You and the Night and the Music," segueing smoothly into "Someday My Prince Will Come." There was another gentle click, and one of the voices returned. It was the angry voice that spoke first; the impatient one who was clearly unhappy with the temponaut. His tone was soothing, cajoling, as if he were the Recreation Director of the Outpatient Clinic of the Menninger Foundation.

"Enoch . . . may I call you Enoch . . ." Enoch murmured it was lovely to be called Enoch, and the first voice went on, "We're, uh, having a bit of difficulty understanding you."

"How so?"

"Well, we're taping this conversation . . . uh, you don't *mind* if we tape this, do you, Enoch?"

"Huh-uh."

"Yes, well. We find, on the tape, the following words: 'frenzel,' 'smelches,' 'nolneg' . . ."

"That's nol*nek*," Enoch Mirren said. "A nol*neg* is quite another matter. In fact, if you were to refer to a nolnek as a nolneg, one of the tilffs would certainly get highly upset and level a renaq . . ."

"*Hold it!*" The hysterical tone was creeping back into the interrogator's voice. "Nolnek, nolneg, what does it matter—"

"Oh, it matters a lot, see, as I was saying—"

"—it doesn't matter at *all*, Mirren, you asshole! We can't understand a word you're saying!"

The woman's voice interrupted. "Lay back, Bert. Let me talk to him." Bert mumbled something vaguely obscene under his breath. If there was anything Enoch hated, it was vagueness.

"Enoch," said the woman's voice, "this is Dr. Arpin. Inez Arpin? Remember me? I was on your training team before you left?"

Enoch thought about it. "Were you the Black lady with the glasses and the ink blots?"

"No. I'm the white lady with the rubber gloves and the rectal thermometer."

"Oh, sure, of course. You have very trim ankles."

"Thank you."

Bert's voice exploded through the speaker. "*Jeezus* Kee-*rice*, Inez!"

"Enoch," Dr. Arpin continued, ignoring Bert, "are you speaking in tongues?"

Enoch Mirren was silent for a moment, then said, "Gee, I'm awfully sorry. I guess I've been linked up with the Cissaldan so long, I've absorbed a lot of how it thinks and speaks. I'm really sorry. I'll try to translate."

The studious voice spoke again. "How did you meet the, uh, Cissaldan?"

"Just appeared. I didn't call it or anything. Didn't even see it arrive. One minute it wasn't there, and the next it was."

Dr. Arpin spoke. "But how did it get from its own planet to $Earth_2$? Some kind of spaceship, perhaps?"

"No, it just . . . came. It can move by will. It told me it felt my presence, and just simply hopped across all the way from its home in that other star system. I think it was true love that brought it. Isn't that nice?"

All three voices tried speaking at once.

"Teleportation!" Dr. Arpin said, wonderingly.

"Mind-to-mind contact, telepathy, across unfathomable light-years of space," the studious voice said, awesomely.

"And what does it want, Mirren?" Bert demanded, forgetting the conciliatory tone. His voice was the loudest.

"Just to make love; it's really a terrific little person."

"So you just hopped in the sack with that disgusting thing, is that right? Didn't even give a thought to decent morals or contamination or your responsibility to us, or the mission, or anything? Just jumped right into the hay with that pukeable pervert?"

"It seemed like a good idea at the time," Enoch said.

"Well, it was a *lousy* idea, whaddaya think about *that*, Mirren? And there'll be repercussions, you can bet on that, too; repercussions! Investigations! Responsibility must be placed!" Bert was shouting again. Dr. Arpin was trying to calm him.

At that moment, Enoch heard an alarm go off somewhere. It came through the speakers in the ceiling quite clearly, and in a moment the speakers were cut off. But in that moment the sound filled the interrogation cell, its ululations signaling dire emergency. Enoch sat in silence, in darkness, naked, humming, waiting for the voices to return. He hoped he'd be allowed to get back to his Cissaldan pretty soon.

But they never came back. Not ever.

The alarm had rung because the disgusting thing had vanished. The alien morphologists who had been monitoring it through the one-way glass of the control booth fronting on the examination stage that formed the escape-proof study chamber, had been turned away only a few seconds, accepting mugs of steaming stimulant-laced coffee from a Tech 3. When they turned back, the examination stage was empty. The disgusting thing was gone.

People began running around in ever-decreasing circles. Some of them disappeared into holes in the walls and made like they weren't there.

Three hours later they found the disgusting thing.

It was making love with Dr. Marilyn Hornback in a broom closet.

TimeSep Central, deep underground, was the primary locus of visitation, because it had taken the Cissaldan a little while to acclimate itself. But even as Bert, Dr. Inez Arpin, the studious type whose name does not matter, and all the others who came under the classification of chrono-experts were trying to unscramble their brains at the bizarre progression of events in TimeSep Central, matters were already out of their hands.

Cissaldans began appearing everywhere.

As though summoned by some silent song of space and time (which, in fact, was the case), disgusting things began popping into existence all over Earth. Like kernels of corn suddenly erupting into blossoms of popcorn, one moment there would be nothing—or a great deal of what passed for nothing—and the next moment a Cissaldan was there. Invariably right beside a human being. And in the next moment the invariable human being would get this *good* idea that it might be nice to, uh, er, that is, well, sorta *do it* with this creature.

Saffron-robed rilOnks entering the mountain fastness of the Dalai Lama found that venerable fount of cosmic wisdom busily *shtupping* a disgusting thing. A beatific smile creased his wizened countenance.

An international conference of Violently Inclined Filmmakers at the Bel-Air Hotel in Beverly Hills was interrupted when it was noticed that Roman Polanski was under a table making violent love to a thing no one wanted to look at. Sam Peckinpah rushed over to abuse it. That went on, till Peckinpah's disgusting thing materialized and the director fell upon it, moaning.

In the middle of their telecasts, Carmelita Pope, Dinah Shore, and Merv Griffin looked away from the cyclopean red eye of the live cameras, spotted disgusting things, exposed themselves and went to it, thereby upping their flagging ratings considerably.

His Glorious Majesty, the Right Honorable President, General Idi Amin Dada, while selecting material for his new cowboy suit (crushed velvet had his temporary nod as being in just the right vein of quiet good taste), witnessed a materialization right beside his adenoid-shaped swimming pool and fell on his back. The disgusting thing hopped on. No one paid any attention.

Truman Capote, popping Quaaludes like M&M's, rolled himself into a puffy little ball as his Cissaldan mounted him. The level of dope in his system, however, was so high that the disgusting thing went mad and strained itself straight up the urethra and hid itself against his prostate. Capote's voice instantly dropped three octaves.

Maidservants to Queen Elizabeth, knocking frantically on the door to her bedchamber, were greeted with silence. Guards instantly forced the door. They turned their heads away from the disgusting sight that greeted them. There was nothing regal, nothing imperial, nothing even remotely majestic about what was taking place there on the floor.

When Salvador Dali entered his Cissaldan, his waxed mustaches drooped alarmingly, like molten pocket watches.

Anita Bryant, locked in her bassinet-pink bathroom with her favorite vibrator, found herself suddenly assaulted by a disgusting thing. She fought it off and a second appeared. Then a third. Then a platoon. In moments the sounds of her outraged shrieks could be heard throughout that time zone, degenerating quickly into a bubbling, citraholic gurgle. It was the big bang theory actualized.

Cissaldans appeared to fourteen hundred assembly line workers in the automobile plant at Toyota City, just outside Yokohama. While the horny-handed sons and daughters of toil were busily getting it on, hundreds of half-assembled car bodies crashed and thundered into an untidy pile forty feet high.

Masters and Johnson had it off with the same one.

Billy Graham was discovered by his wife and members of his congregation having congress with a disgusting thing in a dust bin. He was "knowing" it, however, in the Biblical sense, murmuring, "*I* found it!"

Three fugitive *Reichsmarschalls*, posing as Bolivian sugar cane workers while they plotted the renascence of the Third Reich, were confronted by suddenly materialized Cissaldans in a field near Cochabamba. Though the disgusting things looked disgustingly kosher, the unrepentant Nazis hurled themselves onto the creatures, visualizing pork-fat sandwiches.

William Shatner, because of his deep and profound experience with Third World Aliens, attempted to communicate with the disgusting thing that popped into existence in his dressing room. He began delivering a captainlike lecture on coexistence and the Cissaldan—bored, vanished—to find a more suitable mate. A few minutes later, a less discerning Cissaldan appeared and Shatner, now overcome with this *good* idea, fell on it, dislodging his hairpiece.

Evel Knievel took a running jump at a disgusting thing, overshot, hit the wall, and semi-conscious, dragged himself back to the waiting aperture.

There in that other time/universe, the terrific little persons of Cissalda had spent an eternity making love to one another. But their capacity for passion was enormous, beyond calculation, intense and never-waning. It could be called *fornigalactic*. They had waited millennia for some other race to make itself known to them.

But life springs into being only rarely, and their eons were spent in familiar sex with their own kind, and in loneliness. A loneliness monumental to conceive. When Enoch Mirren had come through the fabric of time and space to Earth$_2$, they had sent the most adept of their race to check him out. And the Cissaldan looked upon Enoch Mirren and found him to be *good*.

And so, like a reconnaissance ant sent out from the hill to scout the territory of a sugar cookie, that most talented of disgusting things sent back telepathic word to its kind: *We've got a live one here.*

Now, in mere moments, the flood of teleporting Cissaldans overflowed the Earth: one for every man, woman, and child on the planet. Also leftovers for chickens and kangaroos with double vaginas.

The four top members of the Presidium of the Central Committee of the Supreme Soviet of the Communist Party (CPSU) of the Union of Soviet Socialist Republics—Brezhnev, Kosygin, Podgorny, and Gromyko—deserted the four hefty ladies who had come as Peoples' Representatives to the National Tractor Operator's Conference from the Ukraine, and began having wild—but socialistic—intercourse with the disgusting things that materialized on their conference table. The four hefty ladies did not care: four Cissaldans had popped into existence for *their* pleasure. It was better than being astride a tractor. Or Brezhnev, Kosygin, Podgorny, and Gromyko.

All over the world Mort Sahl and Samuel Beckett and Fidel Castro and H. R. Haldeman and Ti-Grace Atkinson and Lord Snowdon and Jonas Salk and Jorge Luis Borges and Golda Meier and Earl Butts linked up with disgusting things and said no more. A stately and pleasant hush fell across the planet. Barbra Streisand hit the highest note of her career as she was penetrated. Philip Roth had guilt but did it anyhow. Stevie Wonder fumbled but got in finally. It was good.

All over the planet Earth it was quiet, and it was *good.*

One week later, having established without room for discourse that Naugahyde was neither edible nor appetizing, Enoch Mirren decided he was being brutalized. He had not been fed, been spoken to, been permitted the use of lavatory facilities, or in even the smallest way been noticed since the moment he had heard the alarm go off and the speakers had been silenced. His interrogation cell smelled awful, he had lost considerable weight, he had a dreadful ringing in his ears from the silence and, to make matters terminal, the air was getting thin. "Okay. No more Mister Nice Guy," he said to the silence, and proceeded to effect his escape.

Clearly, easy egress from a 10′×10′×20′ padded cell sunk half a mile down in the most top-secret installation in America was not possible. If there was a door to the cell, it was so cleverly concealed that hours of careful fingertip examination could not reveal it. There were speaker grilles in the ceiling of the cell, but that was a full twenty feet above him. He was tall, and thin—a lot thinner now—but even if he jumped, it was still a good ten feet out of reach.

He thought about his problem and wryly recalled a short story he had read in an adventure magazine many years before. It had been a cheap pulp magazine, filled with stories hastily written for scandalously penurious rates, and the craftsmanship had been employed accordingly. In the story that now came to Enoch's mind, the first installment of the serial had ended with the mightily-thewed hero trapped at the bottom of a very deep pit floored with poison-tipped stakes, as a horde of coral snakes slithered toward him, brackish water was pumped into the pit and rising rapidly, his left arm was broken, he was without weapon, and a man-eating Sumatran black panther peered over the lip of the pit, watching him closely. Enoch remembered wondering—with supreme confidence in the writer's talents and ingenuity—how he would rescue his hero. The month-long wait till the next issue was on the newsstand was the longest month of Enoch's life. On the day of its release, he had pedaled down to the newsstand on his Schwinn and snagged the first copy of the adventure magazine from the bundle almost before the dealer had snipped the binding wire. He had dashed outside, thrown himself down on the curb and riffled through the magazine till he found the second installment of the cliff-hanging serial. How would the writer, this master of suspense and derring-do, save the beleaguered hero?

Part two began:

"With one mighty leap, Vance Lionmane freed himself from the pit, overcoming the panther and rushing forward to save the lovely Ariadne from the aborigines."

Later, *comma*, after he had escaped from the interrogation cell, Enoch Mirren was to remember that moment, thinking again as he had when but a child, what a rotten lousy cheat that writer had been.

There were no Cissaldans left over. Everywhere Enoch went he found the terrific little persons shacked up with old men, young women, pre- and post-pubescent children, ducks, porpoises, wildebeests, dogs, arctic terns, llamas, young men, old women and, of course, chickens and kangaroos with double vaginas. But no lovemate for Enoch Mirren.

It became clear after several weeks of wandering, waiting for a materialization in his immediate vicinity, that the officials at TimeSep Central had dealt with him more severely than they could have known.

They had broken the rhythm. They had pulled him out of that disgusting thing, and now, because the Cissaldans were telepathically linked and were all privy to the knowledge, no Cissaldan would have anything to do with him.

The disgusting things handled rejection very badly.

Enoch Mirren sat on a high cliff a few miles south of Carmel, California. The Peterbilt he had driven across the country in futile search of another human being who was not making love to a Cissaldan, was parked on the shoulder of Route 1, the Pacific Coast Highway, above him. He sat on the cliff with his legs dangling over the Pacific Ocean. The guidebook beside him said the waters should be filled with seals at play, with sea otters wrapped in kelp while they floated on their backs cracking clams against their bellies, with whales migrating, because this was January and time for the great creatures to commence their journey. But it was cold, and the wind tore at him, and the sea was empty. Somewhere, elsewhere, no doubt, the seals and the cunning sea otters and the majestic whales were locked in passionate embrace with disgusting things from another time/universe.

Loneliness had driven him to thinking of those terrific little persons as disgusting things. Love and hate are merely obverse faces of the same devalued coin. Aristotle said that. Or Pythagoras. One of that crowd.

The first to know true love, he was the last to know total loneliness. He wasn't the last human on Earth, but a lot of good it did him. Everybody was busy, and he was alone. And long after they had all died of starvation, he would still be here . . . unless he decided some time in the ugly future to drive the Peterbilt off a cliff somewhere.

But not just yet. Not just now.

He pulled the notebook and pen from his parka pocket and finished writing the story of what had happened. It was not a long story, and he had written it as an open letter, addressing it to whatever race or species inherited the Earth long after the Cissaldans had wearied of banging corpses and had returned to their own time/universe to wait for new lovers. He suspected that without a reconnaissance ant to lead them here, to establish a telepathic-teleportational link, they would not be able to get back here once they had left.

He only hoped it would not be the cockroaches who rose up through the evolutionary muck to take over the cute little Earth, but he had a feeling that was to be the case. In all his travels across the land, the only creatures that could not get a Cissaldan to make love to them, were the cockroaches. Apparently, even disgusting things had a nausea threshold. Unchecked, the cockroaches were already swarming across the world.

He finished the story, stuffed it in an empty Perrier Water bottle, capped it securely with a stopper and wax, and flung it by its neck as far out as he could into the ocean.

He watched it float in and out with the tide for a while, until a current caught it and took it away. Then he rose, wiped off his hands, and strode back up the slope to the 18-wheeler. He was smiling sadly. It had just occurred to him that his only consolation in bearing the knowledge that he had destroyed the human race, was that for a little while, in the eyes of the best fuck in the universe, *he* had been the best fuck in the universe.

There wasn't a cockroach in the world who could claim the same.

From A to Z, in the Chocolate Alphabet

A is for ***ATLANTEAN***

Their science predicted the quake. There had been two centuries of warning temblors. With the aid of genetic engineering, they began a return to the ocean. It would not be a lost continent; it would be an abandoned continent. And throughout the ages that followed, humankind would search for "lost" Atlantis, never realizing that when the earth split and the fires of the underworld seared the land, the Atlanteans would already have developed gill breathing and useful membranes. See, then: Krenoa, capital city of undersea Atlantis. Snug and secure at the bottom of the Maracot Deep. Towers of porphyry and adamantine, lit with lambent flames from within; walls of seaweeds and kelp, altered by chemical means to retain their flexibility yet suitable for buildings; flying bridges and causeways all hollow and shimmering. Krenoa, beautiful beyond belief. And lying in a public square, an enormous lead canister, split open and holding darkness. An alien object dropped into Krenoa from above. See, now: the Atlanteans. Pale blue and great-eyed, gentle expressions and wisdom in their open, staring, dead eyes. What God and Nature could not destroy, the inheritors of the Earth did.

B is for ***BREATHDEATH***

It's waiting for them when they reach space. It grows on virtually every world but the Earth. It is common as weed. The little black flower with the soft red bulb in its center. Its spores fill the atmosphere of gray planets circling yellow stars and burned-out cinders. When the last of the atmosphere has been drawn off into space, the spores will settle. But they will still kill. It is a lovely flower. If one stares into its center one can see many things, disturbing things. Until the aneurysms stop the visions and the blood bursts forth. There is a race on a far star that believes the breathdeath can be ground up and cut with various juices and consumed, and it will give eternal life. No one has ever tried the recipe. It waits.

C is for Cushio

When he was ten, he was savaged by a forest creature they had thought extinct thousands of years before. They killed the beast and put it on display in the largest museum of their world. The boy was taken to Regeneration and they rebuilt him with machine parts and soft things that had been flesh in other bodies. He grew up half-human, and thus never understood what humans wanted. He killed his first when he was fifteen. By his twenty-first year he ruled the continent with a guard of mercenaries as ruthless as himself. He went into space with an armada at the age of thirty and left behind him a route of road-markers that had been lives and cities and thriving markets. The route of embers and mass graves. They stopped him near Aldebaran, and space was littered with wreckage beyond the range of even the most sensitive sensors. They took him alive, and they encased him in amber and they embedded him in the earth of the homeworld, with cameras that never shut down and never let him out of their sight. And there he stayed, forever. The regenerators of his world had done their work well. He would live forever. And mothers of the homeworld, who desired their children to go to sleep, invoked the name of Cushio. They said, "Cushio will take you if you don't do good." And the children were too young to know that could never be.

D is for Dikh

He is sick. He writes his books in the lowest level of a deep labyrinthine grotto. His books are filled with things no one ever wanted to know. Unsettling things. He became part mushroom many years ago, but even the small lizards who come and feed off his body never realize he was once a man. If he were on a desert island he would write his awful stories and send them out in bottles. But there, deep in the grotto, no one will ever read a word he has written; written with shards of sharpened stone in the blood of lizards; written on walls that go deep into the earth. But one day they will need fossil fuels, and they will break through a wall of his grotto, and they will find the books, written on endless walls. And they will find the thing with a tormented face, growing in the moist soil of the underworld.

***E is for* Elevator People**

They never speak, and they cannot meet your gaze. There are five hundred buildings in the United States whose elevators go deeper than the basement. When you have pressed the basement button and reached bottom, you must press the basement button twice more. The elevator doors will close, and you will hear the sound of special relays being thrown, and the elevator will descend. Into the caverns. Chance has not looked favorably on occasional voyagers in those five hundred cages. They have pressed the wrong button too many times. They have been seized by those who shuffle through the caverns, and they have been . . . treated. Now they ride the cages. They never speak, and they cannot meet your gaze. They stare up at the numbers as they light and then go off, riding up and down even after night has fallen. Their clothes are clean. There is a special dry cleaner who does the work. Once you saw one of them, and her eyes were filled with screams. London is a city filled with narrow, secure stairways.

***F is for* Flenser**

Among all the paranormals, the flensers are the most kind. They read minds, they are empathic, and they see all the anguish in those they pass. They wipe clean the slates of the minds they encounter. And for this, they suffer a great isolation. They are the pale people whose socks fall down, the ones you see standing on street corners. They are the ones with pimples and odd conversation. Theirs is a terribly lonely existence. Every day they crucify themselves, endlessly, over and over. Be kind to the pale old ladies and the mumbling scrawny boys you pass in the drug store. They may save you from the terrors of your past.

G is for Golem

Golems are *goyim* that always wanted to be Jewish. But they never suffered enough guilt.

H is for Hamadryad

The Oxford English Dictionary has three definitions of hamadryad. The first is: a wood nymph that lives and dies in her tree. The second is: a venomous, hooded serpent of India. The third definition is improbable. None of them mentions the mythic origins of the word. The tree in which the Serpent lived was the hamadryad. Eve was poisoned. The wood of which the cross was made was the hamadryad. Jesus did not rise, he never died. The ark was composed of cubits of lumber from the hamadryad. You will find no sign of the vessel on top of Mt. Ararat. It sank. Toothpicks in Chinese restaurants should be avoided at all costs.

I is for Ice Crawler

When the exit from the polar ice cap was sealed by nukes and thermite, a few of them managed to escape. They were tracked by land and by air, but their thick, white skins concealed them from all but chance discovery. With the end of the supply of good skins, the fashion died quickly and the return of stripped corduroy-and-velour soon followed. Those that had escaped found channels in the permafrost and tried to return to their land. They had never known violence, it had come to them slowly, only as a desperate last measure; and only a few had learned the lesson well enough to crawl back to their blasted domain. The hunting parties that had come after them had slaughtered thousands before there was the slightest retaliation. At first, they had believed the warm people from the light had come to establish relations. But when their piping language fell on deaf ears, and the harpoons were thrown, they knew they had been discovered to their ultimate undoing. Those who survived crawled back and ate out burrows for their dead. Then they slithered away from that place to a deeper level and began to breed. They would teach their children what they had learned. And perhaps one day they would wear fashionable skins . . . in four or five different colors.

J is for Jabberwock

India conceals many secrets. In the Hindu Kush there is a monastery far back in the low mountains where a sect of monks worships the last Jabberwock. It is a fearsome creature: much smaller than one would expect from reading *Alice*. It has bat-wings whose membranes between the struts are tattered and torn. It is deep red in color and covered with bristly fur from its shoulders to its buttocks. It resembles a bat-eared, winged jackal with incredibly sharp teeth and one good eye. The other eye has two pupils and is a most malevolent thing to behold. Its claws can tear rock, and it screams constantly. The monks are the holiest of holy men. They have tried to mate the Jabberwock to preserve its presence in their midst. They have mated it with a pig and produced a thing that can neither walk nor see. They have mated it with a camel and the offspring was born dead but would not decay. They mated it with swans, with ibis, with auks, and with jackals. The monks keep the children of these unions in glass cages, but they seldom go to look. They mated it with a young girl, a virgin stolen from a small village. The girl died, but the child still lives. They must change the soft cloth in the bottom of its nest three times a day. It sweats blood. The holy monks hope they will be able to find a mate for the Jabberwock before another hundred years passes. What they do not know is that the Jabberwock has sentience, it is a thinking, feeling creature for all its awesome menace. What they do not know is what the Jabberwock thinks, what it wishes. The Jabberwock wishes it were dead.

K is for Kenghis Khan

He was a very *nice* person. History has no record of him. There is a moral in that somewhere.

L is for Loup-Garou

Had Śasa Novácek's parents come to America from Ireland or Sweden or even Poland, he would not have realized that the woman next door was a werewolf. But they had come from Ostrava, in Czechoslovakia, and he recognized the shape of the nostrils, the hair in the palms of her hands when she loaned him a cup of non-dairy creamer, the definitive s-curve of the spine as she walked to hang her laundry. So he was ready. He had bought a thirty-ought-six hunting rifle and he had melted down enough twenty-five-cent pieces to make his own silver bullets. And on the night of the full moon, when the madness was upon her, and she burst through the kitchen window in a snarling strike of fangs and fur, he was ready for her. Calmly, with full presence, and murmuring the names of the very best saints, he emptied the rifle into her. Later, the coroner was unable to describe the condition of Śasa Novácek's body on a single form sheet. The coin of the United States of America, notably the twenty-five-cent piece, the quarter, has less than one percent pure silver in it. Times change, but legends do not.

M is for Muu Muu

One should always wear one if one has more than six or seven arms.

N is for Nemotropin

Irl and Onkadj were the last to enter the Tunnel of Final Darkness. The competition had been more fierce this Contest than any nemotropin could remember. The gladiators had fallen, spears in their thoracic vitals, mandibles shattered, eyestalks ripped out, claws sliced off . . . until only Irl and Onkadj had survived. Now they were closed off in the Tunnel to decide which of them would have to suffer the penalty. The Contest among the nemotropin was the only way they had to rid themselves of undesirables. And as the nemotropin were universally judged the most evil, warlike race in the galaxy, the level of undesirability was a marvel even to the most vicious brigands and hellspawned marauders. They were forced to produce everything they needed for their existence; no other planet or confederation of planets would undertake to trade with them. They were staked off-limits and permitted to breed and kill and live as best they could. But they could not leave their nameless world. With one exception. Thousands of years before, a mission from the Heart Stars Federation had come to their world and had tried to civilize the nemotropin. Just before the missionaries had been slaughtered and masticated, they had been granted the right to send one of the nemotropin off-world. The mission had no way of knowing that time and ritual would alter this grant as an excuse for the nemotropin to weed out those even too despicable for existence in a society of killers and reavers. The nemotropin were at least sane enough never to reveal the nature of their awful duplicity. And so, periodically, they would hold the Contest, and the worst of their number would slaughter and slay and attack each other till only one was left standing. And he would be sent to the shape-changing satellite the Federation maintained, and would be sent to the pilgrim world where he could do no more harm among the nemotropin. And so Irl and Onkadj went into the Tunnel of Final Darkness with their shell shields covering the soft vulnerable spot beneath which rested the gliomas of their brains. Irl wielded a pair of cutters, and a brace of poison bags was strapped to his right side, protecting his wounds from earlier battles. Should Onkadj strike in that area, the bags would spurt poison and kill him. Onkadj was the younger of the combatants, and without peer in use of the broiler spear. Helmeted, their hooves coated with retardant to keep them from slipping on the mossy stones of the Tunnel, they faced each other and the final combat began. It raged for three days and three nights, and on the morning of the fourth day, Onkadj emerged without one of his four arms, but carrying Irl's lower mandible. He was sent to the shape-changing satellite, made malleable, altered into the form of the superior indigenous life-form of the host-planet, and sent away. On the host-planet, Onkadj did quite well. It was a very different world than that of the nemotropin, and Onkadj functioned well in the body. He became a prominent figure. There *is* an explanation for Attila, for Haman, for Cortéz, for Cesare Borgia, for Christie and Speck and Manson and Nixon. For Torquemada. But only the nemotropin know the explanation. And they smile as best they can with bloody mandibles.

O is for Ouroboros

Banished from the Earth, the great worm coiled ever so tightly and went to sleep. One day he will awake. The moon will writhe.

P is for Poltergeist

Essentially very well coordinated. Very few people remember, because of the Black Sox scandal, but in 1919 the Chicago White Sox carried a pitcher named Fred Morris who won thirty games; pitched seven perfect no-hit, no-run games; struck out twenty-five batters in one contest; and replaced every divot in the outfield without moving from home plate. He played only one season, his heart was broken when Shoeless Joe Jackson turned up a creep, and inexplicably vanished from whence he came. He was a poltergeist with a whole lot of love for the sport. Hardly anyone today remembers Fred Morris.

Q is for Quetzalcoatl

He did not come from space. He was not an alien. He did not build Toltec or even Aztec pyramids as landing beacons for flying saucers. His most obvious bad habit was a rather nasty appetite for freshly excised, still-pulsing hearts. It is not true what they say about Quetzalcoatl and the virgins. Take it or leave it.

R is for Roq

The flying city of Detroit (it's up there) was in the midst of its Founder's Day celebration when the great golden roq came to feed. It settled down over the Caliph's Dome (where the roller derby semifinals were in progress) and thrust its ebony beak through the formed plastic and steel girdering. It dipped again and again, bringing up masses of writhing spectators (and blocker "Rumpy" Johansson), their screams feeding into the p.a. system and causing an overload. The great bird's appetite could hardly be satisfied with a few sports fans, however. It rose on enormous, beating pinions, its pink tongue vibrating and its shriek of joy shattering all the facets of the Esso Tetrahedron. The roq's shadow swam across the gigantic flying metropolis as the bird dove on the Servitor Factory. What could have made it seek out such an inedible attraction no one in Detroit (or even Bombay, floating over there a little way off) could ever say. But it settled and began to eat the entire plant, robot parts and all. And when it had finished consuming the Factory, and the millions of individual bits of incipient robot, it slaked its thirst in the Crystal Falls for the better part of a day. And when, hours later, it fell (crushing a whole lot of stuff), and it died, the residents of Detroit were stunned and waxed extremely wroth. The great golden roq of the sky had rusted itself to death and the meat wasn't worth a damn thing, not even for hot dog casings.

S is for Solifidian the Sorcerer

I was an invited guest at the elegant fund-raising party where Solifidian performed his miracles. I'd received the engraved invitation to the party several weeks earlier, but had not planned to RSVP, because I knew they'd be hitting us up for contributions to the political war chest of a city councilman whose position on rapid transit I considered really fucked. But Penny Goldman called first, and tried to embarrass me into coming, and when that didn't work Leslie Parrish called and said it had been so long since she'd seen me, why didn't I stop being a poop, and just come to the party; and I wanted to see Leslie again, so I went. It was held at Larry Niven's new home out in Tarzana, and Larry and Marilyn had really outdone themselves in setting up the buffet and hiring the caterers to erect the big party tent on the grounds out back. The minute I came through the door, a committee worker for the councilman handed me a pledge card, which I promptly folded and put in my side jacket pocket. I'd probably give the slob some bucks, but I'd make damned sure I spent a few minutes telling him if he didn't get off his ass and start formulating plans for a new rapid transit district in Los Angeles he was going to find himself facing a *new* committee . . . one I'd form to beat his backside at election time. So I wandered around and made small talk with people I knew, and tried to corner Leslie, who was buzzing around doing organizational things; and finally the entertainment started in the tent. George Carlin and Richard Pryor took turns ruining my mind, and then they got together and did an ad lib routine in tandem, which had to be the funniest thing since Jack Lemon delivered the line, "Leslie the Great escaped with a *chicken*!?!" in *The Great Race*. Then there was a break while Tom Hensley got set up with the Roto-Rooter Good Time Christmas Band, and I saw Solifidian for the first time. He looked just like Mandrake the Magician. He was about seven feet tall, and as thin as a Watergate alibi; he had one of those hairline mustaches that always made me think of Simon Legree in a stage production of *Uncle Tom's Cabin*; and he had the slimmest, whitest, most beautiful hands I'd ever seen. Brain surgeon fingers with polished nails. He wore a tux with tails, and a top hat. If I'd owned a diner, I'd have hired him on the spot as a sandwich-board man. And after Tom's band had blown everyone away, Solifidian was introduced by "the Candidate" himself, and the sorcerer—because that was what he clearly was—asked the audience to tell him their most secret desires. Nothing big, just something that was personally important to each person. At first no one would speak up, but finally a woman said, "I have a very painful, difficult period every month. Can you do anything about that?" Everyone was startled and a little embarrassed, but when I realized it was Georgina Voss I smiled; she'd say *any*thing. But Solifidian didn't seem to think it was outrageous, and he pointed a long white finger at her and said, "I think you'll find it all better now." Querulously, Georgina looked at him, and then a big smile came over her face, and she stood up and said, "Oh my *God*!" and, laughing like a loon, she rushed off into Larry's house, presumably to the bathroom, to check herself. But no one in the crowd doubted that Solifidian had rearranged her parts so she wasn't in pain. Then I heard a man's voice say, "I can't get a decent shave. My beard is like barbed wire and my skin is like a baby's instep," and I suddenly recognized the voice as my own. "When I even use an electric razor I cut myself and get ingrown hairs and then I look like a forty-two-year-old kid with acne. Can you take care of that, sir?" Solifidian nodded, pointed a finger at me and, as everyone gasped in awe (and not a little horror), every follicle on my face wormed its way out of my skin, carrying with it the root and whatever it is that makes the hair grow back. It all fell on my jacket, and I brushed it off, and rubbed my jaw, and I was as smooth as if I'd just come from the barber at the Plaza Hotel in New York. I led the applause. There was more, much more. He performed a dozen similar miracles in the space of mere minutes. He gave one woman a sensational nose job, made a talent agent's penis larger, cured one guy's color blindness, gave Bill Rotsler back the sense of smell, and restored hair to the bald pate of The Candidate. He was amazing, this miracle worker. Never saw anything like it. He was in the middle of performing a vasectomy on Marty Shapiro when a stout woman wearing an improbable hat came stalking into the midst of the crowd. She stood there staring at him, this *miracle worker*, with her chubby hands on her hips until he was finished. And when he looked around to see who was next, and he saw her, his face fell. "So this is where you are, you asshole," she snarled. He began to fumfuh and wave his hands around helplessly. "Harry Solifidian, get your lazy ass in gear! There's work to be done at the house, and no time for you to be fooling around with these schmucks! Now come *on*!" He looked sheepish, this *miracle worker*, but he followed her docilely. They walked through the crowd, which parted for them without a murmur, and in a moment they were gone. And that was that. And I never saw him again. But, you know, to this day I'm always amazed at the magic hold some men have over some women . . . and the magic hold some women have over some men.

T is for Troglodyte

They live under the city dump, and they can eat almost anything except plastic containers. If it weren't for the troglodytes, we'd be *tuchis*-deep in garbage. There is a whole lot to be said for returnable glass bottles.

U is for UPHIR

Demon chemist and doctor, well versed in knowledge of medicinal herbs, responsible for the health of demons, official apothecary and surgeon to the Court of Satan, Uphir recently had a rather unpleasant experience. Semiazas, chief of the fallen angels with Azazel (no need to go into the subject of office politics) came down with a serious charley horse in his tail. Uphir was called in, diagnosed the problem, and applied the traditional incantations and a poultice of mole paws and liverwort. Just to be on the safe side, he gave Semiazas a shot of penicillin. How was he to know the demon was allergic to mole paws. An unlovely reaction, made even worse by the penicillin. Without volition, Semiazas began to make it snow in Hell. Instantly, hundreds of thousands of foolish promises, idle boasts, dire threats, and contracts Satan had made containing the phrase "It'll be a cold day in Hell" (on which he never thought he'd have to deliver) came true. Uphir was punished by being submerged to his nose in a lake of monkey vomit, while a squad of imps raced motorboats around him, making waves. California is not the only place where it's difficult to get malpractice insurance.

V is for VORWALAKA

Count Carlo Szipesti, a *vorwalaka*, a vampire, having long-since grown weary of stalking alleyways and suffering the vicissitudes of finding meals in the streets, hied himself to a commune in upstate New York where he, with his beard, his accent, and his peculiar nocturnal habits, fit right in with the young people who had joined together for a return to the land. For the count, it was a guaranteed fountain of good, healthy blood. The young people in the commune were very big on bean sprouts and hulled sunflower seeds. They were all tanned from working in the fields, and the blood ran hot and vibrant in their veins. When the count was found dead, the coroner's inquest did not reveal that he had been a creature of darkness, one of the dread vampires of the old country; what it *did* reveal was that he had died from infectious hepatitis. As the *Journal of the American Medical Association* has often pointed out, health is inextricably involved with morality.

W is for WAND OF JACOB

Alfred Jacobi, seventy-two years old and nearly blind, was accosted at one o'clock in the morning on the Sheridan Square station platform of the IRT subway. His grandchildren, Emily and Foster and Hersch, had been yelling at Alfred for years: "Why do you go out walking in this awful city late at night? Crazy old man, you'll be mugged, killed. What's the matter with you?" But Alfred Jacobi had lived in New York for sixty of his seventy-two years, and he believed in the God of his forefathers, and—miraculously it seemed—he had never suffered even a moment's unpleasantness in the streets. Even though New York had become a prowling ground for the most detestable human predators urban America had ever produced, Alfred Jacobi was able to walk where he wished, even in Central Park at midnight, *kene hora*, tapping his way gently with his specially carved cane, painted white to indicate he could not see. But neither the cane nor his age deterred the gang of young toughs with cans of spray paint who paused in their systematic defacement of white tile walls and poster advertisements to attack the old man. They came at him in a bunch, and he extended his cane, and there was a bright flash of light. And Alfred Jacobi was alone on the platform once more. The Wand of Jacob, the stick which preceded the magic wand, that forces spirits to appear or repulses them as did Moses's rod, his Wand of Jacob was still fully charged. If one ventures down onto the Sheridan Square platform of the IRT, one can see a most marvelous example of native artwork. It is a frieze, apparently rendered by an unsung urban Michelangelo in spray paint, in many colors, extremely lifelike, of a gang of young men, screaming in horror. It's a refreshing break from all the obscenities and self-advertisements for CHICO 116 one finds in the New York subway system.

X is for Xaphan

Demon of the second order. At the time of the rebellion of the angels, *he* proposed that the heavens be set on fire. For his perfidy he has forevermore stoked the furnaces of Hell. It is never good to have dissatisfied help working in one's company. Xaphan is steadily overloading the boilers. Pay attention to stories about the melting polar ice cap. Xaphan is programming for Armageddon, and there's not a damn thing we can do about it.

Y is for Yggdrasil

The legendary Nordic ash tree with its three roots extending into the lands of mortals, giants, and Niflheim, the land of mist, grows in Wisconsin. Legend has it that when the tree falls, the universe will fall. Next Wednesday, the state highway commission comes through that empty pasture with a freeway.

Z is for Zombie

Howard Hughes did not die in 1976, no matter *what* they tell you. Howard Hughes died in 1968. It was not a spectacular death, down in flames in the "Spruce Goose" or assassinated by his next-in-command or frightened to death by an insect that found its way into his eyrie. He choked to death on a McDonald's greaseburger during dinner one night in July of 1968. But wealth has its privileges. Johns Hopkins and the Mayo Clinic and the Walter Reed in Maryland sent their teams. But he was dead. DOA, Las Vegas. And he was buried. Not in 1976, in 1968. And Mama Legba, with whom Hughes had made a deal twenty years earlier in Haiti, came to the grave, and she raised him. The corporate entity is mightier than death. But the end is near: at this very moment, training in the Sierra Maestra, is an attack squad of Fidel Castro's finest guerrillas. They know where Hughes went when he evacuated Nicaragua one week before the earthquake. (Zombies have precognitive faculties, did you know that?) And they know the 1976 death story is merely misdirection like all the other death rumors throughout the preceding years. They will seek him out and put him to *final* rest by the only means ever discovered for deanimating the walking dead. They will pour sand in his eyes, stuff a dead chicken in his mouth, and sew up the mouth with sailcloth twine. It would take a mission this important to get the fierce Cuban fighters to suffer all the ridicule: bayonet practice with dead chickens is terribly demeaning.

Eidolons

Eidolon: a phantom, an apparition, an image.

Ancient geographers gave a mystic significance to that extremity of land, the borderland of the watery unknown at the southwestern tip of Europe. Marinus and Ptolemy knew it as *Promontorium Sacrum*, the sacred promontory. Beyond that beyondmost edge, lay nothing. Or rather, lay a place that was fearful and unknowable, a place in which it was always the twenty-fifth hour of the day, the thirtieth or thirty-first of February; a turbid ocean of lost islands where golden mushroom trees reached always toward the whispering face of the moon; where tricksy life had spawned beasts and beings more of satin and ash than of man and woman; dominion of dreams, to which the unwary might journey, but from whence they could never return.

My name is Vizinczey, and my background is too remarkable to be detailed here. Suffice to note that before Mr. Brown died in my arms, I had distinguished myself principally with occupations and behavior most cultures reward by the attentions of the headsman and the *strappado*. Suffice to note that before Mr. Brown died in my arms, the most laudable engagement in my *vita* was as the manager and sole roustabout of an abattoir and ossuary in Li Shih-min. Suffice to note that there were entire continents I was forbidden to visit, and that even my closest acquaintances, the family of Sawney Beane, chose to avoid social intercourse with me.

I was a pariah. Whatever land in which I chose to abide, became a land of darkness. Until Mr. Brown died in my arms, I was a thing without passion, without kindness.

While in Sydney—Australia being one of the three remaining continents where hunting dogs would not be turned out to track me down—I inquired if there might be a shop where authentic military miniatures, toy soldiers of the sort H. G. Wells treasured, could be purchased. A clerk in a bookstore recalled "a customer of mine in Special Orders mentioned something like that . . . a curious little man . . . a Mr. Brown."

I got onto him, through the clerk, and was sent round to see him at his home. The moment he opened the door and our eyes met, he was frightened of me. For the brief time we spent in each other's company, he never ceased, for a moment, to fear me. Ironically, he was one of the few ambulatory creatures on this planet that I meant no harm. Toy soldiers were my hobby, and I held in high esteem those who crafted, painted, amassed, or sold them. In truth, it might be said of the Vizinczey that was I in those times before Mr. Brown died in my arms, that my approbation for toy soldiers and their aficionados was the sole salutary aspect of my nature. So, you see, he had no reason to fear me. Quite the contrary. I mention this to establish, in spite of the police records and the warrants still in existence, seeking my apprehension, I had nothing whatever to do with the death of Mr. Brown.

He did not invite me in, though he stepped aside with a tremor and permitted entrance. Cognizant of his terror at my presence, I was surprised that he locked the door behind me. Then, looking back over his shoulder at me with mounting fear, he led me into an enormous central drawing room of his home, a room expanded to inordinate size by the leveling of walls that had formed adjoining areas. In that room, on every horizontal surface, Mr. Brown had positioned rank after rank of the most astonishing military miniatures I had ever seen.

Perfect in the most minute detail, painted so artfully that I could discern no brushstroke, in colors and tones and hues so accurate and lifelike that they seemed rather to have been created with pigmentations inherent, the battalions, cohorts, regiments, legions, phalanxes, brigades, and squads of metal figurines blanketed in array without a single empty space, every inch of floor, tables, cabinets, shelves, window ledges, risers, showcases, and countless numbers of stacked display boxes.

Enthralled, I bent to study more closely the infinite range of fighting men. There were Norman knights and German Landsknecht, Japanese samurai, and Prussian dragoons, foot grenadiers of the French Imperial Guard, and Spanish conquistadors. U.S. 7th Cavalry troopers from the Indian wars; Dutch musketeers and pikemen who marched with the army of Maurice of Nassau during the long war of independence fought by the Netherlands against the Spanish Habsburgs; Greek hoplites in bronze helmets and stiff cuirasses; cocked hat riflemen of Morgan's Virginia Rifles who repulsed Burgoyne's troops with their deadly accurate Pennsylvania longbarrels; Egyptian chariot-spearmen and French Foreign Legionnaires; Zulu warriors from Shaka's legions and English longbowmen from Agincourt; Anzacs and Persian Immortals and Assyrian slingers; Cossacks and Saracen warriors in chain-mail and padded silk; 82nd Airborne paratroopers and Israeli jet pilots and Wehrmacht Panzer commanders and Russian infantrymen and Black Hussars of the 5th Regiment.

And as I drifted through a mist of wonder and pleasure, from array to array, one overriding observation dominated even my awe in the face of such artistic grandeur.

Each and every figure—to the last turbaned Cissian, trousered Scythian, wooden-helmeted Colchian, or Pisidian with an oxhide shield—every one of them bore the most exquisite expression of terror and hopelessness. Faces twisted in anguish at the precise moment of death, or more terribly, the moment of *realization* of personal death, each soldier looked up at me with eyes just fogging with tears, with mouth half-open to emit a scream, with fingers reaching toward me in splay-fingered hope of last-minute reprieve.

These were not merely painted representations.

The faces were individual. I could see every follicle of beard, every drop of sweat, every frozen tic of agony. They seemed able to complete the shriek of denial. They looked as if, should I blink, they would spring back to life and then fall dead as they were intended.

Mr. Brown had left narrow aisles of carpet among the vast armadas, and I had wandered deep into the shoe-top grassland of the drawing room with the little man behind me, still locked up with fear but attendant at my back. Now I rose from examining a raiding party of Viet Cong frozen in attitudes of agony as the breath of life stilled in them, and I turned to Mr. Brown with apparently such a look on my face that he blurted it out. I could not have stopped the confession had I so desired.

They were not metal figurines. They were flesh turned to pewter. Mr. Brown had no artistic skill save the one ability to snatch soldiers off the battlefields of time, to freeze them in metal, to miniaturize them, and to sell them. Each commando and halberdier captured in the field and reduced, at the moment of his death . . . realizing in that moment that Heaven or whatever Valhalla in which he believed, was to be denied him. An eternity of death in miniature.

"You are a greater ghoul than ever I could have aspired to become," I said.

His fright overcame him at that moment. Why, I do not know. I meant him no harm. Perhaps it was the summation of his existence, the knowledge of the monstrous hobby that had brought him an unspeakable pleasure through his long life, finally caught up with him. I do not know.

He spasmed suddenly as though struck at the base of his spine by a maul, and his eyes widened, and he collapsed toward me. To prevent the destruction of the exquisite figurines, I let him fall into my arms; and I carefully lowered him into the narrow aisle. Even so, his lifeless left leg decimated the ranks of thirteenth-century Mongol warriors who had served Genghis Khan from the China Sea in the east to the gates of Austria in the west.

He lay face down, and I saw a drop of blood at the base of his neck. I bent closer as he struggled to turn his head to the side to speak and saw the tiniest crossbow quarrel protruding from his rapidly discoloring flesh, just below the hairline.

He was trying to say something to me, and I kneeled close to his mouth, my ear close to the exhalations of dying breath. And he lamented his life, for though he might well have been judged a monster by those who exist in conformity and abide within the mundane strictures of accepted ethical behavior, he was not a bad man. An obsessed man, certainly; but not a bad man. And to prove it, he told me haltingly of the *Promontorium Sacrum*, and of how he had found his way there, how he had struggled back. He told me of the lives and the wisdom and the wonders to be found there.

And he made one last feeble gesture to show me where the scroll was hidden. The scroll he had brought back, which had contained such knowledge as had permitted him to indulge his hobby. He made that last feeble gesture, urging me to find the scroll and to remove it from its hidden niche, and to use it for ends that would palliate his life's doings.

I tried to turn him over, to learn more, but he died in my arms. And I left him there in the narrow aisle among the Nazi Werewolves and Royal Welsh Fusiliers; and I threaded my way through the drawing room large enough to stage a cotillion; and I found the secret panel behind which he had secreted the scroll; and I removed it and saw the photograph he had taken in that beyond that lay beyond the beyondmost edge; the only image of that land that has ever existed. The whispering moon. The golden mushroom trees. The satin sea. The creatures that sit and ruminate there.

I took the scroll and went far away. Into the Outback, above Arkaroo Rock where the Dreamtime reigns. And I spent many years learning the wisdom contained in the scroll of Mr. Brown.

It would not be hyperbole to call it an epiphany.

For when I came back down, and re-entered the human stream, I was a different Vizinczey. I was recast in a different nature. All that I had been, all that I had done, all the blight I had left in my track . . . all of it was as if from someone else's debased life. I was now equipped and anxious to honor Mr. Brown's dying wish.

And that is how I have spent my time for the past several lifetimes. The scroll, in a minor footnote, affords the careful reader the key to immortality. Or as much immortality as one desires. So with this added benison of longevity, I have expended entire decades improving the condition of life for the creatures of this world that formerly I savaged and destroyed.

Now, due to circumstances I will not detail (there is no need to distress you with the specifics of vegetables and rust), the time of my passing is at hand. Vizinczey will be no more in a very short while. And all the good I have done will be the last good I can do. I will cease to be, and I will take the scroll with me. Please trust my judgment in this.

But for a very long time I have been your guardian angel. I have done you innumerable good turns. Yes, even you reading these words: I did you a good turn just last week. Think back and you will remember a random small miracle that made your existence prettier. That was I.

And as parting gift, I have extracted a brief number of the most important thoughts and skills from the scroll of the *Promontorium Sacrum*. They are the most potent runes from that astonishing document. So they will not burn, but rather will serve to warm, if properly adduced, if slowly deciphered and assimilated and understood, I have couched them in more contemporary, universal terms. I do this for your own good. They are not quite epigraphs, nor are they riddles; though set down in simple language, if pierced to the nidus they will enrich and reify; they are potentially analeptic.

I present them to you now, because you will have to work your lives without me from this time forward. You are, as you were for millennia, alone once again. But you can do it. I present them to you, because from the moment Mr. Brown died in my arms, I have been unable to forget the look of human misery, endless despair, and hopelessness on the face of a Spartan soldier who lay on a carpet in a house in Sydney, Australia. This is for him, for all of them, and for you.

1

It's the dark of the sun. It's the hour in which worms sing madrigals, tea leaves tell their tales in languages we once used to converse with the trees, and all the winds of the world have returned to the great throat that gave them life. Messages come to us from the core of quiet. A friend now gone tries desperately to pass a message from the beyond, but the strength of ghosts is slight: all he can do is move dust-motes with great difficulty, arranging them with excruciating slowness to form words. The message comes together on the glossy jacket of a book casually dropped on a table more than a year ago. Laboriously laid, mote by mote, the message tells the friend still living that friendship must involve risk, that it is merely a word if it is never tested, that anyone can claim *friend* if there is no chance of cost. It is phrased simply. On the other side, the shade of the friend now departed waits and hopes. He fears the inevitable: his living friend despises disorder and dirt: what if he chances on the misplaced book while wearing his white gloves?

2

Do they chill, the breezes that whisper of yesterday, the winds that come from a hidden valley near the top of the world? Do they bite, the shadowy thoughts that lie at the bottom of your heart during daylight hours, that swirl up like wood smoke in the night? Can you hear the memories of those who have gone before, calling to you when the weariness takes you, close on midnight? They are the winds, the thoughts, the voices of memory that prevail in the hour that lies between awareness and reverie. And on the other side of the world, hearing the same song, is your one true love, understanding no better than you, that those who cared and went away are trying to bring you together. Can you breach the world that keeps you apart?

3

This is an emergency bulletin. We've made a few necessary alterations to the status quo. For the next few weeks there will be no madness; no imbecile beliefs; no paralogical, prelogical, or paleological thinking. No random cruelty. For the next few weeks all the impaired mentalities will be frozen in stasis. No attempts to get you to believe that vast and cool intelligences come from space regularly in circular vehicles. No runaway tales of yetis, sasquatches, hairy shamblers of a lost species. No warnings that the cards, the stones, the running water, or the stars are against your best efforts. This is the time known in Indonesia as *djam karet*—the hour that stretches. For the next few weeks you can breathe freely and operate off these words by one who learned too late, by one who has gone away, who was called Camus: "It is not man who must be protected, but the possibilities within him." You have a few weeks without hindrance. Move quickly.

4

The casement window blows open. The nightmare has eluded the guards. It's over the spiked wall, and it's in here with you. The lights go out. The temperature drops sharply. The bones in your body sigh. You're all alone with it. Circling with your back to the wall. Hey, don't be a nasty little coward; face it and disembowel it. You've got time. You have *always* had time, but the fear slowed you, and you were overcome. But this is the hour that stretches . . . and you've got a chance. After all, it's only your conscience come to kill you. Stop shivering and put up your dukes. You might beat it this time, now that you know you have some breathing space. For in this special hour anything that has ever happened will happen again. Except, this time, it's *your* turn to risk it all.

5

In the cathedral at the bottom of the Maracot Deep the carillon chimes for all the splendid thinkers you never got to be. The memories of great thoughts left unspoken rise from their watery tomb and ascend to the surface. The sea boils at their approach, and a siege of sea eagles gathers in the sky above the disturbance. Fishermen in small boats listen as they have never listened before, and all seems clear for the first time. These are warnings of storms made only by men. Tempests and sea-spouts, tsunamis and bleeding oceans the color of tragedy. For men's tongues have been stilled, and more great thoughts will die never having been uttered. Memories from the pit of the Deep rise to lament their brethren. Even now, even in the hour that stretches, the past silently cries out not to be forgotten. Are you listening, or must you be lost at sea forever?

6

Did you have one of those days today, like a nail in the foot? Did the pterodactyl corpse dropped by the ghost of your mother from the spectral Hindenburg forever circling the Earth come smashing through the lid of your glass coffin? Did the New York strip steak you attacked at dinner suddenly show a mouth filled with needle-sharp teeth, and did it snap off the end of your fork, the last solid-gold fork from the set Anastasia pressed into your hands as they took her away to be shot? Is the slab under your apartment building moaning that it cannot stand the weight on its back a moment longer, and is the building stretching and creaking? Did a good friend betray you today, or did that good friend merely keep silent and fail to come to your aid? Are you holding the razor at your throat this very instant? Take heart, comfort is at hand. This is the hour that stretches. *Djam karet.* We are the cavalry. We're here. Put away the pills. We'll get you through this bloody night. Next time, it'll be your turn to help us.

7

You woke in the night, last night, and the fiery, bony hand was enscribing mystic passes in the darkness of your bedroom. It carved out words in the air, flaming words, messages that required answers. One picture is worth a thousand words, the hand wrote. "Not in *this* life," you said to the dark and the fire. "Give me one picture that shows how I felt when they gassed my dog. I'll take less than a thousand words and make you weep for the last Neanderthal crouched at the cliff's edge at the moment he realized his kind were gone . . . show me your one picture. Commend to me the one picture that captures what it was like for me in the moment she said it was all over between us. Not in *this* life, Bonehand." So here we are, once again in the dark, with nothing between us in this hour that stretches but the words. Sweet words and harsh words and words that tumble over themselves to get born. We leave the pictures for the canvas of your mind. Seems only fair.

8

Rain fell in a special pattern. I couldn't believe it was doing that. I ran to the other side of the house and looked out the window. The sun was shining there. I saw a hummingbird bury his stiletto beak in a peach on one of the trees, like a junkie who had turned himself into the needle. He sucked deeply and shadows flowed out of the unripe peach: a dreamy vapor that enveloped the bird, changing its features to something jubilantly malevolent. With juice glowing in one perfect drop at the end of its beak, it turned a yellow eye toward me as I pressed against the window. Go away, it said. I fell back and rushed to the other side of the house where rain fell in one place on the sunny street. In my soul I knew that not all inclement weather meant sorrow, that even the brightest day held dismay. I knew this all had meaning, but there was no one else in the world to whom I could go for interpretation. There were only dubious sources, and none knew more than I, not really. Isn't that the damnedest thing: there's never a good reference when you need one.

9

Through the jaws of night we stormed, banners cracking against the icy wind, the vapor our beasts panted preceding us like smoke signals, warning the enemy that we looked forward to writing our names in the blood of the end of their lives. We rode for Art! For the singing soul of Creativity! Our cause was just, because it was the only cause worth dying for. All others were worth living for. They stood there on the black line of the horizon, their pikes angrily tilted toward us. *For Commerce*, they shouted with one voice. *For Commerce!* And we fell upon them, and the battle was high wave traffic, with the sound of metal on metal, the sound of hooves on stone, the sound of bodies exploding. We battled all through the endless midnight till at last we could see nothing but hills and valleys of dead. And in the end, we lost. We always lost. And I, alone, am left to tell of that time. Only I, alone of all who went to war to measure the height of the dream, only I remain to speak to you here in the settling silence. Why do *you* feel diminished . . . you weren't there . . . it wasn't your war. Hell hath no fury like that of the uninvolved.

10

Hear the music. Listen with all your might, and you needn't clap to keep Tinker Bell from going into a coma. The music will restore her rosy cheeks. Then seek out the source of the melody. Look long and look deep, and somewhere in the murmuring world you will find the storyteller, there under the cabbage leaves, singing to herself. Or is that a she? Perhaps it's a he. But whichever, or whatever, the poor thing is crippled. Can you see that now? The twisting, the bending, the awkward shape, the milky eye, the humped back, do you now make it out? But if you try to join in, to work a duet with wonder, the song ceases. When you startle the cricket, its symphony ceases. Art is not by committee, nor is it by wish-fulfillment. It is that which is produced in the hour that stretches, the timeless time wherein *all* songs are sung. In a place devoid of electrical outlets.

And if you try to grasp either the singer or the song, all you will hold is sparkling dust as fine as the butter the moth leaves on glass. How the bee flies, how the lights go on, how the enigma enriches and the explanation chills . . . how the music is made . . . are not things we were given to know. And only the fools who cannot hear the song ask that the rules be posted. Hear the music. And enjoy. But do not cry. Not everyone was intended to reach A above high C.

11

Ah, there were giants in the land in those days. There was a sweet-faced, honey-voiced girl named Barbara Wire, whom we called Nancy because no one had the heart to call her Barb Wire. She tossed a salamander into a window fan to see what would happen. There was Sofie, who had been bitten by *The Sun Also Rises* at a tender age, and who took it as her mission in life to permit crippled virginal boys the enjoyment of carnal knowledge of her every body part: harelips, lepers, paraplegics, albinos with pink eyes, aphasiacs, she welcomed them all to her bed. There was Marissa, who could put an entire unsegmented fried chicken in her mouth all at once, chew without opening her lips or dribbling, and who would then delicately spit out an intact skeleton, as dry and clean as the Gobi Desert. Perdita drew portraits. She would sit you down, and with her pad and charcoal, quickly capture the depth and specificity of your most serious flaws of honor, ethic, and conscience, so accurately that you would rip the drawing to pieces before anyone else could see the nature of your corruption. Jolanda: who stole cars and then reduced them to metal sculpture in demolition derbies, whose residence was in an abandoned car-crusher. Peggy: who never slept but told endlessly of her waking dreams of the things the birds told her they saw from on high. Naomi: who was white, passing for Black, because she felt the need to shoulder some of the guilt of the world. Ah, there were giants in the land in those days. But I left the room, and closed the door behind me so that the hour that stretches would not leak out. And though I've tried portal after portal, I've never been able to find that room again. Perhaps I'm in the wrong house.

12

I woke at three in the morning, bored out of sleep by dreams of such paralyzing mediocrity that I could not lie there and suffer my own breathing. Naked, I padded through the silent house: I knew that terrain as my tongue knows my palate. There were rolls of ancient papyrus lying on a counter. I will replace them, high in a dark closet, I thought. Then I said it aloud . . . the house was silent, I could speak to the air. I took a tall stool and went to the closet, and climbed up and replaced the papyrus. Then I saw it. A web. Dark and billowing in the corner of the ceiling, not silvery but ashy. Something I could not bear to see in my home. It threatened me. I climbed down, moved through the utter darkness, and struggled with the implements in the broom closet, found the feather duster, and hurried back. Then I killed the foaming web and left the closet. Clean the feather duster, I thought. In the back yard I moved to the wall and shook it out. Then, as I returned, incredible pain assaulted me. The cactus pup with its cool, long spikes had imbedded itself in the ball of my naked right foot. My testicles shrank, and my eyes watered. I took an involuntary step, and the spines drove deeper. I reached down to remove the agony, and a spike imbedded itself in my thumb. I shouted. I hurt. Limping, I got to the kitchen. In the light of the kitchen I tried to pinch out the spines. They were barbed. They came away with bits of flesh attached. The poison was already spreading. I hurt very much. I hobbled to the bathroom to put antiseptic or the Waters of Lethe on the wounds. They bled freely. I salved myself, and returned to the bed, hating my wife who slept unknowing; I hated my friend who lay dreaming in another part of the house. I hated the world for placing random pain in my innocent path. I lay down and hated all natural order for a brief time. Then I fell fast asleep. Relieved. Boredom had been killed with the billowing web. Somehow, the universe always provides.

13

Like all men, my father was a contradiction in terms. Not more than two or three years after the Great Depression, when my family was still returning pop bottles for the few cents' deposit, and saving those pennies in a quart milk bottle, my father did one of the kindest things I've ever known: he hired a man as an assistant in his little store; an assistant he didn't really need and couldn't afford. He hired the man because he had three children and couldn't find a job. Yet not more than a week later, as we locked up the stationery shop late on a Saturday night and began to walk down the street to the diner where we would have our hot roast beef sandwiches and french fries, with extra country gravy for dipping the fries, another man approached us on the street and asked for twenty-five cents to buy a bowl of soup. And my father snarled, "No! Get away from us!" I was more startled at that moment than I had ever been—or ever *would* be, as it turned out, for my father died not much later that year—more startled than by anything my father had ever said or done. If I had known the word at that age—I was only twelve—I would have realized that I was *dumbfounded*. My gentle father, who never raised his voice to me or to anyone else, who was unfailingly kind and polite even to the rudest customer, who has forever been a model of compassion for me, *my father* had grown icy and stony in that exchange with an innocent stranger. "Dad," I asked him, as we walked away from the lonely man, "how come you didn't give that fellah a quarter for some soup?" He looked down at me, as if through a crack in the door of a room always kept locked, and he said, "He won't buy a bowl of soup. He'll only buy more liquor." Because my father never lied to me, and because I knew it was important for him always to tell me the truth, I didn't ask anything more about it. But I never forgot that evening; and it is an incident I can never fit into the film strip of loving memories I run and rerun starring my father. Somehow, I feel, without understanding, that it was the most important moment of human frailty and compassion in the twelve years through which I was permitted to adore my father. And I wonder when I will grow wise enough to understand the wisdom of my father.

Thus, my gift. There were six more selections from the scroll of the *Promontorium Sacrum*, but once having entered them here, I realized they would cause more harm than good. Tell me truly: would you really want the power to bend others to your will, or the ability to travel at will in an instant to any place in the world, or the facility for reading the future in mirrors? No, I thought not. It is gratifying to see that just the wisdom imparted here has sobered you to that extent.

And what would you do with the knowledge of shaping, the talent for sending, the capturing of rainbows? You already possess such powers and abilities as the world has never known. Now that I've left you the time to master what you already know, you should have no sorrow at being denied these others. Be content.

Now I take my leave. Passage of an instant sort has been arranged. Vizinczey, the I that I became, goes finally on the journey previously denied. Until I had fulfilled the dying request of Mr. Brown, I felt it was unfair of me to indulge myself. But now I go to the sacred promontory; to return the scroll; to sit at the base of the golden mushroom trees and confabulate with astonishing creatures. Perhaps I will take a camera, and perhaps I will endeavor to send back a snap or two, but that is unlikely.

I go contentedly, for all my youthful crimes, having left this a prettier venue than I found it.

And finally, for those of you who always wash behind your ears because, as children, you heeded the admonition "go wash behind your ears," seeing motion pictures of children being examined by their parents before being permitted to go to the dinner table, remembering the panels in comic strips in which children were being told, "Go back and wash behind your ears," who always wondered why that was important—after all, your ears fit fairly closely to your head—who used to wonder what one could possibly have behind one's ears—great masses of mud, dangerous colonies of germs, could vegetation actually take root there, what are we talking about and why such obsessive attention to something so silly?—for those of you who were trusting enough to wash behind your ears, and still do . . . for those of you who know the urgency of tying your shoelaces tightly . . . who have no fear of vegetables or rust . . . I answer the question you raise about the fate of those tiny metal figurines left in eternal anguish on the floor of Mr. Brown's drawing room. I answer the question in this way:

There was a man standing behind you yesterday in the checkout line at the grocery store. You casually noticed that he was buying the most unusual combinations of exotic foods. When you dropped the package of frozen peas, and he stooped to retrieve it for you, you noticed that he had a regal, almost, one might say, *militaristic* bearing. He clicked his heels as he proffered the peas, and when you thanked him, he spoke with a peculiar accent.

Trust me in this: not even if you were Professor Henry Higgins could you place the point of origin of that accent.

Dedicated to the memory of Mike Hodel

THE LAST WORD

All the Lies That Are My Life

For Robert Sheckley
Para mi compinche camarada
duranta mal tiempo y mal.

They buried Jimmy Crowstairs today.

My closest, oldest, best friend: the world-famous fantasist, Kercher Oliver James Crowstairs.

They put him down the rectangular hole this morning, and I was one of the dozen people *inside* the black, plush velvet, upholstered ropes. Also in there among the select few was an ex-president of the United States, for whom I had not voted; also two actresses, one of whom, though age thirty, keeps being cast as late teens beachbait, despite her excellence as a serious thesp, mostly on the basis of her chubby cheeks and a pair of breasts if you'll pardon the pragmatism—only slightly smaller than Bosnia and Herzegovina; the other one I didn't know, but she made a good impression on me when, as we were walking up the hill to the grave from the limos, she graciously waved off a small knot of ghouls seeking her autograph; Jimmy's publisher, whose chief claims to fame are his rejection of Jerzy Kosinski's first novel on the basis that it was morbid and depressing, and his ongoing participation as a panelist on a television game show now into its seventh year of syndication; Jimmy's sister, eight years his senior, whom he had not spoken to for over twenty years and to whom he referred as SylviaTheCunt, all one word; a great bear of an English novelist, a French film director who wore clothes so elegantly it made everyone else feel like breadline standbys, a plasma physicist from Princeton who's up for the Nobel this year because of his major breakthrough in magnetic containment fusion; and two married couples Jimmy considered close friends, mostly because they proved to him, as living examples, that it is possible for Man and Woman to cleave together under the same roof, bound by The Paper (as he constantly referred to it), without emotionally disemboweling each other. How many is that? Counting me, that's thirteen. Well, okay, thirteen, not twelve. Even so, it was a select cadre of mourners.

Set apart by black, plush velvet, upholstered ropes from the vast throng of his fans and idle groupies of the great, the near-great, the celebrated, and the hemidemisemicelebrated.

History tells us that when Victor Hugo died on May 22nd, 1885, over two million Parisians followed the pauper's hearse he had specified from the Arc de Triomphe to the Panthéon, where he was buried.

Jimmy's entourage wasn't quite that large; but for a contemporary author, in a nation where illiteracy has gone beyond mere totemization, well into deification . . . it was eminently satisfactory. Maybe two or three thousand. Not bad at all for a guy they steadfastly called a "sci-fi writer."

You'll notice *I* never use that hideous neologism.

Jimmy spent the last twenty-five years of his life trying to get that ugly categorization off his books and out of the biographies they wrote about him. He wrote fantasy, if specific pigeonholes are needed; but he insisted on being called simply a *writer.* He didn't even like being referred to as an "author." He once told me the difference, as he saw it, between an *author* and a *writer.* "An *author* [he said] is what you put on your passport, because in Europe they think a *writer* is a newspaperman. An author is somebody who gets his name on the spine of leatherbound volumes that are never read; a *writer* is someone who gets hemorrhoids from sitting on his ass all his life . . . *writing.*"

Either way, whatever they *called* him, he managed by sheer dint of hard work and careful manipulation of his public image to become three things, almost always mutually contradictory: a staggeringly wealthy bestselling novelist, a serious artist who was seriously regarded by all the "serious" critics, and a legend in his own time. A household name like Salk or Babe Ruth or Hemingway—or Nixon or Jack the Ripper or Hitler.

And this morning they lowered him into darkness, and wonderful words were read over him by Rabbi Ashkenazi, Monsignor McCalla, Dr. Ehlen, Carl Sagan, and me. Mine were the best.

Naturally: I knew him best. And as Jimmy so often told interviewers, with that abundance of humble largesse that so endeared him to *People* magazine, the *Paris Review*, and the *National Enquirer*, "Larry Bedloe is a good solid writer; he's got a nice little talent working there."

That popped up in my thoughts as I stood there watching them crank down the gunmetal-blue anodized aluminum casket. Right across from me, on the other side of the black, plush velvet, upholstered ropes, was a chubby little woman in basic black and pearls. Her face was all puffy from crying. She was clutching the Literary Guild boxed set of his *Radimore* trilogy. Chances of her getting it autographed were very slim.

Kerch, as everyone but his ex-wife, Leslie, and I called him, was already on his way to stardom when I met him. We were both just turning twenty—I scampered ahead only six months older—which meant that for half of each year he could refer to me as "old man" and I could admonish him to speak with respect to his elders—and we had both been science fiction fans.

Every ingroup coterie has its mystiques, its craziness. Masons have secret handshakes; jazz musicians run a special patois incomprehensible to squares; only in the motion picture industry can you get a laugh when you tell the one about the Polish starlet . . . who fucked the *writer*; antiquarian bookdealers share arcane rituals of buy&sell that bind them in terms of verso, recto, foxing, gutters, and true firsts.

The deranged traditions of science fiction "fandom" are overwhelmingly attractive, particularly to those few boys and girls who are the outcasts of their high school classes because of wonky thought processes, a flair for the bizarre, and physical appearance that denies them the treasures of sorority membership or a position on the football team. For the pimply, the short, the weird, and intelligent . . . for those to whom sex is frightening and to whom come odd dreams in the middle of study hall, the camaraderie of fandom is a gleaming, beckoning Erewhon; an extended family of other wimps, twinks, flakes, and oddballs.

We had never met, though we'd corresponded heavily for several years. The nexus of our incipient friendship was the maelstrom of fannish publishing—"fanzines." Mimeographed amateur magazines of comment about the writers and the works in the genre, and a smattering of dreary fan fiction. His fanzine was titled, with becoming modesty, *The World's Greatest SF Fanzine Including Venus*; mine was called *Visitations*.

But it was at the tenth annual World Science Fiction Convention (neologized as ChiCon II), in Chicago, 1952, that we actually met.

I was walking through the lobby of the Hotel Morrison. Being short on funds, I had arranged to stay in a two-room suite with half a dozen other fans from different parts of the country; and I was looking for the one in whose name the rooms were registered, so I could get the key and dump my suitcase.

The lobby was jammed with a horde of fans checking in, renewing acquaintances, screaming across through the potted plants for directions, rolling in dollies with cartons of used books for the huckster room, making arrangements for cheeseburger dinners that night. And in the midst of that cyclical flow of sweaty aficionados who had driven or flown or hitchhiked or crawled in from Minneapolis and Kansas City and Cleveland, Jake Repnich tracked me down.

I felt a hand grab the back of my shirt as I tried to elbow through a knot of kids divvying up suitcases for the trek to the elevators (thereby saving the bellboy's tip), and I reeled backward as the tension was applied. Then someone clubbed me a shot in the kidney.

I pitched forward but couldn't fall down because the back of my shirt was still wrapped in a fist. So my feet went out from under me and I dropped to my knees. I tried to look around behind me; I was in such exquisite pain that my head wouldn't turn on my neck. Everything seemed to be slipping off the edge. But I could tell from the expressions on the faces of the crowd that something awful was about to happen, and that I was on the visitation end of that unnamed awfulness.

A foot was planted between my shoulder blades and the fist let go of my shirt, and I was booted forward onto my suitcase, which slid a few feet, carrying me as on a raft.

I fell off, rolled over, and tried to sit up.

Conquest, Slaughter, Famine, and Death were staring down at me.

The courageous and loving extended family had moved back to clear a circle in which I could be conveniently stomped to pudding. Erewhon had been invaded.

The nastiest-looking of the Four Horsemen—whom I instantly recognized as Death—leaned forward, providing me with a dandy view of his terminal acne, and (in the pulp magazine vernacular of the period) lipped thinly, "I'm Jake Repnich, you little sonofabitch. You wanna tweak my nose?"

It all became hideously clear what was happening. Six months earlier, among the batches of fanzines I traded for *Visitations* by mail, I'd received an ineptly hektographed crudzine called *Uranium-236*. It was "edited," if one takes semiliteracy, quadruple amputee syntax, and sophomoric screeds against any writer with aspirations of writing literature above the level of shootouts in space as editing, by one Jake Repnich. It came out of Secaucus, New Jersey. Need more be said?

As the voice of reason, I had cast caution to the Four Horsemen (without knowing it) and had responded to a particularly stupid article in which Repnich had said H. P. Lovecraft was a better writer than Poe, with the published remarks that good old Jake had about as much literary savvy as a storm drain, and that someone ought to tweak his nose. The point being that merely slapping his pinkies wasn't due and proper for the intellectual crimes of a pimplebrain like good old Jake, a.k.a. Death.

Now Jake and three of his buddies, who no doubt spent their offhours chewing broken glass and flogging cripples, had come all the way to Chicago from Secaucus, New Jersey, to more than tweak the nose of Larry Bedloe.

The smell of the Jersey swamps was still on them.

And I hadn't, at that point, lived enough of a life to have it flash before my eyes.

With three stories out to market, without even having had my shot at immortality, with the National Book Award and Martha Foley's *Best of the Year* and intimate conversations with Styron, Mailer and Hemingway and Steinbeck just within my grasp, I was about to become a problem for the carpet cleaners of the Hotel Morrison. *Quelle ironie!*

At which moment Jake Repnich's nose spouted blood and he went pinwheeling past me to land in a hideous heap against the check-in counter.

A foot and a half behind the spot he had just occupied stood a wild-eyed, babbling apparition, part vampire bat, part slavering derangement, part avenging Fury. The attaché case he had used to break Death's nose was dangling from one of his little pixie fists. The other fist was balled and seemed to be waiting for a target of opportunity.

Feet planted far apart, this pint-size Zorro, no less than Destiny's Tot, stared at the three remaining teddy boys with eyes that could have triggered an A-bomb. "You want trouble, you pustulent slugs? You want a hassle, huh? You want to come in here where law-abiding science fiction fans are trying to share good times, and start a fracas? Huh, that what you want? Well, we're ready! Right, *everybody*?"

He directed the challenge at the extended family, cowering in confusion and naked cowardice around the lobby.

From here and there in the crowd came timorous responses of "Yeah, you tell 'em," and "We're with you, all the way!"

In that instant I understood the dangerous power of Willie Stark, Elmer Gantry, Jean Paul Marat, and Aimee Semple McPherson.

Gorgo the Small then instructed Conquest, Slaughter, and Famine to gather up the weeping, bleeding carcass of their leader and, with the crowd backing him all the way, in some unfathomable powerpull, he moved the guerrilla band through the lobby, down the steps, across the landing, down some other steps, through the revolving doors, and out onto the street. The potential assassins were held there for a few minutes, I suppose to get explicit directions from the Goliath-slayer how to find their way back to the sewers that emptied out onto the Jersey flats—with detailed warnings of what would happen to them should they try to return to the ChiCon—and then the throng returned.

I was still on the floor.

Peter Pan reached down, pulled me to my feet, and said, with a wide, infectious grin, "Hi, you're Larry Bedloe, right? I'm Kerch Crowstairs, we're sharing the room upstairs. I just sold my first novel, Crowell's publishing it in the spring, it's called *Death Dance on Sirius 7*. You're going to love it, I promise you."

Say hello to Kercher O. J. Crowstairs.

It started raining as the funeral party filed away from Jimmy's grave. I looked up into the slanting gray downpour.

My parents were Wesleyan Methodists. Straight out of the Book of Discipline: no movies, no books except the Bible and the Book of Hymns, no eating in restaurants that hold a liquor license, church four times a week, tithes, and praying out loud in unison till it all melds into a droning chant. Some of the clearest thinking of the early 1700s. God is love and no intermediary is needed to intercede for his children. Not to mention that I confess Jesus Christ as my Savior and Lord and pledge my allegiance to His Kingdom.

From this background I fled Pittsburgh and my family with the cynicism that served as Maginot Line against the rape of my sanity, yet unable to shake the inculcated, subcutaneous certainty that **God Is Watching**; God, the art director; God, the set designer; God, the stage manager.

Who always makes it rain at the most dramatic moments in the burial ceremonies. Just once, I thought, why doesn't the Holy Director go against form, against typecasting, against cliché. A hail of frogs, perhaps. Or a celestial chorus and marching band decked out like a New Orleans jazz funeral, with selections ranging from "Muskrat Ramble" to "Jesus Doesn't Want Me for a Sunbeam."

I stood there as everyone else filed away, directed by the attendants. Since I was still inside the black, plush velvet, upholstered ropes, they let me remain for a moment.

Almost thirty years. I knew you through most of my life, Jimmy. Friends. I don't even know what that means. I'm sure you must have done things for me on the basis of friendship, but I'll be damned if I can remember a single one of them. I remember another time of rain, a night in New York, years ago, when we had dinner together and you left me standing in the wet outside the restaurant, I remember that. You hustled down the sidewalk to your car and popped into the Porsche and drove off uptown, never even thinking to offer me a ride back to my hotel. It took me the better part of an hour to get a cab; I remember that.

But friends. Never occurred to me to question that word as the operative definition of our liaison. But what the hell did that ever *mean*, functionally speaking? You knew almost everything about me, and I knew quite a lot about you, but then so do *all* your readers, what with the confessional nature of most of what you wrote.

I was one of your readers. Every word published that I could lay hands on.

Which is more than we can say for the reverse, eh, Kerch?

You read "The Hourglass" ten years ago, chum; and made a point of mentioning how good it was every time we got together. I wrote that short story *ten years ago*, Jimmy! Ten fucking *years* ago! Nine books since. But by the mute testimony of your failure to mention even one of them, old friend now gone, you told me that it had all been downhill. Ten years ago, Jimmy. That was *it*, right? The one high spot and then nothing but mouth-to-mouth resuscitation, right? Too controlled, that's what you used to tell me on the nights when we'd sit across from each other at the kitchen table, after your staff had gone to bed, when we'd sit and drink instant and reminisce. Too controlled, too cautious. There wasn't enough wildness in what I put on the paper. Right? Right.

You had enough wildness for both of us, Jimmy.

Jesus, I'm lonely without you. Christ, I'm glad you're gone.

I'd stamped muddy spots around my feet. The tops of my shoes were covered. And I looked across the grave, through the rain that was coming down cold and nasty, and Jimmy's ex-wife, Leslie, was staring at me. She'd cried so much her nose had swollen and closed both eyes to slits. She held her head to the side like a little girl who's seen her dolly run over by a speeding car. I couldn't hear the short, sharp thistles of her sobs, but those Audrey Hepburn shoulders went up and down, each intake of breath painful.

You had enough wildness for both of us, Jimmy.

I walked around the grave and stepped over the black, plush velvet, upholstered rope and scuffed through the pedicured grass to her. She could barely see me, but she knew who it was. We knew how each of us moved, even in the darkness.

I took her in my arms, and she buried her face in the hollow of my shoulder. Her dress was soaked through, and she was cold, heaving with sobs but not shivering. The weather report had said nothing about rain.

Every few years I was privileged to hold her like this. Usually, she was crying. We fitted together, in this way, like ancient stones.

"Come on, love," I said, over her head, into the rain. "It's all done now. We've got to go put a lid on it."

She spoke words I couldn't understand, sending them into the fabric of my jacket. Then more words, two of which were Jimmy's name and my name. And I turned her slightly and started to walk her away from the grave site.

"I can't go over there, Larry. Do I have to go over there?"

I said yes, she had to go over there, it was her due, it was the payoff for all the good times *and* all the bad times. I said I'd be there with her, and it would be quick, and then we could both go out somewhere and have a couple of dozen extremely potent drinks, and pretend the past was smoother and kinder than flawless recall permitted us to *mis*remember it.

And the last of the limousines was waiting, and we let the chauffeur hold the door for us, and we got in and went off to Jimmy's baronial mansion to hear the reading of the will.

And Kerch, left behind in the rain, went with us.

Jimmy had been having simultaneous affairs with four women, any one of whom would have been sufficiently daunting to scare even Vlad the Impaler into impotence. One was an Olympic gymnast, no more than twenty years old, what is usually referred to as coltish, natural blonde naturally, and much given to scenes in restaurants where the maître d' objected to her carrying a coatimundi on her shoulder. Her name was Muriel. One was an authority on machine intelligence, in her early thirties, with what used to be referred to as "bee-stung" lips, a mass of heavy, thick black, lustrous hair the shade of thoughts for which one can be jailed without bail, and an intellect that made virtually everything she said incomprehensible to all but five or six of the finest minds on the planet. Her name was Andrea. One was a Cuban actress who had fled Batista's tyranny mere hours before an order for her arrest on grounds of moral turpitude was issued, whose exiled status in America had been guaranteed by the extension of said warrant whose grounds of moral turpitude had been upheld by Castro; not yet thirty, in appearance no more than twenty-five, she claimed to be Chicana, Puerto Rican, Venezuelan, or Castilian, depending on what the casting director was seeking, with a pair of legs usually referred to as "terminating just under her chin," with a voice and range that could have shamed Yma Sumac, and a temper that frequently manifested itself in a splendid right cross. Her name was Edith. One was a consumer advocate for CBS television, a former runner-up to Miss North Carolina in the Miss America contest, thirty years old, rather puckishly committed to a variation on the original Ann-Margret coiffure which, given all proper due, admirably suited her auburn hair, opinionated, contentious beyond belief, and directly responsible for a Xerox price rollback that had cost the firm nearly a quarter of a million dollars. Her name was Mary Louise.

I had been seeing Leslie for three years.

Not until six years after they'd married did Jimmy bother to ask if I'd been troubled by the heat-death of the universe. Simply never occurred to him to worry about it. Not that he was bone-stick-stone insensitive; no indeed: it was that he moved too fast for consideration of the emotional debacles at any given point along the scenic route.

They were living in Connecticut, near Crown Point, in a stately manse brought over from Thomas Hardy country, somewhere near Dorset, brick-by-brick, in the early 1900s by a Dutch robber baron who'd made his boodle in association with Elisha Otis on the development of the gearless traction elevator. It was one of those fumed oak, parquet-floored, wine-cellared beauties all writers dream about owning; just the right setting when one receives the word that one has been awarded a Nobel, or a Pulitzer, or an American Book Award, or a high six-figure purchase offer from Paramount. Two, and almost three, of those came to Jimmy in his stately manse. I was writing a lot of book reviews for *The Village Voice* and *Kirkus.*

He called late in the afternoon; the last spear of light permitted entrance by the surrounding buildings, had almost vanished from the airshaft, and I sat in gloomy relaxation trying to decipher the Mayan Codex that Doubleday charmingly called a royalty statement.

"What're you up to?" he said, without identifying himself.

"I'm locked in non-orgasmic congress with Doubleday's bookkeepers. It's the first time I've ever been fucked by a mindless octopus."

"How about dinner?"

"When, tonight?"

"Yeah. I'm in the city. You free?"

"According to my royalty statements that's exactly what I am."

"The new book isn't doing well?"

"How could it? They must have taken the entire printing, loaded it on barges, floated it out the Narrows, and deep-sixed it. Weighted down, no doubt, by the excess profits from their latest bestselling cookbook."

"You don't sound like the man to cheer me up tonight."

"Sure I am. You can spend my last exuberant evening with me before I establish residency in the nearest leper colony."

"That would be the Carrville Leprosarium. In Louisiana. And they don't call it leprosy anymore. Hansen's Disease."

"Why aren't I grateful for that information?"

"I could stop off at Abercrombie & Fitch on my way over and pick up a nice big bell for you. Or maybe a cassette of Frankie Laine singing 'Unclean, Unclean.' Do wonders for getting you a seat on the subway during rush hour."

Badinage. Brightalk. Never a discouraging word, and the deer and the antelope play. The ritual incantations of those who had resonated to Salinger. I still had my red baseball cap in the bottom of a carton of old clothes, at the back of the bedroom closet. Nostalgia somehow cannot survive the smell of mothballs.

"I'm here; come on over whenever you're free."

"About an hour. We'll go have a steak. I'm paying."

I smiled. Naturally, you're paying. With a five-thousand-copy print-run of Laurence Bedloe's most recent astonishment, *The Salamander Enchantment*, rapidly being carried by salutary sea-currents toward the Bermuda Triangle, naturally you're paying for steaks. Now if you're up for Twinkies and Hawaiian Punch, I'm paying.

"See you when you get here."

"Take care."

"So long."

I listened to the dial tone for about two minutes. Then I sat in the growing darkness, thinking about Arctic tundra. Somehow it didn't make the Carrville Leprosarium seem more attractive.

After a while the doorbell buzzed and I put on some lights and let him in. He had the look of a man who has broken some vows.

"I need a drink," he said. He fell into the rocker with the leather seat, toed off his loafers, and sank down onto his spine, eyes closed. "By the unspeakable name of the slavering hordes of Yog-Sothoth, though Allah be the wiser, I do fiercely need a drink."

"Can be done, chum. Give it a speakable name and I'll put it in your paw in moments."

He rubbed his closed eyes ferociously. From inside his hands he mumbled, "Any damn thing. Largeish, if you will."

I went into the kitchen and opened the cupboard and gave the cognac a pass. This looked like heavy weather drinking. I poured Wild Turkey into a big water glass without benefit of jigger, tossed in a single ice cube, raised the level with a little tap water, and carried the Bomber's Moon back into the living room.

Jimmy was sitting on the floor, in the darkness near the window. I couldn't see him that well, but I could hear him sobbing. I think I grabbed for the doorjamb to steady myself. In the fifteen years we'd been friends, I'd never seen him cry. I'd never known him to cry. I'd never heard anyone mention that they'd seen him cry. It had never occurred to me that he might one day, in my presence, cry. I didn't even know if he was *able* to cry.

He didn't know I was there, staring at him.

Very quietly, I carried the glass over to him, put it down beside his crossed legs, and I went back across the room and sat just outside a pool of lamplight, my face in darkness. I had no idea what to do, didn't want to say something wrong, definitely didn't want whatever I finally said to be banality or homey homily; so I waited. Eventually, it seemed to me, he'd stop, take a drink, and we'd talk.

Eventually he stopped, noticed the glass, reached for it slowly, and drank long and deep; and then he looked around for me.

"Here's a new one for you," he said.

I spoke softly. "Not so new; I do it all the time."

A marvelous waiting silence resumed.

Quite a while later he said, "I never asked you: Were you pissed off at me for marrying Leslie?"

I thought about the right answer. Not necessarily the kindest answer, or the most politic answer, or the truthful answer; just the right one. "I think we were about done with each other."

"That's no answer."

"It's an answer. You want others, I can make up others. But that's definitely *an* answer."

More silence. He finished the drink, I went in and threw a lot of cubes in a mixing bowl, brought the bowl and the bottle, and set them down in front of him. He worked at it slowly. Neither of us would end up alcoholics: we weren't passionate enough about the juice. Oh, hi there, I'm recruiting for Richard the Lion-Hearted; we're putting together a *wonderful* follow-up to last year's big hit, The Children's Crusade. This year it's The Wino's March on Mecca, from the people who brought you the Black Death. You'll just love it—all the Sterno and Grand Marnier you can osmose. Whaddaya say?

Listen, I'll talk to you later. You go save Mecca, I'll have a go at writing the Great American Novel, and we'll meet right next to the big lions on the steps of the New York Public Library two years from now. You can't miss me, I'll be the one *without* the Holy Grail.

"You know, I've always felt like your kid brother," he said.

"It's only six months, Jimmy."

"Always felt faintly ridiculous around you. Loudmouthed, gauche, coming on too strong even when I was purposely speaking so softly I knew people had to strain to hear me."

"It's only six months, Jimmy."

"You know I'm a better writer than you, don't you? Not just sales . . . *better.* There's heat in my stuff; it works, it pulls the plow. *Better.*

"For Christ's sake, Larry, there's nothing but cold dead air blowing through your books. They ought to hand out woolly mittens with every copy of your stuff."

I thought about Arctic tundra. "Six months, Jimmy; just six months."

He started crying again. "For Christ's sake, Larry, *help* me! You've got it all together, you've got the answers, you've *always* had the answers. I don't know whether I'm coming or going, I'm falling apart. I feel like I'm being emptied out, like a hot water bottle; it's all running away from me. I'm going to kill somebody, I swear to god I'm going to run through the streets killing strangers."

"How about some gin rummy, tenth of a cent a point?"

He got up, went into the bathroom, and washed his face.

When he came back, he sat down in the rocker, looking bushed. "You ready to talk about it now?" I asked.

He stretched his hands out on the arms of the rocker until the fingertips were just at the edge. Just at the edge. "This open marriage with Leslie is killing me. I can't stand it."

It was the first I'd heard of it. When he married her, I stopped thinking about anything in that area. I never knew what went on with them in that way. I felt my stomach getting cold. That's the way I respond to photographs of Dachau.

"So get out of it," I said.

"Don't be an asshole."

"It's only six months, Jimmy."

He started yelling. "Give me a break, will you? I've got nobody else in the world to talk to. You're my best friend, maybe the only friend I can really trust. I'm *talking* to you, I'm asking for help!"

What I *wanted* to say was: Come off it, Jimmy! You've got exactly and precisely what you always wanted. You're rich, you're well liked, you're urbane and charming; you've got a beautiful, intelligent wife, a big classy home steeped in authentic antiquity; everywhere you go they know you, your face is on the tube and they don't hold you for the last fifteen minutes of the Carson Show; you go where you want, do what you want, you're a workaholic under the weight of the Puritan Work Ethic, so you get off on slaving night and day . . .

You're who you made you, Jimmy; so come off it.

Wanted to say that. But didn't. Sat there and said, "Go ahead, tell me what's happening." Remember when you were a kid, how awful it was when you bit down on the tinfoil?

And he went on for about two hours, telling me everything about his life, and Leslie's life, and my life, and about how dear I was to him because I was his role model. All of this went in and flowed out again, and I must confess there were even three or four things that disgusted me.

And then we went out to O. Henry's Steak House and had magisterial chunks off some King of the Beasts, and I put ketchup on mine and Kercher Oliver James Crowstairs, the bestselling and critically acclaimed author, winced and said, "That's disgusting, Larry."

And I said: "Chalk it up to improper toilet training."

Jimmy's baronial mansion was not the one in which he'd lived with Leslie. That had been Connecticut. This was Los Angeles.

The Crown Point mansion had been brought over stone-by-stone from Dorset. This one looked as if it had been brought over ticky-by-tacky from the back lot at Twentieth.

But it had a "library." Yes, indeed, it had a library that held the 37,000 books Jimmy had owned at the moment of his death. He read a book a day, summer or winter, bright or cloudy, naked or clothed.

And we gathered there, in the high-arched library, for the reading of the will, the last will and testament of Jimmy, beloved Kerch, American literary treasure.

It was not what I expected. But then, Jimmy never did the expected. There was an evening we spent together at a reception for the Brazilian ambassador to the United States, at the Spanish legation in Washington, during which Jimmy had a meaningful relationship with a gigantic silver Cellini tureen filled with applesauce.

It was not what I expected.

The room had been set up with deep, comfortable chairs all facing an enormous beam-television screen. The projector was hooked up with a Sony Betamax unit. An impish-looking man of middle height, wearing what was clearly a very expensive three-piece suit that had not been properly tailored to the slump of his shoulders, stood before the screen holding a document that was very likely the last hurrah of my friend Jimmy Crowstairs.

Despite the serious manner of the imp in the three-piece suit, intended I suppose to give the occasion the proper portentous ambiance, it was impossible to get away from a festive feeling in that room. Jimmy had been an inveterate collector—of everything. The library was floor-to-ceiling with books, almost all hardcovers, arranged alphabetically by author, from Aeschylus, Aldiss, and Algren at the left of the topmost shelf of the first bookcase to the left side of the entranceway . . . to Zamyatin, Zelazny, and Zola at the bottom of the last bookcase all the way around the enormous room at the right side of the entrance. But there were also glass cases spotted across the room, containing pewter figurines, Makundi sculpture from Mozambique, lacquered boxes from Russia, T'ang dynasty glazes, gold scarabs encrusted with lapis lazuli from Egypt's Middle Kingdom, scrimshaw from whaling villages in New England, Amerindian pottery, German kinetic sculptures flickering and strobing, ceramic statues from the Austrian courts, fantasy bronzes by Enzenbacher, Spacher, and Rumph; and lucite easels with paintings: Kanemitsu, Stamitz, Pebworth, David Hockney, the Dillons, Wunderlich, Bash, Wyeth, Rothko, Kley, Campanile, and Willardson. And in the dead center of the room was a nine-foot-tall model of the Abominable Snowman that Steve Kirk had designed for the Matterhorn at Disneyland.

No matter how hard the imp in the three-piece suit worked at it, he could not possibly overcome the lunatic frivolity of that yeti.

The five chairs were arranged in a semicircle. At the extreme left, already seated, Jimmy's sister, SylviaTheCunt, stared straight ahead, folding and refolding the telegram that had commanded her appearance here. The next chair was empty. And the next chair. In the fourth chair sat Jimmy's friend Bran Winslow, himself a writer, and probably the gentlest human being I'd ever met. He had not been at the burial ceremony. In the last chair, at the extreme right, sat Missy, which was short for Mississippi, who was—and for the past fifteen years had been—Jimmy's assistant, good right hand, troubleshooter, basic office staff, and Person Friday. She let no one call her a "girl," even if the word Friday followed it.

Obviously the two empty chairs were for Leslie and me.

We moved toward the chairs and started to sit down, but the imp stopped us, saying, "Mrs. Crowstairs, would you take the third seat please; Mr. Bedloe, Kerch wanted you to sit in the second seat." We rearranged ourselves. It made good sense: I separated

Leslie and SylviaTheCunt, who looked at each other with the enthusiasm one might evince at the prospect of root canal surgery.

The imp waited till we were settled, then he said, "My name is Kenneth L. Gross; I was the attorney for Kercher Oliver James Crowstairs and remain legal counsel for both his estate and the Kerch Corporation in which Mr. Crowstairs was the principal party of record."

He showed us the document we had all come to hear.

"This document is Mr. Crowstairs's last will and testament, as you might have supposed. However, it will not be read here today."

Why had I suspected Jimmy wasn't finished with us yet?

He waited a moment for the effect, then went on. "Mr. Crowstairs, as you all know, was a rather remarkable man, with a flair for the original. One day, several years ago, we were discussing the preparation of this document, and I mentioned, almost as a joke, that he ought to videotape the reading of his will. Kerch . . . Mr. Crowstairs immediately fastened on the idea and instructed me to look into the legal ramifications of such a videotaping.

"At first there were questions of validity, but Mr. Crowstairs financed the appropriate research, and in a decision handed down just eight months ago by the Supreme Court of the State of California, such a procedure was adjudged permissible, contingent on a written document being prepared as it has been historically.

"Many of the smaller grants in this document will be handled directly through my office, but the principal beneficiaries are gathered here, per Mr. Crowstairs's instructions; and you will now hear your bequests directly from the deceased. This extended element of the basic instrument was videotaped four months ago . . . before any of us had any idea . . . we never thought . . ."

He faltered to silence. I liked him a lot. He had cared about Jimmy.

Then he went behind us and turned on the television set from the projection module, cut in the Betamax, light appeared on the enormous screen, color-bands of leader ran through, and suddenly we were looking at this room, with Jimmy, the attorney, Missy, a tall, thin Black woman I didn't recognize, and Bran Winslow, sitting at Jimmy's desk. It was obvious that Missy, the Black woman, and Bran Winslow were the witnesses to the execution of the will, and I now understood how two people as close to Jimmy as Missy and Bran had been, who had been there only a few months before when this document had been merely an act of preparing for the long, far inevitable future, had chosen not to attend the burial service.

They all sat up there, larger than life, on the screen, and I thought with the faintest flutter of trepidation, *What a field day the archivists will have with* this *little chunk of literary gossip.*

Roll 'em, C. B. It's magic time, I thought. *Break a leg, Jimmy.*

He once took me along with him on what he called a "dangerous mission of research."

Because of the confessional nature of much of what he wrote—Jimmy had believed Hemingway when Poppa said, "a writer should never write what he doesn't know"—Kerch was forever putting himself in crazy situations where raw material for books had to be obtained firsthand, usually at risk of one's life or sanity; or at very least at risk of one's complexion.

He had scaled mountains, raced sports cars, worked in a steel foundry, traveled cross-country on a Vincent Black Shadow with Hell's Angels, marched with Chavez in the Coachella Valley, spent time in Southern jails for civil rights activities, chummed it up with a Mafia *capo*, managed to con a trio of radical feminist lesbians into a four-way sexual liaison, covered a South American revolution, hired himself out to a firm specializing in industrial espionage, and god knows what all else.

He had no secrets when he wrote. He talked about his feelings when his mother had lingered in her endless midnight coma and he signed the order to kick out the plug on her life-support system; he revealed the most intimate secrets of his love life, with Leslie and others; he told stories on himself that men with more humility and a greater sense of shame would have buried in the vaults of their family secrets. Probably because of that open conversation that went on between Jimmy and his millions of readers, his popularity grew and grew. It was possible to trust a man who told *everything*, a man who could not be morally or literarily blackmailed. It made it seem reasonable that he would go to the burning core of whatever he wrote, because he was not afraid of sunlight striking the tomb of the vampire.

And once he took me with him.

I was living in Chicago at the time, doing editorial work on a men's magazine. He called and asked if I was free that night, and if I was free would I like to accompany him on a "dangerous mission of research."

Evenings spent in Jimmy's company were many things, but they were seldom dull or uneventful. I said I was stoked for an adventure.

He picked me up in a Hertz rental at the office, and all he would say was that we were going deep into the South Side of the city, the section commonly known as Back of the Yards. Oh yes, he said one more thing: he was going to see a woman who had given him a case of the crabs.

I think I responded with the remark, "Frankly, I'm underwhelmed."

But when we got there—*there* being a rundown tenement in a scuzzy section—I found an apartment half-filled with card-carrying criminals. They had the appearance of righteous gypsies, some kind of hyperthyroid Romany rejects. Eleven of them, looking like road company understudies for *The Wolf Man*, starring Madame Maria Ouspenskaya.

Four flights up, in what would have been called a railroad flat, had we been in New York and not Chicago, they sat around the kitchen staring at Jimmy and me with dark, hooded eyes. I felt like a cobra at a mongoose rally.

An extremely attractive young woman had opened the apartment door after Jimmy had knocked in a special cadence: two shorts close together, pause, then three more shorts.

"'Open, Sesame' isn't required, eh? How convenient," I said. He gave me one of his looks.

And the door was opened by this extremely attractive young woman, who threw her arms around him and kissed him full on the mouth. I stared beyond them, into the kitchen, and was greeted by the massed nastiness contained in ten pairs of dark, hooded eyes.

He held her away from him and murmured something too quietly for the gypsies to hear. What he said, Jimmy always the romantic, was: "What're you pushing this time . . . cancer?"

She grinned and gave him a playful punch in the stomach—playful enough to straighten him out with a whooze of pain. Then she led him into the apartment. I followed, not happily.

Let me cut through all the subsequent hours of weird happenings. The background was this:

Jimmy had been out on the lecture circuit the year before. In Kansas City the usual gaggle of esurient sycophants who cannot differentiate between the Artist and the Art rushed the podium for autographs and cheap thrills such as the pressing of flesh. In the crowd had been an extremely attractive young woman who, when her turn came to thrust a book and a pen under Jimmy's nose, had thrust neither. She had moved in quickly and thrust *herself*.

Reaching for him, she had put her mouth to his ear and whispered, "Why don't we go back up to your hotel room and see if you can make me groan."

Needless to say . . .

About a week later, Jimmy back home, a phone call on his private line. It was the extremely attractive young woman whom Jimmy had made groan. Her name, she told him, was not Mia, as she had told him. She was not, strictly speaking, a bank teller, as she had told him. She was, in fact, a member of a rather large family that specialized in robbing banks. When they were between jobs, she worked as a bank teller. "Who better?" Jimmy had replied to that one. She was on the dodge, spent most of her time underground with different aliases and different pseudo-lives, and she had had a wonderful time with Jimmy whose books, during those long hours underground, had brought her endless pleasure.

When Jimmy inquired why she was revealing all this to him, she shamefacedly admitted—though he couldn't see her face—that she had probably given him a cataclysmic dose of the crabs.

Without even bothering to check, Jimmy perceived that he had, at last, an understanding of why he had been scratching furiously for the preceding week. As it was his first exposure to *Phthirus pubis*, he dropped instantly into panic. "I would rather," he said later, "have ten thousand years of tertiary syphilis than ten seconds of the crabs." He had an urgent Candygram from his autonomic nervous system, directing him in the most stridently hysterical tones, to rush off and set fire to his crotch.

She had gone on—unaware that Jimmy was no longer within ratiocination range—to say she hadn't known about it herself, that she was sorry as hell, and that she thought it was a crummy thing to do to someone who had given her so many hours of pleasure, both in print and in bed. And *that*, she told him, was why she was calling him to tell him . . . and spilling the beans about herself.

(Which wasn't that big a deal, apparently, because she wasn't in Kansas City anymore; and *he* couldn't very well find her, or the family, if the FBI, the Federal Reserve System, the Organized Crime Task Force, Brink's, and the Pinkertons couldn't find them.)

Ever the polite chap, Jimmy had thanked her decently for taking the time to call on such a piddling matter when she obviously had bigger problems to worry about. Then he hung up the phone, hyperventilated, and sent Missy to the pharmacy to buy copious quantities of A-200 Pyrinate Liquid, Cuprex, Kwell cream, *and* Kwell lotion—and a thermite bomb just to be prepared in the event a scorched-earth policy proved necessary.

Now a year later, the Mia-*manqué* had summoned Jimmy from California to Chicago to act as intermediary in the family's surrender to the Laws (as she called them, reminiscent of the colorful patois of Bonnie & Clyde).

And this once he had taken me with him.

Pseudo-Mia took him by the hand and started to lead him down the hallway toward the rear of the apartment. "Hey!" I said. The sound made by a ferret caught in a clampjaw trap.

Jimmy turned, still being led by the hand, walked backward and said, "Make yourself at home. Strike up new acquaintances. Establish meaningful relationships. I'll be back."

And Not-Mia opened a door to what I presumed was a bedroom off the hall—thereby illuminating her family's liberal, one might even say cavalier, attitude toward her sexual egalitarianism—and she disappeared inside; followed by Jimmy's disappearing hand, arm, body, and face, leaving behind only the smile of the Cheshire Cat.

I turned to stare at ten pairs of dark, hooded eyes that were staring at me.

A man in his thirties got up, stood aside, and indicated the empty chair at the kitchen table. I sat down, not happily.

At almost the instant I realized there was a wonderful, dark brown smell of something baking in the apartment, the old woman—an old *old* woman, shapeless and infinitely corrugated with wrinkles—sitting directly across from me reached behind her, wearing a potholder mitt, opened the door of the oven, pulled out a metal bread pan, and slapped it down on the table between us.

"*Langos,*" she said. She pronounced it *lahng*-osh.

It smelled sensational. Some kind of deep-fried bread dough she'd apparently been keeping warm in the oven. I looked at it. The guy who had given me his seat took a bowl full of garlic cloves off the sink and put it down in front of me.

"Bread," he said. "Rub it with the garlic."

I reached in, took a piece of *langos*, burned my fingertips, squeaked, provoked ten smiles, added an eleventh, my own, and rubbed the hot surface with a clove of garlic. It tasted sensational.

Then the old, old woman began rattling off at me. She spoke uninterruptedly for about a minute. In Hungarian. I smiled. I nodded. She stopped and looked at me, waiting for a response, I thought of Arctic tundra.

A man in his fifties, sitting to my left, said, "She asks if you know if Laurie will marry Vic Lamont and if Cookie will go crazy and will Simon Jessup kill Orin Hillyer?"

I stopped chewing. I smiled. I nodded. I looked from one to another of them, hoping someone would take pity on a man lost in the desert.

The old, old woman, hearing what the man in his fifties had said, added a few more words. I looked at the interpreter. He spoke resignedly: "And will Adam Drake fall in love with Nicole?"

I hoped, with profound desperation, that Mia was neither greedy nor afflicted with the *djam karet* attendant on ownership of a hooded clitoris.

"I'm sorry," I said slowly, "but I don't know what she's talking about." I smiled. I nodded.

There was an appreciable drop in temperature around the table. The man in his fifties said something short to the old, old woman. She snorted that special snort translatable in *any* language as, "Who asked for you, who sent for you; who sent for you, who asked for you?"

And so, every instant anguish, I sat there for the better part of an hour. In Indonesia they have a name for it: *djam karet* . . . the hour that stretches.

Eventually, open covenants having apparently been openly entered into, Other-Than-Mia and Jimmy emerged from the bedroom. It looked like a draw.

I got up at a signal from Jimmy, who drew me aside. I started to whisper my consternation, but he pressed my bicep for silence. Maybe-Mia took my seat, and began speaking in a low, intense voice. In Hungarian. Or Urdu. Or tongues, maybe. What do I know about glossolalia?

She was about fifteen seconds into the recitation when they *all* started replying. Eleven gypsies, all going at it like the Russians were invading Evanston. A hailstorm of babble.

Jimmy leaned in and said, "You know the FBI's list of Ten Most Wanted?"

I nodded. Not happily.

"They just made it to number one."

"Terrific. I'll meet you in the car; say my goodbyes for me."

"Shut up and listen.

"It's a hype. It's a publicity dodge. The Feds never put *anyone* on that list till a week or two before they're going to make an arrest. That way they spread it around about all these dangerous felons at large, and a week or so later the Bureau makes a pinch, making it look as if they're right on top of things. People they *can't* find never even get *on* the list."

"You're telling me Jimmy Stewart's going to break in here any minute with a Thompson submachine gun, is that it?"

"I'm telling you they want to give themselves up; but they're afraid they'll get wiped out if they just wait for the Feds to find them."

"Why don't they run? God knows they're in practice."

"Shut up and listen.

"They want me to be the go-between. To get the press and some responsible local officials in here before they pull the plug."

"Listen, Jimmy . . . they pull the plug and you're liable to lose the baby with the bathwater. I'm referring to *me*, baby, in case you had any doubts . . ."

"Take it easy. I did a docudrama about a Chicago psychiatrist for CBS last year . . ."

I hadn't heard the word *docudrama* before. I was looking at him with confusion. He understood my problem and said, "Fictionalized documentary. Semi-real. Touches truth in at least ten places. Anyhow . . ."

The babble was growing louder. The old, old woman was now silent, watching and listening. The thirty-year-old guy and the fifty-year-old guy were obviously on opposite sides of the question—whatever the question *was*—and I could see the crowd was about evenly divided. The older guy was with Mia, whatever she was proposing, and I had the certain feeling that if the thirty-year-old guy's point of view prevailed, that this baby might go down the drain *before* Jimmy Stewart made one of his rare personal appearances.

"Are you *listening* to me?" Kerch demanded, squeezing my arm.

"No," I whispered, "I'm listening to them. Somehow I get the feeling what they're saying has more to do with my living to a dignified old age."

"Just shut up and listen, for Christ's sake!

"Marvin Ziporyn is his name . . . the psychiatrist. He's the top shrink for the state. Works with the Cook County authorities. Concert violinist, big social mover, wrote a couple of books; he's got access to Kup and the mayor and everybody else."

I was staring openly now. Hell, anybody could get to the mayor; but access to Irv Kupcinet, the columnist; well, that was the Big Time.

"So?"

"So I call Marvin, tell him what I'm into, get him to contact Kup, who'll love it a lot. They pull in a few of the local squires and top cossacks . . . and Mia and the crowd remand themselves into proper custody."

"Before Jimmy Stewart breaks in . . ."

"Right, right."

"I'll meet you at the car. Thank the old lady for the bread." I started toward the door. The thirty-year-old guy erupted from his seat and if there was anything else in that lousy kitchen but the gigantic .45 in his hairy paw, I didn't see it. There is a quality about blue-steel gunmetal that gathers all light in a room; like a black diamond.

He was pointing it at me.

I grinned stupidly, placed both palms against the air and tittered like the village idiot. He seemed somewhat mollified and the barrel of the automatic lowered to the vicinity of my crotch. For a moment there it had been like staring into the mouth of the Holland Tunnel, only bigger.

"Damn it, Larry, stop acting like a schmuck. Let Mia handle it."

"Her name isn't Mia."

"*Whatever* her name is; let her handle it."

So I stood there with him, leaning against the wall, for the better part of an hour while the Sanhedrin decided my fate.

Sometime during that hour I asked him, "Who's Vic Lamont?"

He said, "Who?"

I said, "Vic Lamont."

He said, "Never heard of him."

I said, "Will Laurie marry him?"

He said, "What the fuck are you talking about?"

I said, "Will Laurie marry Vic Lamont; will Cookie go crazy; will Simon Somebody-or-other kill Orin Hillyer; will Adam Something-or-other fall in love with Nicole?"

He stared at me.

"The old lady seemed miffed I didn't know the answers," I whispered.

He thought about it a minute. Then he said, "*The Edge of Night.* It's a soap opera."

I said, "Why me?"

He said, "Because you're with me, and Mia told them I'm a famous television writer, and that means you're a famous television writer, and that means you know what happens to all those characters in the soap operas, because they're not characters, they're real people, and I suppose when you're on the lam the only consistency in your life is the surrogate life of people in soap operas. What'd you tell her?"

"I didn't tell her anything. I didn't have the faintest idea what she was talking about."

He said, "How'd she take it?"

I said, "Not terrific."

He nodded, thought about it a minute, then called Mia over. He took her aside, whispered at her for a little while, then sent her back to the table. She bent down over the old, old woman, whispered in her ear for a while longer, and when she straightened up the old, old woman was grinning wide as a death's-head. Her mouth was a classic argument for compulsory remedial orthodontia.

Whatsername sat down and smiled, waiting.

Then the old, old woman said something sharp and hard. In Hungarian. Everybody shut up and stared at her. Then she said something else, not quite as sharp and hard, and the thirty-year-old guy packing the Holland Tunnel bowed his thorny head, nodded in supplication, and murmured words of acquiescence.

The fifty-year-old spoke rapidly to the Ghost of Mia Past, every once in a while pointing at Jimmy or me, or Jimmy *and* me. Once, damned sure, he was making a threat; and once, damned certain, he was giving warning. She nodded, said okay okay okay every few sentences, added a thought here and there and, finally, it all seemed settled.

She got up, came over to us, and said, "All set. Do your stuff, Kerch."

He gave her a little kiss and started toward the old black two-handed pedestal telephone on the kitchen counter. I asked the Memory of Mia, "What's all set?"

She patted me on the cheek and answered, "They're not going to cut you into small pieces and leave you in garbage cans all over the South Side." Then she went away, to join my best friend, Kercher Oliver James Crowstairs, who had brought me along into the jaws of death on a "dangerous mission of research."

It was not till a week later, after the gypsy bank robbers had given themselves up with attendant headlines and photos of Jimmy leading them out of the tenement into the waiting arms of Irv Kupcinet, the mayor of Chicago, and the bureau chief of the Midwest Regional FBI office (not to mention several thousand cops and G-Men armed for the apocalypse), that Kerch bothered to tell me that what had saved our lives was Mia's imparting to her dear old Granny the information that I was a close family friend of everyone on *The Edge of Night* and that when (or if) Granny ever got sprung from the federal slam, I would introduce her to

Laurie, Vic Lamont, Simon Jessup, Orin Hillyer, Cookie, Nicole, and Adam Drake, *whoever* the hell they were!

"My name is Kercher O. J. Crowstairs," said the Kercher O. J. Crowstairs three times life-size on the screen before us. The camera pulled back into a medium shot and Jimmy up there whipped open the wallet lying on the desk. He pulled out a sheaf of cards and held the first one up to the camera, which obligingly zoomed in for a closeup. Jimmy's voice, off-camera, said, "And this is my driver's license, issued by the state of California. You'll notice it has a rather unflattering photograph of me right here in the lower left-hand corner, which will identify me as the one and only K. O. J. Crowstairs, your friendly neighborhood testator."

The camera had slowly pulled back to include the attorney, Kenneth L. Gross. He was making a small moue at Jimmy's levity. The moue became a stricture as Jimmy held up one card after another:

"And this is my BankAmericard/Visa card; and this is my Master Charge card; and this is my Diners Club card, but I don't use it much; and this is my Carte Blanche; and this one will rent me a Hertz, and this one an Avis, and this one will get me a tacky room in any Holiday Inn across the face of the Earth; and this one is for Neiman-Marcus, and this one is for good old Bloomingdale's, and . . ."

He must have caught the strangled moan from Gross, because he stopped. He dropped the rest of the thick pack of cards and looked into the camera.

"Look: we're doing this videotape so no one, and that means *no one* will be able to raise the question of my competency after I've croaked. By competency they mean was I of sound mind and body, and under no duress, such as being held captive by the Symbionese Liberation Army. But if I played it absolutely straight, and didn't laugh at all this somber bullshit, then anyone who's known me more than ten minutes would suspect I *was* out of my skull.

"Nonetheless . . ." and he said this hurriedly, because Gross was making the kind of strangling noises that, had he uttered them in a good restaurant, would have brought the maître d' running to administer the Heimlich Maneuver, "nonetheless, moving right along to the serious stuff, folks, here's my friend and advisor, the world-famous corporate attorney, Mr. Kenneth L. Gross, who'd like to say a few words. Let's give him a big funeral day welcome . . . *Kenny Gross*!"

The attorney was the color of old toothpaste as he read from a prepared form. "Mr. Crowstairs, you have now established your identity for those who may be seeing this recording at a later date. You have retained this office in connection with estate planning and more specifically to prepare your will. The document I now show you (handing will to client), is the final draft of that will. Would you please take a moment to review it?"

The screen now went to split-frame, the right side being a copy of the will. Jimmy took the document Gross handed him and scanned it. "But this is a laundry list, Kenny." The attorney damned near fainted. Jimmy laughed and hurriedly corrected himself. "I'm *kidding*, I'm just kidding; this is my will; honest to god, I swear it is!"

Gross was breathing hard. I felt for the poor devil. "Is this the document that you have, hopefully, previously read?"

"Yes, it is. But you don't mean *hopefully*, Kenny. You mean *I hope*, or *it is to be hoped*, or *one hopes*. You see, when you use the word 'hopefully,' you're reporting a subjective state of mind; that is, *full of hope*. Your error is in attributing your hope to the object, in this case the will . . . or is the object *me*? I'm never really sure of parts of speech. In any case, if you were to reverse the word, you'd see how wrong it's being used: *hopelessly* I've read it. See what I mean? Good grammar, Kenny; always good grammar. Your mother and I have chided you about this on numerous occasions . . ."

Gross exploded. "*Mister* Crowstairs! If you will, sir! This is a serious undertaking! Now *is this*, or is this not the document previously read by yourself?"

"It is, it is! Nag, nag, nag."

Gross gave it up. He bulled forward. Not happily. "Are you executing this document or prepared to execute this document . . . no, wait . . . I'm out of sequence! Damn it, Kerch!"

Jimmy grinned infectiously. He was never happier than when he was stirring up the soup. He laid a placating hand on Gross's. "Take it easy, Kenny. Don't fumfuh."

Gross swallowed; as they say, he looked daggers at his client, pulled a weathered pipe with a large Oom Paul bowl and a bent stem from his vest pocket, puffed it alight with a kitchen match taken from his *other* vest pocket, harrumphed once, and began again.

"All right, then: In my presence, and in the presence of these witnesses, and cognizant of the fact that these proceedings are being videotaped, does this document reflect your exclusive and entire wishes with regard to the disposition of your property?"

Testator responded in the affirmative: "I respond in the affirmative."

The attorney now turned to the three witnesses. "Each of you has known Mr. Crowstairs for many years. You have been asked to participate in these proceedings for the purpose of further identification. Will you now, each in turn, declare who you are, your relationship to Mr. Crowstairs, and verify that this is, in fact, Mr. Kercher Oliver James Crowstairs."

Camera came in to closeup on the first witness as the split-screen went to solo image.

"My name is Brandon Winslow. I have been a close personal friend, house guest, and sometime-collaborator of Kercher Crowstairs for almost fourteen years; and I hereby declare that the man over there with all the credit cards is, in fact and as he's stated, the Crowstairs he says he is."

Well, well, I thought, *oh my ears and whiskers.*

"Sometime-collaborator." Now there's one phrase I never thought I'd hear in connection with Jimmy. So Bran had been paying off the loans and the live-in companionship with something more valuable than coin of the realm. He had worked on some of the books. That went a long way toward explaining how Jimmy could turn out his novel *and* a short story collection every year as regular as the swallows visiting Capistrano, plus finding the time for all the introductions, newspaper columns, background pieces for *TV Guide*; the lectures, the television talk show appearances, the writing workshops; and the women. He had another laborer in the vineyard. A bond slave.

I cast back through the long list of Crowstairs publications trying to figure out which ones had been *co-written—entirely ghost-written*?!?!—no, it was unthinkable—but then, *collaboration* had been unthinkable till Bran had let the black cat cross the path—and I came up with two immediately.

Bakelite Radio Fantasies and *Fearsome Noises.* They were gentler, more thoughtful than was Jimmy's wont. There was greater lyricism in them, closer in tone to Bran's own solo novel—his *only* novel—*Knowledge of Two Kinds.* They were a couple of my favorite Crowstairs creations.

And my heart contracted in my chest as I realized that in some way Bran Winslow had sold himself to Jimmy, had denied his own career, to add a few more chapters to the myth of Kercher Crowstairs. I didn't want to know what Jimmy had had on Bran, that could make him, seemingly willingly, put aside his own work, to become a secret shadow of the public Kerch.

To me, it was unthinkable. The more I thought about it, the more often the word *unthinkable* burned in the darkness. Unthinkable: Jimmy was many kinds of a man, but blackmailer wasn't one of them. Unthinkable: Brandon Winslow was as fiercely committed to his art as was I, as was Jimmy . . .

Unthinkable!

No one has that kind of charisma. I simply wouldn't go for it. There had to be something deeper, something more potent. It was unthinkable that a writer of Bran Winslow's sincerity and dedication would simply give over his life to Jimmy; it was unthinkable that Jimmy's fever could be passed on to another writer—possibly a *better* writer, a more important writer, an intrinsically more valuable, a *worthier* writer—to cause him to deny the song of his own Muse. But now that I'd thought it, as unthinkable as it had seemed . . .

Kercher Crowstairs refused to acknowledge the night.

He had a quote from Thomas Carlyle taped to the molding of the bookcase right over his typewriter:

Produce! Produce! Were it but the pitifullest infinitesimal fraction of a Product, produce it, in God's name! 'Tis the utmost thou hast in thee: out with it, then. Up, up! Whatsoever thy hand findeth to do, do it with thy whole might. Work while it is called Today; for the night cometh, wherein no man can work.

He refused to cower against the fear of scaled or furry or fanged creatures moving toward him in the night.

He was a sharpened stick.

He was in motion, no sitting target.

He did not play poker, yet he never sat with his back to the door.

But such a level of energy *has* to dissipate itself before it can consume another writer. It has to! Sheer force of will, massed totality of personality, unleashed waves of charismatic power . . . no one has that. No one! Unthinkable goddam you Kerch Jimmy!

What the fuck did you have on Bran Winslow to turn him into your Uncle Tom? Your Stepin Fetchit? Your coolie laborer? Second sax in your brass section? Make-work creative typist?

Oh, Jesus, Jimmy, this is most hateful; and I don't even know what was behind it.

Poor Bran.

Damn! Stop that! Stop thinking that way. There was a reason, a solid, good reason. There had to be. No writer can do that to another writer who knows how good he is, who has the books in him crying out to be released. No one. No damn you, *no one*!

My head was swimming. I felt sick to my stomach.

"Can you hold the tape," I heard myself saying; and then as the film vanished and white screen appeared, I bolted out of my chair and rushed for the toilet.

That dyspeptic old fart Nelson Algren got three out of four. He wrote:

"Never play cards with a man named *Doc.* Never eat in a place called *Mom's.* Never sleep with a woman whose troubles are worse than your own."

Close. Very close.

But he missed a fourth:

"Never let anyone catch you down on your knees puking into a toilet bowl."

Especially not a woman whose troubles are worse than your own.

I should have locked the door. But the bile was pushing as if it were spring-loaded; I barely had time to get into the can before

I felt it coming like the Sunshine Express. Down on my knees, loving the toilet bowl, and then the river of fire.

Leslie was in there, right behind me, trying to hold my forehead, *for Christ's consumptive sake*, with me hurling and heaving like a boa constrictor that's swallowed a Peterbilt. I shoved at her, ineffectually, as she continued to play Lady Bountiful to my bounty.

I flailed my free arm behind me, trying to get her to *back off*. I think in that moment I realized just how insensitive she is. There'd always been hints . . . such as her revelation at a group dinner many years before that she had, as a child, thrown a hamster into a window fan . . . and then, of course, she'd stayed married to Jimmy; that had to indicate more than a *soupçon* of the obdurate.

But the level of insensitivity it takes to force someone in the most degrading condition known to humanity to think that he's being *watched* while he glops up his guts, no matter if it's misguidedly interpreted as "concern" or "out of love," is a bestial level whereon one finds only flagstones or spent shell casings. *Back off!*

After a while I got up, filled the sink with cold water, put my face into it completely, and lay there for quite a length of time, allowing the spittle and other nastiness to float away on the tide. My eyes were burning. I could not, thank god, see my face in the water.

I emptied the bowl, washed thoroughly, gargled as best I could with icy water, and reached for a towel. Leslie was standing there with one in her outstretched hand.

I took it. "Thank you very much."

"How do you feel?"

"Dandy. Just dandy."

"That was awful."

I looked a surprised look. "Oh, really? It usually brings down the house. The awestruck expressions of the crowd are usually upon me." *Back* the fuck *off*!

"My god," she said, "you know you're even starting to *talk* like him?"

Have you never perceived that before, my love? Have you never caught on that my interior monologues are *never* in my own voice, never the way *I* write or speak? They are pure Jimmy. That quick-silver turn of the phrase, all that heat and color; not the plodding, methodical, reasonably reasoned wise uncle with good, solid thinking of Laurence Bedloe, but rather the bold, sure spring of the tiger, and I believe in you. Never caught that, eh? How sad, how sorry: if I were to write up the relationship between the Recently Departed and Larry Bedloe it would be in the assumed voice of Kerch Jimmy. You didn't pick up on that? You're simply not paying attention.

"The hamster isn't the *most* awful I've ever heard," I said, "although it is in the top tenth of a percentile of the most awful."

"What are you *talking* about? Are you okay?"

"The *most* awful, I guess, was something Missy told me. She said that when she was a kid Down South they used to take baby ducks and chicks, and they'd bury them up to their no-necks in the dirt, and then they'd run the lawn mower over them. Now *that* is yucchh."

Her face was all pulled out of shape. "I'm calling the doctor."

There was a brace of silver-backed military brushes on the counter. I picked them up and started brushing back my wet hair. I looked at her in the mirror and said, "Very good idea. You call the doctor. Make it a voodoo doctor, if you can get Inboard to clear a line to Haiti. Get a specialist in resurrection. Tell him we're not sure Jimmy is completely all the way dead . . . that he seems to be clinging ferociously to life . . . *your* life, *my* life, *Bran's* life . . ."

She started to cry. I put the brushes down and turned to her; but I didn't take her in my arms, usually *pro forma.* I just stared at her. She had the heels of her hands in her eyes, and she was starting to get into it.

"Come on, Leslie! Pack it in, darlin'!"

She fell against me, put her arms around me.

"Then," I said, "he pushed her away." And I pushed her away.

She looked at me. She said, "What?"

"He stared back at her," I said, "and said simply, 'We don't walk backward, do we? You're his wife; you'll *always* be his wife, even if you remarry, even if you're canonized; he owns you. You say no, but five years from now you'll make a deal with Simon & Schuster and have poor Bran out there ghostwrite your memoirs—*I Was Kercher's Koncubine.*' And he shook his head sadly," I said, "and he walked to the door and walked out." And then I walked past her to the door and walked out.

Not so hard ghostwriting in the voice of a ghost.

They all looked at me as I reentered the library. I patted the Abominable Snowman on the belly and resumed my appointed seat, ready to let Jimmy have another go at me. Bamboo shoots under the fingernails would have been a happier prospect.

They were still looking at me as Leslie came in. "Something I ate, perhaps. An undigested bit of beef, a blot of mustard, a fragment of underdone potato. More of gravy than of grave. Do let's continue with the show." All but Leslie continued to stare at me, touched by astonishment. Ah, of what good are literary allusions in the Land of Functional Illiterates, close on the borders of the Kingdom of the Blind?

But we continued.

The videotape began playing again, and once again we were in this library, weeks ago, only a moment after Bran had identified Jimmy as Jimmy and caused me to lose a perfectly lovely breakfast from DuPar's Farmhouse. The tall, thin Black woman I didn't recognize now spoke, as the camera came in on her.

"My name is Eusona Parker, and I have been Mr. Crowstairs's housekeeper for eighteen, going on nineteen years; and that's him sitting right there; and don't nobody try to say he's not in his sound mind and body 'cause I have *known* him all these years and he's just as sharp and clean and neat as a pin as he's *ever* been. Is that what I'm supposed to say?"

No wonder I didn't recognize her. Eusona Parker had lost about eighty pounds.

Every Wednesday. That was Eusona's day. I'd only seen her half a dozen times through the years, when I was in Los Angeles and visiting Jimmy. But if anyone knew his state of health, it was Ms. Parker. She had been more of a true mother to Jimmy than his own natural mother. What I remembered best about her was the "hearing aid."

She had a memory that should have been on display in the Smithsonian. It might be three or four years between our seeing each other; but when I'd come out of the blue guest room searching for coffee early on a Wednesday morning during one of my visits, there would be Eusona, dusting Jimmy's vast, endless hoard of *tchotchkes*; and she'd look up and grin as if I'd been there uninterruptedly for years, and she'd say, "Good morning, Larry, sleep good?" And I'd scream at her, "Hello, Eusona, how are you?" And she'd answer, "Doin' just fine, Larry; water's still hot." And I'd scream, "Thanks, Eusona."

The reason I screamed was that she wore a hearing aid. One of those little button things shoved into her ear, the cord trailing down to disappear into the capacious pocket of her wraparound apron where the shape of the battery pack bulged.

And we went on that way, amiably, until one time she stopped me in the back corridor leading to the greenhouse, took me by the hand like a small boy who's been caught eating worms in the schoolyard, and she said, "Mr. Bedloe, why do you always scream at me?"

She never called Jimmy "Mr. Crowstairs" unless he was behaving badly or living with a woman who left globs of mascara on the mirror in the bathroom, and she never called me anything but Larry unless I had left my bed unmade. Ms. Parker made it clear she was a house*keeper*, not a maid; and if I slept in it, I ought to make it when I got out of it. "Mr. Bedloe" was her way of politely saying *pay close attention now, asshole.*

"Why, uh, I'm sorry, Eusona," I said, terribly embarrassed as one can only be embarrassed when one has been caught staring at the empty place between eyes and mouth where a leper's nose has fallen off. "I was speaking loudly because I wanted you to hear me."

"Well, I'm not hard of hearin', dear."

That *dear* of hers: butter would not have melted in her mouth. I've never understood what that meant, it never made sense to me, butter not melting. Whatever it meant, it's what that *dear* was all about. The dear you use when you say, "No, dear, the round hole is for the *round* peg."

"You're not?"

"No, Mr. Bedloe, dear, I'm not hard of hearing."

Mr. Bedloe *and* dear.

"But you wear a hearing aid."

"*Mistuh* Bedloe, this is not a hearing aid." And she pulled the earphone of the transistor radio in her apron, out of her ear and, faintly, like fairy trumpets, I heard the tinny sound of Steve Garvey batting the brains out of the Cardinals' relief pitcher, bottom of the seventh, two out, a man on third.

All that went through my head as Kenneth L. Gross said, "Yes, Miss Parker, that's all you have to do, is identify Mr. Crowstairs."

"That's him. I said it."

"Thank you, Miss Parker."

"Neat as a pin, everything right in place; always been like that, eighteen going on nineteen years."

"*Thank* you, Miss Parker."

"You're welcome, dear."

Then Missy identified him; then Jimmy as testator stated the date and stated that the will being made on that date took precedence over all other wills previously made by him, including any that might be found written in cuneiform on stone tablets by gas station attendants roaming in the Nevada deserts.

Then the roundelay went like this:

Kenny: Are you executing this document or prepared to execute this document with a complete satisfaction on your part that it says what you wish it to say, and that you understand it in its entirety?

Jimmy: Affirmative. And it should be noted for the record that the last person to marry a duck lived four hundred years ago.

Kenny: Choke. Are you prepared to execute this document and accordingly state for the record, in my presence and in the presence of witnesses, that in so doing you are not acting under duress, undue influence, or under the influence of any drug or other substance that may impair your mental capacity?

Jimmy: I had a Coca-Cola about half an hour ago, does that count?

Kenny: No, sir, it does not. Please!

Jimmy: Are you sure, Kenny? I mean, if you take a piece of raw meat and you put it in a glass of Coke and leave it overnight it comes out looking like something from a James Bond movie. You know, all those little piranha bubbles in there, they could chew the shit out of your brain cells.

Kenny: *It doesn't count, damn it!*

Jimmy: Then how about all the stuff I put up my nose just before we started filming?

Kenny: *Aaaargh!*

Jimmy: Okay, okay, take it easy. I'm just clowning. I don't use dope, you know that. Everybody knows it. I couldn't possibly write the crap I write if I was ripped. Having my nostrils Tefloned was just for a lark, you know that.

The attorney laid his head down on his arms and pounded the tabletop with his fist. It was pathetic what Jimmy was doing to this poor soul. We all looked around in the semidark, but Kenneth L. Gross was back there in the shadows, no doubt chewing through the bit of his pipe.

On the screen Jimmy was being upbraided by his three witnesses. They whipped him into a semblance of probity and urged Kenny Gross to resume the proceedings.

The attorney said, "Therefore, in my presence and in the presence of the witnesses, god help us, is it your wish that you now execute the document and that we sign the document as witnesses thereto?"

Client responded in the affirmative.

"I will then ask, Mr. Crowstairs, that you now initial each and every page in the lower right-hand corner . . ."

"I'm left-handed."

"Then do it in the lower *left*-hand corner but for god's sake initial the damned thing already!" He was shouting; it seemed to quell Jimmy. He started initialing. Gross went on weakly, "Up to but not including the signature page. For your information and for the record, this is being done so that no pages can be substituted in the future into this document."

He was standing now, over Jimmy's right shoulder, behind him, turning the pages to verify each one was properly initialed (and possibly to insure that Jimmy didn't sign *Herman Melville* or *Frederick VIII, Duke of Schleswig-Holstein-Sonderburg-Augustenburg*).

It went on that way without hindrance. Jimmy had clearly grown bored with the activity and even bored with the japery that had made the proceedings minimally tolerable. Jimmy reached the signature page and filled in the location of execution of the will, then the date, and then he signed it. Then each of the witnesses signed location, date, and name. The latter two added their place of residence. The will was returned to Gross, who asked if Jimmy wanted the will kept in the attorney's vault and a conformed copy provided to Jimmy, or if the client wanted to keep the original with a conformed copy in Gross's possession. Jimmy waved a hand negligently. "You keep it; send me a copy."

Gross said he would do so and, painfully aware that the juice was running out of the presentation, said, "For the record, the witnesses need not be present during any videotaping portion which is about to occur and the only people who will be present will be myself, Mr. Crowstairs, and the two camera persons."

Yo-ho-ho. Here we go. Up there on the screen Missy, Bran, and Eusona Parker rose, walked out of camera range and damned certainly out of the room, and Gross turned to Jimmy and said, "Mr. Crowstairs, if you wish, you may say some words to your beneficiaries or for that matter, to anyone who may have been excluded by you under your last will which we have just executed."

He placed what was obviously a seating diagram of this room as Jimmy had planned it to be arranged on the desk in front of Jimmy, got up, and backed out of camera range. Now all we had on the screen was Jimmy sitting behind his desk, hands folded demurely, staring out at us, looking right to left as if he really could see us, back there four months ago when he had known for certain that he would live forever.

He looked first at SylviaTheCunt, then at me, then at Leslie, then at Bran who was seeing and hearing this for the first time—which may have been why he hadn't attended the burial ceremonies—and finally, at my right but Jimmy's extreme left, Missy. She hadn't spoken all day.

But I'd make book she knew what was coming.

Jimmy stared at us, and we stared back at him. He kept us waiting. I don't know what the others wanted—vindication, protestations of love, vast wealth, security for their twilight years, remorse, the slam bang of gin and vermouth, a trip to the moon on gossamer wings—but all *I* wanted was to be turned loose. Tempest-tossed, righteous card-carrying wretched refuse, I merely yearned to breathe free. To sever the bond with Jimmy. I heard a sound, I'll tell you what that sound sounded like:

On July 28, 1945, a foggy Saturday on the East Coast, Army Air Forces Lt. Colonel William Franklin Smith, Jr., took off from Bedford, Massachusetts in a B-25 light bomber for La Guardia Field in New York. A few minutes after 10:00 a.m., Lt. Col. Smith crashed his two-engine bomber into the north side of the Empire State Building at the level of the 78th and 79th floors.

On the 75th floor of the Empire State Building an office worker who had come in to do some extra work over the weekend heard a sound. A terrifying, ominous, hurtling-toward-him sound.

He looked out the window to see, emerging from the fog, ten tons of screaming airplane rushing toward him at 225 m.p.h.

I sat staring, waiting for Jimmy to speak to us from beyond the grave. I heard a sound, rushing toward me out of the fog at 225 m.p.h.

This is how Jimmy died.

The story was in all the papers.

It was pried loose, finally, from one of the three *culeros* they pulled out of the other wreck. All three of them lived; one of them lost his left leg; one of them has no teeth. But that was Jimmy, not the crash.

Appropriately enough it was Halloween. That's Bradbury's favorite holiday, and it's mine, and it was Jimmy's. It was last week.

Jimmy had spent the evening at a party thrown by one of the two married couples who had been inside the black, plush velvet, upholstered ropes at the burial ceremonies. Huck and Carol Barkin. She's an architect, he's a writer. They were very close to Jimmy.

Around midnight Jimmy had left. He'd only had a couple of glasses of wine, perfectly sober and, in fact, had been drinking Perrier since ten o'clock. That figures in the story.

He took a cold quart bottle of Perrier with him when he left, swigging it straight from the mouth to his mouth in the car. Then he realized he was almost out of gas, probably couldn't make it back to the Valley and the ancestral manse, went looking for an open station on a holiday, near midnight, in Los Angeles where odd-even allocation is taken seriously.

He found a serve-yourself that was open, but they wouldn't let him fill up because it was an odd-numbered day, and he had license plates that ended in an even number. So he pulled off to one side and waited for the clock to run past midnight when it would be the next day and he could get pumped up.

I wasn't there, no one was there in his head, but I know what he was like, and from the story the *culeros* told, it had to have happened like this. And even if it didn't let's see how well we can get inside the characters, let's see how fluidly we can carry the action, let's see if we can plumb the intricate motivations. This is called sensitive, creative writing; full of heat, Jimmy; pulling the plow, Jimmy; getting the powerhouse up to peak efficiency.

What we need is a good opening, a tough literary hook.

Kerch Crowstairs slumped behind the wheel of the Rolls Corniche, listening to the second movement, the *Allegro appassionato*, of Brahms's Concerto in B-flat major. In the chopped and channeled Chevy beside him the raucous clatter of the Eagles banged uneasy counterpoint . . .

No, too esoteric. Not Hammett enough.

How about this:

He was distracted. Thinking about the past, the future, indefinite times and opportunities passing too fast for analysis. Under him the Rolls hummed softly, waiting for the light to change. Beside him three Chicanos in a decked Chevy raced their motor. Drag for pink slips, mister?

No, too diffuse. Not enough oomph.

I can't do it, Jimmy. I can't write like you! I can talk and think in your voice, because I can *hear you* . . . I've always had phonographic recall. But I can't put it down in your bloodthirsty Visigoth way.

What happened was . . .

He filled the tank. He drove back out onto the street. He was listening to the classical music on KFAC-FM. He was smoking his pipe. He was sitting at the light, waiting for it to change, simply enjoying the cool night air and the pleasant music and the smoke rising from the pipe. The empty Perrier bottle lay on the passenger seat. A car pulled up beside him in the left lane. Someone spoke in the night. He was caught up in the gentle feel of the music washing over him, the sense of ease and leisure. He was relaxed. For once, he wasn't on, he wasn't angry, he wasn't hyper. He was feeling good; and he paid no attention to the voice. But it spoke again, louder, coarser, directed at him. He looked across. Two young men, late teens, maybe early twenties, in the front seat. Another one in the back seat looked asleep. The kid closest to him yelled again. "Hey! *Cabrón!* What're you smokin' in the pipe?" The light changed. He took off. At the next light they raced up, gunned the motor, closer to his lane now. "Hey, man, *de dónde?* I ast you what the fuck you smokin' in the pipe?" He stared ahead. He didn't want any hassles. God, don't these lights change? "Hey, *mamador*, you gonna answer me or I'm gonna come over there an' whip your ass?" He looked at them. If Rick Garza or Pano Del Rio were here, they'd have just the right words to back these clowns off. But he was alone. "I'm smoking Essence of Asshole," he said. "I'm smokin' your mama." And the light changed, and he hit it. They ran up his tailpipe to the next light. Jesus, how many lights are there before the freeway? As he screeched to a halt the one on the passenger side jumped out and came across to grab him. He dumped it into reverse, backed up three feet, threw open the door and knocked the silly sonofabitch flat on his ass. Then he took off through the just-changing light. Behind him the passenger was climbing back aboard as the driver decked it. They caught him at the next light and he thought about going straight through: the freeway was one street up. But now the adrenalin was pumping. He stopped at the light and grabbed the empty Perrier bottle. When the passenger got to his window, he swung the bottle in his left hand with a flat, scythelike movement and busted out the guy's teeth, emptied his mouth and sent him careening backward into the Chevy. *Then* he went through the light, turned sharp left, ran down the side street to the freeway entrance, hit the ramp doing sixty and was on the San Diego before the driver could load his buddy back into the trashwagon. *¡Huo de la chingada!*

They caught him just beyond the interchange of the San Diego and Santa Monica freeways. He was in the fast lane, the number one next to the divider. He was doing seventy-five. The Chevy came up on the right and the berserk latino swung it over hard; lock to lock, maybe not—but hard. The Rolls took it just behind the door, slewed into the cyclone fence, scraped along throwing sparks back in a fan, then shot ahead, as Jimmy floored the Corniche. *¡Puto pendejo!*

Doing ninety, he cut out of the number one lane, slanted across the second, third and fourth lanes, and ran away. The Chevy caught up on the grade leading through the saddle of the hills to the Valley. The *culeros* rear-ended him. Hard; once twice three times. Jimmy braked, speeded up, cut in and out, but the Chevy was hot, it ran him down like a bulldogger. *¡Vatos locos!*

Two miles before the Mulholland offramp the *cholos* said aw, fuck it, and decided to boom him. They came up in the number three, doing ninety-five, went ahead by two car-lengths and slant-drove across his bow. Jimmy stood on the brake, but it didn't count. They impacted at eighty-five, the Corniche went in hard on the right front, ricocheted, spun out and went over the side. The Rolls hit the berm, dropped, and began to somersault. The Chevy was horizontal across the three and four lanes, caught a centerpunch from a long-distance moving van, lifted, went tail-over onto its roof, sliding across the shoulder, followed Jimmy over the side two hundred yards beyond him and came to rest against a low hillside.

Behind the Latinos the Rolls Corniche took one last roll, hit the crumbling hillside, and went off like a can of beer shaken in a centrifuge. It blew apart, scattering hot metal and parts of Jimmy all over the Santa Monica Mountains.

Say goodbye to Kercher O. J. Crowstairs.

“I’m not feeling too giddy about all this, now that we’re alone,” Jimmy said from the screen. “You five are the most I’ve got left. Everybody else has been taken care of; okay, they’re okay; I took good care of them, in the ancillary sections of the will. But you five are the big scores, and I wanted you to hear it straight from me.”

He stopped, wiped his mouth. *Jimmy nervous?* Come on, give me a break here.

“Missy, you’re first.” he said, looking all the way to his left, directly where Mississippi was slouched in her seat, long legs crossed straight out in front of her. “You get the Kerch Corporation and all its holdings.”

SylviaTheCunt gasped, off to my left. The smell of cardiac arrest was there in the library.

Jimmy went on. “You keep it running. There’s the land up at Lake Isabella, we own it free and clear now, and it’ll be built up pretty big within the next five years, they’re putting in that Kern County International Airport. Keep adding to the art, find a place to show it, something nice and stately like the Norton Simon Museum . . . you know . . . something toney and really chi-chi. Set your own salary, keep on as much of the staff as you need, hire more, fire some, do what the hell you want with it. It was just a dodge to keep the tax fuckers off my carcass, anyhow. You make it into something terrific, kiddo. I love you, babe. You watched out for me real good.”

Missy was crying. Toughest woman I ever met, but she—even she—lost it when Jimmy went to work at the top of his form. In Iran there’s a word—*zirangi*—it means cleverness, or wiliness. The Machiavellian quality. It’s much admired by the Shiites. Jimmy would have been a smash in Islam.

"And for the record," Jimmy added, "let it be known that never once in all the years you and I worked together, did we once so much as fondle each other's genitalia. The bantlings will need their gossip, m'love; and they'll fasten first on she who was my amanuensis. Let the slushfaces herewith take note: you and I worked together for fifteen years plus however many more wash under the bridge from the date of this taping before I bite the big one, mostly on the basis of your being the best goddamned pool-shooter I ever met. I would have fired your tidy ass a million times, kiddo, if it hadn't been that you shot the most unbelievable three-bank cushions into the hip pockets."

Missy was dry now. And smiling gently.

Then he turned to Brandon Winslow sitting right beside her.

"Bran, my friend . . . I've done you right, and I've done you wrong. But you never once treated me like a hotshot, and for that I cannot thank you enough. Other people were in awe, or they wanted to drink my blood, or they came sharpshooting. But you were my friend, and my colleague, and you started out as something like my student but went beyond what I could show you. And you maintained, chum. You make the hall of fame for hanging in there. So this house is yours. The house and the grounds and everything in it. Live here, and change it any way you want to make it *your* nest the way I made it *my* nest. I built the west wing full of separate apartments for other writers who need a place to flop. I never could afford to buy San Simeon from the state of California; I always thought the old Hearst castle would be a dynamite place for a no-obligation writers' colony where kids who had the real stuff could come and work without worrying about rent or getting fed. So lay in half a dozen real outlaws, Bran. And the only rule ought to be that they can stay and be happy as long as they *write.* If they turn into leaners, if you catch them sitting around all day watching *The Price Is Right* boot their asses into the street. But if they're producing, they can live here forever. Alone is okay, but loneliness can kill a good writer . . . you know that. Give them a community of sharp, witty minds . . . and three squares a day. You'll be the only landlord who writes books that chew on the hearts of the literary establishment.

"Do it for me and for you, Bran."

SylviaTheCunt was making sounds like the *Titanic* going down.

Then Jimmy looked straight ahead. At Leslie.

He didn't say anything. He just stared.

Leslie took it for about thirty seconds. Then she got up and walked to the side of the room where she stood with her arms folded, watching the screen, still curious, but—once having freed herself of Jimmy's power—unwilling to let him manipulate her beyond a certain point of tolerable terror.

Now Jimmy was staring at an empty seat.

She's insensitive, or maybe desensitized; but she's tough. Which also explains how she could have stayed married to him as long as she did. High-fashion barbed wire wrapped in Spandex.

"Leslie, you did okay in the settlement. But I suppose you rate more than a standard 'I'm sorry,' which doesn't count for shit . . ."

"You can say that again," Leslie murmured from the side of the room.

". . . so the Corporation is depositing a million in the Bermuda account for you; I've signed over ownership of the magazine to your name; Kenny will transfer the chalet at Villarvolard to you . . . so you can keep that ski bum of yours on the string a little longer; and Missy'll find a letter in the safe that transfers a substantial block of non-voting stock in the Kerch Corporation to you. Stay out of the business, take the dividends, and try to remember me fondly."

"Right," Leslie said from the side of the room.

Now he looked all the way to his right, directly at SylviaThe-Cunt, who *had* to know what was coming. There was still a lot in the till, and from what Jimmy had said of her in years past I knew she'd be bolted to that chair till the final farthing had been accounted for; but, for a wonder, she *had* to know what was on the way.

"To my beloved sister, Sylvia . . .

"And that's the first time in over twenty years I've said your name without adding the sobriquet. Seems truncated, but these are formal proceedings and I want to do it without flaw so after I've finished talking to you—which you'll sit through right to the last syllable on just the off chance that I might act like a brother even though we both know I despise you with a pure, blue flame of loathing, and you might be able to cadge a few bucks—where was I? Fouled in my own syntax. Oh, yeah, I was saying you'll sit through all this maleficent defoedation—Kenny, if she needs help with that, stop the tape and get her the definitions—you'll find them in something called *Mrs. Byrne's Dictionary*, in the reference shelf to the left of my typewriter in the office—shit, I lost myself again. Oh, yeah, I remember. You'll sit through it because you cling to greedy hope like a leech on floating garbage. You figure I can't be that big a prick after all these years, and so you'll wait for the last rotten word I'm going to speak to you, sister dearest. And I'm doing this without flaw so that you won't even have a scintilla of hope that you can contest this will. It's solid, Sylvia; ironclad, rockribbed, diamond-encrusted solid.

"And the bottom line is that you get zip.

"Not a cent.

"Not a penny.

"Not a farthing.

"Not a grubnik. (Which is worth 13 cents American.)

"Not even a Blue Chip Stamp.

"Nothing is what you get. Nada, nyet, nihil, nil, nihilum! Nothing, because if I have any dislike of women as a species it comes from you. Nothing because if I haven't been able, my whole life, entirely to trust a woman, it's because of what you ran on me when I was a kid.

"Sylvia, I don't think I've ever had a chance to tell you how deeply and thoroughly I loathe you. No, that isn't even correctly put. I loathed you for *most* of my life, but about twelve years ago I just sort of dropped you out of the universe. You ceased to exist. You were never there.

"I know you can't doubt that, because you were on the other end of the phone that time when—"

SylviaTheCunt screamed.

"Stop it! *Stop him right now!*"

Kenny Gross moved in from the shadowy rear of the library and cut off the Betamax. The screen went white. So did SylviaTheCunt. She was on her feet, the veins standing out in her forehead; a dumpy, big-bosomed woman in middle years. Jimmy always said she was one of those pathetic creatures that had been assembled by The Great Engineer in the Sky without a love mechanism in her. It didn't take a writer to see that. She had the look of old stone walls that had never even been considered for monuments or pyramids or standing circles.

"This is criminal!" she shouted. She clutched her purse to her stomach and kept hitting it with her fist. She wanted to strike out at something more offensive, but that was under dirt now. "I'll fight this! I will!"

Missy came around her chair. She towered over SylviaTheCunt and looked down at her, eyes blazing. It may not have been Jimmy reborn, but the spirit had floated out of the grave, off the silent screen, and had entered the body of his most stalwart defender. "You won't do *shit*, dolly. You *knew* what he had for you. You've always known. He hasn't *spoken* to you for twenty years till now. You'll fight? It is to laugh, dolly! He left the Corporation to me, and I'll put ten fucking *thousand* attorneys on it. We'll block you and tie you up and make you look like the scumbag you are. Wanna fight, dolly? I'm waiting!"

It drained her. Bran came around and took her by the shoulders and took her back to her seat. Missy slumped down, murmuring, "That bitch . . . she hated him . . . she never thought he'd make it . . ." Bran whispered soft things close to her ear and she quieted down.

"For the record I'd suggest you watch the rest of the videotape, no matter how distasteful," Kenny Gross said to SylviaTheCunt. "In the event you *do* contemplate any legal action. Or if you prefer, you can wait in the living room and when the tape is finished I can run this section for you alone."

She stared at him with animosity. She looked around the room at the rest of us, her eyes like slag heaps. Then she went back and resumed her seat.

Jimmy was really putting us through it. It reminded me of the piece he had written after his mother's funeral, where SylviaThe-Cunt had stood up right in the middle of the eulogy he had written and was reading, and had started screaming that Jimmy was defiling her mother's funeral. It had shattered Jimmy. He could almost have forgiven her anything she'd done to him as a kid, as a young man, as an adult: but not that. She was doing it again.

It was posthumous revenge, but it didn't ennoble Jimmy in the least. And it was hell for the rest of us.

The attorney started the tape again, and for the next twenty minutes Jimmy rang every change he could on the woman. How she had brutalized him as a child, with specific deeds that he had remembered with that quirky selective memory of his. Affronts and mean tricks that were almost ludicrous but which, if you remembered how susceptible you were as a little kid, were monstrously cruel. How she had fucked over her own kids, Jimmy's nephew and niece. How she had beaten down her husband, whom Jimmy had liked even though he wouldn't stand up to her. How she had become a deplorable human being—racist, bigoted, coarse, provincial and, for Jimmy the most inexcusable of all, bone-stick-stone stupid.

For twenty minutes we all averted our eyes as Jimmy got into it like a 'lude-stoked jazz musician trying to blow Bud Powell back from the Great Beyond. It was a bravura ugly performance, many riffs, a lot of high shrieking runs and a lot of low animal growls. None of us could look. There are beasts that go right in and suck the marrow, clean the bones to a glistening white.

But SylviaTheCunt looked.

With hard, mean eyes; straight up at the screen; locked in eternal combat with the creature for whom she had seldom felt anything but the most destructive kind of sibling rivalry.

Jimmy once told me how he had gotten SylviaTheCunt to stop pulling his hair. He said one time when she grabbed a fistful of his straight, brown hair he had gritted his teeth and started turning his body in her grasp. Around and around until the hair pulled so tight the pain went all the way to the soles of his feet. It was so horrible, so excruciating, that *she* had been appalled at how painful it must have been . . . and she let him loose. And whenever she would try it again, he would inflict that pain on himself. Until she was so horrified by it that she stopped. "That's how I developed a very high threshold for pain," he had said.

I remember when he got done telling me that . . . I was gritting my teeth.

But finally, thank god finally, Jimmy had had all of it even he could handle. He had turned and turned till the pain was insupportable, even for him. Even my best friend, Jimmy, with that seemingly limitless capacity for revenge, for not just getting even, but for getting a bit more of the vigorish in shylock interest, even *he* had had all he could stomach. And not a moment too soon.

"You can stop it now," SylviaTheCunt said. And she stood up. The screen went white again, lights came on in the library where evening had descended, and Jimmy's sister looked around at all of us.

"You haven't heard the last of me," she said softly, and then she left. *You haven't heard the last of me.*

But I had the sure feeling that we had; we had heard the last of her. Jimmy had called in all the debts from his childhood.

We sat down again, the lights went off, the Betamax went on, and Jimmy turned his head slightly to the left, looking straight at me in my chair. He had saved me for last and he said, "Larry, buddy? You out there?"

We were driving from Chicago to New Orleans in an attempt to make Mardi Gras, which we would miss by a full day, arriving on Ash Wednesday, because in the next five miles we would spin out across the snow-covered highway, escape being piledriven by an oncoming truck by inches, plunge off the side of the road, and bury the Corvette headfirst to its rear wheels in snowbanks fifteen feet deep. But we were still five miles away from missing Mardi Gras when he said the thing I remember most clearly from all the years that we knew each other.

He was driving. He said, "You know the one thing about me that I'm terrified anyone will ever find out. The one lie that makes all of my life a lie."

"I do?"

"Yep. You know it, but you don't know you know it."

"That makes no sense. If I knew it, then I'd know it."

"You know more about me than anyone else, and you have the data; but you don't know how much I fear it, how frightened I am that it might come out."

"I'll never tell."

"You might. Get pissed off at me sometime in the future; I might screw you; you might let it slip without knowing it."

"Never. I'll never tell a living soul; honest to god, you can trust me, Rocco: I'll take the filthy secret to my grave."

"No, I'll take it to my grave. But you might still tell it."

"If you're dead there'd be no way you could protect against that, is there?"

He thought about that for a while. This was before he married Leslie. We were good and close friends, whatever that meant. But he thought about it, seriously thought about this terrible thing I knew that he was ashamed of, the one thing in a life like his so filled with things any normal human being might find the cause of sleepless nights, that didn't bother him in the slightest way. He thought about the knowledge I possessed, this Damoclean sword I held over his life and his career and his work in which he revealed *everything*. Everything except the one bit of knowledge that made all of his life a lie.

And he said, "I'll have to figure out a way to keep you quiet after I'm dead."

"Good luck," I said, laughing lightly; and then we hit the icy patch and started to spin out.

He looked straight at me, having saved me for last.

"Larry, I herewith make you the executor of my literary estate. You have control of every novel, short story, essay, article, review, anthology, and introduction I ever wrote. All those millions of words are in your care, buddy. You're the one they'll have to come to if they want to reprint even one of my commas."

I sat stunned. If he had done me the way he'd done SylviaThe-Cunt, taken this last chance to purge all the swamp animosity of a lifetime . . . or if he had done me the way he'd done Leslie, tried to clear his conscience of real or fancied harm he'd visited on her . . .

if he'd done me as he'd done Missy and Bran, paid off for loyalty and friendship and domination of their lives . . . I wouldn't have been surprised.

But, oh you malicious wonderful sonofabitch! You did the one thing I cannot bear: *you tied me to you forever.*

Malicious? Probably not. It was just Jimmy insuring his memory. Going for posterity, and dragging me along with him, kicking and screaming every micromillimeter of the way. What a mind, what a fucking sweetly conniving mind. I couldn't even condemn him; hate him, yes, revile him, yes, rail at what he was doing, yes—*against which I had no defense*—but he was merely demonstrating as a perfect paradigm for his whole breakneck plunge of a life . . . the ugliness of simply being human.

I sat stunned. And the voice of the turtle was heard in the library: "Would you mind cutting it for a minute?"

Turtle, the voice was mine; stunned, I sat in the darkness. The sound of very old, rinkytink music played distantly in the empty concert hall of my head.

Jimmy had set me up to be either his servant or his Griswold.

Poe. Jimmy got the idea from Poe.

He saw himself as Edgar Allan, cut off in his prime from the benefits of posterity's accolades; he saw me as the Reverend Rufus W. Griswold, but a Griswold who was walled up himself, not free to blacken Poe's name, a Griswold never free of the sound of the tell-tale heart, Jimmy's heart, still beating, his will indomitable, his presence felt until the last moment of my own Griswold-trapped life.

We had talked of this. Poe was one of Jimmy's idols. He was more than an amusing storyteller to me. But Jimmy even had a puppet made of Edgar Allan, had it hanging in the living room as an ever-present reminder of what heights fantasy could reach.

And we had discussed what Griswold had done to Poe.

He had buried him for a hundred years.

What a poor judge of human nature Poe had been. What an ass. But let the critic Daniel Hoffman (Doubleday, 1972) tell it:

> Most of all, [Poe's] own Imp of the Perverse so arranged the history of his career that his literary executor was his most invidious enemy, the Reverend Rufus W. Griswold. This man, an ex-minister, a busybody of letters, an incessant anthologist and publicizer, a failed poetaster fattening on the writings of others as does a moth eating Gobelin tapestries, went to extraordinary pains, after Poe's death, to present the deceased writer in a manner designed to make his name a household word for the dissolute, immoral, recklessly debauched. Griswold falsified the facts of Poe's life, and he revised the texts of Poe's letters, always with this calumnious end in view.
>
> The scoundrel's punishment is this: he is now known everywhere, if known at all, as the maligner of a helpless genius; whereas had he done his job honestly, he'd have won his proper modest niche among the footnotes by which the nearly forgotten are saved from total oblivion.

How better to keep me quiet? What insanity! I didn't even know *which* of the many seamy facts of Jimmy's life was the one that so paralyzed him with fear of its disclosure! I wouldn't have talked about him; I wanted to be *free* of him. I simply wanted to be able to say, when asked, "Yeah, Kerch Crowstairs and I were close friends for over a quarter of a century; he'll be missed; his like will never come again"; the usual bullshit. That's *all* I wanted.

But the crazy paranoid sonofabitch couldn't even credit me with decent motivations *after* he was gone. My god, does fear have a life of its own, to keep feeding on the living after the carrier of the plague has gone down the hole?

"Okay, you can start it again," I said.

Kenny Gross ran it back and hit the PLAY button. Jimmy was in the middle of what he'd been saying when my heart had begun to slam at me. "—if they want to reprint even one of my commas."

He looked so damned innocent up there.

Just chatting with his best friend; just asking his best chum buddy to take care of his memory.

"Larry, you know I'm not afraid of dying. Not that, and nothing else. Not spiders, snakes, being burned, being crippled, heights, closed-in places, ridicule, rejection . . . none of them ever got to me. Very high pain threshold, remember? But it's tomorrow that gets me, Larry. The day *after* you see this tape. Will they still read me? Will I be on the bookshelves, the Modern Library, matched sets in good bindings? *That's* what I'm afraid of, Larry. Posterity. I want a chance to go on after I'm gone. Fifty years from now I want them to come back to my stuff, the way they did to Poe's, and Dickens's, and Conrad's. I don't want to wind up like Clark Ashton Smith or Cabell or the other Smith, Thorne Smith. I don't want bits and pieces of my unfinished stories written by the literary vampires. You've got to promise me, Larry: nobody will ever touch one of the fragments in my file. I probably won't know when I'm going to buy the farm, probably won't have time to get into the file with a blowtorch and crisp all the false starts and half attempts. I've got them locked up, everything that's not finished, all in one file drawer in the office. Missy has the only other key. Get all that stuff out of there and burn it for me, buddy.

"Pride isn't part of it . . . honest to god it isn't! You remember when we talked about Poe how I said he had the right idea, that it was the *work*, it was Art, that held the high road, not religion, or good deeds or friendship or patriotism? None of those. The stories, the books. That's all you can put a bet on. That continues. And I couldn't bear to think of some half-assed science fiction hack dredging up a line or two I started and didn't know how to finish, and writing a whole fucking book off it, the way they've done to poor old Robert E. Howard, or 'Doc' Smith. They even did it to Poe and Jack London and . . . oh Christ, Larry, you *know* what I'm saying. Promise me!"

He waited. He watched that camera and he waited, four months ago. I murmured, "I promise, Jimmy."

"You take care of me when I'm gone, Larry. You're the only one I can trust to do it. Keep me alive, Larry."

And if there was more to that vile videotaped document I don't remember it. After a while I was sitting there and the lights were on, and everybody else had left the room.

He did it. The clever sonofabitch did it. He figured a way to keep me tied to him. He knew I'd do the job.

I'd make sure there were regular retrospectives of his germinal stories; I'd write the best kind of interesting essays and articles about how significant Kercher O. J. Crowstairs had been in the parade of contemporary American letters; I'd set up seminars at the Modern Language Association conclaves; I'd edit anthologies of his work, putting the stories into fresh and insightful contexts; I'd keep him alive through his seriously considered work.

And in the bargain I'd sublimate my own talent. I'd spend a part of every day living with Jimmy. I'd hear his voice and finally start writing the way he did. And if I ever ever ever figured out what it was I knew about him that made all of his life a lie, I'd keep it to myself till the cancer killed me, too.

And at last I know the nature of our friendship.

Say goodbye to Laurence Kercher O. J. Bedloe.

Copyright Notices